From the darkest series of Al Crown

Grotesque Wings

THE ARCHANGEL OF A BLACK FEATHER

TWILIGHT OF DECEPTION

Disclaimer
This novel is a work of fiction intertwined with truth. Characters, names, locations, events, associations, occupations and occurrences are the product of the author's fantasy or are used fictitiously. Any similarity to actual characters, living or dead, incidents or places is totally coincidental.

Historical Facts
In 1513 Spanish explorers were the first Europeans to reach the West Coast of North America, on the Pacific Coast of the Panama Isthmus. This part of the world was considered by Europeans to be the most distant place in the world.
They sailed at the beginning for Cape Horn in South America, and north all the way up to British Columbia, a trip that took more than six months. The English were discouraged at first because of the dangerous and difficult route, and only the Spanish Empire made regular visits, establishing settlements and ports.
The year 1795 determined a change in the colonial history of the Pacific Northwest. After three hundred years of Spanish domain, authorized by the papal bull of 1493, the British Empire finally took over, thanks to the conventions signed in 1790, 1793 and 1794.
Spain at last gave up its claims that it alone could establish settlements in the Pacific Northwest.

The Curse of the Oak Island Treasure
In 1795 three teenagers walking on the island stepped on a hole, discovering the famous mysterious money-pit treasure. From that day, the story has been written in countless books and illustrations, and in time assumed the emblem of a fearful haunted case.
It was a story of gluttony and controversy, overlapping researchers, explorers and corporations of all kinds, lasting for more than 200 years…

PART ONE

In the secret of universal silence the Earth is merged into the emptiness of the spiritual cosmic air, flying continuously in the essence of the perpetual creation. No ground or material stability seems lasting longer than our mere existence. All is shrouded around our unborn life, waiting for the everlasting resurrection of the cosmos, where all stars, galaxies and planets are dying in time.

Al Crown

This is a work of fiction. Names, characters, places, and incidents either are the product of the author's imagination or are used fictitiously. Any resemblance to actual persons, living or dead, events, or locales is entirely coincidental.

Printed in Canada
First Printing, 2019
Cover illustration by Viviana Ceolin

ISBN 978-1-9991275-0-3

CHAPTER I PART ONE

The Expedition

C*aptain George Vancouver* (1757-1798) was a British officer of the Royal Navy, in charge of the famous expedition of 1791-95 (Vancouver Island, Vancouver British Columbia and Washington State were named after him). He had with him a second officer, English Captain Sir Edward Clark, who like him, came to settle in an area originally claimed by Spain, but never occupied.

After passing what are today California, Oregon and Washington State, they entered the Strait of Juan de Fuca and then the Rosario Strait, leaving Vancouver Island on their left…reaching Vancouver's west coast. The ship penetrated the inlet, proceeding between Bowen and Bowyer Island.

The officers landed with their frigates on the coast of the future Vancouver. It was almost springtime, and the crew was admiring the astonishing landscape. A glassy undisturbed ocean was sleeping, shrouded in the bay mirror, reflecting luxuriant mountains enriched with vegetation.

The cliff side soared steeply to the sky, under which were white peaks still covered with snow. Crew members began unloading on land, while a fresh drizzle was falling silently between the tender clouds. It was almost Sunset when Clark fetched his monocular, scanning the mountains above the hills; he pulled a map beneath his shoulder.

"This is where our task begins, the map is clear…one cannot mistake such a beautiful unique place for another. I always imagined this bay in my dreams to be like this, no other way," commented a flabbergasted officer, depositing the monocular in the leather sheath.

He glanced precisely at the map and whispered to his lieutenant: "Tomorrow morning we will calculate the precise coordinates of our point. Judging from the mountains' inclination it will be not easy to reach. We will use our local scouts, as Captain George Vancouver suggested, they are friendly with us now."

"Yes, Captain!" asserted the other young officer, fetching the map from Clark while organizing the sailors' activity.

Natives came to assist the settlers, as they did with George Vancouver's crew, while others were busy working, taking all the materials out of the ship before night. Clark noticed the feeble purplish sunset, after some clouds moved over. The rays were darting toward the mountains to the northwest. He began running closer to the shore, to have a better view of the western part of the mountains. The man was looking for something, and it was at that moment that he felt like a cold blade gored inside his backbone, as if an obscure darkness was emerging from the woods.

He felt a desolated seclusion, a lost emotion of solitude.

"Everything is alright! Did you see something up the hills, Sir?" exclaimed the lieutenant staring at his commander from the lower side of the ship. Clark remained with his serious look glued to the mountains replying, "Yes, Officer! Just a sensation, the landscape is breathtaking, don't you think!" The officer promptly replied, "Indeed Sir, unique!" The expedition was sponsored by the English Anglican church and the Catholics as well. Some members of the Catholic and Anglican clergy were onboard, and while Captain Vancouver continued with the frigate up north, Clark remained focused on his personal mission.

Clark questioned his officer while descending the wooden stairs: "Would you have preferred being with Captain Vancouver rather than here, officer? Vancouver is exploring the northwest coast, as we all know." The officer answered cautiously, "I am delighted to serve with you, Sir! We have an important mission to accomplish here."

An important personality had sailed with the English, an influential figure of the Roman Curia, Cardinal Pietro Ravello, a descendant of the first

Ravello to be ordered in 1600. He paid a large sum of money to accomplish his delicate mission, a wealth he took from his family treasures and possession, stashed in a Vatican vault.

Ravello was sponsoring the education of his two nephews living in Rome, who were worried because of France's rule. In fact, Napoleon Bonaparte was challenging the Roman Catholics' delicate missions... and for this reason he was protecting his family titles, hazing however the real purpose of his expedition.

The cardinal said to the clerics, "We are all here to accomplish the will of our Lord and Savior Jesus Christ. Our faith is once again united at this very place. No evil will divide us, dear brothers, as long as we keep our hope in God. We were summoned to be part of this ordeal, bound by the symbol of the holy cross. May the Lord bless this forgotten land and our struggle," raising his arms wide open.

The Captain was told of an old curse to be broken up the mountains, created by the first Spanish colonists in the seventeenth century, which brought diseases, plagues and death upon aboriginals.

The Church felt responsible, deciding to end the mischief, attempting numerous times since the first expedition of 1610. "Your help will be not forgotten Captain, as will your compensation. This mission we are performing will be remembered for centuries. You are a man of faith! That is why you were chosen," expressed Ravello directing his gaze toward Clark. "Your eminence, I was told this intricate feat would be a perilous one, not that I fear darkness or solitude, but my crew is..."

Ravello interrupted, placing his right hand upon the officer's shoulder, "Trust me! There is nothing to be worried about, God wants it, and we will achieve our victory over evil."

The crew behaved diffidently around Ravello. They heard the legendary tales of the natives, about a powerful evil spirit dominating their land since 1610. The tribes suffered almost two hundred years of mysterious killings, kidnappings and dreadful curses, losing control over the mountain range... neglecting hunting, fishing and camping.

The Protestants offered their help in the name of the Lord Jesus, and Pietro had with him a couple of Catholic priests from France and Spain, whom presence was much needed..

The crew worked with the natives who had lived in that area for thousands of years. The old chief and Clark were studying the map, while the others were sitting around the fire watching the mountains.

The aboriginals were praying in their language, mixing with it some old Latin prayers learned from previous European explorers. The shaman was chanting and dancing with the sacred spiritual guide around the fire, he was radiating, sending up smoke signals. Clark did not show any curiosity about the native's prayers and rituals, while the soldiers were fearfully concerned in hearing those spiritual choruses…eyeing obscure animal-human totems mingled with wooden Christian crosses. One of the guards noticed a few dancing warriors with a strange cross tattooed on their abdomens, a cross with four equal sides; it was a Templar Cross of the 1300s, banned by the church for heresy.

A soldier commented, "Vancouver established a good relation with those tribes, but I don't trust them! To me they are dangerous. I mean, the way they perform those rituals. It is frightening, don't you think?" His face was covered by wrinkles, red-colored because of the bonfire's reflection. A second soldier replied, "I agree with you, I do not trust those people either—or the clerics, they are deceivers."

Ravello told the English colonists that it was a coincidence. The aboriginals could have copied the Templar symbol from mercenaries working on the ships. The bonfire was turning a deep red color, and the sunset was over, with the last light obscuring the valley. It was March 12, and in eight days the expedition would have moved up the hills.

A week later, ten settlers and six natives guided by Clark commenced hiking up the trails…the chief and the shaman behind them. It was dawn and nobody was talking. The scout brought the members to a pathway that created two ways going in the same direction, toward the west. They decided to split in two mixed groups.

Clark ordered: "One group will proceed with me, while the other with the lieutenant. We should meet our point almost at the end of the trail, where the two paths are reunited." The captain gave to his young officer,

James Williams, a copy of the original map, allocating subsequently the clerics in both groups. Cardinal Ravello proceeded with Clark, who approached the chief and stared at his face, saying, "I wish you good luck. May the spirit of the mountains protect you and your people."

March 20 was a sunny day, the beginning of spring, and Sir Clark briefed the crews before advancing into the woods. They were looking for a little lake, hidden somewhere between the trees; it was situated just before the last peak of the so-called Black Mountain (named by the natives).

The Mystic dusk was falling on the valley, and the sun was hiding from the ocean. A mix of rays were crashing into each other between the wood and the long trees, running and rushing in an exhausted way, while everybody felt lost in a sort of claustrophobic sensation.

Clark questioning: "Eminence! Why do the Catholics fear a tiny lake so much? I do not comprehend what kind of evil could be concealed in it." Ravello replied, "Christ was born in a tiny haystack, placed in a forgotten little village. He was the son of God, the Savior of the world. The deceiver of humankind chose the same way, hiding in a tiny lagoon far away from the eyes of the Holy See. Only the grace of the Lord revealed to us its obscure dwelling, following a star, the North Star!" Ravello elucidated while crossing his chest, and blessing the officer said: "This is our last chance, Captain! Our lives, the future of the world, depend on it. God must prevail!"

The officer was overwhelmed by the cleric's powerful speech, staring at his long skinny face. The cardinal was a tall slim man, presenting two sunken dark eyes divided by a little nose. His cheekbones surfaced showily, moving with a sliding look, while his voice was rusty and redundant.

The first group maintained a sluggish pace because of the presence of numerous clerics, while the second was briskly advancing thanks to the aboriginal people. Twilight was regarded with fear by the locals, while the settlers saw a chance to rest and camp.

The light of spring was diminishing!

CHAPTER I PART TWO

Dark Mirror

Clark felt a strange feeling, his head stooped down, observing the sky covered with clouds between the trees. The hindmost sunlight was warming the air, when the officer realized he was discerning that magic horror view from a mirror, a lake mirror, a bloody mirror of death.

Screams, shouts…voices of past spirits were heard all over the mountains, while a wooden stick entered the Captain's stomach, coming out of his backbone, lifting the body up in a macabre agonizing balance. Clark's hands were desperately slipping on the bloody pole, while his voice was a spitting red, suffocated desolation. The creature's convulsions made the corpse collapse, reaching half of the long piece of wood. His eyeballs could see two dark black eyes scanning him as he was dying.

Priests and the Cardinals grabbed their huge crosses and said in a loud voice, "*Vade Retro Satana*" (Go back, Satan). Cardinal Ravello was reciting his powerful exorcism, claiming his right in the name of Christ to expel the beast.

All personnel were trapped in an unnaturally obscure, enchanted spell, hearing around them a chorus of guttural reversed rasping voices. The rutted eerie tongues motioned closer and closer, confusing their lost minds and souls. The first group was surrounded, while the second close to the lake heard the screams. "We have to be prepared for whatever is out there, let the locals advance first, they know better than us this place," ordered James Williams. One of the clerics was trembling with fear, falling into a panicking paranoia: "No, Officer! We should retreat right now! Do you hear those screams? The roots of evil are out there, there is nothing we can do, too late for us!"

Williams restrained the priest. "Father, please! You are a man of God, how can you relinquish from your duties? They need our help, God's help." The cleric stepped back from Williams, while a few natives seized him. "You people do not understand! We are facing the ancestral evil of eternal creation, Lucifer himself! Listen to me, please, hear those exhales and sounds? I tell you now…" A soldier froze mid-conversation: "Shush, you all! Listen! The priest is right, those sounds are creepy."

Lieutenant Williams restored order, boosting his authority, "I am in charge here! Those sounds could be wild animals, we do not know for sure. Regroup now! Ready to advance fully armed!"

It was March 20th (Easter time) and Pietro's cross was clasped by a strong obscure spiral-curled hand that repeatedly stroked the priest's eyes till it smashed inside.

The remaining clerics were drowned soon after, one by one. Trees witnessed people hanged with roots and slaughtered before they choked to death, while others were tossed from the cliff and impaled upon the numerous surrounding pine trees. It was a disgusting, atrocious scene. Few aboriginal warriors escaped, showing on their bellies a Templar cross. They were the only survivors of the hiking mission, now crashing on James Williams.

"What are you doing here, where is Captain Clark? What about the clericals?" The shaman out of breath exclaimed in terror: "The woods revived, the evil spirit of the forest assaulted us. They are all dead, dead! No one survived."

The horrified priest replied, "I told you, fool! We must leave now, before it is too late. There's nothing we can do anymore, the seal is unlatched forever." Williams advanced toward the man in a threatening mode, thrusting people aside and making his way. "What seal! What are you talking about?" questioned the officer while grabbing the man by the collar. "You better start talking clearly, priest! You and Ravello know facts we are not aware of, it is true? Speak, in the name of God! What is hiding out there?" People were staring at the cleric, while Williams released the grasp. "True evil is dwelling in this very place, and it is coming to punish us!" The aboriginal retreated, losing sight of the settlers as the heinous entity was advancing inexorably.

Williams' head was severed by a long sharp scale of rock, while torches died under pouring water. Settlers scattered all over the forest, caged by an abominable fate. Silence fell, and the rending moans of pain vanished, while two dark deep yellow eyes arose from the hill, watching the end of that night, the beginning of a new day.

Those who stayed ashore later accused the natives of the slaughter, sparking a battle that once again scattered the tribes away from the area. The remains of the body were left to rot up in the hills…no one dared to hike in the forest.

Only after Captain George Vancouver returned from his expedition were the remains collected and divided. George could not believe what happened, thinking of a mutiny. "Clark was a young officer, proud and full of himself—very authoritarian, I should say! However, he was a loyal officer. I want to discover the truth, the perpetrators of such infamy cannot be unpunished…we will interrogate every single person," remarked a furious captain feeling somehow responsible.

Subsequently Vancouver arrested and deported those who survived the riots, bringing back what remained of the cardinal's documents and personal objects. He barely manned the two galleons, ready to leave forever that haunted place…and never return.

The galleon of our life was breaking the ocean water,
generating two opposite waves facing each other, evil and
good apart forever, made of the same substance.

Al Crown

CHAPTER II PART ONE

Capitulation

March 20, 2016, Vancouver (British Columbia, Province of Canada) Father Larry Murphy, a sixty-year-old Catholic priest, was in charge of the North Vancouver church situated along the Capilano River, within the Squamish Nation reserve.

It was early morning when Larry was leaving a note to his friend, the sacristan, saying that he could not serve masses or confessions that day because he was sick and needed to rest. He was concealing something serious, preparing himself for a dangerous hike, carrying religious items with him while leaving papers and documents on the sacristy's table. One of the sheets presented the cardinal numbers (from one to nine) positioned upside-down, all related to their diversely viewed graphical meaning. The number 9 in particular was the only one assuming another cipher if turned, the number 6, a cursed digit!

He wrote beside the association with number nine (the Biblical number of the Judgment Day, the perfect movement of God. Christ died at the ninth hour of the day, or 3 p.m.). He placed the 9 under the right side of a cross, twirling it after… uncovering the master of deceit with a satanic crucifix bearing a number six on the left. A note was left: "All is relative to our minds, confusing the truth with lies, we cannot discern from which side to peruse the verity of the existence. Good and evil are faces of the same coin, swindling our feeble heart continuously. My path today is lost in a dark wood, may the light be not obscurity."

He was a tall man with a lean and rangy figure, looking with his gaunt dug face from the window. The clergyman seemed nervous and unconfident, despite his experienced age.

He had discovered in time that Vancouver was an unbelievable intertwining of "line codes," a prophetic modern cryptic cipher city.

Codes appeared in numbers and locations on the south ground city, in major streets, bridges, churches, rivers, islands and ocean inlets, and up north in the mountain range with lakes, creeks, peaks, hills, ravines and trails. There was a natural spiritual balance in numbers, shapes, angles, directions and positions, creating many lines and codes opposing the north to the south, with the sun and moon in between, from east to west.

Larry's calculations based on historical facts and prophecies he had found in Europe, guided him strongly to believe that Vancouver was predestined to witness a biblically prophesied phenomenon very soon. One of the sheets was a drawing he made, regarding the North Shore mountain range, and all the area around. It was done to derive symbolic and geometrical figures.

Larry was reasoning with a content dramatic expression, uncertain of his future life, "I was finally able to uncover the truth. Those churches and scrolls guided me here. That Abbey close to Rome above the Aniene River and those trees around the Stanley Park Lost Lagoon were connected. An absurd distance so far away in time, yet neared by a watered destiny. I am alone now, as was Jesus on the Gethsemane gardens. They are looking for me, I have no choice, I must go up the hill!" said him in a lonely dialogue ignited with courage.

He looked at the sinuous serpentine mountain range of North Vancouver, and at its three major peaks from west to east (Hollyburn Mountain in the Cypress Provincial Park, Grouse Mountain and Seymour Mountain) surrounded by the West and East Pacific Ocean Inlets.

Moving on the northernmost area behind the mountain range, numerous lakes of different shapes were distributed in the surface. Between Cypress Provincial Park and Grouse were situated two little peaks (The two Lions), one close to the other. Several peaks and little lakes were scattered all around. Larry was obsessed by the triangle shapes created by the crest of the mountains.

The Pacific Ocean as seen from the north was a unique shallow horizontal bed of infinity, surrounding the City of Vancouver and crashing against Vancouver's Island.

Larry traced the formation of five pointing-down triangles, followed by five pointing-up triangles, one facing the other. The pointing-down triangle is the symbol of female nature, while the pointing-up triangle is the symbol of male nature.

The major formations were close to the West Cypress provincial park, where Larry spotted brindled, three female triangles. The first two were bigger than the third one, like a protection of the little one; He was thinking about two women guarding the third one, threatened by two male triangles close to the small one. Down, it was as if the three female triangles became one, facing the end two male triangles. The other two triangles, female and male, were facing each other to the east.

On the papers Larry wrote numerous times the same names related to the triangles: Morgair and Ravello (female and male).

He left the church with his car, disappearing in the morning fog, dressed in his cassock. A large cross necklace was around his neck. The goal was to reach the west triangle under Hollyburn peak, and come back before 6 p.m. His nervous face revealed all his fear and uncertainty. He thought, "May God, protect me! I will change my shoes in the parking lot under Cypress Park, those boots I purchased are the most reliable when walking on the snow. I should not worry too much, if lucky the snow will be not so much up there."

He started from one of the many trails present in the area, choosing southwest Whyte Lake Trail at first, and switching to the north trail view-point, North Baden Powell Trail. He was out of shape and out of breath, mumbling to himself about a native lost map of Black Mountain, and a lake he was looking for, seen in a painting. "The Lost Lagoon tree is broken! They know I am here, she knows!" Glinted in fear, Larry thought, "I saw her shining energy."

The mountains have a strong religious and spiritual meaning, they are named five hundred times in the Holy Bible), hiding secrets and lost legends. The most symbolic aspect of a hill is the peak, which is believed to be the closest to heaven (the Greek mythology has Mount Olympus for Gods, the Jews have Mount Sinai for Moses receiving the 10 Commandments, while Christians have Mount Tabor).

Volcanoes were worshipped and feared in the past for their sacredness and fury. Larry was attracted to its profound mystery, learning quickly the aboriginal spiritual feeling of nature.

Streams of water fed plants and animals, which gave the tribes all they needed for life. Natives saw the mountains as a struggle of a love story, a legend of history of creation in a battle over love. The peaks are a living organism on their own, nourished by the power of God's inspiration and revelation.

Larry remembered Mount Tabor, where Christ was revealed to be the son of God, or Mount Olive, where Jesus spent his last night.

The priest did not carry enough water or food, and his body was already suffering for dehydration around 1 p.m. He kept going until coming across the first lake on the left side of the trail, he rushed to drink its cold water, instantly freezing his abdomen.

PART TWO

His stomach was in pain. Larry's muscular walls writhed in anguish, while he recoiled displaying a reluctant expression, "I feel sick! Cramps! How naïve I was. In my mind I have the old crypt I discovered in Italy, so cold and wet inside. The frescoes were my guide, but now! Ouch!"

Thirteen little lakes were spreaded all around the area, down east of Cypress Park, close to the triangle mountain formation he was looking for. Larry one by one tried to distinguish the lagoon for which he was longing, remembering all his notes and studies. He wrote about Friday the thirteenth, and its meaning, connected with the Knights Templar course and the number of lakes up there.

Thanks to the two Lions' peaks, the triangle paring was possible…otherwise the male shape would have prevailed. The summits were seated as if they were scanning the west side, close to Black Mountain. For Larry it was not a mere coincidence, but a prophetic symbol perpetrated by destiny. In fact the lions were a strong signs of universal spiritual meaning, symbolizing the strong fire of love and courage. The lion is a proud emblem, loved and feared at the same time, while the lioness reflects Sun's God and maternal sensuality. Its eyes are always opened and never sleep, to guard and protect the sacred hills. Larry crooked, managing to overcome a wide bush, thrusting his right hand against the abdomen. He then surveyed: "The two Lions peaks are facing the two lions positioned on the Gate Bridge, dividing the north mountain range from the City of Vancouver. From up here it is very clear. The symbol of Christ's resurrection is a lion in the New Testament! While in the Old Testament, lions are depicted as vicious evil. What an opposite meaning and ambiguity at the eyes of God…"

The priest was mumbling, huddling strenuously his feet upon, "I did not expect all this snow, it is killing me and my legs are so tired. My stomach is driving me crazy! I was a fool! I drank the cold water like a little kid."

An oval-shaped lake was the one Larry needed. The lagoons were all different, and the last one was down east of Black Mountain, close to Shore Glades. A light fresh wind was blowing, while the sun moved farther west close to the island. Larry felt a sensation of solitude and isolation, neglecting the time. It was four o'clock and his legs were wasted, Larry was reproaching himself for being too confident in going up there alone. He sat, he quit, relinquishing and admiring the sunset, the last sunset of his life. A cold breeze of darkness was approaching as twilight fell on the ancestral wilderness, covering the triangle above his head. He stood up, trying to find the Baden Powell Trail, while his footfalls briskly advanced downhill. He lost his religious objects.

A severe pain burst in Larry's liver and spleen, forcing the man to walk slowly, while his hands were still alternately pushing against the left side of his abdomen. A silent prayer was following his desperation, checking in a spasmodic way the clock, 6.30 p.m.

An eerie mist grazed upon the leaves, emerging from nowhere. It was the Black Lagoon's grotesque fog searching for the curious impostor. A white dense atmosphere encircled Larry, as if was touching him. He turned, hearing a creepy giggle, a child's giggle. An amorphous figure was advancing, enfolded in the mist, absorbing the humidity while fully shaping. Larry discerned a little girl with long hair holding a red rose, slightly detached from the ground. "It's the girl dwelling in the crypt, the fresco's flower… away from me evil spirit!

The opaque ghost freed the red rose, as if the flower was falling from a cliff. A relented downfall blossom dissolved, as did the girl. The haze condensed, ghost deliquescing in a puddle of water, while a flabbergasted priest felt its wet touch.

Larry merged his numb hand in the tiny pond, feeling a live warm water of life: "It is warm! She was alive! It is not a ghost that I saw but… blood? What is that? My Lord! Petals, those are red petals!" The clock stopped immediately, and sunset came on time. Larry felt a noise from a distance, the northwest side precisely. He whispered, "It is coming! It is true! God help me…courage!"

The resonance was approaching like a distant relentless avalanche of darkness, embodied with rolling rocks, slithering roots and watering slashing…dragging the steps of wet logs. A very strong gale was raging in Vancouver, entering through the sacristy slightly open window; papers were gradually falling on the creaking wooden floor, revealing additional information on the sunset of his life.

Uppercase omega and lowercase alpha letters were positioned facing each other, represented with the number one (the first letter of the Greek alphabet) and twenty-four (the last letter of the Greek alphabet). "1" remained "1" and "24" was transformed into "2+4 = 6."

The previous writing was overlapped by a second one, displaying several ciphers, and the remarked letter Y juxtaposed with a cross. Besides, the letter was reverted as was the cross, followed by two names, mountain names: Mount Elsay, Mount Yasle.

Larry was petrified, clutching his only cross, hearing inverse exhale sighs. He distinguished a muttering double eldritch "suspirium" as one, and when he came closer, he realized was Latin! He was in a state of absolute terror…he was in hell.

"*Ego sum hic*"—Here I am! A voice was swallowing itself in the abyss of pandemonium. Larry turned around perturbed, and two yellow irises closed and opened, while a penetrating cold rock struck his left side, ripping his organs. Larry walked backward, shivering and fainting, feeling water dripping from above. His organs were losing on the legs, while a muffled scream came from his mouth. A hand with six sharp long rocks shattered his skull from the top, rotating inside his brain while still alive. The shattered gathered neurons forming the gray matter were transmitting the last signals of terror, using the smashed axons of the white matter. Water and fat were mingled violently by the rocks' blades. The man fell dead on the ground soon after, while some roots wrapped around his body, dragging the mauled corpse away from that place. A prowling contorted figure was approaching the northwest woods, retreating back where it belonged; hauling and yanking behind its abominable obscurity was the rotten remains. It was plunging slowly in the death pool of endless damnation.

That same evening a person entered Larry's sacristy, stealing from his hidden box all his precious documents and papers, walking soon after brusquely out of the room, trampling on the ground sheets. The imprint of the shoes embossed upon the documents, smearing ruinously a name, a mysterious anagrammed name.

The stranger was reciting a prayer of mourning in his aboriginal language, crossing his chest three times (three as the three hundred years of Christian persecution, before Roman Emperor Constantine recognized Christ the King of Kings).

CHAPTER III PART ONE

The Outsider

September 2016. The West Vancouver sport teams were beginning the training season, welcoming the new players joining the club for the first time. The fields were located between Ambleside Park and Marine Drive, facing the spectacular North Mountains Range, and the Pacific Ocean. Stanley Park was connected to the North Shore area by the Lions Gate Bridge.

The seaside was overwhelmed by people playing volleyball on the beaches, and kids swimming in the water. Some of the guys living in the North Shore had been playing with the clubs for a long time, while others joined later, after they moved to this part of town.

One of them was a 21-year-old Claudio Verallo, who at the age of 19 moved from Italy to Canada with his widower father Giacomo and his best friend, golden Labrador Leon. His mother Lidia died on 17 September 2010 of a malignant pancreatic cancer, whereas his older sister Laura remained in Italy after obtaining a significant position in the Vatican State. Giacomo had a younger brother named Tony (Antonio) who had moved to Canada in 1996, when he was offered the chance to work as an electrician for the City of Vancouver.

After working as an apprentice electrician, Tony acquired the red seal trade certificate, becoming in time a superintendent of his branch; soon after he married Lyan, in love with the Italian history and the beautiful nature of British Columbia.

"How is Claudio dealing with his issue, he is alright?" Said Tony to his brother... "Same, he has not improved; specialists say he will have to deal with it for the rest of his life. Once the damage is done it is impossible to heal it completely. Losing his mother was a profound trauma." Presenting a fragile body, Tony moved his hand to remove the glasses, "He is a good boy, he will find his way in Vancouver and I am sure he will surprise us all. Specialized doctors do not always have the answers to comprehend our minds." With a more strong-shaped body, Giacomo faced his brother: "I don't expect miracles anymore, it is what it is. The boy has always been unsure and unconfident, resembling more Lidia's character. I tried to chisel Claudio in a straightforward manner, but it was useless. Since Lidia passed away, his temper has become even more timid and insecure, afraid to face life."

He caressed his thick foliage down the neck, bothered about Tony insistence on Claudio's personal feelings. He was a realistic man with no illusions about life. "Claudio, just to let you know, has developed a kind of paranoid sense of order, far-fetched from reality. He is obsessed with putting everything in order, you should see his room!"

Tony countered, trying to sober his brother's rough temper: "That is not bad! On the contrary, I wish Michael was the same; his bedroom is like a dump... nothing is in order. Claudio is a responsible young man, and he is trying to cope with a great loss. Give him some time."

After his brother arrived in Canada, Tony moved with his family from the south side of Vancouver to Lynn Valley in North Vancouver, just on the opposite side, separated from the Pacific Ocean and united by the Lions Gate Bridge. They had an only son named Michael (born March 17th), one year older than Claudio (born March 20th, three days after his cousin's birthday). Giacomo moved to Vancouver because the economic situation in Italy was unstable, getting even worse after 2009.

Giacomo arrived holding his permanent resident, adrenalized...waiting for the citizenship application in few years. He was very happy for his achievement, and the chance that his daughter could decide to join the family in the future was palpable.

"I can tell you anyway that Claudio is trying to survive his mother's death, followed by a specialist. Since Lidia passed away, he had horrible nightmares about deaths and grotesque presences. Back in Italy he has regularly seen a psychologist, afamily friend, while Laura was his guardian angel. You know, as I already told you, he was a kid when Lidia died, never forgetting how she passed away," abundantly explained Giacomo.

Tony interrupted: "Don't be sorry! We are talking about your son, my dearest nephew. I want to know, and you need to let out your emotions, you have always been reserved. Keeping our thoughts inside doesn't benefit our health," gingerly observing. "Thanks Tony, I appreciate your sympathy. Claudio has a slow-motion image printed forever in his mind. Lidia died in a respiratory crisis, choking just before him; we tried to give her oxygen, while Claudio was screaming and kicking the air tanks. She was looking for him, to whisper her tearjerker last words. Claudio saw his mother losing forty kilograms in ten months, she was bones and skin. One day by mistake he entered the bathroom, while I was cleaning her : she was a walking dead, a destruction of the human body. Claudio got scared, running away in despair, and acknowledging that cancer was the devil consuming his mother. He saw God forsaking Lidia in her time of need. She was a believer and a humble good person, as we you know," emotionally expressing. Tony placed his hand on his shoulder, as a sign of comfort, "He lost his faith. The wind of death got his lost soul," concluded an afflicted father.

Teammates gathered at the presentation session of the new athletes, now officially engaged with the club. The training was easy and the boys started to know each other better, deciding the roles and the substitutions in case of necessity.

Everybody was trying to impress the coaches and the assistants, showing off their skills and qualities. Everyone stopped on the field, marveled t the bright rainbow created by the light rain, and a timid sun hiding between the tender clouds. It was a colorful passage bridging the field to Grouse Mountain. Claudio's eyes were amazed as he praised that natural painting, while his coach's hand fell on his shoulder, like a welcoming compliment; he felt a strange feeling eyeing the hills under the mountains.

Clouds were darker as if something was moving inside, and a shiver entered inside his body. He felt a fearful sensation of solitude…something was happening but he did not fully comprehend what it was, perhaps the beginning of a new adventure of a young man living in a new country.

Soon after the training Claudio prepared for the welcoming party at the pub. He looked lost and down in his temper, while his father started questioning about his first day of training, and the new friends he met on the soccer field.

"Let me hear how was it! I wish I was you down there, playing my best and…" Claudio looked at his father with profound eyes, whispering something he could not clearly hear, something about a trail and a path going up the mountain.

He left all of a sudden, and running outside…jumped on a car that drove away. Giacomo: "What the hell! Did I say something wrong? If I dared to behave like that with my father, God forbid!"

The night was great and all the boys had a good time. Claudio was introduced to some girls, one in particular was curious to meet him, Isabel from Vancouver. She was a gorgeous twenty-year-old fit girl, with a determined strong-willed temper. Claudio recoiled back in a defensive mode, feeling an infatuation.

Part Two

He was embarrassed, trying to hide the shyness, while his visage was a mirror of truthfulness where one cannot abscond.

"I am attending the university too, and I love running; it makes me feel better and more relaxed. I use this sport to let out my stress and think about my writings," said Claudio. Isabel: "Writings? Are you a writer?" Claudio felt important, and in his insecure thoughts decided to impress that gorgeous, interesting girl.

"Kind of, I write poetry, short ones. I always have a pencil and a little notebook with me. Inspirations are always behind the corner!"

Isabel was flattered by his assertion, and felt well-versed toward him, pushing the conversation more confidential. "Wow! I met a poet, a real poet. I love poetry… only if you have a deep love and passion for life can you create such poems. I like that!"

They liked each other at first sight, and were feverish to inaugurate a new friendship, conversing with the other about their nicknames and favorite jokes. Claudio confessed that back in Italy his friends used to call him Dante, because of his admiration for one of the greatest Italian poets of all time, Dante Alighieri.

It all began when his mother's brother, Loris Rotondi, introduced Claudio to the mystical and mysterious figure of Dante, narrating the obscure times of the Late Middle Ages.

Loris used to sit outside his garden during summertime, adorned with sublime and odorous olive trees, reading with theatrical gestures the three parts of Dante's *Devine Comedy* (Paradise, Purgatory and Inferno). The boy's imagination was mesmerized and frameless, flying with his original fantasy in a dark dream. When his mother passed away, the *Inferno* descended upon his life, sparking a kind of poetic refuge for his damaged soul. Loris's country house in the Roman hills of ancient Tibur (Tivoli, an ancient town close to Rome) became his sanctuary and cultural cradle, isolating the lad from the cruelty of the world. Lidia died in that house, bought by his brother after retiring from the University of Florence, where he used to teach literature.

Isabel's eyes glinted with mystery, "I was scared about the figure of Dante Alighieri, all his mysteries and visions created a unique *Inferno*. I always thought he was a black poet, but I feel that you are a white poet." Awakening from his shyness, Claudio observed: "I can be both black and white, depending on the mood. I was always lured by Dante's obscure side, even if he was a devoted man. His fearful *Hell* is for those who committed horrible and treacherous misdemeanors in life, I should say a positive black side on its own."

Isabel neared the boy, glancing at his shirt, "I like your Italian jersey, very cool!" A pause, "What is a jersey, Isabel?" She explained, "Your shirt, *la tua maglia*, as you say in Italian. Describe to me what is on it, I would like to know." Verallo bent, pushing his jaw against his chest, and pointing his finger on the monuments. "It is one of those cheap shirts you can purchase in Rome's stalls, along the Coliseum. You can see Saint Peter in Rome, Adrian's Villa in Tivoli, and Villa D'Este, also in Tivoli," he elucidated.

Isabel stammered, "Where is Tivoli? I never heard this town before. I did not know those monuments were there. You know, we think everything is in Rome!"

Claudio managed, ruling the guide game, "Most of the tourists discover the province of Rome only when visiting the eternal city, it is normal anyway. My uncle lives there in Tivoli, close to a village named Vicovaro, where a suggestive monastery was built in the sixth century. Tourists who visited the cloister are impressed by the numerous crypts, vaults and caverns naturally formed alongisde the cliff."

Isabel… mesmerized by his tender voice, whispered, "You like this place very much. I mean the isolated monastery, how come?" He was silent for a while, and then said, "My mother used to go there almost every week. She attended services, helped with the charity, supported volunteering. When my mother passed away we celebrated her funeral within that monastery's chapel." Isabel sympathized, "I am very sorry."

Later on Claudio blushed before his father, "Don't lie to me son! Did you meet a girl?"

A shiny full moon was up in the sky, mirroring the hills down the mountain trails.

The obscure shadow of our existence is within the shining light of life, as it is the eternal solitude concealed among us.

Al Crown

CHAPTER IV

The Discovery

The following days Michael and Claudio exchanged some ideas about cardio training. They wished to enhance their heart performance running faster and longer.

Claudio was always watching the mountain trails, and could not wait any longer to go up there, discovering all the paths and lakes of the North Shore. He purchased a detailed map, studying all the areas.

"We should go up the trails before the end of September, I studied the map inch by inch and I discovered so many trails we could go running. We should start from the short ones at the beginning, adapting our muscles, challenging after the others. What do you think, Michael?" asserted Claudio in a euphoric manner. "I think you studied too much! We do not need a map to go up there. We can find the paths just running randomly. There are signs and illustrations everywhere, and the trails are marked with different colors. By the way, I just want to remind you, Claudio, that in Vancouver until the end of October the weather is usually nice, and there is enough light for running."

Claudio was bothered by his cousin's arrogant bragging, "Do you know Michael, how many people got lost around those mountains, hiking without maps or GPS? Some did not survive the elements. I think your attitude in underestimating the serious circumstances will cause problems."

The following long weekend was the best option, given that no games were scheduled. Michael was silence, wearing a look of disapproval toward his cousin's reproach.

Weekend quickly arrived, and the team met at dawn. They warmed up before the trail became too steep, and when up halfway, they noticed few helicopters of the North Shore rescue flying above their heads. Some rescuers were coming down the hill, "Sorry guys, it is not possible to continue on this trail, someone got lost. Those guys up there are forensic police, they are investigating," with a warning tone. Claudio, who was leading the group, questioned: "What happened? Why are the forensic searching the area?" insisting out of curiosity. "I am sorry, but at the moment we are still working on it, and no information can be released. Turn immediately and run downward please?"

The sun was nicely showing upon the horizon, and it was time for breakfast. The group met later for brunch at the restaurant down on 15th Street, across Marine Drive. They were seated at the corner, listening to some people talking about the remains of a person who were found by a lost hiker the night before. The customers' voices sounded concerned and surprised. One of them was an old man, who said, "Nowadays everything is possible here; this place was a safe heaven once and look now. Those remains are old perhaps, nobody noticed them before? We cannot even go up the hills anymore. Police will close the whole area, I bet!"

Something serious had happened, and the next morning Claudio and his friends bought the newspaper, reading about the case.

"A guy went missing last night while hiking toward Cypress. He took a shortcut that was unmarked, pushing west. When he realized he was on the wrong path, he started panicking in fear because the sun was setting. The man later tried to come back, but lost orientation, wandering all night long. When finally the rescuers found him, he told them to go up there over the trail, where bones and a broken skull…"

"I think this man is hiding something. How come no hikers up the trails noticed those remains? What if he killed this person long time ago and concealed the remains, faking being lost and consequently creating a strong alibi?" Michael promptly reacted, countering: "Didn't you read the article properly? They say the remains were found far out off the tracks, where he got seriously lost. That man risked his own life up there!"

Claudio wearing a discordant glance, "He is alive, anyway! Better than serving a life sentence in prison, don't you think?" Michael inappropriately slipped the newspaper from his cousin's hands, continuing to read in a loud voice: "The person was consumed and scared, telling the forensic police about distorted sounds coming from the forest overnight. He thought at first of wild animal fights, and consider they could even be Search and Rescue teams' devices. Only when he saw the human remains, he rushed to find a concealed shelter."

Few weeks later, TV news released the whole story, and Inspector Kevin Mesotti of the West Vancouver Police Department said in a conference that the bones found were those of Father Larry Murphy (an Irish Catholic Priest) disappeared six months earlier, in March. He was executed in a violent vicious way. Mesotti did not specify if Father Larry was killed by a wild animal or perhaps by a person; police did not possess such evidence at the moment. The community assumed that it was a robust strong creature. The inspector spoke with an experienced calm voice: "At the moment we cannot say how the victim died, we discovered his identity after forensic anthropologists studied and extracted his DNA from the remains. It was a really difficult process, really!" One of the journalists asked, "How did the forensics obtain the DNA? We know it is not always possible with bones!" Kevin replied, managing, "The B.C. forensic anthropologists were assisted by an expert tooth researcher, who was able to extract the DNA from the inner pulp of few teeth. The only way was to suck and conserve the pulp, finding with a complex process a good valuable DNA. We have a long list of missing people, and Larry was one of the last."

The interview continued and curiosity was growing around the officer, he served the police for more than twenty-five years and knew a lot about forensics. Kevin answered all the questions regardless: "To be one hundred percent sure about our affirmation, we scanned the skull remains in a computer program, matching and comparing the external points with Larry's pictures. The overlapping comparison determined it was Larry!"

The officer was facing the press chin-up; senseless of the flashes and confusion echoing in the conference room, he had lived those rushing moments a long time ago. He was sure, strong and confident.

"When will be you ready to tell us if Larry was killed or not?" questioned coldly a reporter from a local channel.

"As I told you a moment ago, we have our forensic expert working on the remains. From the skull and the bones we will be able to determine how the cleric died. Let us do our job. Thank you all."

After Larry's disappearance the church was managed by Morris Harrison, the sacristan, and no religious services were conducted.

Every day Claudio read the news about this case, talking with his friends and family about the figure of Inspector Msotti. "I like him, he is humble and at the same time very professional. He is a calm and thoughtful detective. He reminds me of an old investigator back in time," said Claudio following the TV news.

Giacomo was cleaning the sink wearing two plastic yellow gloves, fastidiously whistling. He then took them off, sighing: "Remember that he is a cop! He is a practical man, and only facts and evidence matter to him."

A new interview was released, trying to minimize the gruesome details of the cleric's death. When the truth came out completely, it was clear to everybody that the priest had been viciously murdered.

Giacomo's concern was palpable: "I never thought those crimes could happen in this part of town, I only hope it is an isolated incident." Claudio replied with an ignited tone. "Didn't you know that around the world every country is the same? You told me that once if I am not mistaken." Unfortunately time was changing, and in October the North Shore trails under Cypress were still closed. Police began searching throughout the mountain, hoping to find some traces left by the killer. In the past, several related homicide cases went cold because investigators gave up the research. One of the cases was discovered later to be a serial murder, active for more than twenty years.

Police did not want to commit the same mistake.

CHAPTER V PART ONE

The Priest

After hearing the news, the group decided to quit the cardio training for the moment, waiting for the reopening of Cypress trails as soon as police had concluded their investigation. Soccer and football teams decided to train as usual on the field, while hockey used the indoor ice rink. Claudio decided to introduce Isabel to his father, inviting her for a coffee, extending the invitation to his cousin Michael.

The excuse was to discuss university programs and possible exams to take. It was already evening when Giacomo decided to invite everybody for dinner. Isabel called her parents to let them know about supper plns, while Giacomo turned on the TV, watching the local news. "Hey guys, I will prepare a good dinner for us tonight!" said the man laughing. "I can help and learn something here!" replied Isabel, while Michael sat comfortably on the sofa with his uncle. TV showed the latest interview released by the chief of the West Vancouver Police Department, addressing the unexpected findings of further human remains up the North Shore; those were not of Larry Murphy. "It is clear at the moment that a dangerous, unscrupulous killer is on the loose, and probably a few of the missing people we are looking for have been murdered in the last few years," commented a solemn audible commander.

Everybody was carefully listening to the TV news in astonishment and fear. Inspector Mesotti spoke after the chief of police. He was longing for everybody's cooperation, liaising with the WVPD and the North Vancouver Police. Kevin spoke with a businesslike tone: "We decided to collaborate with the other districts, intensifying our investigation and uniting our skills. After all, those missing people are from different districts, and we need all the information possible. Any clues or details about suspicious people seen on the trails must be reported. We ask of the citizens a constant opened eye." Kevin looked like an old-time inspector. He boasted a long career as an investigator in diverse homicide squads. He worked in the States (California) and Ontario, before attaining a position in West Vancouver, where he was born. A fit man with the pleasure of smoking, especially when nervous or after a coffee, he got a serious, hollow face, showing protuberant cheekbones with thin lips, while his long brown hair framed his skinny long face.

Although he seemed at first sight sober and humorless, Kevin, in his tall figure, revealed a well-hidden sense of humor and sarcasm. His closest colleagues nicknamed him Count Vlad, after Dracula.

Father Larry was moved from his hometown Armagh in Northern Ireland to Toronto in 2010. Subsequently he studied at the Vatican Diocese in 2013, and lived in Rome for three years. He was deepening his theological studies and Latin language at first, intensifying his obsession for the research on religious history and colonial expeditions later.

All originated after the acquaintance of a Spanish clerical friend, who was well acknowledge in the history of religious colonial missions connected to Canada and the city of Vancouver.

Larry exercised a vigorous pressure on the Vatican Clergy, seeking to be transferred back to Vancouver. He wrote several letters addressed to the ministry of the holy order, insisting redundantly until he was finally moved in January 2016… when he lost his life. Kevin speculated on his own, "why the Priest went hiking while snow was still on the peaks, dressed in religious clothes and carrying his sacred objects? To me it remains an unexplainable mystery. He must have come here for a reason, he was looking for something. I am convinced that he was not hiking. The path he took and the material he carried are not those of a picnic. Perhaps he was running away from someone!"

The officer was mind-bending, supposing all the theories. Larry disappeared in no more than three months, neglecting his services and duties. He was clearly dedicated to something else.

At Giacomo's dinner was over… Michael appeared ready to go home and turned in for the night. Claudio and Isabel had made the meal…"You guys are the official cooks from now on!" announced Giacomo.

For Claudio, the meal had been a nice way to relax together and forget about the case for a little while. Now he stood at the window scanning the hills. A half-moon was shining, and a few fluffy clouds drifted overhead. For a moment, he thought he could distinguish the shape of long swaying hair in the clouds.

Thursday was a busy day. After school Claudio's team met at the soccer field for a final practice, going over tactics for Saturday's game. A feeble light drizzle refreshed the players, mixing with their sweat. Claudio was pouring all his effort into playing his position, trying to impress their sober coaches. He was so focused that he forgot about the killings and the news.

Suddenly he realized someone was watching him. A chill went up his spine and he turned his head. It was Isabel, there to watch him practice. He was so happy to see her that he began showing off. His team was playing a scrimmage and Claudio tried to tackle an opposing forward, but the player dodged him while running toward the net. Claudio had no choice but to chase him. He attempted a slide tackle to get the ball, but fell, slamming into the ground. He laughed along with the spectators. "That is it for me, guys, I am in pain," exclaimed the boy.

At the end of practice Claudio joined Isabel outside the fence. "You almost killed yourself! Who were you trying to impress, me or your coaches? I think you need to sober up and have a cold shower." She laughed and slapped Claudio on the shoulder.

"Thanks for caring about me, my dear! I am just trying to show you what an Italian soccer player can do." Isabel stopped and put her hands on her slim hips. She smirked at Claudio. "Do you see any love handles here? Soccer is slow! If you want a challenge, I can take you running up the hills."

Claudio countered, "My God, Isabel…are you serious? I don't dare challenge you, I know you are strong. Who is bragging now?"

Isabel wrapped her arm around Claudio's neck, and put her head against his. "I didn't realize until now that I am taller than you, Claudio. Ha!" They kissed each other good night and left the place.

Meanwhile Police had found the remains of six bodies, apparently killed within the last three years. The sacristan from Father Larry's parish had been arrested, after he lied about several previous accidents, although on the day the priest was killed, he had been with his family at home.

The news anchor was explaining the details: "Today Morris Harrison, the church caretaker, produced a credible alibi while being interrogated by the police. The forensic investigation of the remains suggests that the killer or killers tortured the victims, and then tried to get rid of the bodies by drowning or burning the corpse." The announcer concluded with particular sophisticated laboratory studies, showing that all the victims had both hands and feet perforated by sharpened rocks, followed by signs of water presence inside the bones. Burns appeared on the collagen of fibulas."

Giacomo almost choked on his dinner while listening to this horrible news. He coughed loudly, feeling a rounded portion of pasta stuck in his throat. "Dad, take a sip of your wine, please, you're scaring me!" When he was finally able to speak, he said. "We have a wacko living in West Vancouver! I cannot believe it! This is the quietest and safest part of the lower mainland."

"It was! I told you that before, dad! All places seem safe until the truth starts to emerge. I remember what you told me about the nice and quiet Florence in the eighties, young lovers being killed in their cars."

Inspector Mesotti admitted that police were following more than one hypothesis, a possible single serial killer or a complex network. The identified victims were not part of any religious society. The North Shore forest was checked constantly by the park rangers and police, while some trails were closed and others were opened, waiting for the skiing season to start.

Kevin's face was shown daily on the news, and he had no fear to speak and comment. "At the moment we are still questioning Morris. Some details are not completely clarified. An investigative team has been created in our department, and as I told you in the previous interview, both North Vancouver police and Vancouver police are collaborating with us."

Claudio relented while eating, because his chewing cheeks were muffling the sound of Kevin's voice. He desired to hear every single word the detective was saying.

PART TWO

Mesotti sympathized: "So far we do not think that an intervention of the Provincial Integrated Homicide Team would be necessary, it is too early to assume that. We have three diverse police departments working on it, and moreover, this is the first time in the North Shore that we've had assistance with such gruesome crimes in the North Shore. We need time to investigate and use in a full scale our resources. In any case, the Provincial Homicide detectives are in a standby mode."

A few more questions concluded the police conference. "That is all for today, thank you for your cooperation," said Kevin, in a dismissive voice.

Claudio's eyes were squeezed with curiosity and excitement. Back in Italy he tried to join the military at first, deciding later to challenge the police enforcement, a desire that his father despised. Claudio turned to his father while cleaning his plate with a piece of bread, performing a scraping Italian *scarpetta.*

"What were you saying about Kevin Mesotti, dad, an article about what? Please tell me, I want to know."

Giacomo motioned toward the table, holding a tray of fresh fruits. He started peeling and cutting a peach. "I was saying, before being interrupted, that I read an interesting article about your detective. He was in a popular magazine this week. You need to read more instead of listening to the radio and watching TV, it is good to improve your English."

Claudio was frustrated: "Come on, for God's sake, you are slow! Why every time do you have to go around the matter with your dissertation? I know you can read, ha!" Giacomo put the sectioned and cubed peach in his glass, adding more red wine and letting the fruit rest for a few minutes. "Kevin is a veteran, my son, and he is close to retirement. His story is not a happy one, even if the man looks confident and self-assured. He lost his twenty-year-old son in a tragic accident, and his wife after that tribulation concealed her mind in anguish, committing suicide. I know it is hard to believe, but this is the truth."

Claudio sighed in disbelief, "Are you for real? I didn't know that. When did this tragedy occur?"

Giacomo was meticulously savoring his peach, while speaking to the bewildered youth: "It was not long ago just a few years, if I am not wrong. Mesotti was called with his team to chase a car after an armed robbery in downtown Vancouver; at that time he was working in the city. The criminals escaped from the Lions' Gate Bridge, trying to take the upper-level highway to Whistler. West Vancouver law enforcement intervened to block the car. The vehicle jackknifed and violently hit a car proceeding in the opposite direction. Unfortunately for a strange destiny, Mesotti's son was in that car, driven by a friend. The driver survived, while his son died after being transported to the hospital."

Claudio lost his appetite, moving away the tray of fruits from his view. Kevin's boy was going to be a cop, and was preparing himself for the police academy. It was too sad to hear.

"Who told him about the accident?" questioned a perturbed Claudio.

"No one, he found out! He had permission to chase the vehicle after the bridge, making the criminals drive in a spasmodic way. The West Vancouver police checkpoint did the rest, and when he rescued the other vehicle, he opened the door and saw his son in agony."

For Claudio that was a torrent of emotions and thoughts. It was utterly obvious in his mind that he loved uniforms. Even the military ones were going to suit him. Slowly his brain killed the engine of his numerous speculations, deposing the boy at rest for the long endless night.

CHAPTER VI PART ONE

Fear

Saturday's game was at hand, and Claudio's club won with a large victory. He scored his first goal, gaining an important role as midfielder. The night was spent in a downtown Vancouver live music club, close to Georgia Street. They danced until exhausted, when a taxi drove them back home. Claudio said goodbye to the fellows, while some alcohol was still going around his body. He turned his head to the north, looking for the big ladle constellation and Cassiopeia's starry dots. He was matching their directions, united toward the North Star (the brightest star in the Ursa Minor constellation, closest to the earth's north celestial pole).

The sky was dark and clear, and all the lights were sparkling bright.

A full vivid moon was shining in a fresh October while an obscure wind was blowing on his face…leaves on the trees remained calm.

A yell came from a distance…a wild animal was hiding in the woods. Claudio questioned his cousin, while his head was spinning around. "Did you hear that shriek? It was reverberating down the hills, I am sure of that." Michael replied, distraught, "Not again please, with this story of yours. As soon as people hear something strange, they call for a killer."

Claudio spun around with a serious look, as if a searing bolt had pierced his Achilles tendon. "I am alright, and I am sober. I clearly heard that scream. It was not an animal! What do you think it is?"

Michael moved away from Claudio, jumping in the car while teasing him. "Hey Claudio I think you are right, I bet it was Isabel! Go and save her from the ghosts!"

A little piece of wood flew toward Michael, while Claudio was looking for something bigger to throw at him. The vehicle disappeared and Claudio felt a fearful sensation, a constant threat around him. He froze and could not move…something was grabbing his soul.

He entered the living room motioning toward his bedroom, falling asleep into a reverie of a young gorgeous girl walking barefoot, displaying two long hair braids.

She was wearing a native dress floating like a sailing galleon, advancing in slow motion with her eyes closed. All of a sudden the woman turned, watching Claudio's face: he stared at her in wonder.

Claudio's nightmares did not cease in Vancouver, becoming more frequent and real in time. His father thought that leaving Italy for good would have helped him healing his personal profound wounds, forgetting the troubled times they endured back home. Regrettably, Giacomo omitted one crucial thing: "Sorrow always rests within us, until we die."

The young fellow would have never forgotten his mother's death, as a continuous photogram immortalized in the heart of his soul.

Rooms, trees, scents, churches, colors and seasons connected Claudio with the remembrance of his dear mother.

From March to September, Claudio recollected every single day he spent with her. Six months of hope and tribulations.

Lidia ended her life at her brother's house, upon the northeast Roman hills, where the olive trees grow. Loris was fond of Claudio, and every week they talked on the phone for hours.

He was part of a restricted group aficionado of Dante's Devine Comedy, founded in Florence and transferred to Rome. The group was devoted to the poet's theories and his mysterious life.

While Claudio slept in Vancouver, Loris was conversing with Laura: "I have to call my nephew very soon. If I do not reach him first, he will not! Your father does not even answer the phone calls anymore. He is such a moody person. He left us with a surly expression."

Laura replied, sympathizing, "Be patient uncle, Claudio loves you very much and always talks about you, he misses you. My father has always been a tough man, and after our mother died he got even worse." Loris complied, "Yes I know that, I am only worried for Claudio. It was our younger associate, very smart and open-minded. I miss our readings and translations; we had a good time up here. Anyway, I will read some verses of Dante and relax. I will call you tomorrow, my dear! Bye, now."

Dante Alighieri, the Italian father of poetry, was a white Catholic Guelph, exiled perpetually from Florence (the Republic of Florence) when the black Guelph (devoted to the emperor) disbanded their opponents. Dante never returned to Florence because he could have been burned at the stake. He died in Ravenna, Papal State (there are no precise dates regarding his birth and death).

The poet's devotees affirmed that he was born around 1265 in Florence, and died in September 1321 in Ravenna at the age of fifty-six.

Loris read Dante's biography again and again, comparing his life with that of Claudio. A sinister meditation pervaded him, thinking that Dante never returned to his beloved city; a thought that was dragging down the man in an aura of uncertainty.

PART TWO

Saturday evening Claudio was chatting with Michael, expressing with a blatant charm: "After Lucifer was cast out of heaven, he found refuge in the very center of the Earth, concealing with him all the powerful energy of his survived reign. Fires of boiling ravaged lava were poured into the bowels of the fulcrum terrestrial planet, forcing God to desist in fighting Lucifer and his traitor angels. Dante's *Inferno* is the one under our feet, embedded to our eyes since the creation of human life. A real reign of terrestrial spiritual damnation, connected to the material life more than the heavenly holiness. That would explain why humans are more inclined in sinning then repenting, following more easily the path of perdition. Devil's domain prevailed on earth, without any control in time. Hell has been with us since the genesis of life."

Michael shot his eyes wide open, obscurely flabbergasted by his cousin's contorted speech. "Jesus, Claudio, your ideas are frightening. According to you we are all possessed by the evil spirits, if they exist, obviously. I am not really a convinced believer, but I think your uncle is out of his mind! I like the idea of the mysterious opaque image you mentioned before, but to me it is just a fantastic vision, a dreamer's illusion. Thank God it is not the truth!"

Claudio was hiding his inner disappointment, feeling teased by his cousin. The conversation had no reason to continue, and Claudio left.

Next morning began with a knocking on Claudio's door. It was eleven o'clock, time for brunch. "Hey, princess, are you alive in there? Don't you know that a night as a lion corresponds to a day as a sheep! Your uncle Loris called, he was surprised about me answering the phone!" Claudio woke up, remembering his dream about the beautiful girl. He began performing a portrait of her, almost falling in love with the image.

Giacomo, seeing his son's face, started singing an Italian love song, "That's *amore*."

A couple of hours later, Claudio was on the phone with his friend Ryan Swann, with whom he used to play in a music band. Ryan had heard some news about the murders, and updated Claudio after reproaching him for missing a few jam sessions. Morris (the sacristan) finally decided to talk to Inspector Kevin about all he knew of Father Larry's past life.

Claudio enquired: "Where did you hear those facts, I am always following the case,"

Ryan: "I know you are involved in a certain way, your cousin Michael told me a great deal about it. We miss you, my friend."

Claudio paused and said, "I will be back very soon, don't worry, I was sick for a little while. Tell me about Kevin, please."

Ryan continued, "Morris Harrison asserted that Larry, as soon as arrived in Vancouver, was studying numerous books and documents that he brought from Rome. He was accurately researching here in Vancouver the past colonial history of native legends, starting from 1500 to nowadays. The cleric was obsessed about the old remains of a map, and a papal document he discovered had been kept secret in the hidden archive of the Vatican. Larry mentioned later a drawing that got lost in time."

Claudio implied, "It is not a confession but a clarification. I don't understand why the sacristan delayed in giving the information, perhaps he is hiding something… settling his version."

A surprised Ryan responded: "Wow! You sound like a detective, I should be careful talking to you," Claudio weaved his front as a sign of tension. Mesotti at the end decided to release the sacristan…

CHAPTER VII

Suspicious

Claudio was killing some time, fooling around. He grabbed the receiver and called his sister. "Hey, how are you?" said Claudio, breaking her name. A surprised toned voice replied, "Claudio! What a surprise! I am OK, thanks, I was thinking about you. What are you doing, is it lunchtime there?"

A brief moment, "Lunch is over, sister. What's the news from Rome, I mean in the Vatican? They should be concerned about Father Larry's death."

Laura complied, releasing a few intriguing details. "I have seen Reverend Larry many times in the library, but I never personally talked to him. I know one of his closest friends, by the way, Father Armando Suarez; he is from the Navarre region in Spain, an expert in religious history and theological matters."

Claudio revived, plunging into the conversation. "Apropos of Larry's friends, his verger here gave a full statement related to the time he spent in Italy. Morris Harrison was even arrested for reticence."

Laura reluctantly commented, "Arrested, the sacristan? I do not see any connection with Larry's homicide, as far as I am concerned. It is bizarre." On the other side: "I don't know how to explain my feelings, but I perceive that something else is intertwined with this murder. Larry died too soon, without any logical explanation. Three months in Vancouver! More or less, it is weird, isn't it?"

Laura persisted, "I need to have a meeting with Armando Suarez as soon as possible. Of course Larry's death is illogical! Perhaps the sacristan knows more and I am completely wrong about it!"

The siblings shifted to familiar questions before hanging up the receivers, and Claudio questioned Laura, "Are you thinking of visiting for Christmas?" There was silence for a little while. "Too busy at work, I will try in the spring perhaps. I am sorry, Cla! I know you miss me!" "Never mind, Laura! Spring weather is even better."

A click signaled the end of the conversation.

Leon as usual followed Claudio into the bedroom, receiving a nice long brushing and a kiss on his forehead. Lying down on the soft carpet, Leon began snoring profoundly, pampering Claudio with a nice profound symphony of lost dreams.

The Next day Claudio was driving, accompanied by Isabel, passing by the Catholic Church in the North Vancouver Squamish Reserve.

By surprise the house of worship was opened, and a man was sweeping the patio: it was the released sacristan. They parked the vehicle, and the young couple asked: "Is it possible to pay a quick visit inside the church?"

He replied, "Yes, of course young fellows, you are welcome!"

While guiding them inside, Morris was donning his sacristan's cloak, explaining the history of the church and the relationship with the natives. A beautiful painting of Jesus dressed as a native appeared close to the altar, followed by saints depicted in aboriginal cloths.

Flowers and totems were displayed along the altar, releasing a mix of historical and religious atmosphere. It was an original, well-maintained emblazoned setting.

The sacristan explained, "Father Larry was very active with the aboriginal community, and just in a few months, people attending the church increased exponentially. As you can see, we are scarce in people right now. We are hoping for a new priest to be assigned soon."

He looked sincere and sad at the same time. "I told the investigators everything I knew," concluded Morris adjusting a few candelabras, while dusting the countertop. He was a hard worker. Isabel sensed a shiver of fear in hearing Morris's rusty voice resonating…strongly grabbing Claudio's hands as a sign of protection and trust. He glanced at Isabel reassuring her, feeling after a long time in control of the situation. He muttered: "I am not sure about the other killings, and I will continue to search for the truth. My sister in Rome knows some people who were very close to Larry."

The smell of frankincense shrouded the church.

Morris escorted the couple outside the entryway, and wished them good luck while gazing at them from a distance. He then said loudly, "Father Larry used to say that only when dusk is falling one can discern the truth."

"That Morris guy is strange! Something atypical was in the church, starting with that incense. They use it only when performing funerals or sometimes special celebrations, and yet no one was there," criticized Claudio, whereas Isabel surveyed, "You know what…if Morris confessed his secrets to Larry before he was killed. He could claim the secret of confession." After a brief hiatus, Claudio said, "I never thought about that, Isabel!"

It was a possibility neglected by many.

After leaving the churchyard, Claudio drove along Marine Drive, gazing at the ocean's shore; Isabel sighed, coddled by the romantic view. "What did your sister tell you about Larry Murphy, any news lover boy!" He swiftly glanced at her, glinting, "Lover boy! Ha! That is funny." Isabel lowered the radio volume.

"My sister informed me that Father Armando Suarez will spend two weeks' holiday back home, in Spain. He is following Larry's case, trying to sift through his past life. She speculated that perhaps Larry's death is a mere coincidence, a botched robbery."

"Could be right, do you not think?" Claudio frowned "Do not forget! Police found diverse remains up there," Isabel countered, "One more reason to suspect a random accident."

A vibration distracted the couple. "Is it your phone, Claudio?"

"Yes, but I am driving. Take a look for me, please, it could be my father." Isabel rushed, "It says Laura! What should I do?"

"Put her on the speakerphone, please, and pretend you are not here, Isabel."

A brief hiatus allowed the communication to settle, while a delayed voice burst from the speakers. "Claudio! Are you busy? Can you hear me?" Laura puffed and grunted, membrane vibrating. "Yes, I can hear you, but the communication is not very good. I am driving right now, I am alone."

Laura faltered, "Alone! Why do you punctuate? I think you are not alone, smart boy. Do not tease me, please." When Claudio swore to be the only one in the vehicle, Isabel gestured with a sign of discontent.

Claudio knew that his sister could read his mind. Laura was holding the receiver with her right hand, placing the left on her side... head bent slightly. "Are you there? I cannot hear you anymore, Claudio!"

Communication broke down, and the day ended quickly.

Fall was one of the most colorful seasons in British Columbia. Trees were painted with a myriad of different colors, blasting and modifying within the scattered shards of the sun's rays. Leaves were changing in the mirror of a kaleidoscope, in their varied and subliminally engraved geometric shapes.

Claudio was striding with Leon between Granville and Laburnum Streets, along an array of lush trees, donating warm radiant colors. Leon was sniffing with his wet nose, pointing upwards, capturing the fragrant scents of the pictured leaflets. He closed his eyes, falling in a state of unconsciousness, snatched by the smell of the forgotten past.

Claudio thought of places of never-ending radiant tales, like the one he was living in Vancouver. All of a sudden, he let go of the leash, releasing his trapped mind and Leon's freedom of love. Claudio opened his pupils, admiring the slow-motion running of Leon...a riding, diving in the mystery of life's free will. Leon's head turned, showing a proud, strong, protective face, while the autumn was leaving with its charming colorful poetries, abandoning the dark dead tone of cold melancholy.

Nature was emitting its peculiar love.

"*Midway upon the journey of our life I found myself within a dark forest.*"

Dante Alighieri

CHAPTER VIII PART ONE

Detectives

One week before Christmas Laura contacted her father, "How is my little brother doing? I need to hear your opinion." Giacomo in a puff of contentment exclaimed: "A little bit better if left alone. He is now interested in this obscure case, the novelty of the year. My personal detective…"

Laura directed, "Be patient old man, he will find his path and tranquility sooner or later. Where is he? Last time we spoke he was driving, and the communication died." Her father defined, "He was speaking with your cousin Michael before you called…and left."

Laura enquired, "How is the situation there, any news about Larry Murphy's homicide?"

"I am not really concerned about it. Since Larry was killed, no other people were found dead. Those remains are antecedent. I think it was an attempt to rob him, or something like that."

"I do not like this, papà. Long hiatuses are always a sign of deceit and ambiguity. Remember that after long hiatuses always followed more victims."

He didn't seem to agree with that, dismissing Laura soon after.

The investigation was covered by a shimmering blanket of snow, shrouding all the fuss in a momentary soft slumber. 2017 brought a nice winter, and the ski resorts of Vancouver were sold out. Claudio and his friends went skiing. They spent the afternoon on the mountain, dining at the lodge. From the peak, Vancouver resembled a Christmas tree, adorned by the city lights and the Lions Gate illumination, reflected in the ocean.

Michael took a break, removing his gloves with his teeth. He desired to take a picture. "Look at the view guys, fantastic! The ocean inlet is reflecting the snow, creating a whitewater pool of mystical poetry."

Claudio's eyes were cold and blurred. He was admiring the landscape when a shadowy image lured his attention. The opaque figure was moving on the left side of the ravine where the group was standing. An amorphous, crooked-like female was slowly walking in distortion, as if badly injured. Claudio noticed the high snow opening while she was passing in between, dressed in a grimy white robe displaying long greasy hair. He neared, standing against the safety fence, and before the misshapen creature disappeared behind a pine tree, he noticed some roots sliding over her legs. He saw her bulging neck, which gave him the creeps. He was going to lure his friends' attention, when he distinguished a second figure chasing the previous one.

A little girl paraded before his astonished eyes. She appeared candidly dressed in a white robe, waving her glinting hair. She turned for a brief moment, as if sensing Claudio's presence. In her hands were concealed a red rose, a bloody rose. For a moment the lassie lost her grasp, clutching the flower a moment before it dived into the snow. She smiled at Claudio, vanishing into the woods.

Claudio stood up, moving briskly along the fence. "Hey guys, did you see those women down the ravine? They are lost, I think. A little girl was chasing her mother." Isabel kept looking, "Where are they? I do not see anyone there, it is so dark. Are you sure? Perhaps wild animals..."

Claudio reluctantly answered, "Are you kidding me, Isabel! I am not out of my mind yet. I saw two people down the ravine."

Michael intervened to solve the debate: "Snowshoeing my friend! There are trails for that, and one is just where you pointed your finger."

The group split, sliding along the diverse slopes, while Claudio remained with Isabel on the hill. She was ready to go when Claudio yelled once again, "Isabel, look! There she is! Look now."

Isabel observed a dirty white piece of cloth blowing in the air, like a flying sail. It was changing forms because of the wind, gliding far away upon the snow. "It is just a piece of cloth, Claudio, nothing more. This is what you saw! Come on let's go. I am starving."

The episode slid away as a beautiful skiing, while Claudio started doubting his own troubled mind.

Reverend Armando Suarez was a notorious cleric in the Vatican. He was like a walking library, he knew a lot. The cleric returned to Rome and met Laura a few days later. She was dying to tell Claudio about her meeting with him.

"Uncle Tony contacted me a few days ago. Did you know that?" An ashamed Claudio toned, "No, really! It's been a long time since I heard from him. Is he OK?" Laura in a reproaching mode, countered, "Tony sounded a little bit disappointed with you. He complained about your absence in his house. He is the only relative we have in Canada."

"Yes, I admit it, but it was not done intentionally. Michael lately changed his attitude toward me. I think he's jealous of Isabel." An ignited sister said, "No, come on! He is your best friend and only cousin in Vancouver. Do not say that, please. Promise me you will pay a visit to our uncle as soon as possible. Extend your apology, OK?" Claudio whistled silently, "OK, I promise! Now I have to leave you because there is Inspector Kevin on the TV news, *ciao bella*!"

"Wait a moment, you fool! Let me tell you about my meeting with Armando." "OK, shoot, but be quick, please," exclaimed her brother.

Meantime, Detective Kevin released worrying updates: "We are very disturbed to announce the finding of additional human remains in the North Shore forest. Forensic have established that a few of the bone samples date back to 1999. It seems they were all murdered between March and September, in an interval of six months. We used the same method we adopted with Father Larry's bones, extracting DNA from the teeth pulp and bone powder. Specialists filtered and purified the DNA at room temperature of 20-23 degrees Celsius, thereby reducing further degradation of the already damaged DNA."

A common misconception assumed that those months were the favorite seasons of the killer, striking almost every year.

The inspector managed, "A public profile of the maniac was made by the expert profilers, less ostentatious than the previous one."

Mesotti showed his rigid facial muscles, glinting, "The slayer could be a young strong person with a good education, who perhaps has had a past trauma in his childhood. He is a local, because he can move on all the mountain trails without losing orientation. Conceivably he could be a hunter, or an expert hiker with a military background, bewildered by his macabre chronicles of sadistic pleasures. The alert is at a high level."

The officer was questioned, answering with his expertise to all the inquiries. "The Provincial Integrated Homicide Team will officially step on the case, supporting us. My assistant, Agent Robert Jones, will liaise with whoever has information related to this specific case," concluded him while pointing at Robert, who was smoothing his mustache.

Claudio was still on the phone with Laura, "It all started when Armando and Larry discovered some historical Spanish manuscripts related to colonialism and Catholicism in modern Vancouver. The period was the seventeenth century. Several documents were found in Rome."

Laura calmly continued: "At the beginning Larry was only curious, but after a trip the two made in Spain, the conservative cleric became obsessed about this topic, using all the time he had to research and investigate. Larry visited Spain, England and France, stressing insistently the clergy to be transferred to Vancouver."

Claudio enquired in a rush, "Where did he go, precisely, and why?"

She managed, "In his coherent stringent research, Larry spent time in the northern region of Spain, the province of Navarre, precisely. He reached the border of France."

Claudio was completely absorbed by this inquest. Too many coincidences were followed by the outlandish feeling that something was trying to whisper words of mysterious time.

In a moment of exaltation he remarked, "I suspected that Larry's death was connected to Rome, and moreover…"

Laura abruptly said, "Hold your horses, Colombo! Do not fantasize. We have to wait and investigate on our own. Patience is a refined quality."

PART TWO

In February, Claudio bravely attempted several times to contact Inspector Kevin. The boy was denied, deciding instead to speak with his friend Ryan. Claudio left a message on his phone: "Ryan—how are you my friend? Long time I do not hear from you. I was wondering if we could meet sometime and have a beer. I need to talk to you about the murder case, call me back when you can, please. Thanks."

Ryan received the message while driving, and decided to pull over. Claudio, reading Ryan's name on the phone's screen, eagerly fetched the device, and with a smirk of enthusiastic joy said, "Hey! Are you still alive, Ryan? I am so happy to hear from you again, what are you up to?"

Ryan replied, surprised, "Wait a moment, Cloudy! Sorry, I meant Claudio, or perhaps I was right the first time. You are the one who vanished for weeks, like a cloud in the sky. You missed all our music jam sessions this month and we had to use some random guitarists."

Verallo felt guilty for the second time, "I am sorry, I admit it. I was busy with Isabel and the university. I should have at least called you, even if I am not that type of guy. I will be back soon, I promise."

Ryan Swann was nodding his head while listening to the speaker, rotating a drum stick with the fingers of his left hand. He was timing Claudio's voice. "What the hell are you doing, Ryan? Playing music? I need you big guy!" sentenced the Italian.

"Do you need me for real, Claudio? I am all yours, what can I do for you, my crazy friend? Speak, please." A moment of uncertainty followed a flattering voice: "I need you to introduce me to Inspector Kevin! I have to talk to him."

Ryan silenced, after a hiccup surfaced him. "Are you out of your mind? You will never be able to meet him, unless you possess the keystone of the crime scene. Everybody wants to talk to that man. He is too busy dealing with the Provincial Integrated Homicide Team…"

Claudio cut off Ryan: "Yes, I know. I am following this case very closely and I know lots. I just need a chance, and you are studying to join the police, aren't you, Ryan?"

"Remember that I am just a cadet. I know lots of policemen, of course. Mesotti is very important right now, and is highly quoted because of the investigation. He is coming to our police academy next week, at the justice institute of B.C. in New Westminster."

Claudio hesitantly said, "Are you for real? Could you invite me?"

Ryan countered, "It is not possible…it's a session about crime scenes and serial murderers' behavior. Wait a moment, boy! Perhaps there is a chance for you outside the institute, after the assembly is concluded."

"Please, Ryan, make it real. I will offer you lunch and dinner, I swear to God! I could join the police department if my father agrees. I wish to do what you are doing right now."

Ryan surveyed, "It is a lengthy process. Before being a detective, you will spend years on patrol chasing criminals. If your father can support you at the university, stay there. It is better." Claudio was twisting his front hairs, while caressing his head.

Having healed the wounds with Ryan, he decided to pay a visit to his uncle, calling Michael to see if he was at home. Claudio parked along the street, advancing with a hint of contentment, gazing at Michael standing on the balcony. Tony bent over the balcony displaying stretched opened arms: "The return of the prodigal son, we thank you God!" exclaimed enthusiastically. A second wound was mended and Giacomo embraced Claudio like a son. The two entertained an interesting, long conversation, whereas Michael stayed aloof on his computer, surfing the internet. "You guys must be very careful from now on in approaching the trails. There is a serial killer in the area, and this is a bad omen for all of us. This community has never witnessed something like this before. I heard that forensics found remains almost twenty years older!" said Tony.

Claudio bragged, noticing his cousin peeping: "Very soon I will meet Inspector Mesotti, thanks to a friend of mine."

Tony in bewilderment: "Seriously? The guy is a real notorious personality. He was born in the North Shore, but his grandparents came from Italy, did you know that?"

Claudio adrenalized, replied, "Yes! I know everything about him. I want to be a detective! I need to…" Michael entered the room suddenly, grabbing an apple and breaking into the conversation, “Your father will never allow such a travesty, do you realize that, Colombo?”

Tony abruptly interrupted his son: “Mind your business, Mr. Internet, Claudio is big enough to decide his future, and we all know that Giacomo is always playing the role of the stubborn.”

“Thanks uncle, I am happy for your support.You got my point!”

CHAPTER IX

The Encounter

A week later, outside the police academy: "It seems our detective is surrounded by a storm of cadets. You need Ryan's intervention, son. Everybody is happily having a photo with Kevin," resumed Giacomo…Isabel was impatiently rolling her eyes

Ryan gestured at Claudio, while Isabel poked his shoulder. He suddenly darted toward the inspector, anticipating a few cadets ready to raid the man.

"May I introduce myself, sir? My name is Claudio Verallo, from Rome. I am so happy to have the possibility to talk with you today. I was invited by one of my best friends here, Cadet Ryan Swann. He is standing over there."

Mesotti paraded a compliant look, while gently depositing his phone in the right pocket of his elegant gray jacket. He noticed the other cadet retrieving a few steps away.

"*Puoi respirare quando parli ragazzo*! You can breathe when talking, boy," said him, surprisingly mentioning a few Italian lines with an English accent. "I still know some Italian. I am impressed with your straightforward decision to burn the others. You know what you want. I like that. What can I do for you, Claudio?"

The boy was blushing, flattered by Kevin's comment. He called to Isabel and his father, introducing them. Claudio was very attentive, noticing Kevin's elegance. He introduced to Mesotti the figures of Laura and Reverend Armando Suarez.

The officer without any hesitation, and boasting a grinning smirk, told Claudio, "I know about it! Italian police have been collaborating with us since Father Larry died. Nothing was found in Rome related to his homicide, and the documents police found were just historical facts."

After a short hiatus, he said, "Nobody ever threatened him or had a problem with Larry. He was reserved and obsessed with his studies, searching for spawned legends of the middle Ages," concluding with a guttural, rumbled voice.

Giacomo speculated, "Do you know Inspector, how difficult is to be transferred in a different diocese when studying in the Vatican?" A pause followed. "Not really," replied Kevin, while Giacomo insisted, "It seems as if the clergy was eager to send Larry to Vancouver. It took only six weeks for the blissful upper echelon of the vicariate to arrange Larry's departure from Rome. Outstanding!"

Kevin's eyes riveted in a pale doubtful face: "I do not know about the clergy affair, and I want to rely on what you are saying, given that you guys are from there," answered the perplexed officer.

Claudio's father sounding arrogant and accusing, said, "They even hesitated when looking for the previous curator of the church, who was there before Larry. How come he was moved so quickly?"

In hearing all these logical and consequential questions, the inspector yanked with a tweak of uncertainty; he needed a way out with his smart guests, cutting to the chase and unveiling confidential information. "I think you did not come here for a signature or a photo, am I wrong? Anyway, I appreciate all the comments and criticism about this intricate case. If you know more, please let me hear it, I will give you my phone number just in case."

Claudio was bewildered in hearing Kevin's comments. A moment before he thought Kevin was going to liquidate them, after his father's conceited behavior.

CHAPTER X

Roots of Evil

1604 Region of Navarre, Spain…

Doctor Daniel Morgair had two daughters, Elysa of twelve and Elena of six. His wife died of a mysterious virus that he desperately attempted to cure, and for this reason his sister-in-law moved to their house, helping and supporting the family with her glistening, shining positive attitude.

Daniel deepened and perfected his medical manuscripts, studying alternative natural cures, introducing herbal treatments, religious spiritual mindful rites and therapeutic potions. He taught his older daughter the doctor profession practice, and the secrets to quickly heal sick people in need.

"Give me the gauze, please, I will show you how to place it. The first part is important, calm and gently, like this. I swabbed the surface before so that it is clean and disinfected, there we are," said the doctor, assisted by his older daughter, who was attentive and eager to perform.

"Could I try to cut the rims further? I think I can do it," Elysa asked.

"No rush, you need more time before practicing, be patient and observe what I do."

The patient remarked, "I am sure you will be one of the best doctors in town, Elysa, you are such a lovely, disciplined girl. We are very proud of you!" The little lassie blushed, hiding under her father's arm, while a dusty candelabra accompanied the pair to the exit. The job was accomplished. Doctor Morgair was of Irish origin, and his father left Ireland in 1566, when England conquered the island. He was a Catholic, and had to escape because the English Protestant settlers were converting all the Irish people through violence and torture. The rioting Irish rebels were caged and obliterated in the name of the pure Christendom.

It all began in 1536, when King Henry VIII imposed the Protestant Reformation on Ireland. While the king broke with papal authority, his son Edward VI of England moved further, breaching with the conservative papal doctrine completely. The Morgairs found refuge in the sentry Catholic Church of Spain, and their son Daniel was born a free, blissful Catholic in the Navarre Kingdom.

At that time, healing with medicinal plants was very common and safe for educated doctors, but at the same time dangerous from a religious point of view. *Mandragora or* mandrake herbs had been used for centuries and were one of the most important and powerful plants in sorcery, witchcraft, spiritual rites and herbal medicine. Some herbs of the nightshade mandrake plant contained hallucinogenic, sleepiness and narcotic alkaloids. Daniel taught his daughter how to treat patients, introducing the use of ointments, potions, oils and leaves.

Elysa was really interested in the subject, always travelling with her father visiting around the cities and in the province. She was studying and learning all she could about medicine. Elysa was very passionate and clever but could never forget how her mother died in pain and despair.

"Remember, my love, never to tell anybody about those roots and herbs. We live in menacing times, and cannot trust those who want to hinder the real medicine. If we keep it a secret, no one could impede us to experiment the real essence of healing, I mean saving lives!" explained Daniel to her. She questioned: "Did our mother die because of those thick-headed ignorant father? You could not cure mom from her illness."

"Yes, it is true, love! They obstructed our analysis! Now let us focus on our topics."

Elysa had light warm brown eyes, long dark-blond hair and a soft tanned skin. She was called by the patients "*d'angelo pelo*" or "angel's hair" for her beauty and kindness. She was very fervent and naturally gorgeous, attracting intensely the youths who easily fell in love with her energetic sensuality. Elysa's sister grew up in the shadow of her sibling. She had poor health, remaining in a form of undeveloped growth. Elena was not regarded as important as Elysa, staying at home with her aunt for domestic services: she did not get along with her aunt, despising her.

Elena was considered cursed, the haunted projected image of Elysa. Numerous inhabitants of Logrono used to embed the girl within such a despicable emblem.

A patient of Dr. Daniel was conversing with the cleric of the town about Elena: "That girl is a bad omen for the whole community. She is spoiling day by day her family's reputation. We should send her far away, reverend! I have to confide an incident I witnessed outside the Morgairs' house. I exited Daniel's dwelling after he gave me some medication, noticing Elena torturing reptiles."

The priest enquired, "What do you mean 'torturing?' Be more specific."

The embarrassed male pointed out, "I saw with my own eyes that little imp thrusting tiny scales of wood inside the lizards' heads. The reptiles were writhing in agony while she was laughing, displaying a giggle of contentment. I cannot forget that snigger, a sinister one!"

"What you are telling me is mischievous, contorted for a little girl,"

"There is more, your eminence! A friend of mine told me that she saw Elena smashing frogs with flat rocks along the lagoon; she was disgusted and vomited. Elena Morgair is always harming little helpless animals, talking to herself. She could be a..." "A *bruja*... witch!" replied the cleric while the confessional portal closed behind him. Elena was carried in front of the church sentry soon after, forced to gaze at the Holy Mary's obelisk a few yards from the altar. She was forced to recite a haunted spell in order to obliterate Elysa's devilish seventeen birthday ciphers...1609. The priest helped by the verger restrained the imp.

"Why don't you show yourself, Lucifer? Dwelling in this little arrogant brat? Release her, and free her family from this curse. In the name of God, I expel you! It's he that gave us the authority," yelled the cleric, while Elena was kicking and booting hysterically, screaming, "Let me go, please, let me go! It is my sister the devil, not me! I want my father, help me!"

The situation was out of control. Daniel ran to the cathedral to rescue his feeble daughter, after being alerted. Moments later, Elena briskly escaped outside the sanctuary layout, screaming and threatening to attempt suicide by plunging into the river.

She was able to get free, feeling betrayed by her own family, "My aunt! She is the one who hates me! Elysa, I despise you! You both are a *desgracia* (disgrace)," screamed a furious Elena in distress. She was venting years of anguish and jealousy, drooling like a possessed soul. The priest was crossing his chest and reciting the exorcism, while Daniel in panic attempted to save her. He said: "Elena, I love you. I am your father, please! Forget about your aunt and Elysa, I am here for you, little princess. Calm down and do not act like that!"

Daniel climbed to the cliff and dived in the river as soon as his daughter jumped. He saved her life. From that day on, Elena never spoke with her sister again.

In time Elysa had acquired a wide knowledge of medicine and natural treatments as well, using various manuscripts and notes she made in those years assisting her father.

Three weeks before her birthday, their aunt got sick, and the two girls had to stay at home with her. Daniel went northeast to San Sebastian for an emergency. In the afternoon a wagon with horses from the monastery arrived outside the Morgairs' dwelling, asking for help. One young student was seriously sick and could not breathe properly—the novice was part of an important devout clerical family, and was assisting his uncle in his profession. They came from Rome to Spain for a couple of years.

A man faced Elena on the doorstep. "We are looking for Elysa, they gave us this address, it is very urgent, please!" Elena stared at the male with an ugly face and answered, "I do not know her!" She stepped back, while Elysa introduced herself to the stranger.

"We need your help, please, we were told you are as good as your father. There are no doctors available. We went to the closest villages, and everybody mentioned you."

Elysa grabbed what was at hands, collecting everything in a bag. It was the end of August…dark and raining outside. They rapidly approached the monastery, while someone from the window said in a loud voice, "The magic healer is coming up." Elysa was scared and in a state of agitation. For the first time she was going to assist a sick person without Daniel's support.

The big heavy portal opened with a sound of crunching hinges, while the angel was brought swiftly into the novice's room. The young fellow was mumbling because of high fever, rumbling with a hard respiration. He was confused and in a state of delirium.

"He got sick all of a sudden! He got worse yesterday, and today, as you can see…" The girl replied, "I know what to do, I just need your assistance to move him…It is not too late!"

Elysa suspected it was a virus, perhaps an infection, deciding to utilize several herbs to make an infusion. Her goal was to lower the fever, freeing the neophyte's nose and throat. She spent all night in the room, and at dawn he opened his eyes and saw the angel who had saved his life, an angel he would desire forever. "What a gorgeous young lady God sent me—she is an angel fallen from the sky. Whoever you are, you saved my life," the young novice whispered, eyeing the gem. Her eyes were those of a fawn, largely deep with a wider expression. Prolonged eyelashes moved like sails, giving origin to the wind of passion.

At the beginning he could not properly hear the people conversing around him, spellbound by the gentle dance of her full lips, whispering in silence. He was struck by Elysa right inside the heart, admiring her long wavy hair descending upon a dream of lost love. He was distraught and confused, lost in melancholic deep emotion.

Elysa was asked almost every day to come and visit her patient. She was attracted by his kindness…a mutual respectful feeling of love, which soon after spread around rumors of a scandalous affair. Daniel came back one week later, having cured numerous people affected by an unknown disease. He was so pleased and proud of Elysa for taking care of those medically in need.

"I am very glad for you, my love," he told Elysa. "You took the best part of your mother's personality. You deserve much more from your life, much more. I will tell you about my patients' illnesses and how I treated them, but first your story. How did you save this young fellow? I heard he is part of an authoritative, wealthy family, which means you brought luster to the Morgairs!" Daniel kissed her, saying that only she could have saved her mother, while behind the slightly opened door, Elena was peeping in a distressed, hateful agony.

She was wishing Elysa a horrible *desgracia*! Elena's jealousy toward her sister was growing every day, especially when rumors about the lovers' affair became redundantly persistent. The eleven-year-old started conspiring within her troubled soul, concocting a cold, malicious revenge in time. Daniel and Elysa went home to celebrate the event, while two envious eyes full of covetousness were staring in darkness outside…a sight of fear…

CHAPTER XI

Mysterious Island

Inspector Kevin did not intend to lose time on pointless, unproductive fact-findings, he needed real consistent evidence, and for this reason he decided to locate the antecedent chaplain of the North Vancouver reserve. On the other hand, Giacomo had all the reason to raise doubts about Larry's sudden transfer, because not enough explanations were given by the Vancouver diocese.

Toronto investigators rapidly traced the chaplain, who provided police with a series of documents produced by the Roman Vicariate, in which he requested personally to be moved close to his family. He needed to assist his sick old mother. As a solid reason, he presented a medical certificate to the officers, clarifying the whole confusing scenario. However, even if the cleric had never met Larry, for being in Vancouver and Toronto in different times, he had something curious to tell: "Larry loved writing, making innumerable manuscripts and coded scripts, especially in his favorite old Latin. He left in the sacristy crypt a notebook dedicated to the Oak Island mystery. His findings referred in particular to colonist expeditions and local aboriginal legends. Larry strongly highlighted that the island was placed on the 44th parallel north of the earth's equatorial plane, crossing Europe, the Pacific Ocean, the Atlantic Ocean, and the Mediterranean Sea. (Washington State Vancouver is crossed by the 45th parallel north.) It was a line of prophecy, as Larry wrote on the parchments, remarking that the island has a weird animal shape. Someone called it 'the Omega'."

The priest paused, overwhelming the officers with the information. He sipped some fresh water and continued, "Larry speculated that in 1795 when Captain George Vancouver returned to England, interrupted his trip remaining on Oak Island, where a mysterious pit was found thereafter." Cops observed the reverend nervously consulting notes and papers, as if he had previously studied them.

"The puzzling crater was an old booby-trap conundrum, protecting its precious contents from looters and ransacking. It was accurately built in leveled hard surfaces, and was approximately 666 feet from the Atlantic coastline, had a depth of more than 166 feet, but flooded when they tried to dig further. It was connected to the ocean by a complex system of tunnels, as a secret water seal."

The police were trying not to lose track of this unusual information, thinking of Larry as a visionary. The inspector glanced at his colleagues, wearing an antagonizing look. He then questioned the priest: "What about those theories you were mentioning before! The BC law enforcement needs every piece of solid information. We rely on facts and not mere considerations." The reverend faked a calm and sober expression, continuing: "Among the many theories suggested by scholars, Larry sustained the most possible of all, that indeed the Knights Templar may have been in the New World a century before Christopher Columbus arrived. It all began in October, Friday the 13th of the year 1307, when the king of France, Philip the Fair, ordered to disband all the Templar order in his realm, accusing them of heresy, idolatry, corruption and sodomy. As…"

The officer sharply interrupted: "Wait a moment please! I am losing it. Are we going back to the fourteenth century, here? Do we need to be schooled once again, Father?" The priest started losing his marbles: "You told me police needed all the information, and that is all I have here, officer!" "Ok, Father, at least try to slow your pace, please."

The priest paused a brief moment, and then continued: "The king, with the pope's consent (Clement V), was eager to steal the notorious treasure of the order, although the Templar managed to escape with their fortunes. As is well known, they possessed a large fleet on the port of Rochelle in the southwest of France, where after passing Brittany and England, the Templar proceeded to Scotland, joining the cause of Robert the Bruce trying to overcome the English."

The cop puffed, affirming, "Money, always about money and gold; sacred and the profane in every part of society…always!" He frowned, donning his cassock and concluding, "Larry consulted several parchments concerning the detection of various stone plates, retrieved from the pit. Symbols and cryptic ciphers were engraved on the tables, as were opposite triangles, circles, wind roses and numbers (1, 2, 3, 4, 6, 7, 17, 20…in sequence). The parson was researching in a counterclockwise rotary system, positioning back in time his watch hands, beginning from nowadays to the fourteenth century, in a intertwined codification maneuver of lines, numbers, geometric figures, constellations, and Biblical references. He realized that police were timing the recording of his explanations in order to send it back to Detective Mesotti.

The latter noticed Larry's remark on the symbol of the reddish Templar cross (the equal-armed cruciform was a lavish symbol of honor and décor in a harmonic balance). It is claimed that the locals of Oak Island still tell tales of white men coming from over the seas, dressed in their traditional customs. Mesotti was reading, weaving his meaty lips. "The locals adopted the Templar's emblem, painting on their skin a red cross. The treasure concealed inside the cursed pit could be that of King Solomon's Temple. Three people found the pit in 1795, while six died in time researching the riches. The doomed legend said that when seven had died and only one tree would have remained on the island, the Templar secret would finally be revealed." Kevin paused, whispering profoundly, "I shouldn't be reading this. If it is a curse I could die! Better let the recording run."

Although Kevin was a practical dude, he was a little bit superstitious, as all Italians are. His blood was cold, deciding to play the recorder and let the reverend talk about it. The voice appeared distorted, as if someone was relenting and accelerating the electronic device, making Mesotti's face very serious about this old Friday the Thirteenth malediction.

The recorder played again, "Jacques de Molay, last grand master of the Knights Templar, before being burned at the stake put a curse on the pope and king of France. A few months later, they both died in baffling circumstances. Larry spent three weeks on the island, mesmerized by this fantastic discovery that enlightened his mind and heart, researching the truth shrouded in the centuries by the Vatican. From that day on the cleric's life was devoted to the historical facts of truth."

Kevin stopped the recorder, suspecting that perhaps Larry Murphy was overshadowed by the ordained powerful embossed seal of the clergy, which obliged him to accomplish his secret mission in a trustworthy, vowed fidelity. He could have been the eyewitnesses of an earthshaking enciphered hidden truth; a concealed treasure...valuable historical contents. As the inspector was speculating about the Toronto police report, he looked doubtful, furrowing his brow. "What was he looking for, up the North Shore?" mumbled Kevin in an inaudible, feeble voice. "I cannot see any connection between the Oak Island mystery and Vancouver, except the colonists' expedition and the aboriginal people!" Kevin appeared frustrated, framed in a sense of foreboding. He lunged toward the whiteboard, observing all the symbols and numbers. "Did Larry try to leave a pivotal encrypted message on the board for everyone to know? Or was it just a mere personal query, a sole purpose?" The detective smiled inwardly, retreating on his desk.

The bureau of investigation was still far away from the truth, and the chief of police's homicide squad secretary went to see Kevin Mesotti. His car hummed smoothly, while parking in the yard building. A long conversation took place in the detective's office, confronting a man he seldom worked with. "Our Homicide Special Squad pretends a most efficient connection between the diverse Police Departments of the North Shore with the VPD. We do not like personal investigation in this province. We know you received some materials from Toronto that you should have sent to all the other headquarters," the secretary asserted in a serious fashion. "I am responsible for liaising with all the teams here, and even if your district is the one in charge of the investigation, we are now the pivotal source. Next time we won't be so nice!" The two men argued until the secretary left the office, nodding apprehensively, and shutting with a robust thud the door behind him.

On the board Kevin was observing the number 1 (only divisible by itself, independent of any other numerals, yet the basis for them all. In the Bible it symbolizes the unity and domination, the oneness of the only God.

It represents the unity between God the father and Jesus his son, sacrificed for our sins in the name of Christianity), The number 2 (which conveys the meaning of a union, Christ and the church, the Old Testament and New Testament)

Mesotti's face was a furious one: "Those youth without experience think they can teach you how to investigate. They do not even know where to begin. I am 55 and demand respect. I will talk to my chief and clarify this incident. For few papers they get mad, unbelievable."

The center of investigation was soon reorganized in downtown Vancouver, where a wide ordered room was staged specifically for this case. Kevin said to his chief, "So from now on we have to show up every morning at the new office, is it true?" The chief replied, in a mandatory way, "Yes, make sure to be on time, I do not like the high echelon calling me and complaining about my man efficiency. You must follow the provincial homicide, they are officially in charge of the case and we have to corroborate by all means. Every major detective will represent his branch and district, assisted by an agent."

PART TWO

CHAPTER XII

Whispering Scrolls

Archivum Secretum Apostolicum Vaticanum, the Seal of the Vatican Secret Archive, the central repository in the Vatican City for all of the acts promulgated by the Holy See, is owned by the pope as sovereign of the Vatican City until his death or resignation, when it is passed onto his successor.

Laura knew a lot about the Vatican, and was explaining to Claudio how difficult it was to obtain permission to read or study historical documents. The secret archives contained about eighty-six kilometers of shelving and thousands of books and documents; the oldest surviving document dates back to the end of the eighth century.

Claudio was amazed about the archive, even if he never had the chance to visit the Vatican's secret collection. He asked Laura, "How is it possible to find or reach an old document after all these centuries?" Laura replied, "There are very strict limitations for researchers and students willing to enter the archives. However, I discovered that in the seventeenth century, under the orders of Pope Paul V, the secret archive was separated from the Vatican Library, and coincidently, Father Larry was researching documents of that century.

Later, in 1817, the Vatican Secret Archives were brought back to Rome from France (after Napoleon removed it from Rome), and again, Father

Larry made a personal trip on his own to France. In addition, in Spain between the sixteenth and the seventeenth century, numerous papal bulls were emanated and hidden in secret, yet Larry went to Spain twice to research." Claudio was listening carefully, imagining all those long, dusty corridors stepped upon by heavy secrets of the past. His sister continued indulging the boy: "I think that Larry knew what he was looking for, following a specific line of connection to his new discoveries. A specific expedition, an exploration map and documents related to the facts." Laura kept speaking of other secret archives hidden in several churches of Rome and outside Italy. It was an impossible challenge to track all those manuscripts and scrolls back in time, and Larry surely had pushed himself to achieve that. He had discovered an important historical secret dated back to the sixteenth century. Claudio was silent and thanked his sister for the information. He looked perplexed and was confused in his mind.

The time for the university exams was at hand, and Claudio with Isabel spent the last two weeks reviewing their topics. February was almost over, and people could feel the fresh breeze of the ocean growing warmer, while a blowing cold wind was drifting away. The sky was clean with bright stars and magic love was flying over.

Claudio rejoined his band as a guitar player, making Ryan happy again. He was ready to play while glancing outside the window, noticing the spectacular view of the obscured, cloudy North Shore hills. It was a nice area, boasting beautiful long sandy beaches located to the southwest, opposite of West Vancouver's ocean shores. In summertime after playing, they used to spend the rest of the evening practicing beach volleyball friendly tournaments on the seaside.

At the beginning of March, police announced the presence of a new person in their custody, investigated in relation of Father Larry's murder. Following police scrutinizing on Larry's phone, tracing all his contents and movements, detectives decided to take a precautionary measure on the suspect. He was a native who used to live at the North Vancouver reserve. "The suspect went hiking more than once with Larry, he was well-versed in surviving the elements. He possesses a great range of expertise in moving through the woods, knowing the mountain's trails and its wide-open area. The last day of Larry's life, he was seen with the cleric at the church, as a few witnesses told us. Moreover, spiritual objects were found close to the crime scene...in particular a modest wooden homemade totem, emblazoned with a Templar cross that the suspect used to make and sell," observed the North Van police officer exhibiting a think folder "A vast number of sheets engulfed the native's dwelling, hidden behind a picture. Larry's writing was on them, showing different dates and notes. Our experts evaluated all the manuscripts, finding complex research and mathematical calculations the priest computed methodically, following a faultless line. For the examiners additional documents were missing, given the fact that the order of pages was confused. One record was more complete and interesting, regarding the geographical structure of North America and Europe," continuing. It was unusual to see that Mesotti was no longer the sole protagonist of the interviews. The officer motioned, introducing a symbologist-cryptographer, who took over and explained, "Father Larry, in his documents, was speculating about the two major oceans embracing the north part of the Earth. He compared the North Atlantic and the North Pacific Ocean as two water-sealed symbols," pausing.

"To Larry it was the water sealing the Earth, and not the opposite, as the spirit embracing the body. The Earth dies without the water, while the water can live on itself, as the body dies without soul, and not vice-versa." The expert continued, followed by a skeptical pessimistic ambience: Kevin's face was briskly shoved by the cameras, he glowed ominously. "Our rector compared the present time to the Pacific Ocean, and the past to the Atlantic Ocean. Both are joined in time by their destiny, as the oceans are united by the same water. It is a dissertation related to Biblical prophecies, connecting the world through its basic focal components (*water and earth).* Larry Murphy is leading us throughout a mysterious journey, in an inverted past-present passage trail."

Provincial homicide detectives appeared motionless despite the symbologist's dissertation, as if obliged to let him talk. For the hardcore investigators those documents were not directly related to Larry's tragic end. Why kill him over mere scrolls of paper? Larry mentioned Vancouver as a prophetic revelation—the New World's city situated far west, dividing Canada from America, ideally.

Vancouver was level with Europe in a precise line, standing at the beginning of the Pacific Ocean, the largest and deepest of the world (covering almost fifty-nine million square miles, and containing more than half of the water on Earth). Larry calculated in his cryptic secret code that all the world's continents could fit in the Pacific basin, paring the two basic elements of life. The "Alfa" and "Omega" letters found inside his drawing were united forever in the beginning-ending of creation, Earth and water, in comparison with Vancouver's Ocean inlets and shores.

The provincial homicide squad, away from those literary speculations, supposed that the suspect could have killed Larry for money or revenge. The Catholics' mendacious behavior in residential schools was an example. Being just a born killer, very well experienced in this wild green territory was just impossible.

CHAPTER XIII

Macabre Frequencies

March 17 was Claudio's twenty-second birthday, and he directed with his friends to Whistler, celebrating and enjoying the massages and baths of the pompous Scandinavian Spa. In the evening he offered dinner and drinks to all, coming back home late the same night. Way back on the upper-level highway, Claudio screamed frantically, making Ryan swerve dangerously. Isabel said loudly, "What's the matter, Claudio? You scare the hell out of me! Did we hit an animal or what?"

He spasmodically answered, "Did you see that thing on the roadside? She was… for God's sake."

Ryan flabbergasted: "Are you serious? We almost got astray, do you want to kill us all, with your jokes!"

Isabel, in the backseat, grabbed Claudio's hand and felt he was shaking tremendously. She asked, "What did you see, my dear? You look scared. We should take a look outside, perhaps." Ryan denied: "No! Are you crazy, guys! It is dark and we need to call our friends in the second vehicle. If they don't see us, they will think something happened." Isabel insisted, "What if someone out there needs help? You should go before us. Come on, you're the one who's going to be a police officer." Claudio courageously: "I'll go, I have no fear. I know I saw something out there—a girl, I think." "A girl, are you sure. If so I will follow you," supported Isabel.

The two exited the car and walked carefully back to the side of the road, while Ryan approached the rest area. A light mist was flowing along the border of the North Shore woods, as if tracing them. Claudio advanced and spotted a shadowy figure concealed behind a bush…Isabel stayed far back. He motioned swiftly toward the woods, when the image moved, luring Claudio in a desperate chase along the forest's perimeter.

Isabel rubbed her scalp. "Wait! I cannot see you with this fog, don't run, please." She was reaching Claudio from a distance. He saw the girl, presenting her shoulders. She was emitting a sinister crying, and Claudio realized she was an adult with the voice of a child…hands moving outward clutching a red rose.

Isabel stopped again, calling for Claudio, as a grown-up shape revolved. An old woman was bearing the head of a little girl! Claudio screamed loudly when she spread her arms, displaying a mantle made of dirty roots, hanging like innards…dripping fluids. Her feeble, eerie childish voice emitted a sound. Claudio, blinded by the fog escaped, running into Isabel and making her fly over the roadside.

Ryan suddenly retrieved the youths in the car, escaping with a sound of screeching wheels away from that place. "You guys are tricking me! What did you see, a ghost? I don't buy it," disconcerted. Isabel turned to Claudio, "What did you see out there?" Claudio could not forget that horrible confused figure shrouded in the mist, and began describing her to his friends, luring them in a creepy sinister nightmare. Soon after the radio switched on by itself, and a contorted childish voice was heard reverberating in the speakers as if coming out the membranes; a watered sound coming from the abyss of darkness, a moment that scared the vehicle's occupants very much, confusing them about its provenience. Ryan said, slightly abashed, "You cannot trust those frequencies. Mischievous fakers are able to enter the antennas of the apparatus easily those days. It happened to the police enforcement too. I swear to God!" That voice continued…releasing its swishing rustled sounds.

When in his bedroom, Claudio recollected the red rose incident, the same flower he saw while skiing.

The incident was forgotten when Giacomo and his brother Tony were ready, surprising Claudio with a trip to the Seattle Rock Museum. They left early that morning, driving from north to south. For a moment they drove on the Second Narrow Bridge, parallel for a distance to the Lion's Gate Bridge.

The second Narrow Bridge connects the municipality of North Vancouver to the town of Burnaby, and consequently to the city of Vancouver. Claudio was facing backward while the vehicle was almost on top of the bridge. He could see a yellow blurred moon setting on the south-west side of the Pacific Ocean, whereas a shy rising red sun was opposing the earth's satellite. He sensed as if part of a slow marching, while the car was relenting, and his cousin was sleeping beside him.

Moon and sun were creating an evocative atmosphere that the boy could feel for the first time in Vancouver. Perhaps all the answers Larry wanted were here. The priest was going northwest following the early morning celestial signs of guidance, the stars were exchanging from east to west, revering the North Shore mountain range. "What was hidden up there, in the wood?" The constellations overnight and the star of Venus in the early morning were pointing north. "Why was Larry going there?" wondered Claudio in his dreaming mind.

All appeared so schematic and geometric between the ocean and sky: city and mountains, people and spirits, a continuous opposition balancing our existences, revealing the only impossible truth, one in need of the other in an everlasting contest of prevailing survival.

Claudio crossed the Canadian-American border, feeling excited being along an historical line that would show his destiny. The New World was waiting its revenge.

The day was spent at the Experience Music Project Museum, where Claudio could play and perform on a made-up stage, joined by Michael. Later Giacomo told his son, "I am going with Tony for a few days trip to San Diego. Can you survive without me, without getting in trouble?" Claudio teased his father showing his black hair, a shiny crew cut chiseling sharp his medium-tall stature, while two deep green eyes divided his little nose, displaying a little scar on his face. Michael on the other hand adjusted his light brown hair using a comb hidden in his pocket. A tall skinny fellow, who in time had developed some nervous tics because of a premature birth.

CHAPTER XIV PART ONE

Spring Sighs

Screams of terror and pain cursed the mountain range, welcoming April the first, 2017, that was not April fool's.

Sirens were heard Saturday early morning up the trails of the North Shore mountains, while once again a few of the search and rescue helicopters were flying on the east side of Cypress Park. The radio was releasing the breaking news, a body was found near Eagle Lake area, very close to the trails.

A couple of young fellows who had hiked at dawn discovered the remains of a body along the tortuous hedges, suffering panic attacks soon after. Claudio, still in bed, was awakened by Giacomo. He jumped from bed and went downstairs, monitoring the local news. The boy was proud in front of his father, claiming that he knew. The killer was still on the loose and the native was used as a scapegoat to reassure the community. "I told this to Michael! He thought the native was guilty" said him bragging. Giacomo heaved his eyes to the sky and whispered, "We have a new inspector in the house!" Claudio nodded, "Yes, sir!" Giacomo replied, "Surely a wild animal could be the cause this time, I am confident on that because the man was almost dismembered, according to the news." Claudio stood up, and with a serious, ominous face, stated, "It is spring dad, and if I am not wrong the killer..." He got dressed rapidly and went out to see what was happening in the neighborhood. Some people were discussing it at the square bar of West Vancouver, hoping it was an accident.

Nobody at the moment knew the identity of the victim or when he was killed. Police were very prudent in releasing information, while the forensic specialists were performing an extensive effort.

At Vancouver International Airport the jolt of tires hit the long runway. Laura arrived on time in the middle of a windstorm investigation, while people felt utterly bewildered and confused from the uncertain news. Brother and sister spent a peaceful Easter together, surrounded by their glimmering relatives.

Laura and Isabel liked each other very much, going out together almost every afternoon. Isabel was pleased to show Laura around. Vancouver was a modern growing metropolis, merged in the infinity of the past historical Pacific Coast, dressed in a colorful green nature capped by a deep-blue sky. The North Shore coast was a delicious environment enriched with wild animals, lakes, parks, hills, and beaches. Seals and killer whales were seen often in the ocean. It was unique.

Laura, who lived all her life in an historical, ancient, chaotic city, fell in love with beautiful British Columbia. She was charmed and startled at the same time, knowing that she could move there whenever she wanted. Laura expressed: "I do not know how to thank you Isabel, for your time. I love this place so far away from the chaos." Isabel was flattered: "I bet you would do the same for me in Italy."

Laura's joy was blurred by the local TV news, when at lunch she heard Mesotti releasing gory details on the latest vicious murder. "The victim was identified as an unlicensed hunter, who was leaving with a friend outside Vancouver. His buddy is missing. The male was assassinated by the Mountain Spring Butcher, as the police homicide team labeled the monster. The horrific onslaught left some parts of the body to be processed and studied. How the victim was transported up there remains unclear at the moment. No trace on the ground was found, except the scattered blood of the victim," continuing

"The ballistics exam revealed an unending number of shots fired by the hunter, who completely unloaded his rifle on the killer. The bullets hit the top side of an oak tree, where he was killed originally. To be sure of the rounds, we cut the tree, extracting the bullets and analyzing them. We can confirm that only the victim's rifle was used."

After his intervention, Kevin was speechless and diverted his eyes from the specialists, touching his shoulder holster beneath the jacket. He was squeezing the top edge of the inserted clip, as if he felt threatened by an uncanny presence. "Why had the huntsman shot so high? What did he see between the misty weather elements, blazed by the crimson of sun rays?" Kevin sighed, watching his assistant Robert.

Police were surprised by the strength of the killer, who was able to carry the body from such a distance, unafraid to be discovered. The forensic analyst took over after the officer's intervention, and technically elucidated, "The cadaver showed two holes on the wrists, made by two long sharpened rocks piercing both hands from side to side. A major clear enlargement of the flesh was displayed upwards; he was clearly crucified! The slayer used a tree as a cross, and the victim suffered for at least three hours before dying (three hours, like Christ on the cross, noticed inspector Kevin, mentioning on this occasion the Templar cross on the little totem). The victim's feet were missing, cut brutally with a sharp and heavy rock blade, manipulated by a vigorous fierce hand.

The eyes were grotesquely removed, replaced with muddy water." Laura left the table nauseated, rushing to the bathroom, while Claudio banged his glass on the table, spilling the water. "Destiny has bestowed upon Vancouver a haunted curse," pronounced Claudio spontaneously. "A sequence of homicides out of any logical explanation," he concluded.

Furthermore, the maniac had pushed some roots instead of the feet, boning the inner parts, eviscerating the poor victim soon after from the top down…when he was still barely alive. The grotesque masterpiece was concluded, and the remains were thrown in the water of an unknown lake.

It was just unbearable to listen and hard to believe that such macabre and perverse cruelty happened so close to the community. An Anti-Monster Special Squad was quickly announced and created the same day of the press release. For the second killer's profile, the support of FBI experts was requested.

PART TWO

Andrew Devine, the suspect in custody, was finally released. Every hint and line was followed, banning for the moment any kind of hiking upon the longer trails. Life was not the same anymore, and the massacre changed everybody's tranquility forever. This was a different and symbolic riddle, like a nightmare of the past.

Kevin, meanwhile, received Morris in his office, after the cryptographer found another symbolic ciphered anagram on Larry's manuscripts, acquired at the reserve. Kevin was disclosing foggy feelings: "What I don't really understand, apart from the encoded symbols, is why your friend the chaplain scattered all those parchments around, rather than considering to keep them in a vault; Toronto, Rome and now Vancouver, why?" He continued, observing Morris's reaction: "The provincial homicide team has set aside the personal matter of Reverend Larry, now that other victims have been butchered. However, I have some questions for you. Did Larry ever mention to you or Andrew Devine a secret crate, concealed somewhere in Europe or Canada? Perhaps he indicated an emblematic symbol or a sort of personal code-breaker?" Morris answered with his burled, contorted face, rigid as a log: "The last few months I personally had fallen out of touch with Larry. From being his obliged watchman, I became a perfect stranger."

Kevin unhooked the clasp of flat box, raising the lid, and shuffled a paper in Morris's face. "Do you know what this is?" asked the officer in a thundering voice. "No," said the sacristan. "I will tell you then. It is a clever anagrammatic writing of our dear friend Larry, followed by geometrical shapes and numbers as well. Andrew Devine told us that Larry asked him to keep safe his manuscripts, in case something unusual happened to him. He died, for God's sake! Was someone threatening his person lately?" Morris nodded in distress. "All I know I already told you, I swear to God,"

Kevin showed Morris a series of triangles with a circle inside, the pointed-up ones had the number six on the angles, while the downward-pointed shape had number three; all had the number one inside the circles and number two within the triangles. The geometrical figures were pointing at the four major wind rose positions. North and east had the number six, while south and west the number 3.

The number three is used four hundred and sixty-seven times in the Bible as a spiritually perfect number. In the New Testament there are twenty-seven books that signify the integrity of the holy trinity (three, three, and three, in multiplication). Jesus died at three p.m. followed by three hours of darkness and three day of resurrection: three is a holy number. The number six in the Bible symbolizes man and human deficiency, as a sign of Lucifer. Man was generated upon the sixth day within his sinful life. The temptation of Satan is number six, shown as the mark of the beast.

Morris was quiet in his sad slumber, while Kevin was reading a produced printout of Larry's scrolls. "At first glance, I can tell that you are worn-out Morris," exclaimed the officer exhaling with relief, stressing purposely the man with his reading. "The printing displayed an elaborate theory, based on connected historical facts. Larry, after using the symbols, explained his thesis, joining three diverse subjects related in time: the Templar, the prophecy and the Black Plague. The Knights were disbanded in 1307 (persecuted until 1312) by an infamous conspiracy, while a mysterious prophet, who perished in 1148, predicted an evil haunted revenge perpetrated by the order of the "equal cross."

Larry was convinced that the predicted curse was the outrageous and notorious Black Plague, delivered by the Templar. The plague began from 1347 until 1353, six years of hell (almost sixty million perished), forty years after the Templar's termination. Morris was overwhelmed by Mesotti's torrential information: "I am a simple man, I do not know about those things, it is like I am back at school," Kevin kept reading anyway.

A draft glided across the scrolls, rotating one of the sheets. The number 6 appeared as a 9, revealing the rampant active angel of darkness.

CHAPTER XV

Dante's Visions

Laura was confabulating with Isabel, expressing her concern. "I feel an intense intangible presence within the city, especially when closer to the natural elements. I cannot say if it is just an internal emotion or a state of freedom of the soul for being merged in a free natural wilderness. I sense there is something supernatural between the sky and ocean here, touching the spiritual past of the heart of land."

Isabel was amazed about Laura's poetic speech, recognizing her truthful originality. Laura felt the need to confide in her new friend, continuing the deep disquisition.

"The ocean water here creates misty hazy clouds, which subsequently feeds the astounding lakes and rivers. Paths of fluidity that brought back in time the history of this land, a new prophetic world!"

Isabel replied, "You can feel better than me the sensation of this place, because you are seeing everything for the first time. Your soul's eyes are like those of a child, they always see the truth hidden behind a lie."

Isabel mentioned Claudio and his passion for Dante's *Inferno*, imploring his sister to tell her more about the subject. "Yes! I can try to elucidate Claudio's passion for Dante, but I cannot expose his unusual mind," Simpered Laura, looking pleased, "After our mother's demise, Dante's opera became Claudio's safe fantastic refuge for his broken soul. Our Uncle Loris started calling his nephew Dante, convincing him later that our dear mom was not in paradise, but in limbo. She was still there because she decided to follow her fragile little son, lost in the obscurity of the woods. The forest was seen like the *Inferno*."

Isabel criticized Loris's perturbed behavior, harmful to the boy, in her opinion: "Why create an unreal macabre dimension for a little child?" Laura placed her delicate hand on Isabel's shoulder, continuing, "Loris is a susceptible man, very fond of Claudio. He is like a son to him. This fantastic fable tells about Lidia waiting for him before entering Heaven, coming back from death if necessary, and saving her child from darkness." No more was said about this tragic event, because Laura's holiday in Vancouver was over, and she had to leave the city. She was worried and concerned about her family. An invisible, ruthless murderer was still on the loose, and perhaps more than one, given the dynamics and complexity of the way in which he had carried out the massacres. She thought of a satanic league for the rituality of the assassinations, like those seen in Italy, or maybe just the opposite, a fanatical, extreme religious movement cleansing the sinners. The Mountain Spring Killer had made his infamous fame like the others.

Vancouver International Airport is on the south side of the city, between Marine Drive and the Fraser River – Richmond, to be more specific, where a new brand outlet has been built. People go shopping there while the airplanes fly over their heads. Laura was spending the morning there, and after lunch headed directly to the airport departure gates. A few tears flowed from her melancholyc eyes.

The sky was clean with a few clouds, and the massive airplane flew above the North Shore, where Laura could see from the porthole the vast green, dense vegetation. Numerous reflections of big and little lakes sparkled all around, mirrored by the sunlight, creating windows hiding behind their reflection of mystical deep, undisclosed realities. Laura commented in apprehension, "They are searching for a needle in a haystack."

The first flight landed in London, the second in Rome, where Laura could finally rest. In Vancouver, a massive research started, employing specialized military teams in support of police and the Royal Canadian Mounted Police (RCMP). Helicopters, night-vision goggles and thermal cameras were used by the personnel. SAR dogs units and trackers joined the operation, following the instructions of the headquarter control building in Vancouver. GPS was given to all in case of emergency, or if someone needed to be retraced and positioned. The Anti-Monster Squad was sure that the so-called Mountain Spring Butchers were still aiding in the woods, in a well-hidden area…a tunnel or a cave not visible.

The chief of the operation declared, "Given the gravity of the matter, the provincial government of B.C. has full support from the federal authority of Canada. New funding has been allocated to support the financial part of the whole operation. We can now rely on our technology to catch those criminals, if more than one." Meanwhile a friend of the last victim contacted the Vancouver Police from the town of Regina in the Saskatchewan province of Canada, where he went for a couple of weeks, paying a visit to his parents. He was forced to stay longer, supporting his father on the farm. Police were waiting for his return to have a talk about the victim's personal life: "Why did he go hunting in the late afternoon alone?" What could the hunter have had in common with Father Larry and the other victims? Forensic discovered after a more specific examination of his wrist that the wounds were showing a diverse method of crucifixion, despite the usual one.

Mesotti had an afternoon appointment with Dr. Lewis, the forensic pathologist handling the autopsy of the victim's body. The inspector slowly put on his coat, and gathered his keys and phone. He always dreaded going to the morgue, especially after lunch. He then directed toward his car. Soon after he entered the autopsy room and saw Dr. Lewis bent over the cadaver, overlooking the wrist. Dr. Lewis exclaimed: "Take a look at this, we can confirm that the victim was crucified, but in a different way this time, always on a three-cross. The wounds' enlargement exposed an atypical equal cross, same sides." Kevin walked over to the table, fighting his nausea, interrupting the doctor for a few seconds: "It is a Templar cross!" The expert nodded and continued, "Intestines were not totally cut, but left hanging by one of the internal pieces." He straightened up and looked at Mesotti, his brow creased. "I am no expert of the occult, but this looks like a clear act of satanic ritual, disclosing a defying message directly for us."

Kevin ran his fingers through his hair and said, "That explains why they brought the body so close to the trail; it is a warning of future hideous acts. What kind of contorted mind would do this?"

The pathologist responded, "An evil one!" with a dashed hope, shrouded in frustration.

"Those so-called emissaries of deception elaborated their macabre rites without hesitation, convinced by a contorted strength of mind. It took time to martyr the victim in that technique, binding his abdomen within roots, upon the center cross; a whimsy caprice of perfection. Hands stretched violently from the top to the bottom, nailed parallel to the tummy, whereas feet overlapped each other, hammered by rock spikes." Lewis was disgusting Mesotti with his dissertation. "The slaughterer didn't show the minimum symptom of mercy upon the prisoner, undergoing a relentless painful torture of death." Kevin: "This new garnished fashion of crucifixion is a coincidence or a blustering, well-planned scheme?" Lewis: "It was done on purpose, meticulously, as an emblematic supernatural symbol; in fact the hands close to the belly represent a female sigil—perhaps the murderer is a brawny woman, or the next victim will be a female." This line of inquiry was a possible path to follow at the moment, while Inspector Kevin was ready for a comparison between the sacristan and Mr. Devine, before closing their part in this case. The juxtaposition of parts brought up a new interesting element, the planet Venus!

Larry wrote on a few occasions that he was following also the rising and setting of Venus, to calculate his celestial secret predictions. He knew that Venus was close to the Sun, and could only be visible shortly after sunrise (around six a.m.) and sunset (around six p.m.). The planets Mars and Mercury were difficult to see, while Jupiter could be seen slightly (around eight a.m. to eight p.m.). Venus had the perfect time and light, acting as a guide. The number six was suspicious, named and written many times by Larry.

"I think Murphy knew his assassin, and went to meet him in the woods. Perhaps he was trying to convince him to surrender and admit the crimes, offering after a free confession and forgiveness. The last detail could explain why the religious objects were carried by the clerical," said the officer, omitting to strengthen the spiritual meaning of the planet. Venus is often referred as the Earth's Twin or Earth's Sister, and has approximately the same size, density and composition of the Earth. It is the second planet from the Sun and is well known as the "Morning Star" and "Evening Star" (day and night for Larry's research; in his Babylonians studies: bright queen of the sky). In ancient Rome Venus was known as the "Goddess of love," leading to seduction and desire, attraction and repulsion.

CHAPTER XVI

Lost Soldier

The newspaper's front page reported a weird surreal accident that happened to a couple of team patrols. When close to Cypress's west ridge, the soldiers heard a repeated eldritch screech. It was as if a wild animal had fallen into a trap, spasmodically trying to get free. A chthonic beast was running around the area, while the cracking of branches and shuffling of dry leaves alarmed the pair. Perhaps the creature was not ensnared any more.

The patrollers were positioned in a shadowy steep area with high alpine trees, in the dim late-afternoon sunlight. Soon after, an eerie swish of feathers was rapidly flying on their heads, dropping a warm wet drizzle. One of the members saw a shadow sliding behind the bush, and started advancing with his loaded rifle, while the other moved to the opposite side. The first remained alone, in a trail that clung to his side with a dense blowing wind. He staggered, when he noticed the path closing on him, as if two symbolic mirrors were in front of each other. A dark shadow was covering up, as a misty layer.

He retreated, stepping into a bog, whereas a mendacious quietude shrouded the woods.

His eyes were hypnotized by the rippling water, agitated by a sudden draft of disconcert. An opaque silhouette mirrored on the tiny pond, it was him eyeballing his reflection. The soldier walked slightly, feeling a profound silence, realizing that his reflection did not move an inch. Goosebumps burst on his body as he observed his watered twin living in another dimension. It was like watching a movie on a liquid screen.

The soldier stood petrified in the forest, while within the swamp he revolved his frightened look, advancing toward a tree. The grove was possessed by the afterlife realm, and a grotesque entity spellbound the terrestrial time, chaining the lost souls of the strangers. The male assisted to his slow decapitation, when a tight thick root ensnared his neck against the tree. The reflection showed two macabre burled hands pulling violently the root from behind the tree, while he was desperately sliding his nails along the muddy tuber.

His tongue surfaced, and his face became violet, foaming from his mouth. The pressure reached a tremendous force, cracking the root and releasing the clasp, while the helpless body suffered convulsions.

The shady presence translated facing front, terminating the slaughter with a shining stone blade. Blood was gushing from his throat, while dripping down the body and pooling in the pond's inner circle. The rock's scale severed completely his head, throwing it into the water. A splash of blood and water splattered on his face, as if the head had been tossed into the pond from the outside.

The soldier brought nervously his hands to his head, losing his rifle and running after randomly. He lost orientation, running helter-skelter for more than thirty minutes, while his GPS showed that he had not moved at all. Claudio Verallo was literally eating the article, turning frantically the pages, wishing to find some similarities with his accident. Doctors thought the soldier suffered dehydration stress, fatigued by the long work shift, while his colleague remained unaware of the mishap. Claudio, reading his mind, "There is something similar! The victims are always left alone, as are the witnesses. I was alone when I saw that figure or heard that creepy sound, as was the soldier. Whatever is out there, it is a soulless chthonic creature, able to deceive one's proper mind."

It was a warm sunny May.

A few days later, Claudio was returning from a concert talking with his friends: "Did you see guys, the Lost Lagoon? In the dark it looked really creepy." No one commented, trying to stay awake.

Claudio added, "It seems the soldier who had the accident up the hill was dismissed. He served overseas in Afghanistan, and rumors say that he witnessed a few beheadings before being traumatized irreversibly. He made up that accident to play with the army and get some money out of it. I am sure he decided to quit purposely."

A few minutes later Claudio contradicted himself, recollecting his events. The night was quiet and silent, though a light wind blew on Claudio's dream. It was her, the native beautiful girl gliding along the ground, moving toward him. A noise was heard from a distance, which the boy could not comprehend, while she was showing open eyes full of black rippling water.

Claudio glimpsed from a window, seeing the girl floating on the snow. He was observing the lassie so close with his eyes that he fell in the water, drowning in a nightmare.

When awake, Claudio painted his dream's portrait, noticing Leon agitated behavior.

Claudio tried to move it away, but the dog for the first time in his life turned to him, growling with shiny teeth…scanning him with blood-soaked eyes. The youth stood back, afraid, not understanding what was going on, moving away from the painting.

Leon was paralyzed, and Claudio observed his wide-open orbs, when all of a sudden Claudio's mother's carillon started playing, as if someone was fastening—relenting the eerie notes.

Leon barked furiously when the checkers and chess pieces moved… playing alone. Claudio rushed outside the house, wishing to expunge his bedding frustration…seeking peace. That was a strong obscure lashing… hatred begetting hatred. "I'll regret later to have abandoned Leon up there!" said him feeling a coward. An overture of terror had just begun…

CHAPTER XVII

Abyssal Irises

Vancouver Police was a boiling pot, striving to manage the diverse sectors involved on the manhunt.

Kevin was joined full-time by Inspector Robert Jones, supporting him while on the field. He needed to liaise with the investigators and forensics.

The FBI's behavioral analysis of violent crime in serial murders was cooperating with the police. There were thirty-six estimated cases still open in the States to study, despite the historical past thirteen in Canada. Forensic investigation units joined their knowledge at all times to extract any useful clue. Claudio developed the same idea, feeling inside his soul the need to persevere in his will, calling more often his sister and pushing her in the involvement of Armando Suarez, as a triangular joint-venture research.

The portion of mountain where the last accident occurred was completely surrounded and seized, using olfactory dogs units, trackers, special unit police and sonar (to detect any noises or signs underground).

Morris Harrison and Andrew Devine were finally pulled out of the investigation after being confronted. "Did you hear the news? Police finally freed from every suspicion both Morris and Andrew. You were right, Claudio! They are not involved in those criminal events. I was almost convinced that they were part of it," informed Ryan speaking to the phone.

"I just guessed! Pure luck!" observed Claudio snubbing his own tenacious intuitions. He was yearning to perform his personal investigation, driving once more to North Vancouver Squamish reserve. When there, he noticed a sign exposed outside the church…an exhibition was organized inside the aboriginal community center, held by the new parish.

There was a vast array of artifacts and wood works, enriched with paintings, masks, images, carvings.

Claudio gladly convened with Morris, meeting soon after the new parson. The youth wished to purchase a few original articles, helping the local community. He acquired a gracious little totem crafted by Andrew Devine, hoping to talk to him, although visitors overwhelmed the hall.

Claudio was not in a rush, and started looking around, until his eyes went across the painting of a girl. She was dressed in aboriginal cloths, displaying a pair of hair braids and a collar cross.

The young female had brown eyes and a tanned skin.

The figure was painted facing forward with flowers in her hands, while a red rose was glistening within the bunch. She was surrounded by water and sinuous mountains.

Claudio inquired of a local seller, "Who is she?" The vendor answered, mastering, "She was the first Canadian-American beatified in 1980 by Pope John Paul II, and canonized in 2012 by Pope Benedict XVI. Her native name was Tekakwitha, and she became Saint Kateri, she was born in what is today New York around 1656, and died April 17, 1680, in Quebec, Canada. She contracted smallpox during an outbreak, surviving, while her whole family perished. Her beautiful face was scarred because of the illness, and at the age of nineteen she converted to Roman Catholicism, dying in perpetual virginity."

Claudio was surprised to learn that some miracles were attributed to her. Thanks to her holy intercession, she endured the beliefs of offering and suffering.

Beside the first portrait stood a second painting, endowed with suffuse and obscure atmosphere. Claudio felt an embezzling feeling toward it, despite the one he saw previously. It was as if no one was between him and that image he was admiring, while a mendacious quietude merged around him. Claudio was shrouded with a sense of isolation and infantile feelings, sucked in by the image and the colors.

Mountains were painted at dusk with a weak sunset spring, while a mirror of water was reflecting the image of a well-shaped girl dressed in aboriginal cloths. For a moment he remembered…dream's vision. Her shoulders were painted, and she was positioned between the sun and the mountains.

The water was dark, and her feet were under it, like she was in a macabre dry sea, eyeing high on the hills. She had short hair, her arms placed slightly downward.

Claudio was enthralled by this image, as if it was real, and when a hand touched his shoulder, he jumped in fear. Andrew Devine was surprised at Claudio's reaction, feeling sorry. The youth enquired, trying to hide his scared face, "Is she the same character, I mean the native saint? Who is the author?" After a brief interlude, Andrew followed:

"This icon is not the same character. The old artist was one of the most talented in the native community, until one day before 2000 he left, and never returned. The representation is called the Eclipse of the Soul, and was completed by the artist long ago. It is an original icon, but the reproduction of an older wood-carved masterpiece that was performed by a young boy in a residential school back in time. The old artist never sold the painting or revealed who was the little boy who carved the original in the institute. People speculate that is an old warriors' legend handed down over time. It cannot be replicated or sold, worth a treacherous curse of the past."

Andrew Devine, in his fifties, was explaining it to Claudio…floating his arms all around. He was gesturing like an orchestra director, while Claudio was hypnotized by his waving hands that now and then touched his long dark hairs.

Devine kept the pace, "The girl exhibits a shaman's garment, while trapped in between the sunset and the mountain, obscuring the sun's light and consequently darkening the hills, creating an eclipse."

Claudio had a delayed reaction in his mind, recalling a run he did three days before. It was along the Ambleside seashore, on the path between the North Shore mountain range and the Pacific Ocean, facing Vancouver's Stanley Park. It was late afternoon, sunset, when he took his phone to shoot some amazing pictures, realizing that a huge cruise ship was passing between him and the sun.

For an instant he paused, watching an extraordinary cruise ship eclipsing the sun and blackening the view of Vancouver.

He discerned instantly the name of the majestic ship displayed before him, like a queen of the sea, recalling… "Elysa of the Sea."

Claudio felt a searing bolt of sorrow.

The public started leaving the place, whereas Claudio shook his hand to the organizers.

In the meantime a car stopped by Claudio's, idling impatiently: Isabel was waiting, looking annoyed and distressed. "What happened to him?" thought Isabel…dress billowing around.

Evening was approaching, and a fresh breeze was blowing with the wind, while waves crashed on the rocks as a sound of conflict. The echo spread along the cliff, and whispers were heard mixed with the flying leaves and cracking branches; voices of a spiritual nature. Claudio was absorbed by the splashing sound of the ocean, falling asleep in Isabel's arms, reasoning about something he misplaced within his eyes on the last depiction he saw at the exhibition. It was a detail he distinguished in his mind, but could not discern with the eyes. Isabel had forgiven his lateness…absorbed by a hinting, invisible presence.

"Is everything all right? You lied to me! You are not looking good at all, Claudio. Those visions you pretend to see are not a positive sign. I know about your fears and…" insinuating in his emotions

He perceived a ubiquitous criticism from her, placing himself in a defensive mode. "Are you trying to affirm that I am insane? That I need a shrink? Not that I have never seen one before." "Do not act like a child, please! I am trying to help you out."

"Ho yes sure! My personal psychic—no, sorry, I mean psychologist. Are you deepening your thesis on me? Perhaps you are studying my brain for your final exam? Control freak!"

Isabel lost her patience. "Stop it! You are pathetic! You already spoiled our day. What a fool!" Claudio said, again, "Our date? You mean our session!"

The argument degenerated, ending in an opaque twilight of discontent…snow melted on the high peaks, while the smell of summer was approximating.

CHAPTER XVIII

Innocent Eyes

March 20· 1610, Vancouver, British Columbia…

Pacific West Coast First Nation: An indigenous child was running, hiding from an open trail. He was crying and his desperation was heard by the elements of the living nature. He clutched in his hand a cloth, concealing something within.

Dusk was falling upon the dense forest, and it was time to find a safe haven before night approached. He was pushing through the bushes, scratching his body with long thorns and acuminated branches, revealing a face marked in pain and anguish.

Although spring was a mild season, nighttime on the hill was cold. A shelter was later found inside a big old tree, and the little warrior could rest safe and sleep.

"What did they do to my father and sisters? Those bad people will be cursed by the spirit of the mountains! Such cruel and merciless behavior," whispered silently the lad while pulling out thorns one by one. "Ouch! I hope they didn't get my younger sister; she was hiding with me behind the forest. She saw what I saw. The spirit of darkness surfaced!"

From a close distance, screams of desperation and agony were heard within the woods, while terrifying afterlife distortions lifted from the ground; steam of ancestral macabre hate fell on the forest.

"Hear that horror! My father told me about the forbidden site. Revenge will erase them all." He was crying because part of his family had been murdered. The boy froze, plugging his ears from that horrifying obscurity… an obscene bloodbath.

When morning repulsed the night, he was finally reached by his sister, dressed to celebrate an important day. "There you are! I was losing hope. I thank the good spirits that protected you," said her in tears.

She grabbed his hand and went back to the village, walking among the dead bodies scattered all over the field…two Spanish galleons were waiting along the coast.

"Those strangers attempted to escape after the spirits of the forest rose, sealing their fate forever. I am going to tell you what I saw with my own eyes, brother. I witnessed something unique and fantastic…" The girl was interrupted: "I saw that too, sister! I remained close to the lagoon. We should report this to the people downhill." She replied, "No! We keep it a secret; we will tell the elderly when time is ready, let us leave this disgraceful site."

The couple took whatever they could from the field and ran away, far away, without looking back.

CHAPTER XIX

The Research

"Why do you always look so worried, trembling in fear?" Said Isabel… "I confusedly remembered to have seen that depiction before the showing. Perhaps in my dreams or…" reluctantly expressed Claudio. She assumed, while tuning the radio and driving out of the block, "Often we think to have seen or lived something previously. It is a mere illusion, a déjà vu," delicately revealing a genuine beauty.

Claudio's phone rang…it was Michael, proposing to rent a boat at Sewell's Marina, by the ferries.

The pair walked to the parking lot, while Isabel said: "I will see you tonight, then," Claudio marveled, "Tonight! You are coming with us—we are going home?" Isabel countered, "You should have told your cousin of my presence, he wants to stay with you, I think."

Proceeding with Claudio, Isabel arrived at the marina, where Michael was choosing the best boat. His face transformed into a fuming dragon when he noticed Isabel approaching. He faked a smile and commented, "We could go to Bowyer Island and then up to Lions Bay, what do you think?" Claudio replied embarrassed: "I guess so."

Isabel broke the ice: Let's go! What are we waiting for?"

The trio jumped into the boat. Claudio whispered in Isabel's ear, "I am just feeling kind of weird. Let's go now."

As they were getting up to leave, the Rocky Mountaineer train thundered past on its way to Whistler, shaking the ground. Sitting in the stern of the boat, Claudio stared at the reflection of the trees in the water, while Michael yelled, "Look at that seagull flying above us, it is so fat, it has something there." The bird lost a piece of food that plunged into the water, creating undulating waves, changing the contours of the trees' reflection. For a moment one of the trees seemed to transform into a macabre figure, motioning toward the boat, half-animal and half-human. Claudio jumped, almost falling off the boat, making his cousin lose his balance.

"Hey, watch out!" Michael said. "What's wrong? Did you see an orca?" added Isabel peering over "I am not sure what I saw. It was a creature in the water."

Before leaving the bay, Michael criticized Claudio. "I think you need to stop thinking about the murders on the mountains, it's messing up your head!" Claudio stared at him with crazy eyes, "I am tired of your criticism... you are pathetic!"

Isabel positioned between them when Claudio tried to face his cousin, "Stop arguing! You are acting like kids, let it go now!"

Michael did not hesitate and stung Isabel: "Kids? Who are you to judge, you were not even supposed to come with us."

Claudio said again, "You are a weirdo, Michael! You should stay at home with your computer, your best friend." Isabel grabbed Claudio, pushing him away, while the youths continued offending each other.

Father Armando Suarez was still in Spain, in the province of Navarre, following Father Larry's writings, reaching the Cathedral of Saint Mary the Royal, a Roman Catholic Church in the archdiocese of Pamplona. The church replaced an older Romanesque one that was demolished in 924 during the Islamic invasion, and was rebuilt in the sixteenth century. Armando was reading, while his voice resounded, "The number seven in Christian denominations is considered to be a sacred number, since Genesis affirms that God reposed on the seventh day, while man was generated on the sixth day. Jesus performed seven miracles on God's holy Sabbath day to confirm its enduring holiness to God and to the life of believers." He ascertained, "We know that!"

The cleric, for a moment absent-minded, rose his head and admired the cloister and the French Gothic mysterious architecture, shrouded in the mystical voices of the past. Larry arrived at the Diocesan Museum, where old pieces of religious art and documents of other Navarre churches were kept, and found a reliquary of the sixteenth and seventeenth centuries related to the Holy Church of Rome. It was a document of 1610 that authorized a Spanish expedition to the northwest coast of Canada, after the papal bull *"Inter caetera"* of 1493 granted Spain the exclusive right to colonize the entire Western Hemisphere, including all of the west coast of North America.

Armando came back to the documents, commenting, "Larry learned that in 1513 Spanish explorers were the first Europeans to reach the west coast of North America, all documents and authorizations were clear and readable, while the one he was looking for of 1610 was missing information, and was part in Rome and part in Pamplona." Armando placed his pen on his lips, showing a dubious look, while speculating again. "In Rome, Larry had found only the long navigational map, the papal bull authorization, and the mission to be accomplished, while in Spain he missed perhaps this pivotal church, after leaving Italy for Canada." Armando was frantically searching inside the reliquary, and in those of the seventeenth century found another papal bull related to the expedition, regarding some passengers on board being treated like dangerous criminals, and for this reason deported.

The ships were cargo fleets used for transporting a wide variety of items like gold, silver, gems, pearls, sugar, silk and all the goods they could find. Natives of that part of Canada were mentioned as people to be converted by all means to Christianity, for their sake and salvation.

They used to send religious people with the crews as a justification for the military conquests of Spain and other European powers.

Papal bulls were used to authorize the conquistadors to enslave the infidels and those who opposed the Holy Catholic Church.

Armando read the last document: "Here we have the names of the crew members and the regular passengers, but not those of the condemned to deportation. Perhaps they were lost in time."

There were a number of Catholic missionaries. The head priest was not named. Furthermore there was a strange, faded papal seal with the Spanish crown and the Vatican's cross insignia.

Suarez was merged in a quiet atmosphere, when a phone call distracted him. One of his friends was informed by Armando about the findings.

"All those passengers and criminals were from the province of the old Kingdom of Navarre, which became the Kingdom of Spain and after, in 1620 the Kingdom of France and Navarre, because of dynastic dispute...documents were lost or ruined." He took pictures with his phone, while the flash light showed on the back of the last paper another seal with an oval shape. It was completely empty, bearing an equal cross.

The sigil was unfinished, as if the old curator was in a rush to close the relic. Armando was satisfied with his further discovery and returned to Rome, exposing later the news to Laura.

She commented: "There are also accounts related to Larry's personal objects that police returned to the vicariate, did you know that Armando?" He seemed unaware, "No! We should take a closer look at those items,"

The only manuscript Italian police left in Larry's office was a sketch depicting the world grid map. Parallels and meridians of the Northern Hemisphere were highlighted, overlapped by different triangles pointing from Europe toward North America, and from North America to Europe; while some over Canada were pointing north.

Father Armando entered Larry's office accompanied by Laura, where he studied the parchment: "The 49th Parallel North is a circle of latitude 49 degrees north of the equatorial plane, marked by Larry for his central main guideline. It crosses Europe, North America and the two major oceans. As we can see, numbers are mixed with symbols, lines, triangles and circles...creating a cryptic geographic web diagram; a time-zone grating is clearly visible here." Laura bent over, observing three numbers on the 49th parallel that united in a unique perfect line: Europe, North America and the Atlantic-Pacific oceans.

CHAPTER XX

Cursed Numbers

Armando seated again after stretching his back, "They refer to the World Time Zone connecting British Columbia, Washington State and Europe. There are 9 hours of difference or contrariwise divergence between Vancouver and Rome, while from the East Coast North Atlantic we have a disparity of 6 hours from Rome and 3 hours from Vancouver," explaining to Laura.

"The astonishing result is a 3-666 number in which Larry reversed the two west-east 9s and left the 6 in the middle. Larry coded the sequence obtaining a 666 devil's macabre number, opposed to 3, God's spiritual number. "Laura was astounded: "A cursed line of evil running along our timeline signifying what? What is the real meaning of it?"

Armando replied, "If we could only tell!"

The methodic calculations were sliding along the 49th parallel, toward Vancouver. Something was evoking this city from the past.

Hours later in Vancouver a vehicle was driving west, on Highway one, before Lions Bay. It was Saturday night, and a couple of friends with some drinks on were singing and listening to loud music. They were carefully driving to see if police patrols were around, stopping in a rest area close to the hill. "What's that? Did you see that thing?" The other replied, "What are you talking about, see what?" A big shadow motioned upon their heads, while an odd strange misty rain was descending. Nature's elements were closing up and the two freaked out, turning their heads all around.

"I told you something is wrong, we better leave now!"

The driver entered the car while his friend came closer to the woods.

Car lights revealed a spectral-shaped tree positioned in front of the beams. The driver's orbs discerned a treacherous voracious figure scanning them with dark yellow eyes, melting soon after in the woods.

It was running in a distorted creepy way, releasing a demonic kind of sound they could not understand. One of the fellows got a sick grudge sensation, panicking with fear, while his friend pushed the accelerator and drove directly to the West Vancouver police station.

The police officer on duty said, "Calm down, fellows, I will assist you right away, you two look in distress, what happened?" a second officer was checking their documents, advising them to contact their parents to let them know about their anomalous misadventure.

Police completed the boys' statements, remembering the previous accident that occurred to the military personnel. One of the former soldiers was in a serious stress syndrome.

Teams patrolling the mountain were called rapidly, checking the area carefully. Nothing was found. One of the officers was expressing his opinion to one of the investigators: "Those guys are not reliable, I think they are just acting silly to attract the attention, and besides, everybody knows about the previous accident and what happened." One of the boys insisted, "I will never forget that noise, a sound of the past, a pouring left din, a metallic whim, a distorted squeal." After that, the youth started yelling and trembling, pushing the hands on his ears…squeezing his tongue strongly.

An ambulance drove him to the hospital, where he was sedated and kept under observation for the night.

Investigators had to distinguish by their long experience those who were genuine witness and those who were not, without relenting the enquiring.

Claudio was watching his reflected face on the bedroom chandelier, when suddenly recalled something he saw in the painting. It was like a half-moon reproduced on the fluids, but not visible in the sky. Someone had made two portraits on the same frame, hiding some features. He evoked in his mind the two circles of water around the girl's feet, as if she had dropped something previously; it was a mind-bending effort that ended with the last aspect he could possibly remember: there was another oval circle of water around the two, and was touching the last one.

Claudio's voraciousness in enshrouding the truthfulness was becoming an obsession. He thought, "I need to see Andrew Devine as soon as possible. That canvas is hiding something from our eyes, and I sense it could be connected with Larry's murder!"

He could not wait, and left home at dawn with his bicycle, going along Marine Drive, passing North Vancouver and aiming for the church. He was gasping when getting off the bicycle. Father Duncan Wilson, the new priest, was preparing for the early mass service when he noticed Claudio. "Good morning Father, I am looking for Andrew Devine, I was interested in a few paintings he possessed." Surprisingly one of the operas was still in the rectory with several artifacts, all closed in a safe box.

Duncan agreed, "Come inside, it is so early! I cannot assist you right now because I have to serve the morning mass, but you can look for yourself here."

He guided Claudio inside the sacristy, opening the safe, and after adjusting the artifacts and one of the paintings…he stood in front of Claudio and said, "Beware of darkness, my son!"

Claudio remained there, while the priest went to welcome the early comers.

He advanced…contemplating the reflection on the ocean: it was the suffused face of the native girl. Her eyes were revolving backwards, shining with tears, trying to see who was behind her; Claudio's blood died!

That explained why the water had the circles. The unclear half-moon was only visible on the water, while the feeble sunset and the assorted clouds were just there. It was like a twin painting, and the more he observed, the more details emerged…he took few shots with his phone and left. Claudio's bicycle kept spinning and disappeared through the increasing traffic, while Duncan and the sacristan were cautiously whispering outside the church. People were entering from the gate and the view moved toward the hills, up the mountains.

CHAPTER XXI PART ONE

Predictions

At the end of May police enforcement and military deployment had their results. The murderers, wherever they were hiding, desisted on committing further brutal crimes; nobody wanted to let their guard down, they could have been still in the woods, or more probably closer to the city, the sonar used by the specialists did not reveal caves or tunnels built underground. The lower trails were opened carefully because summer was approaching, and hikers wanted to enjoy the marvelous nature of the B.C. parks.

A feeble twilight killed the day.

Late night in Vancouver saw a new Monday morning in Rome, where the congested traffic was making Laura neurotic for being late to her appointment with Armando and Father Maurice Fredel, a French deacon serving in the Vatican. She was driving on Santo Spirito hamlet, after passing the beautiful Castel Sant' Angelo on the Tevere River, than she turned on the main Via della Conciliazione on Saint Peter's Square and parked beside Saint Carlo Palace.

The Castle of the Holy Angel, or Mausoleum of Hadrian, was built around 123-139 A.D. by the Roman Emperor Adriano as a mausoleum for himself and his family. It was the favorite imaginative place of Claudio, who viewed it as an enchanted, towering cylindrical fortress, used later by the popes as a castle (it is now a museum).

Once it was the tallest building in Rome, featuring at its top the bronze statue of Michael the Archangel. Lidia used to tell Claudio that at night the angel came alive, descending from the highest point of the city, protecting Saint Peter's Church from the evil raids. The lad, when sleeping, felt safe and sound, peeking outside the window...overlooking the long sword of the archangel wielded in the shadow of darkness...

Father Maurice Fredel had met somebody at the clergy offices who allowed him to consult the personal objects of Father Larry, brought back by the Italian investigators.

One fact struck Maurice as bizarre, raising his curiosity. "Why had the police closed Larry's inquiry so soon, without scrutinizing his notes and documents?" said him to Laura, mentioning a name Larry deciphered: Saint Malachy!

Armando unleashed all his knowledge and mentored: "Malachy was a holy prophet who lived four hundred years before the birth of Christ, when the Jews returned from Babylonian captivity. He was the last of the Old Testament Minor Prophets, and for this was called **The Seal of the Prophets**...The Seal!" Stressed him...

The cleric brought the fingers to his upper lip, rolling his eyes while continuing, "He predicted the coming of John the Baptist and that of the son of God, he was venerated by the Jews and by the Catholics like a bridge between the Old Testament and the New Testament. His name, Malachy, meant Messenger of God. His life remained a mystery."

Father Larry insisted on writing this passage about Malachy being the last sigil of the future coming of Christ, he was also called the exiled prophet because he suffered under Persian rule and the destruction of the Jewish Temple. He later condemned part of his people to be exiled, because they lost their faith and betrayed God. According to Armando, Larry found a papal seal on a document related to a conviction of criminal heretics in Navarre, Spain. The seal was a circle with Saint Malachy's name and writings in Latin: *Sigillum Finalem Exsilium*, with a cross on the side and the Reign of Spain badge in the center, *final seal of exile.*

The image of the saint and a phrase on the other side of the seal read, *Malachia Ultima Monizione,* the last warning of Malachy.

In his diary Larry wrote to have found this old paper in the Vatican's secret archive, it was missing more parts lost in the centuries, and was approved by the pope at that time.

He was sure it was part of an expedition from Spain to North America's Pacific Coast. The map they used to reach the place was missing.

PART TWO

Lousy conversationalist friends were playing beach volleyball, whereas Isabel was examining Claudio's shots. Her eyes glimmered, "The three circles of water on the portrait should have the same shape and diameter if made by the same falling substance. Instead the first circle is totally different, created before by a difference…"

A red warm sun was going down the hill, standing on a dark tree, while black crows flying merged into it. A scorching coin was leaning at the verge of the ocean, with the sleeping clouds burned on the last rays that warned the moon, twilight!

A patrol member was waiting for sunrise up the hill, while the moon was still warned and the silence became loneliness. He saw something moving on the tree's trunk, like a liquid sliming web.

Coming closer, he was surprised to observe a large dark smear defying gravity, was it water? His face felt attracted by this old dirty liquid mirror, adapting in a flattened oval shape. The liquid was floating, standing inside the frame like a sealed opaque film. He could not see his own face reflected. His hand oddly stretched to touch this mesmerizing activity, as the sun gave off its first rays, shining on the sealed water.

Something was moving frantically inside, as a sealed womb, and when the hand touched the mirror, it was swiftly sucked. Harmony of the soul was felt by the man, freedom of life and a sense of swoon and sleep; it was like ecstasy of rebirth, after which became cold and fear, for a substance was feeding on his blood.

Screams of terror opened his eyes, which observed something coming from the living nature, like a mirror of truth, reflecting revelations of the past. Rippling dark water wrapped his corpse, as a swarm of bees enfolded him. An extreme cold paralyzed his brain, ceasing the heart beating, whereas soon after it became hot like hell. A cloud of steam vanished!

Someone was missing.

"We think the patroller got lost because of his dead GPS. He is trying to find his position and will come back for sure," reassured the officer in charge.

A few days later a couple of real estate agents were showing a fancy house up in the British Property in West Vancouver, between Chartwell Drive and Millstream Road, when they noticed different animals running down the hill and remaining surprisingly on Shields Dam Park, along the road. Jack Rouschel, one of the real estate agents, immediately called the West Vancouver police: "We noticed something uncommon up here, a certain number of wild animals are just having a reunion on the road, they seem afraid to retreat, as if a threat is nearby. I can see them right now, they are looking around confused. Can you please send someone to check what is going on?"

The alert was launched and a nearby patrol shifted around the area. One of the operators radioed the central communication station: "I confirm we found the animals…out of the blue!"

Jack's partner in business, Luca Socovich, noticed a few sea eagles flying in a perfect circle over the mountain pines. He expressed in wonder: "Take a look at those flying angels, it is fantastic. Today nature is like rebelling up here. What's going on?"

"They say animals can sense earthquakes and catastrophes, and a big upheaval along the west cost was predicted!" affirmed Jack.

CHAPTER XXII

Obscure Woods

It was only the day after, when searching dogs found what was described as a macabre living tree, a scene hard to believe even with their own imagination. The missing person was found inside the remains of an old tree, close to the trail where the animals were scattered.

Both feet and hands were missing, roots inserted into the flesh… attached to the internal part of the plant.

The homicide division's forensic pathologist, Dr. Lewis, released an interview after exiting the morgue, with face showing concern: "Even if you can judge this phrase as a stereotype, I can affirm that in my long career I have never seen something like that. Those roots were pushed inside the belly of the victim, after the poor guy was quartered and all the organs were left hanging with the tubers. Two little slashes on the back of the corpse formed two opposite-shaped triangles. His eyes and ears were perforated, as was his throat, jammed after with rootstock which, like cables, connected the living body to a dead tree." People around him were embarrassed to hear such abominable description, noticing the nervousness of the coroner; what he was describing was something he touched and examined for real. A questioned merged: "What about the eyes?" Dr. Lewis answered, "No eyes left, but water inside. The body could stand straight because it was bound tight and hanged with a big noose, a root around the neck. It was wet and drenched with a mix of water and blood. It looked like a piece of modern horror art that only a sick mind could perform. It was an inhumane, criminal act. Moreover, I have to point out something unexplainable at the moment, because it was not possible to perform such an act up the hills. The victim was first frozen and then boiled…from the inside!"

Reporters commented in disbelief: "What, frozen…boiled, how?"

The criminal scene was seized, and Kevin, assisted by the provincial homicide squad, worked with the support of forensic pathologists, taking pictures and collecting evidences for the investigation.

In the meantime, at the Vancouver headquarters' operational room, the chief of the homicide squad, Jim Carter, illustrated: "We need to consider the possible consultation of esoteric experts and spiritual symbolic professors at this point. I need a generic list to be sent to our prima donna, Mesotti. He has time, and can decide who to contact. We keep him busy, right, so that we can work on the real core of the case."

The secretary, enquired: "Do I have to go there again personally or can our ballerina come downtown?"

The chief answered, "No! Send everything by mail…they will know what to do."

Robert received the communication and printed several lists regarding plausible occultist experts to be contacted and subsequently selected. He prepared the peeling thin sheets all over the office, waiting for Kevin, who entered the doorway in a hurry and placed his folder on the desk, looking at the pile of charts and notes prepared by his assistant.

"What the hell is going on in my office—did you drop a bomb?"

Robert said, "We have to work on this right now, and we must move fast!"

Mesotti: "Hey! Hold your horses, champion! Who said that?"

He replied, "The boss of the boss!"

Mesotti asked, "Who, Al Capone?"

Robert laughed and replied, "I need some help interpreting all of those papers—we are looking for some fortune-tellers and magicians here!"

Mesotti approached his desk, glancing at the list, understanding what the bosses were trying to do. He lost his temper and in a single cleaning movement threw the papers on the air. His eyes wore a clamorous look when looking at the falling sheets…he was going down, too.

"Do not behave like that—come on! It is only a different task, nothing personal," commented Robert.

Kevin, furious, asserted, "They are trying to keep us apart from the main investigation. Since Jim Carter and his secretary settled in Vancouver, we had their breath on our shoulders. They are wrong! I have no intention to retire yet. I will find you a valuable help…you can do this for me alright!" "Alright boss, I'll go through the documents myself," noticing an interesting biography about Meredith Hampton, an experienced 54-year-old professional psychic. She had her own office and a few collaborators specialized in diverse sectors. Robert thought, "There it is! I killed two birds with one stone! We do not need to look further."

Later that day, "Please call her and set an appointment for tomorrow if possible, we need to be active and proactive in this," remarked Kevin when consulting with Robert.

Next day Kevin met Meredith in her office, surprised in discovering that few family members of the victims had already contacted her…she knew everything about the case.

She explained to the skeptical officer, "In almost all religions and cultures going back thousands of years, the tree means life in a symbolic way; for example, you have the roots that dig deep, the branches that reach out for sustenance, the leaves that collect strength, and the fruits that give of themselves." He sighed, as if preparing for a long boring lesson, while the medium continued: "The murderers are saying that they'll feed from those trees, until victims will sustain them. The casualties suffered and died while feeding the dead trees coming back to life. Plants are the breath of life for the earth, involving fire, ground, water and air, all spiritual powers of nature."

Meredith affirmed that in the Bible was said, "If you ate of the tree of life, you would live forever…Adam and Eve ate from the branches of temptation to be condemned for their sins, never feeding again."

She continued, "The two triangles, if overlapped, formed a kind of pentagram, a satanic symbol in this case, even if in Christian faith it could represent the five wounds of Christ. The body was positioned as if crucified, but this time he was not."

He sarcastically interrupted, avoiding being rude: "In all this doctrine of catechism, what do we have to assume about those symbols? I am confused!" She patiently answered, "We have an astrological symbol with a man inside a pentagram, covering the five star's point with feet, hands and head; for what I see, the slayers are telling us of their spiritual fraudulent twisted ambiguity, serving God and Evil at the same time. Demonic adversity is deceiving…leading us always in an illegitimate false overindulgence…it cannot be trusted at all." Meredith then escorted the investigator outside the building, talking about her personal impressions and considerations. He noticed a mousy voice erupting at times out of her mouth.

He glanced at the mountain range and said: "I wonder where they are hiding right now!"

The ocean was playing a tender splashing melody, while a duet of seagulls were flying on the winds of solitude.

Leon was dragging the leash trying to jump in the water…Claudio forcing his arm to stop it. The airstream was bringing sea foam on their faces, and the eyes could still see all the water surrounding Vancouver.

Meredith was mentioning the book of Genesis and the separation between Good and Evil, elucidating: "Jesus is seen as the tree of life for Christianity, the opposite of what occurred on Vancouver's hill. Natives in the past had widely complex forms of sacred and supernatural beliefs, significantly altered by the influence of Christianity, settlers and missionaries; some communities resulted in hybridizing religious practices, while others tried to maintain traditional spiritual practices. Some natives believed in the spirits of transformers, one part good, one part evil, like two brothers. The first created the sun, moon, fish, animals and humans, while the other created snakes, valleys, mountains and anything else that would make life difficult for humans. The tree of life is connected to Mother Earth and the spiritual part of their history. Roots are absorbers of the ashes and wisdom of ancestors, while plants and land are gifts that don't belong to the natives...but the natives belong to them."

Robert requested, "Could you slow down, please? I am a little bit lost." She rewound and continued: "Nature is a part of them, and the body inside the tree is an evil sign against Mother Nature, an act of defiance versus the presence of goodness in the woods."

Robert thought, "Kevin was damn right! This part of the investigation is boring and confusing, a sting in the eye. It is an impasse for us, without the chance to come back. I do not know where all this information will lead us."

CHAPTER XXIII

The artist

Claudio decided to find a part-time job during summer, unleashing the wrath of his father. "You don't need to work right now! Why don't you concentrate on your studies," said Giacomo.

"I don't want to beg for money every time, dad! I can do it! Even Isabel has a part-time job as a personal trainer," folding the hands in his pockets. "She is younger and in ahead of you at the university—you cannot compare the two of you! You need to focus more on studying," replied an impatient father, arms nervously floating on the air.

Claudio persisted: "The only person I know in Vancouver who doesn't have a job is my cousin, and only because he is too lazy."

Giacomo, altered: "Don't mention Michael, you should apologize to him!" Claudio, hearing that comment, left the living room and exited the house, heading to pick up Isabel.

He escorted her to the British properties, searching for the two real-estate agents. Luca Socovich was alone, verifying some details on the property, when he saw new possible clients coming toward him. The couple introduced and explained the real reason of their visit, sitting in relaxation and admiring the astonishing view they had up there. Claudio was like a river in a flood, and went through all the details with the real-estate agent. "That is why we decided to contact you guys—you have assisted at some strange events, like us, something serious is going on up there. Mesotti is the closest person we can keep in touch with, he needs our help! Did he question you?"

Luca said: "No, he didn't, the homicide squad did," deciding to follow the new friendship.

Claudio asked, "Are you done with your job for today?" "Yes, we can go for a coffee and meet Jack later." Claudio insisted, "No time for coffee! I want to show you something more interesting, let's go!"

Quickly the trio reached the church's reserve by the Capilano River, overlooking for Andrew Devine the artist. Claudio solicited some local people, "We are really interested in buying some art works from Andrew Devine, do you know his place?" A man said, "Yes, it is just behind the corner, I will show you." They were brought to his shop, an open garage with pieces of lumber scattered on all sides. Paint easels and canvases overwhelmed the carport, as Andrew came and welcomed the visitors, introducing himself to Luca and Isabel. He was more friendly this time and relieved, telling that the original painting of the native girl was made by a fellow in a residential school around 1959.

"Thanks for visiting me, and appreciating my work, this is all I have left for my ancestors and family. I live thanks to my hobby and traditions. The painting you are looking for is the most important piece I possessed... it is also part of family memories."

Isabel spoke: "Do you know the artist who made the painting?" He said, "Yes, I know! He was my missing father, when living in residential school; although I never told this personal matter to the police." Residential schools were government-sponsored religious structures, established to assimilate indigenous children to Euro-Canadian culture, and were opened from around 1886 until 1996.

Andrew's father, during his permanence at the institute, suffered isolation, denigration and some health conditions. Moreover, he had problems with the new religion he faced and learned.

He apprised his son in what he painted originally, inspired by an old masterpiece of woodwork made by an unknown native artist. The wood-carved artifact disappeared when Andrew was born in 1967 and was never found.

The group of friends was moved in hearing such a troubled and sad story, bought some artifacts from Andrew, and promised to be in touch.

Devine managed, "If you want to see the painting, you can ask Father Duncan, if he is in the sacristy. I don't know his complete schedule."

Claudio added: "Never mind, it is late for us and we have to go. Thank you again, Andrew."

Later, their vehicle was heading west, turning on Taylor Way. The radio was on. Claudio was explaining his thoughts, eyeing an old woman crossing the street. "A woman!" he exclaimed. "Do not worry, we saw her on the walkways," replied her. Claudio again: "Not that one—I mean, Andrew's mother. Who is she and why he didn't mention her?" The young couple looked at each other with curious wonder, reflecting their visions deep in their eyes.

Luca exclaimed: "You almost scared me, guys! Sooner or later I want to see that painting. Jack! I am sure is waiting for us at the coffee club. We should pick him up and let him know what we are doing." Isabel said to the boys, "Shush for a moment, please! The medical examiner is talking on the radio about the last murder. Let me adjust the volume here."

Ears were tuned and erected like those of alarmed cats, although the antenna was losing the signal at times. The reporter said, "Could you explain to us, doctor, what do you mean when you say unfathomable."

"Yes, sure, I will try to be more incisive. Those criminals—and I say criminals because they are more than one—used a source of energy never seen before. I personally performed the autopsy, finding the internal organs in an unnatural energized state. They were frozen and boiled with a swift energetic transformation, a fast passage of antagonism. How can one perform such a thing up the hills? What kind of energy is that? It is beyond belief."

Claudio was glancing at Isabel from the rear mirror…thinking about the luminary intervention, while silenced lips were cautiously sipping a hot steamed coffee, hazed by a vapor of concealed mystery.

CHAPTER XXIV PART ONE

Incriminations

Kingdom of Navarre, 1609

Two irises reflected from a shining moon deep in darkness, closed their eyelids and went to sleep. A new day was ahead in the Province of the King of Navarre, and Daniel Morgair was leaving the house after assisting his sister-in-law. Outside his dwelling threatening armed guards requested him to follow them to the vicariate. It was a legal investigation about the credibility of his profession.

"I do not comprehend! I am a legally recognized doctor here, everybody can vouch for that. I am a serious professional specialist! Why does the vicariate want to see me?" The captain of the guards replied, while dismounting from his horse, which was kicking and whinnying nervously: "I received an order, doctor! I was told to escort you for questioning, by the holy vicariate. I suppose it is about your profession." Daniel was astonished and worried about this deployment of forces, trials and accusations that had begun to rise all over Spain at a huge level.

He speculated: "Perhaps it is about my daughter! She cured a young novice, dwelling in the cathedral, and she is not a certified doctor yet. She was asked because I was away and..."

The officer abruptly interrupted Daniel, moving his head as a sign for the guards. Armored hands seized the doctor, while the captain spoke: "Whatever it is, you will know pretty soon! Let us go directly to our holiness!"

The horses abandoned the estate, while a little girl was watching them from behind a bush. It was Elena, wearing a morbid smirk and motioning to the backyard. It was cold, and she was walking barefoot, her childish cassock bellowing. From her feeble left hand a flower appeared, deposed soon after on a tombstone. It was an off-season red rose, preserved for her mother. Petals were falling one by one, covering in sequence the name engraved on the family gravestone. The last petal had a different color.

The doctor was escorted in front of a commission, in which part of the court was formed by members of the church. Judges were handling and shuffling papers of evidence and confessions against him and his family. He was seriously questioned by components of a different tribunal, who after the cross-examination took him into custody. Daniel was given permission to express, "I am at your service, your grace! I don't know about these false accusations. Where is my family? They are not part of my business, except my older daughter. She randomly assisted me now and then."

A cleric countered sharply, "That is a lie, doctor! Your daughter attempted to cure a young novice living at the monastery, and he was spellbound by her magic tricks. The youth is still sick, worse than before!" Daniel furiously tried to defend Elysa, "No! She cured him from his sickness. There were numerous witnesses who complimented her, why don't you question them?"

One of the leading cardinals shushed the conversation. "That is enough! We are tired of your facile nonsense. We heard those people, and they are all against you and your daughters…a discord!" The man of God screamed with a resonated voice: "You are consuming our holy patience, Daniel! You and your family will be judged by the holy tribunal, away with it!"

A disturbance propagated within the court chamber, while Daniel was arrested with an ecclesiastical court authorization. His family was questioned by the same religious delegation and taken to a different place.

For a few days the Morgairs' house was searched, and more people were threatened and questioned. Evidences of suspicious occult affairs perpetrated by the whole family surfaced, bringing them before a more complex trial. Numerous people cured by the doctor, and in particular by his older daughter, confessed under threat of torture, accusing the prisoners of using magic rituals and deceitful potions mixed with poisonous herbs. Animals and obscure objects were nominated by the accusers, while those who tried to belie and retract were jailed and processed for witchcraft.

"Daniel's younger daughter, Elena, is a little necromancer, everybody has seen her torturing animals and reciting macabre invocations before killing them; she clearly despises the creatures of God!" yelled a witness surrounded by the guards. "I saw her many times with my own eyes! One day, your holiness, she lured a little kitten by the lagoon and strangled it with her little creepy hands…abominable!"

The crowd murmured with a bombastic "Oooh!" The cleric continued, "What about her older sister, Elysa, she could be responsible more than Elena is. We found horrendous evidences!" The man bent his head as a sign of fear and submission, than replied, "I cannot say too much about Elysa, except that she cured me a couple of times and…" A second observer said, "She cured you with her hideous misdemeanor! She never healed me once!"

The disturbance in the courtroom was rising, and controversial testimonies were confusing the holy consistory. The leading cardinal intervened, raising his hand, "Be aware of what you say! Here we speak in the name of the Lord, no lies will be tolerated. Evil is concocting its malignant plan in Logrono!"

A third witness declared, "I once saw Elena conversing with the black crows of the lagoon, she was talking to them! I remember she was circled by black feathers, creating a circumferential shield of protection, and she was not harming the birds."

The cardinal expressed his fury with a satisfactory voice: "Of course she did not! Those animals are a sign of evil, a mark of the black magic. We all know that witches are capable of transforming in those creepy feathers, and they are there in the lagoon!" People clamoring once more…

"Elena cannot harm crows because they are evil, she is a little witch! I am sure that she was mesmerized and indoctrinated by her family; they are the culprits here!" Concluded him while the court adjourned…majority were screaming "*Bruja! Bruja! Hechicera!*

Daniel, along with his family, was followed by prisoners before the tribunal of the Holy Spanish Inquisition, which had worked since 1609 at the

Basque witch trials. It was one of the most ambitious attempts at rooting out witchcraft ever undertaken by the Spanish church.

Andres Salazar was the junior inquisitor delegated to examine the matter at length, armed with an Edict of Grace for those willing to recant and accuse the evil ones. He had travelled across the countryside, mainly in the vicinity of Zugarramurdi, near what is now the French-Spanish border, where a cave and a water stream were said to be the meeting place of the witches. Thousands in Zugarramurdi were accused and tortured for their evil doings, as were those at La Rioja, Burgos and Soria. The most overwhelming evidence the Holy Inquisition had about the Morgairs was Elysa's secret diary.

Five years of writing and drawing of any kind, about what she had learned assisting her father and performed herself. From twelve to seventeen years was all recorded. There was a painting of the herb *Mandragora Dioscurides* or Mandrake, a very common medical plant described as male and female for the different species. The Mandrake root formed the shape of a human body, and was believed to have the power to control a person, such as wealth, desire, conception, vengeance, protection and spells. One figure Elysa painted was a root, figured as a naked woman with long hair. Her hands were crossed in front of her abdomen, while on top leaves were coming out of her head.

A name was written in Latin between the roots: *Mors Resurges Lysae…* from death you will rise Lysae. She was her dear dead mother (Irish: Lysagh Smith), who died of a mysterious virus, and for this reason they accused Elysa to be matricidal.

Salazar, eager to make his rampant career, commented on those findings: "No doubt she is the devilish mastermind of the family! Not Elena but Elysa, indeed, is responsible for the misdemeanors. The holy court was right in investigating the facts. Elena was an easy scapegoat for that sorcerer. She was swindled by her older sister. She will tell us—Elena will confess the truth. Remember you all, as our Lord declared, it is from the mouth of children where the truth is whispered!"

According to the Inquisition, Elysa performed her mischievous ceremonies to gain evil power over her family and the weak, maneuvering the will of Lucifer. For this reason she was immediately sent to Pamplona, where Pierre

De Lancre, the Holy French judge of Bordeaux, was conducting a massive witch hunt ordered by the King of Navarre, Henry IV.

Manuscripts, scrolls and documents related to Elysa Morgair were scrupulously studied by the Holy Inquisition. To them she was the most dangerous source of evil in Spain, given her young age and the people she enchanted with her fraudulent, devilish mysticism.

Even Daniel was at her service, assisting her in killing his own wife.

For the judges she used adulterated potions, which a young religious novice was seduced with. The accusations were endless, as were the confessions, and Daniel was forced under torture to admit his daughters' guilt.

The doctor tried to save the two girls, denying the charges, whereas persecutors continued with their extreme torture, until the male died. His agony was atrocious, as were his averting supplications.

"It is me! Only me! I am responsible for all the happenings. I murdered my wife! My daughters are innocent please, no! I confess, I truly confess," cried the man in agony, while a twisting press was cracking his spine, the noise making a fierce sinister sound. His body's external parts were already burned, as were his torn nails, and his breast was hardly beaten.

"Confess your daughters' responsibility, Dr. Morgair! You are going to die a sinner and a liar! The witches! Confess," yelled mercilessly the guard, while a final crack broke Daniel's neck, ending his writhing contortions.

Torturers terminated Daniel before he could save the two girls, while the other prisoners were hanged and burned at the stakes. Elysa, unaware of all of this, was dragged ahead of the Supreme Spanish Royal Court of the Holy Inquisition…it was December.

PART TWO

An Inquisitor was sent from Rome (Cardinal Ravello Pietro).

Elysa entered in chains, parading with a royal stride—every person inside the court was mesmerized by her young beauty and sensuality, feeling in a contorted way, attracted. Dark blonde hair flew down her head, framing a regal view. A proud pure figure appeared in the chamber, while grumpy and ugly faces were staring.

Elena was kept away from her sister, surrounded by armored guards. She was a mute traitor ready to conspire, cradled by evil. Metallic medieval knights shone their armors, reflecting the evening's reddish twilight. Elysa's eyes for a moment glanced at them, appearing of a deep intense red color.

"Look at her evil eyes! They are full of blood! My God, she is a witch! A witch," screamed a peasant standing along the arcade.

Elysa kept staring at the bright armors, terrorizing all the spectators with her evil purplish irises. A knight was glancing behind his helm's visor at the prisoner, attracted and spellbound by her natural beauty. He opened the brim slightly, meeting the angel's pupils…a look of passion and love.

The judges questioned Elena while hidden behind a tall cuirassier. She answered with an innocent, crying disquieting voice. "She is the daughter of Lucifer, that's what she told us!" "She assassinated my mom! She bewitched my dad, too, she was always treated as the princess of the house," continued her whimpered…grabbing one of the knight's dissonant legs.

Her innocent eyes crossed those of a valorous soldier, who whispered, "I see the innocent look of evil now, while moments ago I saw the ghoulish face of pure love!" His heart pounded.

The court read all the accusations, and by the will of God decided to sentence Elysa to death, without any possibility to recant or be forgiven. She was for the Holy Catholic Church a diabolical deceit, a daughter of Satan—*the* daughter of Satan!

Cardinal Ravello put the wax papal seal on the sentence: "May God have mercy on your disfigured soul. You are a disgrace to humanity!"

Elysa was cautiously escorted to the town's prison. She was to die of hunger and thirst in the lowest dark dungeons of the city, chained alone in solitude and desperation. Her blasphemous beauty had to be consumed slowly, along with her vanity.

She was brought down in chains on a gloomy spiral stairwell, which was long and dark as hell. The steep strides and spectral walls were guiding her in the midst of a slow gruesome agony.

Lamentations and crying were heard all over the fortress, where prisoners were slowly dying of hunger and thirst. Cold and wet were falsely pampered by the dim red light of the torches, positioned along the edges of the rotten vault.

She finally arrived at the deepest point of the dungeon, where not even the torches were fired. A vicious smell of death and hopelessness made Elysa cry, begging and imploring the warden to spare her life: "Please have mercy, I am innocent! I don't want to die!" The jailer replied, "You are already dead!"

Motionless and merciless, the guards violently threw the young girl into the little claustrophobic crypt, described for such a sinister monstrous aspect, only by the forces of evil.

A dauntless heir of the Knights Templar wielded his long sword to the sky, mirroring her purplish vaporized tears of passion…floating on the ground.

CHAPTER XXV

Sacred Methods

A document was found by Kevin regarding Andrew and his missing father, who had attended the Residential Catholic School in North Vancouver, escaping later to Vancouver Island. He was seventeen years old when moved to Port Alberni, where both Tseshaht and Hupacasath First Nations were sharing the territory. A United Protestant Church was burned and rebuilt twice as soon as Andrew's fugitive father moved there.

The certificate was a statement in which Devine's father accused the previous Church for being after him because he had discovered important historical facts concealed in a manuscripts hidden by the Catholics. Only a few papers survived the first fire, and were taken into custody by the priest in charge at that time, before the school was closed in 1976. Kevin was able to retrace this information, looking at the history of native residential schools in B.C. .

Kevin: "The original document was kept after to the Port Alberni United Church, and found by police. It was an English expedition dated 1795, which sailed from the port of Bristol in 1971, and reached what is now Pennsylvania and Vancouver. Sir Edward Clark of the Royal Navy was the second captain in charge of the English Frigates, while George Vancouver was the headmaster and discoverer of numerous locations in the West Pacific Coast. The mission spent twenty-one days at the settlement of Bethlehem, founded in 1741 and named after the Biblical town of Bethlehem of Judea, the birthplace of Jesus the Son of God (Bethlehem is a city in the Lehigh Valley region of the east part of the U.S. state of Pennsylvania," speaking to Robert who dubiously questioned. "Do you think this historical document is really coherent with our investigation? What if it will lead us astray? How can you be so sure?"

Kevin replied firmly, "We have to give it a try! Nothing can be neglected here!" "Later on they reached the West Coast of Vancouver, where they planned to stay twenty-one days as well, although something went wrong. The documents kept by the settlers recalled of a curse to be broken.

Natives living in the area had been threatened and killed by a mysterious evil ancestral spirit. The settlers were later found on the mountains brutally slaughtered."

"How can those killings date so far back in time? Perhaps native revenge on the settlers or toward the Christians—although aboriginal people were killed, as well," observed Robert. "We better show this to Meredith," suggesting to his boss.

After deeply consulting and observing the writings, Meredith deduced: "It's a forgery, it's not possible! They were all killed with specific methods used by Holy Inquisition," clutching a white sheet. "This one had his arms tied behind his back and was hooked with roots on a tree… .The Ripped torture, the second was seated on a sharpened piece of wood… .The Pyramid agony…" Kevin and Robert looked each other.

The psychic added: "What I don't comprehend, is why Anglican religious documents were concealed for years in a Catholic structure. This line shows a strong relation between Bethlehem, Jerusalem, Pennsylvania, and Vancouver; three diverse cities far from each other, with their own history." The conversation went on longer than expected, until the medium provided the last details.

"The gruesome murders, according to the methods, are those used specifically in the Spanish Holy Inquisition."

The Inquisition, in all its changing and forms, lasted for more than five hundred years. Who may have been committing those crimes remained a mystery.

CHAPTER XXVI

Holy Trails

Armando and Maurice were able to trace the identity of some clerics of the 1795 expedition. Surprisingly some of them were Catholics from Spain, France and Rome.

No documents or writings were found about this English expedition that involved both the Christians and the Catholics.

After deciphering some Latin writings and papal seals written with the Benedictine formula—*Vade Retro Satana* —it was clear that the purpose was to eradicate evil from that place, expurgating it, liberating the locals in the name of the Almighty, so that the house of God could be built once for all.

At the Vatican, Father Maurice retrieved the true line that connected all the cities touched by the ship. It was a religious apocalyptic sign, as he explained to the attentive Laura: "The original Bethlehem was the birthplace of Jesus Christ, who died in Jerusalem. The sea travels from Europe to the Atlantic Pennsylvania, where the religious Protestant Moravian missionaries founded the city after Jesus's birthplace. Vancouver is the last one and the youngest, ruled by the King of Spain till 1795 when the British took over."

He drank a glass of water, breathless, "The Moravian reformer John Hus used to preach at the Bethlehem Church, contrasting the Roman Catholic clergy and the hierarchy that after a long Holy inquisition's trial burned him at the stakes in 1415, provoking riots and protests supported after by

Martin Luther. In 1520 Pope Leo X excommunicated Luther and all the Protestants with the papal bull *Exurge Domine Por Causam Tuam*, similar to those bulls we found on the documents of the 1795 expedition." Laura expressed: "What about Malachy, then?" He readily answered, "Father Larry talked about Malachy and his prophecy regarding the last warning, the last prophetic seal…the new water of life; water we saw on the last scene of killings in Vancouver."

Meantime Claudio found his courage and burying his shyness, he contcted Mesotti. "What a pleasure young fellow, you took your time to call…?" said the officer. Claudio flattered, "My sister has found some evidences that connect Larry's murder to Europe—the clerics confirmed it. I have all the information scanned in my computer. I can send it now!" A busy Kevin appreciated, promising to catch up very soon. He liked Claudio because he recalled his lost son, an introverted, clever, attentive boy, full of life… willing to realize his dreams.

"Dates of centuries, old anagrammatic languages and religious scrolls, a puzzling conundrum of time," whispered the officer reading Claudio's evidences. He was eavesdropping in amusement outside the window glass of his office, when simultaneously a flying shadow of fear mantled his troubled mind, curling the wrinkles on his face.

A little butterfly was candidly flapping the wings, turning around a feeble light bulb, creating a trail of shining wind. Kevin's blood froze instantaneously, pivoting with a stunned, frightened appearance, as if expecting to be smashed by an obscure presence.

His look shifted and the creases on his visage relaxed in a delighted manner, observing the fleeting butterfly vanishing within the room's shade. Kevin's beating heart was proved seriously, revealing a lack of fitness. "If I got scared by a harmless butterfly, how could I possibly face those monsters up there?" the dubious officer murmured, arching his eyebrow; his sight returned again to the window, projecting Vancouver's sinuous range in full display. Its lost secret was fast asleep

The elegant austere persona mirrored in the glass window, looking unsettled: "Evil—what is evil for real? Our daily endangered life? We all suffer and fight to be better and survive in this world. Evil can be the loss of someone you loved or cared about, a malignant cancer, a broken family, a denial of God, a betrayal and hundreds other things. Evil can be around us every day, as well as goodness. It is upon us to distinguish and choose which one," his face blank and moody, his eyes shining with the reflected beams of the light bulb; a trembling, rough, elongated hand turned off the switch, generating outside a sense of perilous dynamic thriving.

CHAPTER XXVII

Codes

The mysterious inverted map grid encoded the number, 3-666 (God-Evil). Larry unfortunately could not conclude his mapping of the prophecy, because the truth he was looking for absorbed his life in darkness.

The scattered manuscripts were never joined to exhibit the entire meaning of its verity. A puzzle missing a piece will never be completed, shrouding its real content at the eyes of reality…Kevin was groping in the gloom of the unknown.

If connected (world connection), the two encoded gridlines of parallels displayed two different triangles: One pointing down (female) with number threes on the angles (333), the other pointing up (male) with number sixes on the angles (666).

The grids revealed a beltline, sliding from the 44th Parallel to the 49th Parallel, involving six Parallels (6); and from the 41th Parallel to the 49th Parallel, involving nine Parallels (inverted 9 = 6). The cipher obtained (6 and 9) were solved as 9-6 = 3. A 3-666 line of ambiguity.

It was a zone attaching the history of Christianity (Europe) and the New World (North America), a bridge with its middle point at Oak Island, Nova Scotia (Canada), and Bethlehem, Pennsylvania (USA).

Half of June was gone and in Vancouver Jack Rouschel was waiting for a client, while reading a science journal with Luca. The two came across an article regarding a precise religious astronomical prophecy written by John the Apostle, the Revelation 12 (3) signs.

It was an apocalyptic belief of the New Testament, regarding a star alignment of the Virgo constellation to the Leo constellation within all the planets (a line). Jack focused his eyes on the paper as if captivated by the writings, reading : "The alignment starts from the moon under the feet of Virgo (V as a triangle) and ends with Venus (V as a triangle) under the leg of Leo."

He then read in a loud voice the original Revelation: "And a great sign appeared in heaven, a woman clothed with the sun, with the moon under her feet and on her head a crown of twelve stars. She was pregnant and was crying in agony, giving birth."

Luca: "Do you want to impress me? It looks like you are sermonizing at the Sunday mass!"

Jack said, "You cannot be serious, except when you are working, Luca! Do not you get why I was reading this passage to you? Let me finish, please," There was a moment of silence.

"The prophecy seems real because planet Jupiter will be for its apparent retrograde motion nine months inside Virgo's womb, exiting from the lower part of it. The prophecy was almost fulfilled in 2011 but the alignment was not perfect, while around the 17th of September 2017 (20, 17) it will be in perfect alignment." Jack solemnly concluded: "They are talking about the coming of something cursed, who will unleash death and damnation. A supernatural entity! The West Vancouver police are considering the presence of a satanic guild acting on the hills, doesn't it ring a bell to you?"

The client was late, and after showing the house and its renovations, the realtors went looking for Isabel and Claudio, explaining briefly what they found in the magazine.

Hours later, Claudio and his friends were escorted to Kevin's workplace, submerged in a sea of pictures and documents gathered throughout the case. He was nervously twiddling his thumbs, nodding and watching the fellows, trying to sort out all the inner thoughts in his chest. "I don't want to neglect any aspect of this riddle. Underestimating the enemy has always been a terrible mistake. I believe in what I see and feel, even if seldom one can discern the reality," externalized him with serious austere gaze.

A wide wall embedded a detailed geographic map of the North Shore areas, signed with dots and dates.

Jack showed the cop the article, telling him what they thought about all those coincidences, "Dates between 2011… 2017 (a difference of *six* years) where the homicides increased, the period from spring to September (*six* months), the water and the trees like a spiritual sign, plus the Satanic hate for mankind and the Church. It could be perhaps a mixed religious group of locals, a hybridized band perhaps, inspired by the assassinations of the past."

Meredith stood up, illustrating, "A secret congregation following the prophecy of the apocalypse, like those in the States committing massive suicide!"

They had to rely only on the historical confessions of the survivors, and no real proof was at hand, except: "Those criminals only used side-arms, well-crafted natural weapons. Wounds and fractures revealed their effectiveness and power. They are local people, able to procure food and shelter… the more we try to squeeze them in the circle, the more they hit with fierce determination…marking their territory."

Claudio was fascinated by the detective: "At least we know where they are! The mountains area is huge, that's why they can hide and move without being detected."

Kevin candidly paused the youth, contesting, "Perhaps, but that doesn't explain why if possessing such a technology they prefer to use primordial weaponry to kill. It is an ordeal, and they need lots of energy to make effective those rudimental tools. I have doubts about that!" Meredith suggested, "Those weapons are used to confuse us, and lead us astray from the real path."

PART THREE

CHAPTER XXVIII

Beastly Presence

North Vancouver Regional Park, late evening…

A film crew was shooting a fantastic television series, adapting the woods down Grouse Mountain as an original background. At sunset they stopped for a coffee break, the night shooting was tiring and the security guards were a little bit nervous after the latest episodes. The film company was authorized to shoot only in that secured area. One of the actors was donning his costume, assuring that his spare pants were pleated and ready after the display. He sat on a piece of log, smoking a cigarette and sipping a hot coffee.

A burning reddish fire was consuming his smoke. Every mouthful appeared more luminescent and vivid. The last puff was intensely deep, and enlightened the dark shade of the woods behind his shoulders. A sinister contorted shadow slithered along the disappearing embers of the cigarette, emanating a liquid sound framed by a loathsome smell that allured the man, pervading his opened nostrils.

He revolved, observing the blinded obscurity of the forest, when he felt like a squeezing coarse snake slinking around his throat, sensing an unstoppable lack of oxygen. He was dragged along the surroundings, enduring a treacherous adventure. He woke up feeling a sharp, agonizing pain, procured by his hauled figure violently bouncing on a gravel trail. A groaning voice was coming before him, as if he was dragged by horses. His rotten corpse resembled that of a chastised man, slashed hundreds times without mercy.

Faster and faster the monster was running, careless of the human being's desperate condition. He fell in a state of unconsciousness, fainting for the loss of blood and the atrocious torment

The actor awoke for the last time, watching in semidarkness two tenebrous, wicked dark-yellow eyes coming closer. A small, glassy lagoon blinked to a feeble being, smoothly emanating a dubious breath of afterlife.

He screamed with all the remaining strength he had left. His face and mouth were repeatedly smashed upon trees…rocks cracked his skull open, that was his last scene.

The crew director informed the police, while security guards were looking for David, finding only the shreds of his costume. No blood or traces were found in the vicinity, and police decided to continue the search at sunrise—as they explained, "Maybe David got lost while going in the woods for a nap or for an extra smoke. We found a few butts on the ground where he was last seen."

The crew experienced a sleepless night, thinking of David's disappearance, and in the morning they were anxiously following the search, while the breaking news created a new sense of fear among the community. Reporters announced: "Yet no trace or sign of the actor near the park, the wish is to find him still alive on the loose. Today will be a pivotal point for the research!" The same night helicopters with signal lights flew all around the North Shore, trying to scout David and bring him back home.

It was only three days later when his corpse was identified by a helicopter equipped with thermal chambers. It was tied up halfway on a tall pine. Search and Rscue climbers had the infamous task of taking it down without altering the scene.

Jim Carter was escorted personally to the morgue this time, releasing a peculiar interview after receiving Dr. Lewis's postmortem report. He spoke into the microphones, making clear everybody's roles.

"There were no perforations on his feet and hands. Nothing else was severed like the previous one, except some signs on his belly and a little piece of root inserted inside the abdomen. A sharp piece of rock was used to draw the strange composition that Inspector Mesotti will analyze for us with the support of an expert in symbolism— small circle above the navel and a tiny root inserted in it."

While the interview was widely broadcasted, a pair of workers on a job site close to Capilano Park, made a statement to the West Vancouver police, describing what they saw the day David went missing.

One of the laborers accounted, "We were moving some sheets of plywood on the unfinished second floor, when we observed on a trail that opened a little portion of the mountain, a tall figure running backwards, as if its legs reversed...but not the body. About five, six seconds, and was undulating, covered with branches and leaves. We thought it was a special effect used for the TV series they were shooting." No special effects were used that day...

Meredith deciphered what she thought was a message, comparing the battered corpse wounds positions with the Earth, Sun and Moon. She obtained a solar eclipse when the body was reversed!"

Meredith was unfolding her big blue eyes while adjusting her glasses, her quivering lips showed a sense of discomfort, knowing that those within the room were dubious and skeptical despite her dazzling theories.

Lots of questions were summoned and Meredith gave her final dissertation on the slayers message: "Killers, not killer! Those are prophetic murderers, with knowledge of the Holy Scriptures. The eclipse is a clear meaning of the coming of someone throughout time."

She placed the last sheet on the desk and concluded, "The Book of Revelation of John is another piece of the puzzle—they are killing to fulfill the scriptures, bringing doomsday closer here in Vancouver. The eclipse was found in a reverse position, as well as the crucified body."

Everybody reacted in different ways, but one thing was clear, they had never been so close to the truth. Mesotti left the office while conversing with Robert: "We should inform the press about our report; it is time they talk about our backstage investigation. If Jim Carter thinks we will just stand aside and watch, he is wrong" "The boys are back in town!"

CHAPTER XXIX

Old Pictures

News exploded all over B.C, involving other provinces of Canada and the West Coast of United States. Many titles appeared on the first pages of the provincial newspaper: "The Hills of Evil, the Spring Butcher's Range...Woods of Terror...Devil's Eyes of green Vancouver..." They were just running out of imagination. Some were speculating about the real presence of the Sasquatch-Bigfoot.

Claudio, after consulting with his friends, decided to pay a visit to Port Alberni residential school.

After checking in their motel, the group drove to the infamous institute, where indigenous people were forcefully taken from their families, suffering abuses. They walked across the parking lot toward an imposing brick building. Isabel shuddered and took Claudio's arm while commenting, "I can't help but think of all the children who suffered here." Claudio observed a tall man coming closer, mumbling: "I am Thomas Joseph, the director, how can I assist you?" He reached out to shake Claudio's hand. "We would like to visit the school, we're university students," said Claudio. Thomas agreed and took the lead, "The institute was closed in 1973... three years later the land was given back to the Tseshaht Nation. The dormitory was over here," pointing the finger. "In 2009 our community tore it down, and we had a special ceremony to drive the presence of evil out!"

Silence was dominating around the visitors, eager to cross the large lobby and enter the old library. On a conference table were photo albums and newspaper clippings. The man, with a pompous gesture said, "You are welcome to look through these. I'll be next door, let me know if you have any questions."

The group sat around the table and started paging through the albums. The room became very quiet as they read about the sad history of the school: the mistreatments, the two fires, the rampant illness and malnutrition. They sat side by side looking at the photos… Luca sighed, rubbing his forehead, "Who is the real evil here? How much those children had to suffer, for God's sake."

They saw a picture dating 1918, where young locals were granted some prices for their woodwork. One of the boys had beside him a carved-wood portrait that resembled Andrew's drawing; it was a surprise!

Claudio convened with the school keeper, asking information about the kid in the picture. He answered with a smirk, "Too many documents were lost here because of the fires. Although I cannot give the boy's identity, I can instead show you his woodwork." Claudio felt a strong emotion, as if the girl in his dream was waiting for him, "Do you have the artifact here in the school?" Joseph said, "Yes, sir!"

Inspector Mesotti, when first investigating the Port Alberni school, rushed directly to the church's archive, spending most of his precious time searching for valid elements; instead at the school, he paid a brief casual visit. The fellows, with their stubborn obstinate perseverance, found the probable original wood-carved artifact copied by Andrew's father, "There is a resembled in his facial lineaments," observed Claudio. "Andrew's grandfather?" said Isabel.

Claudio came closer, approaching with Isabel, observing the meticulous artifact, while others were trying to lecture the details. After a while Isabel, using her acute introspection, dominated the differences between the engravings and etches, "There is something else on the water, more dense and red-colored, not the sunlight but blood, and it is close to the bewildering half-moon. The reflection on the fluids shows dripping from the girl, but nothing more can be seen, apart from the turning face and the eyes almost watching back toward us."

Jack: "She is in a lake! Don't t you see guys, those pines all around, confused between the clouds reflected on the water." The opera was a lunar eclipse, explaining part of its title. A lunar eclipse is possible only with a full moon, but in the image the girl was acting like the earth, because her feet were under water and sunset behind her. It was similar to the one found on David's body. In fact, when watching the images not reflected on the water, no moon was visible; instead, when observing the half-falling moon on the lagoon, it was possible! The lunar eclipse was called the blood moon for its reddish color, because of the umbra or penumbra of the earth—in our case her shadow.

Meredith added her comments: "It is a sign of the prophecy when you have astronomical events. In the Hebrew Bible, the Book of Joel is about revelations bound on the lunar eclipse, and reflected the apocalypse of the time—Judgment Day, the coming of Christ, or something worse like the antichrist. Joel, like the prophet Malachy, was part of the twelve Minor Prophets; and while Malachy is the last seal, Joel is one of the first."

Joel's prophecy: "His prophecy said that when the sun will be turned to darkness and the moon to blood… be prepared for the dreadful day."

Claudio observed: "Why follow the minor prophet books and not the others?" Meredith answer: "They are called minor not because they are less important, but because the content of their books is less!"

CHAPTER XXX

Two Lions

Smallpox of 1862 and 1924 killed almost fifty percent of the native population of Canada; thousands of children died and more than 1,500 reserves were built.

Hundreds of residential schools were opened. Bands and tribes were mixed and children were taken away from their families. It was impossible to go back to their identity. Andrew was born in Port Alberni, while his father originated from North Vancouver

Claudio and his friends were apprised by Andrew, "In our culture… legends, history, spiritual belief and traditions are passed by word of mouth. My father, since I was a child, used to disclose the genuine spirits of the mountains…cursing with their revenge the mischief of mankind.

Claudio was gulping a cold beer, seated in a local pub, saturated by Devine's disquisition, and while turning the glass a reel formed a root going down. He felt a vibration in his pocket. His sister sent a message… a new breakthrough.

After weeks researching in the Vatican library, Armando traced the name of several Catholic priests on board of the 1795 Vancouver expedition. One in particular was a Roman inquisitor with a long career…

Armando crested, "The whole matter hinges on a line, and we have to find the beginning to see the end. That's why I requested the access to the secret files of the library, on the subject of the 1610." After reading his message, Claudio's muscles commenced laboring at their maximum oxygen capacity...guided by sonic pulsations. He adjusted the waistband, "Everything alright?" asked Isabel. Andrew fetched a paper-bag, "You have been good friends to me, today...thanks for listening," while Claudio answered back to her: "Good news from Laura, I'll tell you later!"

The step-ladder of retrospections friendly ended, trading back their painful memories...followed by a wind of fragility.

Darleen Satin, one of Meredith's employees, had a passion for astrology, stars, and supernatural events. She enjoyed participating in spiritual sessions and paranormal activities. Since Meredith got involved in this conundrum, she tried to be part of the team, contacting Claudio at Meredith's request.

He was dazzled about Darleen, rapidly regrouping with his friends. "I think it's a great idea—we have more freedom to express our ideas, and above all, our information," said Claudio to the group.

Luca expressed: "Better be careful with the police. They don't like private intruders!"

Meredith exposed a modern alternative line, involving Vancouver's bridges, "Burrard, Granville and Cambie, they all run north-west to the Lions Gate Bridge. The other, the Second Narrow bridge... positioned between Grouse and Seymour Mountains, is an alternative escape to the east side of the city."

"From west the scoundrels enter, from east they escape. At sunset they enter and at moonrise they escape!" said her staring at them. "Sunset and moonrise, like a secret eclipse," adding.

Darleen uncovered to the team the meaning of the "Lying moon" and its deceiving aspects during time.

The two lions' eyes were swindling the truth. Moreover John the Baptist said that he had to descend and Jesus to ascend, like Sunset and Moonrise.

CHAPTER XXXI PART ONE

Envisions

A few days later Claudio was driving, facing a long avenue of colored trees overwhelmed with leaves. He arched his neck forward for a moment, trying to set the radio station, while the wheels were crushing some rocks.

Proceeding inside the tunnel of trees, he heard the echo of dripping water, observing the branches closing on his car…a vigorous breeze was blasting the alley. He sensed a claustrophobic feeling, discerning at the end of the burrow a squeezing mouth-bush sucking his car. Eyes of black water appeared along the sides on the trunks, while the branches were curling like creepy creatures. Burls of deformed growing knots were moving as if sealed in wombs. The boy yelled, sprawling his worries in his innermost recondite mind. Darkness was eating his soul at the end of the street, while a sermonic loud voice merged underwater, sounding his name.

He woke up with shortness of breath, sweating and humid as if he had gone running. He shrugged in a dubious manner, bracing his legs within the head. He motioned soon after, grabbing the door's handle, heading to his father's bedroom. The man was sleeping profoundly, while Claudio was standing on the doorstep, observing the obscurity.

He clasped the knocker, the one Giacomo placed for his son's nightmares, whispering in the penumbra, "Let him sleep in peace, your father has been alone for years…a long, sad solitude, a painful life."

A thud of small trotting steps converged along the shadowed corridor, advancing with menacing grinding teeth and two dilated yellow pupils. Claudio perceived a fatigued troubled breath, closing in a tumultuous, menacing behavior. He was rigidly gelid, unable to move and hit the knocker, as if he was experiencing one of his bad dreams. (He used to scream for his mother's intervention, hoping to be saved from the creatures chasing him.) His throat was paralyzed, as were his vocal cords. A sinister figure approached, crawling behind Claudio, poking his impeded cramped calves…Leon was behind him, flipping its tail!

"You scared the hell out of me, noose dog!" he knelt, caressing a wobbly Leon with genuine affection.

Next morning at Meredith's, Claudio was welcomed with a warm coffee and a piece of homemade apple pie. Darleen Satin was peeling an apple, slicing the fruit and adding layers on the cake. "Wow, you really like apple, don't you?" specified Claudio with a clever smirk. "Yes! You can say that, my friends at school used to nickname me *Pomme,* the French translation for apple," replied her.

Darleen fetched a plan she had been working on, displaying a timid, demure visage: "Armando Suarez's line is completed!" Claudio stoned: "What do you mean completed?"

Meredith said, "We found the closest Bethlehem church on the water here in East Vancouver—it is the Bethlehem Lutheran Church," and was very close to the street where Claudio had his last nightmare.

He could not restrain his emotions, revealing last night dream-vision. Satin placed her hands on his forehead, "Do you think I have a fever, it was just a nightmare!" said Claudio. "Let her read your mind, she knows what she is doing," advised a well versed Meredith.

Darleen whispered as Claudio was falling asleep, "Your brain is releasing an intense warm energy shrouded in a cold dream…it is trapped! Something is trying to use it. I cannot absorb… it is sliding back to you."

"Something is assimilating my thoughts—oh no! What a bad sensation—my God! I see those eyes staring at me! I see a girl, a red rose…" continued her, while Meredith sensed a cold shiver, as if the temperature was dropping. She checked the thermometer and realized that from sixty-eight degrees they had dropped in no more than five minutes to forty-nine degrees.

Claudio awakened, perturbed, "What's going on here, why it's so cold?"

The medium came back to her senses, affirming: "Ghosts and spiritual entities absorb the energy around them, dropping the temperature. I felt a one-way energy exchange in your case. Your body was keeping and not giving."

Meredith clapped her hands and chopped the conversation…everybody was ready to leave…looking for that church. Her bobbed hair moved from one side: "The fact that a church named Bethlehem is here in Vancouver is a sign itself! The name, the line of time… as in old Latin… *Tempus Fugit* or Time Flies.The truth of every prediction comes at the appointed time. We know about the 1795 expedition and now we found the church right here!" Claudio added, "It means something is coming closer and closer, itinerant from the past."

A draft of cold wind breathed on Darleen's neck, making her leap up as if someone was standing behind her. "Ouch! What's wrong with you? You just stepped on my foot?" exclaimed Claudio gazing at her. Darleen: "Sorry! I felt someone sighing, a cold whisper!"

They left the church and drove away, while in Meredith's apartment, the ventilator activated blowing against an invisible energy. A sinusoidal sound flew around the space, a wet sinister frequency.

Hours later, Meredith concluded the research: "Sunrise is on Mount Seymour side at 6:30 p.m… 76 degrees east, sunset around 7:36 p.m. at 276 degrees west past Cypress on the Pacific Ocean. Moonrise is seen around 6:40 p.m. at 116 degrees southeast, and moonset at around 4:06 a.m. in the southwest. We should see the exact position from Vancouver's Lions Gate Bridge, at the Prospect Point Lookout-Stanley Park."

Claudio asked, "What are we looking at…coordinates?"

She answered, "A possible passageway to the slayers' sanctuary, a sort of star comet leading us to them!"

Darleen: "Are we ready for this? Let's call the other and go," said her grinning. "Hope Isabel doesn't bring my cousin, I don't like him be part of our tem," thought Claudio checking his phone.

PART II

A moment of silence was followed by a natural, enchanted eternity.

The first beams of moonrise and the last rays of sunset appeared in a full-moon phase. Darleen took some notes with her to estimate the angulations and the coordinates of the lights seen on the mountains. They were positioned to the south of the Lions Bridge, eyeing sunset from the west, while the rays exploded…spreading toward the center of the ocean, between Cypress and Grouse Peaks.

The moon was displaying her magic presence, beaming lights reproduced on the water between Grouse and Cypress once again. They were closing on each other upon the water, like two diverse essences of shades that were never equal—one warm and penetrating, the other mild and suffuse. Close upon their confused eyes, immensely distant in reality like water and fire, day and night, God and Evil.

Only the luminous shaft of the moon, and the sun's wake, reproduced in the middle of the veiled water a shining trail pointing toward Cypress Peak.

Darleen traced the shaft perpendicular to the mountain, establishing more or less the hypothetical extremity, very close to Black Mountain's spike. What the fellows could not discern was that only in a peculiar given angle, the glimmer of both lights were penetrating the woods, striking and encountering two threes merged in a tiny lost lagoon (unknown to people).

A distorted dusk was falling on the silenced woods, the same that embedded a former soldier under a severe stress; a tragic ending reported only by the local news of his hometown, far away from Vancouver.

The accident was classified as an announced suicide, lengthening the list of those soldiers who took their lives because of post-war trauma. A few weeks after his dismissal from the clinic, the soldier was having sleeping problem, urging his leaden legs to move. He walked in a sluggish way on the spiraling staircase of his tiny attic, glancing skyward, and standing on the banister. He reached the bathroom when it was 3 in the morning, switching on a feeble, dim light, inching his feet to the verge of the sink. He opened the tap, observing the cold churning water forming ringlets of fluidity. Head down, he was holding the flowing water in his trembling hands, recollecting what he saw a moment before.

In the obscure ambience, he discerned a figure on the mirror…a gray tunic.

The soldier's blood froze in fear, sensing an entity behind him. A grotesque sigh gusted, whispering a soulless opaque sentence. Water was escaping from his fingers, as if frightened, while the youth wished to be part of it. There was no time to react or fight. He revolved all of a sudden, no one was there! His shiver sobered. Returning his look on the mirror, he could not see his image. The glass vibrated as if made of water… trespassing the other dimensional frequency, denying his vision. . He breached throughout the door of the supernatural realm, cutting his body with shards of glass.

Behind it, she was waiting, folding his lost face within her hands, sighing horribly. The soldier was forced to grab a long spike of glass, inserting it into his throat. It was violently pushed inside, while he started writhing in anguish. The piece than, pierced his abdomen as a mendacious wedge, slaughtering his guts. Organs slid on the floor while blood flooded the bathroom.

She then boiled in vapor, vanishing from the sink, while the mirror remained broken in pieces and a few red petals were left, mingled with drops of blood.

A cruel suicide had happened, disgusting in the way it was accomplished.

The reflection of our shining material world is behind our vision, erasing the real essence of the intangible dimensional domain, as a shattered mirror of myriad desires.

Al Crown

CHAPTER XXXII

Lagoons

Downtown Vancouver…Lost Lagoon.

It is a shape of water inside the woods, settled on the west side of Georgia Street, near the ingress of Stanley Park. In aboriginal language it means "get dry at times," symbolizing its ambiguous presence in dryness and fullness. The pond is embellished by the encounter of mute swans, ducks, Canadian geese and blue herons, all living in the park.

Claudio for a mysterious reason loved that magic place, amalgamated with the city and shrouded in the forest. He was always feeding the friendly smart raccoons concealed inside bushes…alone.

According to Claudio, after his mother's death, "God and Evil are embedded in a secret relationship for me, signed by a perpetual encompassing truce that divided the world between their boundless powers. Our brave existence is balanced by those dynamic energies, opposing each other since the Genesis of Universe. Our life is a fascinating disillusionment in the eyes of the youth, as depicted for some aspects in Dante's *Inferno* (demonkind's inhabitants of Pandemonium)."

"Abandon all hope ye who enter here." Dante Alighieri

A weak twilight of July could not assist a group of runners training halfway down Mount Seymour Road, on the east side of the park, along the perimeter trail close to the old buck track. They met for a medium run, a standard group of six, mixed between men and women, preparing for their next marathon race. They were rushing down cautiously…it was late and the path was slippery. The team leader and coach was an experienced personal trainer who was motivating the athletes, keeping up their morale. Minutes later, an unusual sound was heard…a noise of rocks reeling behind them. They stopped, believing someone had fallen. One of the girls was left behind. Paul, the head runner, told them to stretch while waiting for their return. He proceeded uphill, retrieving the previous steps. The man could barely see the dirt, brightened by a soft moonlight. He saw the girl standing before a tree, relieved, trying to grab her shoulder. When turning, he saw dark blood on her face, a broken neck…arms stretched and torn by roots, bracing the trunk. Paul cringed, disgusted, revolving in bewilderment, when a grotesque beast hovered…munching his face with ferocious bites.

Screams were heard…they ran out of control, trying to stay together: "Stop! Stop! Where are we going, we should help him!" A second runner countered, "Are you out of your mind? Didn't you hear those shrieks, for God's sake?"

The last bites detached…chewing meat, swallowed with voracious arcane hatred to satisfy the beast.

Paul, the leader, began squealing again like something was grazing on him, the last nibble took his throat and tore his vocal cords, clattering, while a curled burled hand was inserting in a spasmodic momentum… roots inside his trachea.

"We should go up there!" yelled one of them, "There is nothing we can do with wild animals!" said the other. "The butchers, those are the butchers!" affirmed a terrorized woman.

They merged in amazement on Mount Seymour Road, almost at the end of the park; praising God with mirthful eyes…destiny had spared them.

An obscure entity was embezzling the sundown of uncertainty, when cars appeared on the road… suddenly obstructed by the runners begging for help. North Vancouver police were alerted and a patrol moved slowly to that area, far away from the previous ones.

"Why did those guys go running up the hill so late?" declared Officer

Ron Taylor, in charge of the North Vancouver investigative team. "They got lost I suspect, nothing more," added the short, chubby 43-year-old inspector.

Police performed an encompassing research; both Grouse and Seymour Mountains were part of North Vancouver area. Ron said to his assistant: "Give me the phone, please! I need to reach out Mesotti. The investigation is a joint operation, and we need his valuable support."

The assistant suggested, "I don't think it is a good idea! Jim Carter doesn't like Kevin." "We don't need to inform Carter right away, am I right?" replied Taylor.

Paul's disfigured body was found six days later…no trace of the girl. Forensic pathologists were looking for evidences or traces of any kind, hoping to obtain a possible DNA.

As Ron Taylor explained, "the victim was killed on Seymour Mountain and found at Kennedy Lake on Thunderbird Ridge at 1,200 meters' altitude, behind Grouse Mountain's Eye of the Wind." Kevin folded the hands on his face looking desperate, when the TV news eye framed his image.

A journalist asked Taylor, "What can we do to stop those slayers? How did they manage to bring the body up there?" he hesitated for a moment: "They subjugated us I guess!"

Mesotti decided to step in, helping his colleague: "We are doing everything in our possibilities, using all the resources…three joined districts with different visions and tools."

North Shore Police suspected the killers were hiding in the lakes, using perhaps specialized diving materials—after all there were many lakes in the area. The victim was brought near Kennedy Lake without leaving any trace, apart from the furrowed drag marks on the ground. The homicide's headquarter was a steaming chamber…Jim Carter's head was whistling. "Did you hear that goof talking? All because Taylor was speechless! I cannot believe it, divers up the hills!"

Roger: "They don't know what they are doing up there, releasing such information was stupid!"

Carter repeatedly banged his first on the desk, resounding outside the glass panel, where people observed that tense situation… something was going to happen.

CHAPTER XXXIII

Scrolls of the Past

"The assassins pushed themselves on the east border of Mount Seymour, committing the murders, recoiling soon after to Grouse Mountain. When trapped, they tried to exit east once again. The tortured corpse of Paul was left there for a specific reason, overlapping the esoteric and satanic signs this time—it was a clear warning for the victim, who had probably seen the slayers. He couldn't speak the truth because he didn't have his vocal cords anymore; they were removed…roots replaced!" elucidated a tiny shaped Meredith, candidly folding her hands. "They live, speak and survive in the woods, because they are part of it," reinforced her for Claudio.

After leaving Meredith's residence, Claudio went to Eagle Ridge path, a safe area not located in the forbidden zone. He could see the ocean between the trees, and the Yacht Club. The trail had on the left a wall of rocks and on the right a little ravine. Unexpectedly, various rocks rolled down, hitting Claudio on his legs. He was reflecting about Meredith's speculations, when realizing something was moving on the way. He got scared and bumped down the ravine, tumbling while his legs got caught through the roots.

Thanks God was only an accident, committed by an inattentive boy.

In Rome, another handwritten book was closed with a soft thud…a whisper of content. Armando Suarez had found the missing document he was looking for, retrieved in a different file of the same year: 1610. It was the last parchment of the Spanish expedition, embellished with the papal bull approval, and the names of people onboard of the galleons. They were in a different folder because when Napoleon Bonaparte gained power, the French Revolutionary government took interest in developing a systematic method, controlling all the archives in Europe by consolidating them in Paris.

Armando illustrated to Maurice: "Most of them were those of the Vatican Archives, seized with the first campaign of 1796 (Clark's expedition was March 1795, archived in 1796), followed by the 1798-99 document seizures. Six months after Napoleon became Emperor, the National Archive was renamed *Archive of the Empire*, and lots of paintings and artifacts were brought to the Louvre Museum in Paris.

In 1809, Pope Pius VII excommunicated the governor of Rome, General Miollis, who reacted after Napoleon's orders, arresting the pope and putting him in captivity, moving soon later all the Vatican's archives to Paris.

Many scrolls were embezzled in other places and churches after Napoleon lost his war, most of them returned to Rome with the Restoration, while others remained in France or Spain (from 1610 to 1620 the crown of Navarre was merged with the French crown under the rule of King Louis XIII. Napoleon could have claimed those papal documents). Maurice was bewildered and commented: "No wonder why hundreds of historical documents are still missing!"

Armando had discovered that Inquisitor Ravello born in Rom was nominated cardinal in 1606 by Pope Paolo V...after serving the Holy Inquisition. He was the nephew of the bishop of Cathedral of Saint Mary of the Assumption in the Puglia Region (Italy). They were in blood lineage, protectors of the Holy Womb of the church.

Maurice reacted, "a bloodline of inquisitors?"

Suarez again: "Yes, and comparing the document of 1795, I denuded that the Roman inquisitor on the ship was a cardinal...descendant of the Ravello family's blood line. However, he never came back from the expedition, as his nephew Francesco reported." A brief moment followed, "The conundrum deepens my friend. Larry is guiding us to the truth!"

Maurice was firmly convinced that the two expeditions (1610-1795) were strongly connected...but why the Holy Spanish Inquisition was summoned three times to arbitrate the same trial? To the clerics' surprise, two Elysa Morgair appeared to be aboard of one of the Spanish galleon, undergoing a misconceived, defamed destiny sealed through divergent papal sigils. "I have never seen so many discrepancies in a document," said Armando candidly rubbing the hand beneath his chin. He was eyeing upward the luminous chandelier in a dubious look, mentioning the third incomplete seal found in Pamplona. The hefty, solid ligneous portal of the library, embellished within numerous adorned bas-reliefs, closed in a pretentious thud, echoing the secrets of the past along the corridors.

Frescoes and mystical images have been reigning in the Vatican Palace for hundreds of years: the four rooms of frescoes, Michelangelo's ceiling painted in the Sistine Chapel, the Last Judgment and the transfiguration of Raphael.

The wise voices of the portraits were heard, speaking in Leonardo Da Vinci, Giotto, and Caravaggio; all eyewitnesses of their faded images. Laura and Armando walked between the colonnade, discoursing about the doctrine and the subsequent indoctrination of the seventeenth century, while Laura rapidly severed her frenzy pace, revolving back.

She was feeling as if an invisible entity was scanning her through the frescoes' visages, releasing whispering voices of old times. A susurration was slowly bursting out from the fresco's frame, as a warm-colored warning.

"*Tempus est promptus*!" (Time is ready) was heard in the Vatican's arcade.

CHAPTER XXXIV

Dungeons of Despair

1609, Dungeon of Pamplona

One month after Elysa was defamed and thrown in jail to die of hunger and thirst, the prison guards were ordered to remove her disfigured body and burn it. Torches were cautiously descending the helical castle prison staircase, breathing profoundly the wet smell of death. Metallic noises resounded inside the chambers, while swords were banging on armor as a menacing sound of silenced darkness. "What a disgusting duty we have to accomplish, soldiers! Disposing of those rotten corpses will infect us sooner or later. Their abominable carcasses! May God protect us all, brothers!" said the warden while opening the dismal portal. The squeal of the old key was opening the rusty metal gate and the claustrophobic obscurity within. A torch entered and saw the remains of the consumed corpse of the girl. Purplish-colored blood was on her legs, forming a circled pond of desperation; at that moment the armed sentinel advanced dubiously, closer and closer toward Elysa, lighting up with the fire.

"Disgusting, we should burn it right here! The whole cell should be set on fire. This is not like the others."

A pale, afterlife visage awakened suddenly, turning her bloody consumed eyes front face. A stark, menacing scream of ominous resurrection ruptured in the chamber with the last strength left. The torches were tossed up the walls and the soldiers fled, screaming at the devil's presence, and the resurgence of darkness.

"Away with it, save yourself from damnation, soldiers! We better leave this haunted place once for all. The devil, the devil is dwelling here!" yelled the sentinels, flying above the stairs.

Elysa was incredibly, still alive. She survived because she desired to live and loved her life, drinking the urine, humidity and the leaks of rainwater coming through the old bricks. She ate worms, rats and bugs inside the dirty place and slept all day. Although she got very weak and sick, she survived.

People believed she was possessed by the Devil and got horrified by the power of Satan. She was indeed the daughter of Lucifer. Many prison guards gathered with the Holy Spanish Inquisition emissaries. They were sent fully armed down the dungeon, to seize the girl and burn her at the stake. "We descend these steps of darkness protected by the holy hand of the Lord. Do not fear the evil one, you are all blessed!" preached the cleric. Elysa fainted, and the sentinels believed the inquisitor's holy words.

Soon after, the inquisitor spoke with the doctors, who carefully examined Elysa. They decided to get rid of this malevolent curse forever. She was a powerful alchemist, resurrected by *Diabolus* (the Devil) and eternally cursed.

One of the physicians said, "I have never seen such an evil resurrection; she must have died, resurrecting after! Only a supernatural intervention could be responsible for this; an obscure one, your holiness. We must proceed according to God's sacred law."

Ravello was subsequently approached privately by the doctors, "Your grace! There is something more serious and delicate you need to know, something really abominable! There is only one explanation for this, only one." The cardinal, astonished, enquired, "There is more? What can it be? Speak!"

A whisper was heard in Ravello's ears: "The evil spirit of darkness entered in her!"

"Sacrilege and blasphemy...that is a desecration; It is the sign the church was waiting for!" commented the clergyman, disgusted.

A special commission was summoned again, and Cardinal Ravello sealed the final sentence: "*Exurge domine enim exilium a Deo*" (Rise, God, and cast this evil from your creation).

Elysa was sent to the farthest place known at that time on earth, the west coast of Canada, where she would be exiled everlastingly among the evil spirits of the savages.

The expedition was due to leave the coast of Spain in a few days. Pope Paul V and King Philip III of Spain, allowed the prisoner to be shipped with those two galleons from the port of Santander, northwest, soon after Bilbao.

The young novice cured by Elysa was fighting with his conscience in a concealed place. Although he was forced to accuse her in front of the holy inquisition, he discovered he loved her more than he thought. The news about the queen of evil exiled from the civilized world spread throughout the kingdom of Navarre and elsewhere.

Her troubled chronicles were foretold by numerous parchments. The youth was informed by a monk about Elysa—she was still alive.

"I must see her. I cannot let her go away! It is my fault if she was condemned. They forced me to accuse her, don't you understand?" said the man to his informer.

"How could you possibly rescue her? She was sentenced by the inquisition, it is over. Her fate is doomed forever. What happened between the two of you? Why do you wish to save her…risking your own life! The tribunal would burn you at the stake for this" Replied his worried companion.

"I cannot tell you now! I will explain to you later. I was deceived and threatened by the cardinal, I was a coward! They told me that she would have not been condemned…" replied the novice, escaping late at night from the Abbey of Bilbao. He broke in to the horses' stable, and pilfered one of the guard's, fleeing in the obscurity.

"May God forgive you and protect you, brother!" exclaimed the informer.

A hundred kilometers separated him from his forever love, riding all night against the falling moon and the rising sun. The wind was bringing the smell of love and the breeze the sound of hope. Sun was rising while the Ships could be seen from a distance, the sails of Galleons were inflated by the drafts, showing red crosses dancing and going away. The exhausted horse brought the novice on top of the cliff, upon the port, while the vessels were leaving the shores. It was at that moment when his eyes saw a thin figure with a white garment, enriched with long gold hair waving in the wind. She was in chains with other prisoners captured in her city, members of the evil Guild she created.

The ships were turning to exit the Santander harbor, and Elisa saw her lover on the cliff.

It was a span of time and their eyes crossed each other, reflecting their eternal love on the infinity of the ocean of life.

Elisa screamed with all the strength she had left, while a sad slow motion image froze the time: the young lover hoisted upright, jumping in desperation from the high cliff, while seagulls were wailing and flying over the nostalgic seashore beaches.

The birds were observing the undulating tunic billowing and blowing on the air, falling ruinously on the rocks. A purplish sun plunged in the red sea, as a blood of life and love that never dies.

"You came to rescue me, my love! You did not betray our love. I promise you that your blood will not be lost in these shores, but regenerated at the end of the world; we will live forever," poeticized Elysa fainting in despair, while Ravello came up from the ship, unaware of the accident on the cliff.

The two galleons, named San Malachias, carrying three masts and Spanish flags, disappeared from the known earth going on to the end of the world; there the abyss of the abandoned dark sea was sleeping. Water was cleaning the torn body of the man, shattered and dismembered into many pieces by the spikes of the rocks, while his head was severed and lost in the ocean.

Only weeks later the novice's older brother went searching for his remains, accusing the family of the condemned of revenge and conspiracy versus his dead brother and his noble family.

"That is how they repaid the holy justice of the Lord, throwing an innocent young novice from the cliff of the ocean. This is the work of the devil! Lucifer is dwelling in this region. We need to purge and cast away once for all this evil presence. We must find those possessed people, and hunt down the malevolent witches," spoke with words of vengeance the brother.

A new witch hunt was launched by the Catholics, hunting down all the parents and relatives of the sentenced heretics. The brother's fury was uncontainable, sending to the gallows elderly people, women and even children. His eyes were red colored, like the fire he used to torch the sufferers.

Gruesome details came out about his ruthless methods of execution, showing a deep hatred for humans. He was later summoned by the Vatican Vicariate (warned by the Spanish Holy Inquisition for his extreme brutality, regardless).

In those days of death and darkness, a light of hope was shining on the water of life!

CHAPTER XXXV

Flooding dreams

A long corridor with marble columns was sauntered by a young man with long hair. He was wearing a grimy white robe, carrying a robust wooden cross on his scourged shoulders. His bare feet beat in sorrow and pain the cold impassive travertine, revealing a discouraged head bent down, adorned with a crown of thorns dripping in blood. His hands and feet were perforated. Frescoes and masterpieces of the past were all around his chastised body: Michelangelo Buonarroti, Leonardo Da Vinci, Lorenzo Bernini—all were contemplating the man inside Saint Peter's Church, falling three times on his floundering knees.

He appeared outside the main patio's stairs, in front of Via Della Conciliazione, slowly raising his face, displaying to his lost eyes a scene of natural freedom.

The cross was lifted and the pupils admired the North Shore mountain range of Vancouver's west coast, a warm sunset enlightened his wounds, while several rays came across the pierced gashes. Soon after, moonbeams created a glowing halo around his perimeter. The ocean water was now flooding Saint Peter's Square, and the cross was drifting like the galleons of time. The man discerned water on his feet mixed with blood and sun rays, whereas darkness became a deep-red nightmare. His face rose completely and the long hair mixed with brown eyes revealed a surprising young girl.

Their eyes met. The lassie was extending her bleeding hands toward him, mumbling incomprehensible, distant Latin words! Water was drowning Rome…

Claudio woke up with a scream!

After settling materials for the three diving teams, Kevin and Taylor announced the beginning of the operations. "The zone is divided in three areas—Cypress, Grouse and Seymour—that fits our three teams. The lakes were spotted and chosen carefully by the use of helicopters, maps and GPS. Each team is divided into three little groups, for shift work and resting time. The high elevation (300 meters is considered high altitude) of the majority of lakes would vary depth and duration of diving, because atmospheric pressure is different than it is at sea level, as you know."

Questions and doubts surfaced. An interviewer enquired, "Are you going to inspect every single pond? It seems an impossible mission, costing a great amount of money." Kevin was aware that they needed time in order to do that, hoping to find the missing body of the girl. He then replied, "We are going to explore only where needed. Police require helicopter support in remote areas during all the diving operations (from 8 a.m. to 5 p.m.) in case someone gets in trouble making descent and ascent in the water. It is a hazard area and far away from hospitals and hyperbaric chambers."

Ron Taylor continued the illustration on the big board: "Crew assistants are needed outside in case divers are seriously entangled or snagged under lagoons, using special lights and cameras throughout deeper immersions. This is the first time police have sustained an operation of this level!" affirming with a proud voice, making clear the big effort they were facing.

Mesotti emphasized on the map: "Cypress is the most sensitive area because most of the victim's remains were found in that extremity (Whyte Lake, at 166 meters' altitude and Eagle Lake at 406 meters are the lower lakes, while West Lion Enchanted Lake, Hanging Lake and Brunswick Mountain Lake are higher). Grouse Mountain has the big Capilano Lake at a lower level, while Palisade Lake and Rodgers Lake are at a higher level on "Cathedral" Mountain. The last name *Cathedral* is up of suspects. Mount Seymour boasts the big and long Deep Cove inlet and the Indian arm, till the Iron Bay East area. Seymour Lake is east (the long, thin shape close to Mount Bishop)."

Meredith and Darleen, meanwhile, were working by suggestion rather than speculation. They mentioned suspicious allusive names that killers could have used to communicate with the police. Robert was working closely with them, reporting later the results to Mesotti. "Such as encoded evocative names like Enchanted Lake (Mystery), Hanging Lake (Murder), Cathedral Mountain (Spiritual), Mount Bishop (Religious). The final result we have is *mysterious religious murder in the spiritual lakes* (maybe the missing body) or *religious spiritual murderers on the mysterious mountains* (where they hide). Priority must be given to those places, in this lose-lose situation."

Kevin's fear surfaced rapidly when listening to the expert's report: "I do not like this probable misconception, we are continuously scrambling," commented him, nervously shuffling the papers. "From my experience, I feel that all those anagrammatic, encoded allusive messages, have a diverse purpose!"

Meredith was then summoned to Mesotti's office. Her hazel irises appeared foggy…she felt ridiculed by Kevin's mood, replying: "I would like to hear your theory about those allusive dissertations! What's your idea and new line?"

Kevin pondered his derisive temper and stated, "I think the slayers don't want to communicate to us where they are hiding or where the victims could be, neither when the next homicide will occur. I assume they are just announcing who they are! Clearly who they are! We know all the aspects about the victims and the way they were butchered, yet we don't have a clue of the real motive!"

The psychic left the office unhappy, remaining friendly anyway…understanding the stressful responsibility weighing on the detective's head.

CHAPTER XXXVI

Winds of Water

Giacomo's car was parked outside Tony's residence, and Claudio, with an uncomfortable feeling, greeted his aunt. She happily expressed, "So happy to have you here guys, I prepared a special dinner for you. Go upstairs, Claudio—do not be shy! Michael is waiting for you." He embraced his uncle, who was glad to see his nephew with his brother: "You will not regret the invitation, my man! Go up!" Claudio plunged into Michael's room. Michael said: "Hey! Look who is here! I have something to show you!"

Michael was reading some articles about the last operation up the hills, and easily involved his cousin in the reading. Dinner was spent talking about the case and Claudio's private investigation, which negatively surprised Giacomo, who later told his brother: "I asked you to help me with Claudio! Not to make things more difficult, pushing him! What's wrong with you?" Tony put a hand on Giacomo's shoulder and said, "The more you want to pull him away, the more he will be pushed into it. Youth are not rational, they are driven by instinct, and you know that. Believe me, if you let him do it, he will get tired on his own."

A few days later Claudio and Isabel bought some oil paints, frames, brushes and two tripods, ready to perform a portrait of the Eclipse of the Soul.

Claudio used pictures taken from Andrew's father painting, while Isabel that of Port Alberni wood sculpture (made by the grandfather). It was an interesting hobby, and they decided to paint the native girl, to discern better the two different perspectives of the opera. Unfortunately Isabel got sick, and three days later…fever and weakness made her desist from the work.

Claudio had almost finished the contour, and was beginning with the girl's visage, when he saw a shadowy illusion rising from the canvas. It was a dark, contorted shape, coming from nowhere, defining herself. Leon was frantically barking and woofing from outside the garden, trying to leap over the fence. Claudio felt a sense of sleepiness, the usual ones he used to endure. He could not hear Leon anymore, and his eyes were closing in tiredness and abandon. He fainted on the ground, unconscious. Nobody was in the residence, except him and the obscure figure walking on the floor, a wet floor!

Water was dripping as a sound of bells, drop by drop on the youth's forehead, like a Chinese torture, mixed in tears and gore. Something was tenderly watching him in an abominable love duality, an unspeakable, ambiguous presence. Claudio was in a transitional state, in a limbo of existence, as if the image overlapped the terrestrial dimension with her powerful essence.

It was late evening and Giacomo was busy at work, while Leon, outside, attracted the attention of neighbors. A man came out of his house and tried to ease the dog, when he noticed a shadow motioning in the Verallo's house. Leon could not desist on his guard duty, calming only when the neighbor rang the doorbell, awakening Claudio from his profound, lost delirium. The shape walked distortedly backward, merging in the innermost dimension of the shadowed portrait, dissolving in Claudio's misty eyes; he fetched the frame and threw it out the window, while Leon was barking and jumping like a mad dog.

The neighbor shouted, "What the hell is going on up there? Are you ok, young man? You almost hit me! Where is your father?" Claudio apologized: "I am very sorry, I just wanted to ease the dog, I am sick with a fever and my dad went to the pharmacy for medications. Sorry about that."

The man left and Leon was free to come up.

He called Isabel right away and told her to forget this attempt, while she replied, "Why? I can continue if you like." Claudio countered, "No thanks, it was a mistake, a bad omen, I think. And by the way, it is useless!"

The next morning Claudio received n alert on his phone; the cost of flights to Italy were going down, and a nice last-minute two weeks trip to Italy was a dream come true in August. He told his father and he agreed. Giacomo thought, "That is a blessing! Tony was right in at the end, he will get tired on his own." Claudio asked Isabel to go with him to Rome. She smiled and said, "Are you serious? It is too expensive!" "No," replied the boy, "You would only have to pay for the flight, and I found a cheap one!" She jumped and said, "When are we leaving?"

A hot August wind was howling on the plants, blowing summer in Vancouver, crashing against the plane flying over the Rocky Mountains. It was like a hand trying to stop the couple, rising from the horizon of the forest and whispering words of hope and sadness. From the windows they could see the shining lakes behind Vancouver, reflecting the sun's reddish colors up in the sky. Claudio was mesmerized by the glittering water, distinguishing images moving all around. A shape was coming out of a big lake and Claudio saw with his eyes a light game of imagination.

The plane landed in Paris after a nine-hour flight, and the second flight continued to their final destination. Laura was waiting outside the arrivals gate and embraced the couple as strongly as she could, driving subsequently on the highway.

"I was dying for this moment guys, you two are here! We'll have lots of fun," Isabel exclaimed with surprise: "Look— the town!"

From a distance they could see the hill where Tivoli was located. Isabel felt love mingled with emotion, and only at that moment could she understand the same feeling Claudio sensed for Vancouver: Love at first sight. We are all like children when discovering new things, eyes wide open and mouth spread wide. The hills were full of olives and vineyards, the ground dry and hot—it was still 34 degrees Celsius at five o'clock in the afternoon. Isabel could glimpse Rome behind her, and Tivoli coming closer, indulging in the medieval walls mixed with the oldest Roman town, Villa Adriana.

The Renaissance part appeared on one side, and the modern city on the other side. They exited the highway, paying an expensive toll—Isabel could not believe how much expensive was driving on an highway!

Claudio exclaimed, "God bless the free highway of Canada!"

Finally, they reached uncle Loris's residence. A long uphill curved road with fruit trees to the side, ended in a large spacious yard bursting with olive trees and vineyards all around. The old house was on a low hill placed onto a promontory. It was once an old country farmhouse owned by an ancient Roman aristocratic family, which in time lost their noble titles due to fraudulent bankruptcy.

A family friend who worked in the Vatican had suggested Loris to buy the fancy property with all the land. He participated in a Judicial Sale Auction, making the right offer at the right time. Isabel esteemed the place very much, finding herself in a historical fairy tale. Loris came out the property, running and cheering at the boys with his loud voice. Kisses and presentations were overpowered by Loris's vocal box. The man like a classic Roman character was showing off, making fun of everybody: "Hey! My dear you're here finally!" Long time no see! You brought the most gorgeous of the Canadian girls…let me kiss your hand, princess?" Isabel was flattered and amused by that crazy character. Loris was like Claudio's mother, extravagant and funny at the same time. He had never married, and as soon as he retired from his professorship, he decided to live in the province of Rome, where the pace of life was slower and the cost cheaper.

The first week they walked through the history of archeological sites, drinking water from the so-called big-nose fountains and driving to Saint Peter's at the Vatican, where they encountered for the first time Father Armando Suarez end Father Maurice Fredel.

Isabel sensed the real magic atmosphere of Rome, spending all day sightseeing and visiting the church. They climbed to the top of Saint Peter's Basilica Dome, 551 steps in total, admiring a fantastic, dizzying city's panorama all around.

Isabel in a breathless sounded voice, said: "This was a fantastic workout—I am exhausted!"

Claudio followed, "When I was nine years old my mother used to bring me on the top of Saint Peter's, walking all the steps up, trying to convince me that was an act of repentance for our sins. Do I need to take the stairs today?"

Isabel replied, "So! Are you a saint?"

The Holy Angel Castle and the Tiber River were moving like a snake all around Rome. Michelangelo's Sistine Chapel (today it is the site of the papal conclave) impressed Isabel very much: "What a masterpiece!" she said. Before they left, Claudio remembered for a moment the dream he had few weeks earlier—the colonnade, the corridor, the travertine stairs and Vancouver in front of his face.

"Isabel! You are Vancouver," exclaimed Claudio, understanding for a moment that he was walking where the bleeding girl was standing, feeling the need to stretch his hands toward Isabel. He perceived a sense of distress and almost fell on Laura's shoulder. She was forced to guide Claudio outside the stairs, begging him to sit.

"Too hot," said Laura. "You should drink more!"

Claudio knew that a dream had come true.

CHAPTER XXXVII PART ONE

Burning Fires

The first week of August in Vancouver began with warm temperatures that provoked wildfires all around B.C. The media reported the largest blaze in the province's history, with numerous evacuation alerts and orders. The haze and smoke were all around the city, and police was forced to suspend the diving operations.

Ron Taylor, the African-American investigator, gave a quick interview: "Until the smoke is vanished, it is not possible to continue our operations. We regret the delay. We'll continue as soon as possible." The chubby officer killed the press without giving more information. He was sliding his hand on his bald head, wishing to go home, while Mesotti from his office heard the news.

He commented, "My God Ron, you just apologized like a kid, too afraid to speak."

Smog was traveling like the news in Italy, because a dark cloud was wrapping Vancouver in darkness! Fires burning like tongues of hell!

In Rome, Isabel was afraid about Vancouver's wildfires, while Claudio was conversing with Armando, "Do you see! Those are strong signs of prediction, happening for real! Not only dreams or mere speculations." Armando gave a spiritual explanation about Claudio's dreams and fires, "Water and fire can be seen both like good or evil, depending on time and history. In Christianity we use the water for the cleansing of sins, baptizing the reborn, as well to symbolize the troublesome times in life." Maurice explained about Genesis and Noah's Ark, when the water flooded the world and God spared only Noah, his family and a remnant of all the world's animals. The apocalypse is about the end of the world and the power of water destruction. "Fire," replied Armando, "can be a symbol of God (Moses and the burning bushes of God in the Old Testament), or the second coming of Christ (Paul in the New Testament). John had a vision of Jesus with eyes like blazing fire."

Armando challenged, "For all of us, it is not always possible to distinguish the presence of the divine or evil in those signs. We know about the fires of hell for sinners and infidels, but at the same time John the Baptist predicted that Jesus would baptize with the Holy Spirit and with fire (fulfilled on the day of Pentecost)."

Maurice specified, continuing, "What is right or wrong is not on us, but in time the truth will be revealed."

Claudio and Isabel were a little bit confused about the teachings, while Laura was quiet. A blanket of smoke was flying in the sky because of fires, while the sun turned red in Vancouver, telling at the wind the Bible saying: "The last days of doom will turn the sun a blood-red color." Evening appeared, and after a delicious supper the couple left Rome, returning to the town of Tivoli. Isabel, feeling exhausted, went to sleep, while Loris, waiting to be alone with his nephew apprehended him, commencing a serious critical discussion.

A bright full moon was exhilarating the creepy goblins on the hill, while their twirling, winding hands looked like shrouded olive trees. Loris fondled his dark blond hair, arranged on one side, murmuring at the moon: "Maria, Maria…Queen of the Moon!" He gradually swiveled toward Claudio and whispered, "Now! I can talk to you, my dear. You are like a son to me after your mother passed away. How are you! Do you still have your incubus?"

The youth affirmed, "Yes, uncle, always with me since mom left."

Loris knew that already, and continued, "I have something very important to tell you, but you must keep it a secret. Only you and your mother are part of this revelation."

"What is about, an inheritance?" asked Claudio.

"Kind of, my dear, a more important legacy, I should say." Loris cut to the chase and said, "About those killings in Vancouver—be very careful in what you are doing, try to follow your instincts. Your nightmares are a warning, and your mother is communicating with you. It is not a mere coincidence your presence in Vancouver today, time and destiny are something above our will and we can only try to fulfill it!" Claudio felt muddled, sensing a thin line amid two opposite dimensions, Loris on one verge and Claudio at the other.

"Don't worry, my dear! Your mother was aware of those religious historical secrets inside the Vatican, never revealed to anybody before. What I don't understand now, you will remember later, dreaming of Lidia."

An eloquent Loris clasped the boy, fondling his forehead like Lidia used to do on the porch, in front of the hill.

A warm wind began to whisper, coming from the sky, brushing his beloved little boy, keeper of the undisclosed riddle of life and death.

The first week of holidays was almost consumed, and they spent the next day visiting Villa d'Este (of the sixteenth century), the palace and gardens of Renaissance culture, with more than 100 fountains.

They reached Villa Adriana later, a classical building created in the second century A.D. by the Roman emperor Hadrian.

The heat was intense, and Claudio told Isabel, "It is time for me to pay a visit to my mother's burial place." Isabel replied, "I was wondering why you didn't mention your mother so far, and I can understand the reason." Claudio focused, "I always wait several days before going. It helps me face the reality that she is not with us anymore."

He revealed to Isabel about Lidia dying at his brother's house.

"She passed away in one of the rooms close to the garden, and since then, Loris has not moved any objects or furniture from that chamber, leaving everything as it was originally. Lidia is buried in the family chapel, at the Verano Cemetery in Rome (the cemetery was founded at the beginning of the nineteenth century)."

After the visit they decided to remain in Rome, aiming for the Coliseum. Isabel saw the Anfiteatro Flavio for the first time and said, "There it is, Vancouver's library!" Claudio smiled and took her inside for two hours.

Laura joined them later after work with some interesting news about the Spanish trial documents. It seemed that a friend of Father Armando in Spain had found something. Laura said, "He was asked by Armando to take a look at the history of the Holy Inquisition of the seventeenth century, including all the churches involved in keeping religious files, in case Armando missed something.

She was very intriguing and Claudio begged her to continue.

"His friend is a history teacher in Pamplona, and discovered that in the well-known Basque witch trial of the seventeenth century, two important locations appeared (Zugarramurdi and Logrono), the last one had something very relevant. The figure of the mysterious Elysa Morgair appeared for the first time in Logrono, in northern Spain on the Ebro River, the capital of the province La Rioja. Her father and the so-called heretic witches were judged and executed there in Logrono. Elysa, however, was conducted to a second trial in Pamplona and sentenced there."

Claudio and Isabel glanced at each other.

PART TWO

Suarez received an important email from the Cathedral of Santa Maria de la Redonda in Logrono, after his friend in Pamplona requested those documents for historical study.

Suarez told the fellows, "An email with the photos of two original distinguished documents of 1609 was forwarded yesterday. The first is a sentence of the Spanish Holy Inquisition with its seal—the crown of Spain with a cross in the middle, a sword on the left and a branch on the right—followed by a second seal of the Roman Catholic Holy Inquisition (signed by Cardinal Inquisitor Ravello) in Latin writings, naming Saint Malachy (the Prophet) and the name of Elysa condemned to death for being a powerful evil witch. (The Spanish Inquisition was established in 1478, ending in 1834), the sentence was issued by the Tribunal of the Holy Office of the Inquisition in Spain, December 1609, Pamplona."

The cleric paused, deposing the document in a white folder, while extracting the other one. "The second parchment is a death certificate (*Documentum mortis*) of Elysa, dead in the dungeon of Pamplona, January 1610, and cremated after—*Corpus briciato* (the inquisition used to burn the bodies of the condemned, even if they died under torture).

Armando finally obtained the complete document, a well-defined, important parchment!

Claudio and Isabel spent the last night in Italy, when two distant cultures met in their sensual loving encounter, abandoning the senses in a sexual natural freedom. All happened in a rapid expanding hot moment, inside that quite place perching on the luxuriant Roman hills, when their thoughts crisscrossed the minds. Claudio moved close to Isabel's waving hair, kissing her soft neck few times; while she removed Claudio's shirt, touching his solid muscled chest. She was at the zenith of her erotic stimulation…breathing constantly around his ears; he closed the eyes caressing her velvety breast. Irresistible glamorous excitement, ignited by an almost full shining moon. Clothes were completely removed, standing on the warm floor…trampled by the young lovers. Isabel slid under the light blankets pulling him over, avidly squeezing his turgid buttocks while scraping his skin with her sharp nails…releasing a storm of emotions and impulses all over his body. On a pure free will the youths pressed their intimacy to oblivion, hands clutched together in a unanimous endless pleasur. He slammed his fists down to the bending mattress, venturing deeper inside her falling abyssal eyes, into the beating passionate universe. Moon, stars and constellations were upon a celebration of love, their sweating caged bodies and their pure free souls…

CHAPTER XXXVIII

The Vacationers

In Vancouver, smoke eased, and police could resume the research upon the lakes. Palisade Lake on Cathedral Mountain was the one police found some evidence of previous diving, accomplished by unknown subjects. Mesotti described, "The name Palisade could have been connected with the carnages for its meaning (stockade, impaling), and investigators, moreover, found some torn wetsuits, broken diving masks and a used underwater spear gun, unusual for mountain lake activity."

Diver teams meticulously fathomed the reservoirs without any plausible findings, no trace or evidence of the missing body.

They concluded the operation, waiting for the helicopter to pick them up, while a 747 airplane from Rome was flying above of the lagoons, turning on the west side and preparing for landing at Vancouver International Airport.

Late afternoon, the vacationers from Italy landed in B.C; Giacomo was waiting for them outside the arrivals. His car was ready to escort the couple. He said: "Holidays are over, boy! Back to reality now! I am just kidding, summer is still here."

Isabel commented, "Your place in Italy is amazing! Do you miss Rome, Giacomo?" He replied, "Yes, a bit. Did you enjoy the province as well, Isabel?"

"Yes, very much, I had my tourist guide, here," she said.

Giacomo asked, "Did you see the village of Vicovaro too, the one where Lidia's funeral was held?" An embarrassing hiatus followed.

"Not really! We didn't have enough time to go there, even if it was a stone's throw from Tivoli," responded Isabel, with a gnawing, apologetic sound.

Claudio was trying to mend.

"Next year we'll go, and I will show you the two amazing monasteries of Vicovaro and Subiaco villages, built upon cliffs. Lidia spent so much time up there."

Giacomo opened the dashboard, extracting a tourist booklet of the province of Rome, and handed it to Isabel.

"Claudio please, next year I do not want to miss those places, look at those cloisters. I love the historical emblems," she said. Isabel glanced at Vicovaro's coat of arms, noticing the castle, the river, the bear and a red rose. Giacomo said, "Keep it, Isabel." After a moment, she said, "Thanks."

The haze of smoke was completely gone and the temperature was twenty-eight degrees. News released on the radio that B.C.'s heat wave could break 100-year-old temperature records in August. Claudio remembered the last longest cold winter snap in over thirty years—all signs and prophecies? The trip to Rome gave the young fellows a strong stimulus to continue in their own investigations, focusing on their missing conjunction ring: Father Larry's inexplicable death.

Jet lag this time did not impede Claudio to encounter his friends on Monday, especially Ryan Swann, who was waiting for him.

"That is how you follow your case, going on holiday?" he said, shaking Claudio's hand and joking about it. "You know! I met Mesotti last week at the institute. He was explaining the operation up the hills as a topic for our next exam. He told us the logistics and the cost of such an ordeal—out of mind! So complex and expensive that one cannot believe it!"

Claudio brought Ryan to Meredith's and introduced her to the figure of Elysa, one of Larry's first discoveries while living in Rome.

The psychic remarked, "That's an historical figure for sure, but it doesn't ring a bell to me! I never heard of that name before—perhaps Armando will disclose more about Larry."

Darleen stated, "at least we have a complete document and a few names this time!"

This was all they possessed, not much really, while police after all this time were groping in the dark…a dark ocean broken by the roar of two Spanish galleons going toward the farthest place in the known world.

CHAPTER XXXIX

Galleons of Discord

Spain 1610. The two Saint Malachys left Santander's Harbor in Spain, crossing the Atlantic Ocean and facing a long, hazardous journey.

Ninety-nine people were on board, including the sailing crew and commanders, plus 166 soldiers with their officers, and nine prisoners. With so many passengers and animals (kept for fresh meat, milk and eggs) crowded together in a small place, conditions on board were extremely unpleasant. Personnel became sick, dying before reaching the Atlantic's shores, raising the possibility of a curse launched by the witches. The ocean was in full storm because of winter-weather conditions, while the waves seemed monstrous creatures coming from the deep Sea of Hell. A sailor yelled in oblivion, "A curse possesses this ship…we will die in agony if we do not get rid of those evil witches—the ocean is revolting against us all, brothers! What are we waiting for?"

After those bombastic words, soldiers and sailors commenced torturing and executing a few of the prisoners before reaching the East Coast. Fear unfurled among the crew, and although Cardinal Ravello tried to persuade the captain to punish the heretics, there was nothing he could do to restrain their fury. "Alonso! You must stop this massacre. The prisoners are supposed to be executed on the West Coast—restrain those sycophants of yours and spare the women. The will of God must be fulfilled," argued the cardinal, speaking to the captain in vain.

On one of the most dark and bloody nights on board, three of the prisoners were tied up with a big rope, and repeatedly slowly drowned in the cold water, under a full moon. The fourth convict tried to escape, screaming for the cardinal's protection before being hanged up the central mast. "You cannot overcome the Lord's will! You will pay for this," exclaimed the clergyman over Alonso's shoulder—the same person who had condemned the women.

The oldest victim knelt, accusing Elysa of being responsible for everybody's conviction, begging the executioners, "She is the one you are looking for, responsible for all our misfortunes—he knows! The cardinal knows the truth about her—why don't you talk, priest? You are the one who sentenced her and us all!"

The sycophants revolved mendaciously to Pietro, who felt an atmosphere of fatal rebellion, thinking over his next action. He then replied with authority, distracting the agitators, "You are a fibber and an evil perjurer, trying to accuse the others and blame your own guild. The one you just outlined in front of us all never denounced anybody, you..." He could not finish his reproach.

The captive was brutally beaten to death without mercy and torn to pieces by the obliterators. The cardinal could only save Elysa and a second captive, leaving the last two victims to the angry mob of the first Saint Malachy. They were horribly stretched with strong cables and split in two. Of the nine consigned prisoners, only two were spared for specific order of the inquisitor, reaching number "seven" of fatalities.

The crew was firmly convinced to eradicate the evil curse and the beastly number "six," purifying the ship.

After the storm of the first fraction of the journey had melted away, the second part saw the galleons navigating on the Pacific Ocean. Things got worse than before, and the crew was in a state of oblivion. For them, the two last witches had to be killed and smashed to pieces. "The clerics lied to us about those demons. We are all going to die in damnation here! We must kill them all and save ourselves. Think of your families back home, do you want to see them again?" preached one of flattering conspirators.

A mutiny burst on the first Malachy's galleon, while the cardinal gave the order to execute those deserters.

A controversial insurrection divided the personnel on board, until the second ship came to help. An unavoidable bloodshed restored order in a cursed, dark night. Bodies were tossed in the water, and personnel of the second ship did not want to split on the other vessel.

Everybody was afraid and believed in the evil scourge.

On the order of Cardinal Ravello, the shipboard reported a different version about those deaths, saying that they occurred because of illness and sickness.

The galleons reached what is today Vancouver almost at the end of February, and of the 400 people on board, only 299 survived (the most daring joined the second boat to navigate).

The natives appeared along the shore, recognizing the Spanish flags and welcoming the settlers (the Spanish first came to this part of Canada in 1513). Ravello had the duty to bring those witches alive to the New World, on specific order of the Supreme Sacred Congregation of the Roman Universal Inquisition. The Holy See of the Roman Catholic Church was upon him. Pietro had in custody two books with him, the Bible and the Malleus Maleficarum (the Hammer of Witches, written by the German Catholic clergyman, Kramer, in 1478, the year that the Holy Spanish Inquisition was established).

Under Catholic monarchs Ferdinand II of Aragon and Isabella of Castile, the Spanish Inquisition began, with the goal of maintaining Catholic orthodoxy in their kingdoms and to replace the Medieval Inquisition, which was under papal control.

The Portuguese Inquisition was the third one in order, after the Spanish Inquisition; however, Ravello had the highest power given by the Roman Inquisition above the others.

Spanish colonies in Europe and in North, Central and South America, were under the Inquisition's control.

March would have seen the fulfillment of a universal spiritual event, chosen by the will of God in the novel world. Ravello repeated this prophecy, drooling in his mind, waiting patiently for March the 20th. He throttled back, closing the books...than he went speaking to the clerics. They were as if casted out from the world, partway along the corridor of infernal abyss... wider apart.

CHAPTER XL PART ONE

Resting Corpses

Rodgers Lake was very close to Palisade Lake, and something unusual was noticed by the divers—a tree root was exposed, hanging down in the water like something was bound to it. Divers went deep down and discovered the missing body of the young runner attached to the germ penetrated inside her navel, her neck was broken and her eyes were missing. She was unrecognizable, swollen from the water, while her feet and hands were bound to tubers so that the corpse could not move. Her belly was sewn up with thinner roots, as if something had been deposited inside the victim. In opening her during the autopsy, they found three little squirrels wrapped with one another, forming a three-ring spiral. The disfigured corpse was decomposing and medical examiners tried to find valuable evidence. It was unusual that assassins had managed to take the cadaver up there without being spotted by the patrol teams.

Jim Carter got the report from the scientific laboratory and sent all the files to the districts of the North Shore, while Robert Jones sent the folder to Meredith, hoping in her ability this time to read between the lines.

Ryan was conversing with his friend Claudio about it: "Since you came back, things have started to move again—I think you are the killer, ha!"

Claudio said, "You better watch your back, cop! I am going to…"

Ryan: "They found the body far away this time! Very bad sign—they are in control of us."

Luca and Jack joined them later for a walk, commenting about the last gruesome discovery. Ryan said, "By the way, I found a curious article about a ghost seen in the Port Alberni school around 1970, it was described as a girl." Luca observed, "Do you know how many ghosts and legends are created around those schools? Many my friends," Claudio declared: "Nobody ever mentioned this fact at the school, perhaps it is. What kind of policeman are you?" Jack stated, "We have to go, Meredith wants to see us in her office—it's the first time we're so many!"

Ryan added, "I found out that Port Alberni has several natural vaults and caverns along the shores, one was beneath the school and another under the church, but they were closed because they were perilous. They have been inaccessible since then." Claudio: "We went there, and yet nobody told us about that!"

A few days later, up on Crown Mountain, close to Kennedy Lake, a big bear was seen from the helicopter digging a hole. Soldiers approached the area, but the animal seemed not to care about the noise and kept excavating. When the helicopter later landed close to the open area, the bear ran away, leaving a wide pit. Crews continued shoveling, until they uncovered a mass grave. Mixed human bones were found—broken skulls, sternums, pelvises and little pieces.

The pit was more than seven feet deep, made a long time ago—the ground did not look different. Forensic anthropologists and examiners were too busy and overwhelmed by the findings. Maniacs seemed to kill even when resting: New bodies, new troubles. Forensic nthropologists were assisting with the identification of those remains, supporting forensic pathologists and the homicide investigators.

They began studying the skeletal abnormalities to potentially determine causes of death, past trauma and the manners in which the people had been slain.

Kevin and police staff had to wait for the results with patience, while maintaining the search for the killers.

Samuel, the older brother of the last victim, released a dramatic and touching interview on TV, asking for the community's and police's help in bringing those monsters to justice. He was a guest of Kevin at a police conference, later put in contact with Meredith; who meanwhile had discovered something spine-chilling.

As she explained: "The three little rodents were positioned inside the body alive (as the doctors discovered), while the girl was already dead. The root was like a reverse source of life because the animals were feeding the woman (it was the meaning of that macabre ritual). But more astonishing was the spiral ring we unfolded. The three rings were different—the first and second were circles, while the last one was oval." Meredith knew that the circles were similar to those found on the painting by Claudio at the church. She decided to keep it a secret for the moment and think about that.

All were in the water (a girl in the water).

Meredith later received her friendly team, expanded by Ryan and Michael, and expressed her outspoken opinion: "Larry Murphy spoke about a painting, and Claudio had dreams of it. We have to be more open-minded and follow the lines Larry discovered. Those monsters are something unusual, never seen before. They want to impress the public's opinion."

She then concluded, "We now have this name, Elysa, a mystery!"

Later that night Claudio opened his phone thinking about that name, and began copying the image once again, spending all afternoon painting and listening to music.

Dinner was later eluded by Claudio, with an excuse of sickness. When night came, he finally got what he wanted, trying to see his work from all angles and with different lights fired on it.

Diverse colors and perspectives seemed to change the aspect of the depiction as noticed in the original. He came closer, trying to see her face again. When by an optic effect he saw her appearance turning to scan his eyes, he was petrified...blood frozen, and for a moment in his deepest profound subconscious saw her look with his blinded mind! He could not remember, as if something like that already happened.

The colors he used on the girl started melting, as if water was dissolving them, creating a mix of pigments and circles around her feet; three circles—two round and the last oval. He stood up like she was trying to communicate with him, a powerful spirit of art, painting herself in the truth. Claudio then recalled his previous incident and Leon's barking, speaking and asserting, "Who are you? Where are you? Why can't I see you?"

Silence was shrouding the room until Giacomo came. He said, "Claudio please, if you are sick, go to bed right now. I have to get up early tomorrow—I have to work, remember?" "OK," he replied, facing the painting and placing it to rest.

When he neared the icon, he saw inside the circle mixed with the rings of colors, her face painted while trying to scan the girl's pupils!

Night was sleepless, and he assessed, "I went to learn a name while in Rome, Elysa, and now here we are: Elysa!"

In the morning Claudio conducted Isabel to Meredith's office. The drawing was folded with a cloth ready to be shown, but when it was uncovered it appeared to be a disaster of colors and shapes without any definition. Isabel declared in dismay, "What is that mess—oh, my goodness!" Claudio elucidated to them what had occurred the night before, while Meredith interrupted him and said, "Never paint it again. It is for sure a bad sign! We do not need that, and after all I can assure you that Kevin will never believe it." She added, "Kevin has lately become skeptical about everything. The only thing he wants is to have a search warrant and prosecute something tangible."

Isabel looked dubious and said, "Is Kevin tired of all this womanhood that now he doesn't trust us anymore?"

Claudio countered, "Womanhood?! Manhood! I don't think Kevin really cares about it—the only thing he desires, as she said, is real evidence. Be honest, please! So far we've got absolutely nothing—flies on our hand, zero!" However, either Meredith or Isabel had some doubts regarding the canvas incident, even if that icon was a mystique riddle (Claudio knew that something supernatural was working there, as his mother used to say about the reality of God and Evil).

PART TWO

Dr Levis: "We counted six different kinds of bones (six victims) of diverse parts of the body, with the time of death dated between 1984 and 1998, and only in two cases it was possible to assert with a certain degree of certainty the cause of death.

The first victim (from skull remains) was squeezed slowly until his head was smashed, while the second (the pelvis remains) was impaled. We could describe by the examination of the bones the real detailed tortures, similar to those perpetrated in the Middle Ages!" Kevin glanced at his friend Ron, who was devastated because he knew the similarity with the historical carnage of 1795. The pathologist kept going: "According to the ways of executions, we can say that we have two distinct murderers that used two different ways of killing; one was inspired by those of 1795 and stopped around 2000, the other started after 2000 with his sick rituals. Later on, the second slayer took over (police thought they were working together, and the youngest is the leader now)."

Kevin, after this latest unexpected twist, dismissed Ron and told Meredith in trust about the rare possibility that killers could have known about the 1795 homicides' secret files.

"It is impossible! Who is inspiring those criminals—who, for God's sake?" yelled the inspector. "So far in B.C., only the Highway of Tears Murders dated back from 1969 till today (forty killings and more missing people)."

The inspector, in a state of frustration, added: "If they remove me from this case I will be pleased—instead of solving the mystery, we are mixing everything again and again. I am waiting for Carter's next move. I bet he will accuse us of wasting time on the diving operation. That guy is a troublemaker—the boss of the homicide squad, my God!"

Claudio was half-asleep in his bed, shrouded within blankets, falling into a state of unconsciousness. His thoughts fell to the void of the gloomy universe, watching from above-ground. The noise of a train in the distance, followed by a strong honking sound, woke him in distress, omitting for a moment where he was for real. When he was a child, before going to sleep his mother always used to kiss him and wish him good night, while sometimes the train from Rome to Naples passed close to his house, blowing its siren.

Lidia used to say: "My love, this is the train of life, one day you will catch yours that will bring you far away in search of adventures, yet you will never forget what your mother said to you this very night."

He remembered that day, sleeping in a silent cry.

CHAPTER XLI

Scotoma

In North Vancouver, Andrew Devine was reproducing the Eclipse of the Soul. He was allured by a desire to replicate the image, which had drawn Meredith's attention.

"That image is like a continuous improvement. A friend of mine confirmed it two days ago," said the psychic. Claudio questioned, "Who is this guy? How does he know?"

She replied, "He is a professional in authentication and art appraisal, confirming the originality of the painting after Andrew Devine showed it to him. He sustained that it was painted in different times, judging from the colors and shades, perhaps because the artist decided to do so. Many details were added later, and he was convinced that the woodwork was done in the same way, perfecting and improving day by day."

Darleen Satin shouldered Meredith, illustrating a very important technical factor, while the guys were listening with attention. "The professional introduced us to a new, curious scientific aspect called 'visual disorder,' or 'visual impairment,' technically defined as scotoma (from the Greek, meaning darkness, obscurity)."

She paused for a moment to read a paper, mentoring: "Scotoma is an area of partial alteration in the space of vision, when our view is partially diminished or worse—completely degenerated—even if the surrounded zone has a well-preserved vision."

She made some practical examples with several artifacts and continued, "Every one of us possesses a scotoma, or blind scope of vision. In this blindness there are no photoreceptor cells on the retinal cell and optic nerve, which elucidate our misreading of certain details."

Isabel replied in a confident tone, "So we can affirm that the more we are observing the canvas, the more we can detect those missed blind spots? That would clarify why we unveiled those features time after time within the distortions and melting?"

"Yes, my dear, you said well, and moreover, if you like we can affirm that with the scotoma there is no conscious awareness of it, and we would rather assert that the details we missed disappeared on us," concluded the expert, giving a wide perspective of the visual and mental aspects of our eyes and brains, a dubious illusion.

Meredith, at the end of the session, spoke with Isabel about Claudio: "Scotoma could have misguided Claudio in judging his hallucinations and distorted visions, did you know that?" Isabel replied, "Yes, I got that, but I have to tell you that Claudio suffered anxiety disorder and abnormal disquietude, which however responsibly augmented his future disturbances—an upheaval of growing degeneration flew within his unstable life after his mother died."

If gathered, all those afflicted imperfection in Claudio's life, could have resulted in a dramatic, paranoid chain reaction.

Meredith said to Isabel, "If we are able to eliminate all those false perceptions in our troubled state of mind, considering solely the reliable evidence, we could extrapolate the essential facts we really need to evaluate."

Claudio, in the meantime, was afraid of Andrew's new attempt to reproduce his father's work. He was scared, deciding to discourage his friend from this cursed task, even if was a family tradition. Meredith later suggested Claudio forget for the moment about this portrait and concentrate on the last murder case—she had another eerie detail to tell.

The little rodents inserted into the abdomen of the victim, according to the psychic, were three in number, which not only underlined the three water allusive seals seen previously, but also stressed a kind of deeper religious meaning (the holy trinity, the resurrection and the three days Jesus spent in hell) Next day Claudio and Isabel drove east of Chilliwack, and when on Highway 1 before the Harrison Hot Spring exit, Isabel asked Claudio to converge on Exit 135 and park at Bridal Veil Falls Provincial Park. The landscape encompassing the park mesmerized Claudio, who began running upward, while Isabel implored him to wait and hold his horses. When up at the very end of the trail, the hearing-impaired youth realized he was eyeing something never seen before and yet dreamed of: It was a girl made of magic water.

Those Bridal Veil Falls are fantastic, he thought, astounded! For a moment he felt like someone was there before in time, a girl washing on the falls, free and pure, a bride with a white water veil ready to mingle with the spirit of nature. He almost cried, whispering, "I love you!" turning to Isabel with teary eyes. She embraced him and went down the trail, while Claudio kept watching the water crashing on the rocks, spreading a loud grave voice, a desperate voice.

Losing his mother in that pitiful way changed his young life forever. The materiality of death showed to his soul the fragility of life.

The day ended on the divan, watching TV, while several programs began talking about prophecies of the past and the signs of current warning, such as earthquakes, storms, flooding, hurricanes, wildfires, hot temperatures, cold winters and wars.

Claudio was listening, concentrating with his impending English, detecting a pronounced mysterious name: Saint Malachy and the prophecy of the popes! "Malachy, the one Armando was talking about, the papal seal in Spain. I never heard this prophecy before." He neared the speakers, while the preacher was radiating a palpable message of warning. "There were two Saints Malachy…in history, and both were prophets. Today we talk about Malachy the second (1096-1148), the one of the apocalypse. He was the first native-born Irish saint to be canonized, he died in France!" Claudio mumbled, "France? Larry went there!"

"Malachy was Archbishop of Armagh…attributed with several miracles. He was called the Saint of The Prophecy of the Popes, and finally, more important he prophesied doomsday," concluded the preacher.

Malachy used secret, cryptic Latin code to hide the truth—lots of them were lost, as were his remains, moved in different places over time. The first Malachy's seal was the closure of the first millennium and the Old Testament, while the second Malachy was the closure of the second millennium and the New Testament (our millennium today).

Claudio shouted in an accomplished tonality, "Yes! We have found the two seals! Don't you get it, man? It is not an allusion this time but a real fact. Remember Larry and his findings, the depiction, the maps, the scrolls and the colonists. The seals of the prophets are for an unfathomable reason connected with the murderers and the discovered portraits."

Claudio huddled his doubts after his positive excitement: "Yes, sure, but we don't have any clue about this hypothetical second seal!" After a moment he said, "Wait a moment, fool—yes, it is written here, France, Clairvaux Abbey, where the Saint Prophet died (Northeastern France)."

Saint Malachy's Last Prophecy:

> *"In the final persecution of the Holy Roman Church, there will sit Peter the Roman, who will pasture his sheep in many tribulations, and when those things are finished, the city of seven hills (Rome) will be destroyed, and the dreadful judge will judge his people…the End!"*

CHAPTER XLII

Deceitful Seals

The seals of waters, the seals of prophets, the seals of mystery, the seals of life and death: They found two of them but not the third, the final one…the last was seen on the water!

It was a rainy day and Andrew spent all afternoon at the garage, painting and observing his father's work. He had almost ceased the girl's contoured shape, although he had no idea how to complete and make her face more realistic. He remembered his father's story about the autochthon lady's sealed event, and how she became a legend in the time being. His father was told back in lineage by his old ancestors. Why her shoulders were painted remained a mystery, except for a detail his father revealed to him before disappearing. "Whoever tried to reproduce her true countenance was found dead back in history."

That is why she was later depicted only on her shoulders (in time her real face was lost in the memory of the natives, and nobody knew how long ago she lived, she was a powerful shaman). Andrew focused on his childhood, and nothing came out, only one doubt. How could one tell for sure if the shape was that of a girl?

Claudio was still following the TV program, mesmerized by the evangelist's words: "Pope John the XXIII was called a priest and sailor and before becoming the pope in 1958, he was the Patriarch of Venice. Paul the VI was called flowers among flowers and his coat of arms was a lily among lilies. John Paul the II was appealed as the sun's eclipse and he was the only pontiff on the list to be born and to be entombed in an eclipse. Benedict the XVI was named from the glory of the olives and the Benedictine order is symbolized by an olive. According to Malachy this pope will precede the last of the Apocalypse (Peter the Roman, and today we have an Italian pope)."

Claudio's face assumed a tense expression, thinking about Rome. "Could 2017 be the long-awaited day of judgment? It seems all so unreal and true at the same time," he remarked, while watching the next program.

A reporter appeared on the channel, questioning inspector Kevin during a previous interview. "Is it true you wished to be removed from the case? Nothing to be ashamed of, I would probably do the same if I were close to retirement." Mesotti looked proved and in distress: "I deny that! It is not my style—I never quit, nor would I relinquish my career. I'll work on this case until it is solved and…" He was interrupted again: "You quit once, when passing the case of the Vancouver armed robbery. There was an accident that your team caused on the North Shore and you…"

Mesotti's face showed a profound indignation, he suddenly screamed at the journalist, "I lost my son that day, you moron! Your useless job, you…" Ron escorted Kevin outside the conference room, while people were trying to sober the deplorable incident.

Claudio could not believe it, commenting, "They are trying to cut out the North Shore police enforcement, provoking our investigators. Those are blows flung beneath the belt, shameful!"

Claudio could not see what happened after the regrettable interview. Kevin was furious, arguing with Ron, "That peasant, exploiting my son's death to provoke me! I know Carter sent those parasites. I am sick and tired of this case."

Ron encouraged him: "No, that is what he is hoping for, we will shoulder you. We need to change tactics and be more reserved with our things. We're not giving up!"

On the other part of the world, Armando Suarez discovered that Catholics over time authorized other expeditions to Vancouver, sending their cardinals and pastors on ships (always Roman, French and Spanish). One name was always insistently reported on the Vatican's inventory list, a Cardinal Ravello, a lineage descendant!

Armando was reading: "The 1610 expedition was followed by others:1650, 1690, 1730 and 1795, all over forty years and in the spring-time. Another bizarre fact was that after the 1795 expedition, Ravello's name disappeared from the Vatican's cardinal genealogical tree, vanishing to nowhere. No documents or records, as if the family line was extinct (he died on the West Coast from a virus contracted during his last trip, but on the records he had died in Rome)."

Maurice commented, "I think Larry discovered something very important to such an extent that it deeply bothered the Catholic Church. The Ravellos' name could not vanish like that, after centuries."

Laura agreed, mentioning the historical adversity and battles that occurred back in time between Protestants and Catholics.

"Those Catholic priests could have been killed by the Protestants or something else happened there. From 1524 to 1648 religious wars in Europe were at the highest level, until the onset of the Protestant Reformation in Central Western and Northern Europe, followed by the Peace of Westphalia that recognized three separate Christian traditions in the Holy Roman Empire." Maurice clapped his hands, while Laura continued, "Those three traditions were Roman Catholicism, Lutheranism and Calvinism (known as the reformed tradition). Since the end of the wars and the beginning of the eighteenth century, rivalry between the different traditions continued to this day. To the Catholics, the antichrist in history was brought by the Protestant reformer Martin Luther, excommunicated with the papal bull in 1520—'*Exsurge Domine*'—while to the Protestants the antichrist was the pope, who raised himself above and against Christ. The Pope was seen as the usurper of Christ."

Armando thanked Laura and added, "When the king of England, protestant, took over and the king of Spain, catholic, lost the war, things became even worse for the colonies."

CHAPTER XLIII

The Mediums

Meredith Hampton, working in the peaceful atmosphere of her office, was explaining to Darleen, "The West Coast was considered the farthest place on earth after Columbus discovered the New World, away from civilization and God. Natives and local people were considered not only uncivilized, but also savage people living with the evil spirits. Later on they were forced to repent and embrace the true faith of God. For the Catholics at that time, sending prisoners or heretics away from the real world of God was the worst punishment they could inflict. They sent on ships the most hated and dangerous enemies of God, never to come back."

Darleen Satin reacted, "Never to come back—how cruel and sad?"

Meredith glinted, "Yes, I know, at that time it was horrible. Over time things changed because of the war's power and the Protestant Reform. The Catholics were no longer in control of the so called New World, and the papal control diminished. That is why, I think, Catholics tried to keep something secret here, but failed and spoiled everything. After all, the recent scandals of the church in Europe and Canada are examples."

Satin enquired, "Why those other expeditions after 1610? Why every forty years and in the spring?" Hampton mentored, "Forty years, I think, is something related to a kind of religious belief in the Holy Scripture. We see this number numerous times: forty days before Moses received the stone tablets, forty years of the Jewish people wandering the desert, forty days Jesus spent in the desert after being baptized by John the Baptist. Jesus was dead forty hours before resurrection, forty days of Lent—you name it."

"So who did they bring here?" replied Darleen.

Meredith responded, "Who said they brought somebody here? Maybe they found something already here!"

Satin persisted: "What about springtime?"

Hampton laughed and said, "Come on, dear, spring is Easter, and also the resurrection—like a spiritual renewal, a good omen. In this particular period Jesus duplicated himself in the Holy Spirit, descending at first and ascending after…a novice newly reborn in God. We also cannot forget the Annunciation of the Blessed Virgin Mary, which many Christians observe on the twenty-fifth of March (Elizabeth's John the Baptist, six months of pregnancy), when the 1610 expedition took place."

Meredith was a raging river: "We can conclude, assuming that all the information and details were chosen by the Catholics for a specific reason. We have to continue to investigate and try to keep inspector Kevin on our side."

Satin said, "He is with us—in the end we are searching for the case! By the way, I wonder again about this character Armando discovered—Elysa Morgair, right?" Meredith responded, after a brief pause, "Right!"

Satin asked, "How can we place her in our story? Who is she? Armando didn't say enough. I will try to do some research from home later."

It was 5 p.m. when the helicopter boarded the divers and flew them down the mountains. At 6 p.m. silence plunged all over the range. Dusk was coming… . It was coming… !

A creepy, gurgling water sound was heard emerging from the very depth of Mother Earth, a seal of liquid infuriated life, feeding the roots of existence and the tree of the past; soil mixed with blood protecting the distorted beating heart of gloomy spirits, as an obscure form that rises from the origin of creation and travels between night and day, seen from the stars and space.

A certain number of animals were running frantically, escaping a creature chasing them. Dusk was falling between the woods, while two deformed, dark-yellow eyes were scanning the warm escaping silhouettes. Hands of living bark were filled with sharp, sinister rock nails, and twisted, hard roots formed strong, dreadful bloody legs. Cordons of ancestral material were feeding the nightmare of time, advancing inexorably toward us!

Night of living day, day of living night... eternity of horror

Darleen Satin left the office while Meredith closed the main gate. She was headed home. "I will see you tomorrow morning, then—I promise I'll take a shower and go to bed, no homework!"

The hinge turned at Darleen's place, echoing with a strange energy present in the house. She deposed her stuff on the table, and took a hot shower. She froze when she sensed a shiver behind her back, a sigh of the past. The female revolved with a silent scream, nothing was there.

The phone rang...she jumped! "Hello! Meredith, you scared me to hell!" Meredith asked, "Why? Were you already sleeping?" Satin said, "No! I just felt a loss of energy here, the same occurrence we experienced in your house, remember?" Meredith faltered, "Mind the research."

The water was warm and relaxing...Satin was caressing and cleaning her fit body when she noticed a shadow coming closer from behind the shower' curtains. She sighed, "My God, it is cold in here! Who is there?" A dark hand touched the drape, pushing it against her. Darleen yelled, "No—please!" The hand touched her and vanished, deflating the cloth. She turned off the water and opened suddenly the drape; no one was seen. "My God, I am having hallucinations here, I better sleep soon." Before exiting the bathroom she sensed something pulling her long, blond hair, it was like an invisible finger twirling and pulling violently on her head. She could see from the mirror the pulling, screaming even more, "What is going on here? Help—I need help—God!"

The horrified woman escaped the bathroom and directed to the living room, fetching the phone and contacting Meredith. "Come on! Why is the receiver not working, for God's sake," Darleen said. A depiction of Jesus was on top of her bed, something was happening! The colors melted and a brown purplish liquid began dripping from the Lord's pupils, it was so scary.

She commented, "I feel the evil spirit we sensed at Meredith's place. Claudio's painting...it is you! I can feel your creep—noo!" The medium rushed outside the room, trying to exit, while the energy closed the bolt and locked her in.

She was panting and sweating nervously…the entity was within that place. Darleen revolved and saw a girl shoulders, the lassie was wearing a long, dirty white tunic, with blood stains on it. She was slowly walking backward, turning her cracking neck. Satin grabbed a crucifix and pointed it toward the girl, while backing into her room.

She swiftly positioned the hands between her mouth, distracting Satin from her vision, slowly tearing it… slashing completely the flesh. A tongue was tossed on Satin, who screamed out of her mind, closing the door violently. Electronic devices started working, while the entity turned her neck completely. The little shape displayed a sinister, wrinkled grumpy face of an old woman, aging in a consuming horrible way.

She vaporized, sliding beneath the door and reappearing behind Darleen. The entity opened her ebony-colored eyes, moving her dark bloody lips in a creepy sigh. "Darleen..!" was heard, when a purple tongue all of a sudden entered frantically her throat. A fire was set in the apartment…a pyre of the past, consuming her fainted corpse abandoned on the floor.

News hit the community early morning…Meredith dropped her coffee cup: "Did you hear what happened to Darleen? Who killed her?"

Mesotti with an audible voice, said: "I am so sorry for your friend. Ron Taylor called me late night. The blaze was an accident, a tragic one."

She insisted, "No! I do not think so, I left her last night and she was concerned about something. I even called her later on, when she was back at home. I swear she was frightened." Kevin said, "Meredith—listen to me! It was a terrible accident. There is nothing to make us believe she was killed or that she could have committed suicide. She woke up when the smoke was already around her. She could only exit the bedroom and faint on the living room…a tragic destiny."

PART FOUR

CHAPTER XLIV

The Calling

Sunrise welcomed a new day, and Andrew Devine received a strange phone call. A woman claimed to be his only sister, and was living in Port Hardy, northeast of Vancouver Island, with 35 percent of the population of First Nations descent.

Kwakiutl and Quatsino First Nations are both present in Port Hurdy. She warned him about something, questioning. He answered confusedly, "Get lost with those jokes, loser! I have no family anymore. Be ashamed for bothering honest people." He was upset and muddled at first, but later he thought of his friend making silly pranks about the painting curse. The next day the mysterious woman insisted, contacting Andrew once more, and telling him that they were all descendants of the Squamish First Nation of the North Shore.

He demanded her telephone number, so that he could be sure it was not a made-up jest. Andrew called the woman back, she answered!

"Why should I believe I have a sister I did not know? My father never told me…I don't even remember!" She replied, "Are you painting her!" Andrew remained mute for a moment, shaking in a confused state of mind. Her straightforward voice was new to him.

"Who are you?" questioned Andrew.

"I am your sister and our father is with me here," replied the familiar outsider, with a warm sound. Andrew conversed with her for a couple of minutes, deciding to travel to Port Hardy. It was too much to believe. Tanis Devine was her name (meaning moon in native language). She astonishingly narrated past family events. When the residential school in Port Alberni (400 kilometers from Port Hardy) was closed, they were divided…their mother committed suicide. Their father brought her daughter to his mother's First Nation band… up north, while he moved Andrew to his First Nation in North Vancouver. Later on, he was forced to come back with Tanis for reasons he explained to her later. He remained with his daughter ever since, getting sick in his mind because of the painting he copied. Andrew felt hallowed and numb at the same time, reasoning about a possible family reunion. "I need somebody to drive up there, a friend I can trust…Claudio!" thought the artist…

Few days later, Claudio and his cousin agreed to bring Andrew to Vancouver's island. Upon their arrival at Port Hurdy, they converged into the street and went looking for the reserve, when a woman on her fifties was standing in the middle of the way; she named Andrew and hugged him while crying.

The two were moved…introducing themselves, following Tanis to her place. A humble, well-maintained dwelling with a wide porch presented in front of group. She accompanied them inside, offering some desserts with refreshing drinks.

"In a moment you'll meet our father," said her shoving a wheelchair from kitchen, where he was seated in a state of paralysis. "He suffered a severe stroke years ago and the blood supply to his brain was seriously reduced," declared Tanis to her abashed guests.

She was at the point of contacting her brother at that time, but at the end…she didn't. He was in a state of confusion, sleeping most of the time; however, when he saw Andrew… smiled and recognized his son.

"What about that figure on the canvas—why had our grandpa carved her in the wood?" enquired unexpectedly Andrew; Tanis, noticing Andrew's friends staring at her, decided to reveal the mystery. "That figure was our great-grandmother, the mother of our grandpa (who did the wood carving)." Claudio and Michael were surprised, and noticed Tanis trying nervously to balance her story in any way, while the old man was staring at her.

Michael observed a painting of a native warrior with a Templar cross tattooed on the abdomen, "What does this writing mean?" asked him.

Tanis answered, "Guardians of the everlasting spirit." Michael again: "Who are those natives worshipping the Templar cross?" Tanis continued, "It is an old story, I think—some of those warriors saw the Templar cross long ago, brought by unknown European settlers. They were touched by the story of the devoted Templar and their catastrophic end, generating a small outfit of devoted cross warriors." The boy was out of belief, confused by those unusual sentinels. "Never heard that before," he said.

Tanis countered, "On the East Coast, near Oak Island in Nova Scotia, there was an old tribe worshipping those Templar. It is said that in the fourteenth century they brought their fortunes to the east coast of Canada, and subsequently the Spanish, after retrieving it there, moved the treasure to the West Coast."

Claudio for a moment felt a weird feeling, like a magnet with opposite poles trying to push each other. Michael saw his cousin's face turning pale and lost. Claudio's face was pointing to the door beside the bathroom, the one leading to the basement. His mind was pushed away in the opposite direction, like a strong pulsing magnetic wave.

"What is wrong, Claudio?" questioned Michael. Claudio said, "I think she is lying about the real identity of the painted figure." Michael: "Why?" Claudio said, "If you mde a portrait of your mother to remember her in that particular everlasting moment, which part of her would you like to see forever?" Without hesitation Michael answered, "Her loving face!" That was a logical human answer.

Andrew stayed with his family for the night, while the fellows resided in a motel behind the town's harbor, close to the marina club. Even if it was not comfortable like home's bed, they went to sleep late that night, collapsing in a warm, intense dream…a reverie

Claudio was running in a quiet obscure warmth, when some rocks fell close to him. He turned, careless, as a bleeding bark hand filled with sinister sharpened rocks ripped the side of his body…deep inside.

Curled, grotesque, elongated fingers were trying to pull out his entrails, inducing an excruciating pain that saw the youth falling down the ravine. His eyes rolled in the middle of a confusing situation, discerning a macabre figure advancing, its dirty legs intertwined with bloody roots and slimy guts. He was wrapped in a fetal position, breathing frantically, face-down. Suddenly its horrible right hand raised his head, slowly cutting his throat, utilizing his honed, rocky left hand, until he was completely beheaded. Claudio screamed as blood was spurting all over the place. His head was held by the hair. The infamous murder turned the severed cranium toward its malignant presence, so that Claudio could see his disfigured face mirrored inside the beast's eyes.

Looks exchanged by an instant glance, and in that moment the lad died, resurrecting on his dreadful, bloody bed.

A spasmodic "No!" yelled Claudio in the middle of the night, making his cousin jump like a rabbit. "It killed me! It killed me!" asserted the young man in a terrorized manner. "It killed me for real this time," perpetrated Claudio, while touching his throat carefully. Michael clutched a glass of water, trying to sober him. He was out of his mind and utterly drenched in a state of post-hallucination.

"Did you not hear my screams, for God's sake—I was calling you? I yelled and named you! I could not move from the bed! I thought that creature was here!" Michael enquired, "Did you ever have a transitional reverie of this kind before?" Claudio asserted, "Yes, unfortunately—many times since my mother passed away." He replied, "Did you ever consult a specialist or a doctor to try a healing treatment?" Claudio said, "Yes, I was prescribed pills and therapy sessions, but none of that ever worked." Michael then looked outside the window, exclaiming, "Thanks God, morning is coming and sunrise will disband our nightmares—or, if you like, our daymares."

Sleep paralysis is defined as a temporary inability to move or talk, and happens when a subject is awakening or falling asleep. It is not harmful to the body and lasts a few minutes; however, it can be very frightening. Claudio developed this kind of symptomatic disorder as a consequence of his dreadful nightmares, remaining in a state of awareness with inability to move. Claudio's depiction of sleep paralysis was perceived as a demonical visitation, revealing obscure, beast-shaped shadows heavily shrouding his corpse while in bed. He was diagnosed back in Italy with narcolepsy, obstructive sleep apnea and sleep deprivation. That is why he experienced hallucinations in hearing, feeling or seeing things that were not there in reality; those events triggered in his youth…fear of dark.

CHAPTER XLV PART ONE

Depictions

Tanis Devine neared the basement's door, escorting her brother downward. She turned the light on, brightening the muggy ambience.

A portrait appeared in the northward side.

"The icon," declared Andrew, "you are replicating it!"

Tanis said, "Yes! I started not long ago and it is almost completed. This will be the last and final depiction of our ancestral family line."

Andrew was confused and asked his sister what she meant.

She replied, "Get near the drawing and look with the spirit of memories." He approached, noticing new details added by his sister. The figure (if he was not mistaken) seemed to turn her face more insistently, despite the previous depiction, and her right eye disappeared entirely from the reflection in the water, almost completely displaying the shaman's face. The left eye instead was still slightly reflected in the water. Something was depicted within the eye, transforming the pupil, iris and sclera in planetary orbits.

The orb was admiring the universe, where it was merged.

Tanis revealed to her brother, "Truly the image is not that of our great-grandmother, but instead is a historical figure dating back to the seventeenth century. A powerful spirited shaman, a legend! We do not want to reveal this secret to the Western society, because it is an important family tradition handed down over time, more than four hundred years, Andrew." Tanis afterward showed her brother a tattoo on her middle, it was a Templar cross. Andrew, in astonishment, asserted, "You are one of the guardians of the sacred mountain, aren't you?" Tanis firmly replied, with a proud affirmative vibrant voice, "Yes, I am, and you could be one of us." The man was perplexed and enquired more: "What are we defending up there?" Her response was an unfathomable eerie silence.

Andrew promised to keep it a secret, and to be back when the final painting was completed. He then kissed Tanis and embraced his father, feeling part of a new, rediscovered adrift family. The tribe observed Andrew leaving in a rash with his friends, while Michael was driving the car, and Claudio was sitting beside him, sick with a fever.

Back in Vancouver, Inspector Kevin had to manage again the diving operations, neglecting Meredith for a while. She was mourning and crying for a lost paranormal professional, and a friend.

Isabel, concentrating on Malachy's popes prophecy, had discovered that Pope Benedict XVI shocked the world in February 2013 when he became the first Pope to resign in almost six hundred years. What most impressed the womn, was the fact that in reality the pope, in a secret Conclave, decided to resign unofficially already in March (springtime) 2012, as Malachy predicted.

She was reading, "The Prophet had the vision of the popes outside the church of Saint Peter, and he predicted that after the last pope had resigned, Peter the Roman would come to end the Church." Claudio's fever was rising, and back home the doctor gave him some medication. He needed to sleep and rest for a long period, while at the North Vancouver reserve Andrew was chatting with his friends about his family's business. Morris Harrison and Father Duncan Wilson questioned him about the painting and his father.

He answered furtively, "My father is an old, sick man living with my sister, very disappointing to me…nothing fancy."

Morris expected a different reaction from Andrew, leaving the sacristy. "I knew it was going to happen sooner or later—Claudio got sick chasing his stupid investigation, instead of dedicating himself to his studies. He is losing time after those fools! I told you that Tony! He needs to be steered straight. Youth are like horses running on the steppe."

Tony, in dismay, said: "I am sorry! I thought I would do you a favor by letting Claudio decide. I admit it was a mistake. Michael has fallen into the same trap…he went with him on the island." Giacomo asked, "Did you see what happened to that friend of Mesotti? She died in a fire, she was collaborating with the police, and I know she was seeing Claudio's friends."

Tony said, "Yes, I read the article, it was confirmed to be an accident by the forensic analyst technician. I told my son this case is cursed!"

Andrew, too, was worried for Claudio's health, clutching the brush and continuing working on the representation, recollecting what Tanis privately said to him, confusing his mind: "The more we reproduce the artifact, the more we turn away from its truthfulness."

"The pupil, the iris and the sclera—they are like planets!" thought Andrew, trying to work minutely on the details. He began painting the face of the girl completely backward, trying to imagine her visage…the inner part of the left eye. He suddenly stopped, "I need a magnifier!"

The only person who could help him was Father Duncan, who suffered from presbyopia. Sometimes he used a magnifier for reading the Holy Bible. Duncan was cleaning the canonical and saw Andrew running, soliciting for the magnifier. The cleric entered his office and gave it to him, asking, "What are up to?" Andrew said nothing and ran as fast as he could, while Duncan suspiciously closed the office and went chasing him.

The native was reproaching himself: "Why I never thought of using a magnifier to see the reflection on the water? My father used to say that in the dark you can see the true light, in the little space you can see the infinity of the universe!'"

He entered and turned on all lights, directing a strong flashlight toward the original image. "This is not a trivial matter!" exclaimed.

A slow-motion movement perceived his eyes pointing on the visual rendering, looking with scanning research the vision reflected in the lagoon. He focused more and more, until the left eye appeared hidden between the rays of sunset and the visible piece of moon, wrapped in the red color of the blood and the shadow of the eclipse of the soul.

He distinguished, merged in the kaleidoscopic reddish pond, between the sun rays and the blood, tiny rose petals. It was there, cleared by the magnifier and uncovered by the light of truth…that Andrew's gaze fell through the eclipse's pupil, discerning the gravitational planets in an optic, confused effect.

It was at that moment when he saw a light line shoot from the eyeball, dividing the iris in the middle; it was perfect as if unreal. He moved the magnifying glass backward a little, realizing that from that position the eye assumed another shape! A shape of truth! A form! Andrew was speechless… It was watching!

His eyes focused persistently, blurring the vision. He needed a break, softening the lights, while tittering as if a flashlight had been shot in his face. Andrew recoiled in the shade, appeasing his sight, when he noticed an opaque contour swiftly parading along the room. He returned back, walking calmly, and glancing at the foggy image, while a hazy, grimy shade moved around.

The icon came alive, moving in a misty steam from a distance.

A scream was heard by Father Duncan outside Andrew's home.

He ran up the stairs and tried to open the door, it was locked from inside. The cleric furiously began kicking and pushing the gate, using his legs and shoulders. He attempted numerous times, when finally he slammed the door, breaking the hinges. He entered loudly, eyeing Andrew seated on his chair.

PART TWO

"I am sick and tired of your blustering bravado, young man! You decide what to do once and for all with your life. I have to think of myself —I have a life, too!" said a fed up Giacomo

Claudio stood up and replied, "I made up my mind long ago, dad! I want to be a police officer, here or back in Italy. I am tired of losing time on the books."

Furiously shouting: "Is that so! Now we don't want to study anymore, it is easier! How convenient! Forget I am going to pay for your courses. I have already wasted so much money to see you changing your mind. This time you are on your own."

The boy challenged, "I have been on my own since Lidia died. I can take care of myself better than you, old man!"

Giacomo accusingly, "I quit my career in the military to give you a better future, and this is the result. I started from scratch here, working like a carpenter in all weather conditions. You should be ashamed of yourself!" Claudio lost his wits, feeling he was right, "I can leave the house if you like! I don't need you anymore, as I don't need your money!"

He left the room slamming the door, while Claudio remained paralyzed, dressed in his pajamas.

What Duncan witnessed minutes later was a brutal crime scene. Two long, thin rocks were crammed in the artist's eyes, while a long bundle of innards and roots had strangled him so tightly that his tonsils burst out of his throat. The tongue was cut and put back in his mouth, while the colors were dripping from his hands.

Duncan nervously fetched the phone and called 911, turning around the room in a state of terror. He saw the depiction and the girl, when all of a sudden he dropped the phone and observed the shape moving, revolving her face rapidly. He heard a scream of horror! A voice: *Tenebrae Vobis* (Darkness be with you). Abruptly, two long, sharpened rocks were violently thrust in Duncan's ears, so that he could be lifted while still alive, his face munched completely. A contorted sigh mingled with a loud, lustful gnawing, ripping the reverend's throat, sucking blood from his body. A long, raspy, sharp tongue stretched perversely out from the mouth, pushing upon the larynx and playing a contorted macabre sound with Duncan's vocal cords.

He was disfigured, while the local neighbors, attracted by the noise, began running into the house. Police arrived, alerted by Duncan's phone call, and what they saw later was disgusting. The reserve was seized and patrolled all night…a curfew was ordered.

In the morning, publishers had no time to release the news about the misdemeanors, while TV channels were exploding with tormented information concerning the slayers' presence in town. Half of the police force was transferred from the mountain range to the North Shore community areas. The Lions Gate Bridge and the Second Narrows Bridge were partially closed and checked carefully. The ocean shores were patrolled by police, coast guard and SAR. The executioners at the end should have been struggling…they had enough of the tough life in the wilderness. The only feasible escape was the water, and police suspected they came down in the night, using the creeks and the rivers (Capilano River, Seymour River, Lynn Creek)

CHAPTER XLVI

Templar

Jim Carter rapidly overlapped the North Shore police enforcement, slowly launching his revenge. He talked into the microphones: "Forensic examiners collected all the evidence found at the crime scene, such as blood, liquids, pieces of flesh and the murder weapons. Fingerprints were taken all over the area, and the painting was evaluated and photographed. The colors were mixed with dirty water, after being spun around, forming an ensemble of circles, a vortex. Two opposite triangles were crudely painted on the vortex with blood, while nothing was removed or stolen. Whoever killed Andrew Devine did it for a specific reason, while Father Duncan could have been killed only for being a random eyewitness standing in the wrong place at the wrong time."

A journalist enquired, "What about the consultation of new esoteric experts? Are you willing to utilize their expertise?"

The chief responded, "We are working on it, replacing the ones used by the North Shore police. As you know they were forced to retreat after a tragic blaze killed one of the psychics." Photographers were exploding their flashes all around the conference room, framing the sidelined Kevin Mesotti and Ron Taylor. Their faces were pale and unhappy.

August was over, and Claudio with Michael dropped by Mesotti's office in West Vancouver. Robert accompanied them inside, it was a difficult moment. The youths told the inspector about Andrew's family discovery and their trip to Port Hurdy.

Mesotti reacted, "Why did you not tell me about it? Why had you guys kept me out of it?" They answered together, "Devine told us to keep it a secret for the moment." The officer countered, "Did you see what happened to Andrew, as soon as he came back from your secret journey? We are almost cut out from the investigation. Darleen, Andrew and Duncan died in our community. Jim Carter has no limits now!"

Claudio replied, "That trip was a coincidence, and the only strange episode I can remember was that I got sick soon after Tanis Devine offered me a drink." Claudio and Michael recalled all the details, and Kevin decided to pay a second visit to Vancouver Island, this time reaching Port Hurdy. He was accompanied by an investigation squad, especially after Claudio mentioned the Templar worshipper and the Oak Island connection with the band in Port Hurdy. Kevin believed that a relationship could have been possible between the two tribes, joined by the ocean bridge along Vancouver Island.

Equal Cross Band Adorer

The sarcophagus of obscurity opened at last, while dawn sped its glorious purplish rays, warmly filtering through the branches and the leaves of the forest. Light beams widened in the gloom of nature, reflecting the origin of life from the sky. Water was dripping from the shaman's sacred hands, bestowed in wisdom by the gracious spirits of local ancestors. Splashed water created myriads of mirrored shards, enlightened by the reddish fire of the blessed sunrise.

Tanis Devine placed her hands above the humble head of an aboriginal youth novice, blessing his soul and confirming his holy oath. A new adept had joined the guild, a worshipper of the sacred Templar cross. Port Hurdy's forest, within a lake hidden up the hill, saw the ceremony of a new reborn soul, surfaced from the past; a new day for them all.

(Knights Templar used to perform their ceremony of secret rites of initiation at dawn, as a meaning of rebirth and regeneration…a new resurrection blessed by the sunrise of eternity.)

CHAPTER XLVII

Inverted sequence

Meredith was placed officially behind the scenes after Darleen Satin passed away, remaining in contact with Mesotti and her friendly team. She could not relinquish completely now that Darleen was dead. She involved her last employee, an old friend, an expert in the cryptic and paranormal; he was a teacher and a symbologist who had spent a few years researching in Europe. They observed and speculated about those signs, circles and triangles found at the last crime scene.

"The triangle in Western society, most often has a highly Christian meaning, when used in a religious context," explained Chan, the pundit. "The Christian God is a Trinity (Father, Son and Holy Ghost united in a single godhead). The circles instead, as we can see here on the pictures, commonly represent unity, wholeness and infinity. It has no beginning or end, without sides or corners, associated with the number one. In this case with all these vortexes, we have many circles and there is a distinction between the ones inside and the ones outside."

Chan continued, showing his professionalism and passion for the subject: "The message of the murders is unambiguous; circles in this case are protective symbols, shielding something inside from supernatural dangers or influences outside—in other words, keeping a secret that we cannot perceive, but yet is there."

Chan added that the circle is the symbol of the sun (the astrological symbol of the sun is a circle with a dot in the middle), protected inside the other planets and solar system as well. Meredith asked the man about the two triangles, and why they had opposite directions. "Triangles also have physical meaning other than spiritual, such as fire, air and water (present at many crime scenes). The two found on the painting are different and opposite. The first is a pointing-up triangle (strong foundation and stability, rooted on the ground) associated with male energy (air and fire) it means ascension toward the spiritual world. The pointing-down triangle represents female energy (water and earth), or descent into the physical world," replied Chan with a robust belief.

He tried to cut to the chase, concluding, "The interpretation is that inside the circles something was kept secret and protected, while outside two opposite spiritual energies were confronting each other; God and evil fighting up to infinity." Chan stood up rigorously and said, finally, "This is a lucid and distinctive missive for all of us! They will never stop killing unless we free them from their own evil." Meredith showed Chan another fact that emphasized his point: all the murders were committed in a period of six months (March to September), from past 6 a.m. to 6 p.m., forming for the umpteenth time an abominable, 666 death sequence, the number of Azazel.

They all agreed that the satanic esoteric line was the only one possible to follow, natives or non-natives! Those numbers showed by no coincidence many times.

Chan revealed a theory previously endorsed by Larry Murphy: "The number 666 in reality is a number in readiness for the devil, most lethal when inverted—999—because from preparedness it switches into action. The 666 has its head down, as if evil was resting, while the 999 is hoisted, as if ready to attack. Take a closer look at the numbers, the '9' is walking as a deceiver of the past. The '9' is the number of the beast! 999!"

Meredith appeared flabbergasted…a shiver of truth entered her mind.

Meantime Kevin arrived at Port Hurdy. It was a warm, sunny day, and Tanis let the police enter the house. Some locals were giving condolences to the family, while the community clung around them. Tanis did not hesitate and told Kevin all he wanted to know, explaining why his father disappeared and why she lived away from her brother all those years.

"Why did she show up only now?" thought Mesotti.

Tanis moved to the bedroom and opened a drawer, picking up a few documents. She had in her hands two birth certificates, one with her name and the other with Andrew's. She then explained to the investigators, "We were born from the same mother but with a different father. My father is the one in the wheelchair, while Andrew's real father was a sexual offender working at Port Alberni residential school (he abused my mother). The rapist was part of the Catholic school educators and left the place when the institute was closed. Andrew was taken away from his mother and brought to North Vancouver. My father is a descendant of the North Vancouver First Nation, while our mother was inheritor of the Port Alberni First Nation; Andrew was born half-native!" She was crying when telling this sad story, while Kevin comforted her, saying, "The only thing we want is to bring to justice those sadistic criminals!" She continued, speaking about their mother's suicide at the school and the disappearance of a third sister (who became ill with tuberculosis): "Later on, after the two fires occurred in Port Alberni school, lots of documents and papers went missing."

The portrait affair surfaced at the end of the conversation, when the investigators searched the basement and discovered the artifact. "Could we take a closer look at the portrait?" requested the inspector. He remembered the magnifier found on Andrew's floor.

For a moment he fathomed the piece. Everything looked the same except the right eye was more visible. Kevin distinguished a smudge inside the pupil, a dark circle in the circle. "A well-detailed eye, after all," mumbled the officer quickly dismissing the parade, continuing his research around the aboriginal estate. Nothing more was left to see, until they abandoned the scene. As they left the site, driving, the detectives noticed a small group of locals wearing similar shirts, embellished with black and a red Templar crosses facing each other. "Is everything all right?" asked one of the officers. "Yes right! Never mind, keep going, we have already lost enough time here." Forensic examiners handed out the latest results obtained at the laboratories. Dr. Lewis announced, glistering with optimism, "Two types of blood were found on the floor (Andrew's and Duncan's blood) while two more blood types were located on the portrait! For the first time the assassins made a mistake! They rushed to kill and neglected to clean the scene." For Jim Carter, this was a success—finally the murderers went too far, making the classic error. Lewis added, "The forensic laboratory needs a few more weeks to acquire the unknown blood types' gender, and eventually the DNA, also studying the fluids and the pieces of flesh left at the scene."

Police were waiting anxiously for a possible DNA sample, and Carter's idea was to take all the community samples, comparing them with the one found in the house.

Jim Carter spoke after the doctors, saying, "It worked in many cases! The last incident of DNA comparison was in Italy. An entire village was DNA-tested and Italian police were able to identify the suspected murderer, arresting him."

A reporter asked Carter, "What about the divers sent up the hills, did we waste our money up there? Now police came out with these massive DNA tests! Do you not think we are losing time and resources?"

Claudio was watching the news, seriously focused, when Jim answered: "Every piece of the puzzle is needed, and we joined many pieces. The criminals moved back to the city, feeling trapped and lost. Their mistake is the first and the last—in two weeks we will finally…" Claudio's phone rang, it was Laura! "Maurice is in France, searching for Clairvaux Abbey, the place where Saint Malachy died in 1148) how it is going there?" Claudio replied: "Not really well, as usual! A storm is coming from the investigation. We are on our own, and Mesotti is retreating."

Laura said, "Uncle Loris is with me, he wants to talk to you. Did you have a chance of conversation with our father after the argument?"

Claudio puffing, "I do not want to talk about that now, let me talk to uncle." Loris on the other side, asked, "How are you, my dear! Do not worry too much, we already got the antipope once, and the world is still here." Claudio was confused, "The antipope?"

Loris explained that the antipope was another name for the antichrist, the opposite of Saint Peter on earth, the Devil.

Claudio quickly ended the conversation, hung up the phone and drove to the North Vancouver Public Library. He needed to read and distract himself, spending all afternoon in there. After searching on the computer library's files, Claudio came across Loris's historical foretold antipope episode. It was written: "Distressed by factionalism in Rome and pressed to come to France by King Philip IV, Pope Clement V moved the papal capital to Avignon (at that time belonged to vassals of the Pope), which in 1348 became direct papal property. In the period all seven of the popes were French, as were the 111 French cardinals of the 134 created. French power was growing, centralizing administrative offices and controlling agencies."

CHAPTER XLVIII

Schisms

Isabel reached Claudio later. He was ready to read her the last part of his research. He continued soon after, "Once again France was on the list, England and Germany were against this papacy change, which later damaged the prestige of the Catholics all around the world. After Gregory XI reestablished the papal capital in Rome, a second pope was elected in Avignon, creating the infamous Great Western Schism and the succession of the antipopes."

Claudio was astounded about this part of history, and moreover the schism, which lasted from 1378 to 1417, almost forty years of Antipopes (the number forty again, he thought). It was written that for a period, three men simultaneously claimed to be the true pope. At the end of this dramatic page of religious history, France remained in time the capital of antipopes; never again was it written in the Vatican archives about it. Only with the coming of Napoleon, the Catholics thought of the real Antichrist." Isabel observed: "It's a very interesting part of the European history, but I have to tell you another important fact of our past here. Do you know Captain George Vancouver?"

Claudio wisely replied, "Yes, I read about him on the citizenship test book, he is the one who discovered and gave the name to Vancouver."

Isabel declared, "He was one of the greatest explorers and navigators, dying in an unclear condition in 1798, three years after his last expedition at age of forty! No official cause of death was stated, as all the medical records belonging to Vancouver were destroyed. One doctor named John Naish, claimed that George died from kidney failure, while others believed it was a hyperthyroid condition. A document was found later on, inside his sarcophagus in the churchyard of St. Peter's church in London, England."

Claudio's curiosity increased and his hand touched the chin. Isabel continued, "The scroll found was conserved secretly by the Protestants at first, but after Vancouver's last expedition, it was stolen and burned by the Catholics soon after Napoleon's defeat."

Isabel paused, "It is said that the parchment ascertained a mysterious death, caused by a cursed sickness contracted in Vancouver after he named the city." Claudio marveled, "Forty years the antipopes' schism, forty years the lag between the voyages and now forty years of age, it is quite stunning. Do you think George Vancouver died because of a curse? He is not mentioned in any documents or religious scrolls." Isabel followed, "He is buried in a Protestant church called Saint Peter's, the same name of the church where you were born and raised. What kind of coincidence is this, Claudio! Don't you see? Maybe your visions and nightmares are a warning sign for all of us. Even your uncle seems convinced of that." Claudio said, "Did he tell you something about it?" Isabel replied, "No! He was just concerned and preoccupied for you and your family."

That information about George Vancouver was well-known in the history of British Columbia, though no one except Isabel had noticed it. Furthermore, the explorer discovered Seattle, founding a second Vancouver in the U.S. Washington State, close to the Columbia River and Mount Vancouver, a not-coincidental affinity.

CHAPTER XLIX

Trials of Time

George Vancouver, at the end of his expedition, carried with him in London both Ravello's secrets and the expedition's parchments. He established a good rapport in time with the indigenous people and European hunters, showing a high degree of sensitivity to natives. George received a wooden sculpture of the shaman girl, and when back in England he felt the need to reproduce the article, getting sick soon after… vanishing forever.

He brought the keys of the mystical obscure entrance of Saint Peter's in London, while Claudio subtracted it by his destiny, and took the keys back to Vancouver from Saint Peter. "*By Sea, Land and Air We Prosper,*" is Vancouver B.C.'s motto. "*A Colorful Past, a Bright Future,*" is Vancouver Washington's motto; united in the present by the past, the future of the natural prophetic elements.

Andrew's and Duncan's funerals were postponed because the forensic exams and autopsies still had to be completed. The bodies had to be reassembled and made presentable.

Armando, after a long lineup, was granted permission to comb through the last documents of the Inquisition files, another secret archive specially created for the sacred. The cleric informed Laura, "For over 600 years the Inquisition enforced Catholic orthodoxy around the world, producing records that in time have been locked away, becoming the subjects of myths and legends. In 1998 the Vatican for the first time opened the special archive of the Holy Sacred Office on a limited basis; only twelve scholars within the archives received authorization at the beginning, increasing the number later." Armando was looking for those documents regarding the complete Basque Witch Trials in Logrono, from January 1609 until December 1611.

He found the completed folder of the trials, and some parchments were similar to those found previously in the Vatican Secret Archives, while others were supplemented or tailored afterward. After reading the copious places where the Spanish Inquisition put its powerful hands, he finally met the final hearing concerning the Morgair's family in Pamplona: a new evidence was the condemnation of two girls, as he explained to Laura.

"Elysa Morgair and the indefinite Lysae were condemned," he told her. "Who is Lysae?" asked Laura. Armando answered, "In all the documents this name never appeared before! Perhaps a relative! It is a mystery, although the death sentence for both was the same. The church perpetuated those girls' images as evil ones." Laura exited the room, waiting outside the archive. Armando left minutes later. He looked abashed and exclaimed, "I do not like the clutter of all those documents, lost and found after 400 years." Laura opined, "I think that Elysa was executed, and Lysae could be a mistake of bureaucracy because Elysa had undergone two different proceedings in two different places." Armando nodded, showing all his dubious thoughts.

The lab, however, had some interesting news. Even if DNA results were not ready yet, the blood found on the portrait disclosed the same types of blood cells (*A-positive*, the second-largest blood type in Canada and Europe). What shocked most the specialists was discovering that it belonged to two different women, and only one was of a living body. The second sample was old, dead blood, deposited on the scene by the killers as an act of defiance. Some qualms were expressed by the investigators in regard to the other sample. Murderers could have purposely left both the blood types in the room, along with the other evidences. Jim Carter had to continue anyway, pausing for the DNA values to be compared with the whole community. Having more blood to trace meant having more unidentified victims.

Meanwhile in Clairvaux in northeastern France, Maurice Fredel arrived at the abbey, a Cistercian monastery founded in 1115 by Saint Bernard. He admired the brawny walls, furnished at intervals with watchtowers and other defenses, like a protection of the old Holy Secret.

The man passed then through the gateway, while monks and visitors entered the outer court of the inner ward, staring suspiciously at him. The great cloister was on the south side, surrounded by the chief monastic building, Maurice entered where the Saint Prophet died in 1148, while a powerful organ was playing a mystical song followed by a deep melodic choir. He felt as if someone was waiting for him after all this time.

The prior escorted Maurice and described, "It is under the abbey's crypt where Saint Malachy's body remains were entombed originally. Some parts were later moved to Ireland in 1194 and put in a reliquary. Later during the French Revolution, the reliquaries unfortunately were destroyed and scattered in different places."

Maurice was impressed that Malachy had no peace for his remains after his death, it was like a Devil's revenge for such a good prophet, and his prediction remained a strong sign for all of them. The prior showed Maurice the thousand-year-old Archive of the Abbey, releasing him the access to study what he was looking for. That day changed his life forever. It was there on a papal sigil, a single document with the final Saint Malachy's second seal, closing everlastingly what was opened with the first Saint Malachy's seal of the Old Testament. It was composed by Cardinal Ravello of the Inquisition.

Maurice read, "The last Malachy's prophecy will be fulfilled in the second millennium (Peter the Roman and the last Pope), 400 years from now; we seal for the salvation of humanity and of the Holy Church, the true antichrist to come forever in the new lost world. Elysa is exiled in the farthest place on earth, among evil spirits and uncivilized savages. The princess of darkness, the daughter of Lucifer will not prevail."

Maurice noticed the original seal with the image of Malachy the second, and the year December 1609, Christmas time! He whispered in his mind, "Elysa did not perish in Spain, but was instead exiled to the West Coast, today's Vancouver!"

The priest felt two cold hands on his shoulder and a thrill inside his body. Outside a vigorous rain was pouring due to the high temperature.

Maurice came back to his papyrus, and with a sense of fear felt something was changed forever.

Talking to himself he said: "400 years from 1609 will be 2009, we are in 2017! Malachy always said millennium, 2000—something is missing here. Wait a moment! There is a number on the scroll... Elysa, age seventeen!" He heard a voice inside the crypt, similar to water playing on a piano, a natural piano, an instrument of the past. The rain was beating the sliding time, flew between Maurice's hands. Hours passed shrouding his foggy reality.

"Seventeen years and 2000 years..." sighed

He focused on the number 2017, as the sigil appeared hazed and he got bleary-eyed. The rain seemed to fall inside the crypt closer and closer like a barefooted downpour of the past. He was mesmerized by a presence within his imagination, running away through the colonnade and aiming for the main imposing portal. The church was closed in a claustrophobic framed silence; everybody was gone, ignoring his presence. That sound was a watery slinking, ascending from the crypt and following the priest's brisk steps; his eyes squinted as if a strong light was upon his head. His figure motioned reversely, escaping upon the church tower bells, clambering the prolonged helical stairwell. The male was out of breath, observing an allusive figure climbing behind him. He accelerated and frantically reached the top tower, undergoing vertigo and dizziness that found him circled by numerous old brass bells playing an overwhelming melody of death, an infernal, macabre loudness that created confusion. He esteemed the height and the graveyard beneath, realizing he was witnessing a baffling inexplicable landscape.

It was an ancient environment of the past, as if time was reversed, the year 1610 whereas the church aged suddenly.

Maurice in his deafening sensation revolved the eyes toward the stairs, as he saddened and fell from the tower; that entity had appeared front-face, scaring his soul to death. His body smashed upon a gravestone far away from that place—a tombstone was placed there, with a name engraved... Elysa Morgair! Maurice was reading while emanating his last puffed breath.

A hand fell on Maurice's shoulder. "Sir, sir are you ok?"

Maurice leaped up, scared out of his mind, throwing the scrolls near the rostrum lectern. "I—I was... I was," mumbled the man. "You fell asleep, I guess, after reading for so long. You better come back tomorrow morning, you must be very tired," asserted the caretaker. Maurice at that moment apprehended the real vision he experienced as a collateral, intangible dimension—he had encountered her! The cleric left all the scrolls around the room, running far away from that place, away like the two Spanish galleons landing in the North Pacific.

In the Bible the number 17 symbolized "overcoming the enemy" and "complete victory," as had Noah's ark and its eight passengers when the immense vessel rested upon the hills of Arafat on the 17th of the seventh month. God flooded the earth with rain on the 17th of the second Hebrew month. The number 17 is directly related to Christ's resurrection.

Number 20 represented a perfect waiting period of time, expecting liberation, justice and judgment from God. It is an old biblical number.

CHAPTER L

The Anagram

February 1610

The environment of the northwest coast of Canada was very diverse, and often extreme. The two surviving prisoners were escorted to the closest native village up the hill, protected by the trees, with a view overlooking the bay. A rugged coastline extended all along the deep fjord, forming wide and narrow beaches down the mountains. A multitude of little islands were displayed astonishingly in front of the bay. In the inland, lakes and rivers were spectacularly exploited by the local people, while spruce, cedar and fir forests enriched the whole area. The inhabitants had lived near the water for basic survival.

The two detainees were disposed and delivered in custody to the chief and shamans of the village, before the Holy Inquisition sentence took place in March. They spent one month living with the aboriginals, experiencing a tangible sense of love and friendship.

"We have to teach those women how to survive and deal with the elements. They have to integrate with our culture. I was told by their spiritual leader, Ravello, that they will never return back home," said the head authority of the tribes, touching the rim of his nose with a feather.

"I will guide them through the woods, showing how to dodge the adversity of nature. They seem pretty insecure," added one the hunters.

The natives were fishing every day, providing food for all the people ashore, building houses and canoes using the cedar trees. Prisoners were helping the tribe with their chores, feeding themselves with their hard work. Hunters used to capture deer and elks in the woods, favoring and gracing the spirits of transformers for their precious gifts. They used to preach in complex social and cultural customs, addressing the sacred and the supernatural.

Day by day, the captives became absorbed as a part of the tribe, away from the delusion of Spanish colonists, which had segregated them because of their misconception. Elysa passively was adapting to the new lifestyle, while the other was snitching, "I would escape, rather than live with these cold-blooded brutes, look at them! They look like..."

Elysa interjected the snitcher, tired of her complaints.

Again she accused, "It's your fault if we were confined here! Think about all those people who suffered and died because of your family's name. I don't want to live with you in this cursed land."

Settlers were busy trading and converting the local community, exploiting the rigid orders of Pietro, who was mistrustful of all the natives...in his eyes they were performing distorted rites, utilizing monstrous masks resembling demons—"the indigenous realm of haunted specters."

The shaman had a fourteen-year-old boy, and two daughters, ages seventeen and nineteen. His wife was respected by warriors and chiefs of the tribes (she cured and saved lots of people from sickness and illness, using local herbs and natural treatment). Elysa was noticed more than one time aiding and assisting the local people with extraordinary skills; she had not forgotten what her doctor and alchemist father had taught her before he was barred and expelled.

Without informing the settlers, the chief adopted Elysa as his daughter, conducting a special ceremony. She was welcomed as a new adept of the sacred shaman committee of eight. In the chief's eyes, only God could have endowed her with such power and grace.

The lassie conserved her delicate beauty, despite the hard punishment and deprivation she endured. Elysa regained some health, eating more than ever, protecting herself from stress and fatigue, as if she was thinking of doing something unusual. She was often seen alone with the shaman's oldest son, fomenting the other prisoner's jealousy of being not considered.

"She is a real witch, then! The church was right! Only now can I see her deceitful plan, selfish hag! I'll not shush this time, I'll have my revenge," said the prisoner disclosing Elysa's affairs. The clergyman was convinced that Elysa was converting herself into an aboriginal evil spirit, mesmerizing the locals in the real and only power she had; the devil's authority of hell.

"Your grace, don't let me in the hands of Lucifer! Elysa is the one to blame. She is conspiring with the natives against us. They will attack you and your guards soon!" spoke her in a dramatic attempt, bending on his knees.

"If what you are saying is true, God will change your destiny," replied the cleric.

He and his followers were furious, deciding to persecute and condemn the shaman's group without provoking a reaction among the tribes. They were more than 200 people, while native numbers exceeded the thousands.

To fully honor the reborn, the chieftain renamed the extremity of the northeast mountain, tricking the settlers with a simple anagram: Elysa became the anagram Elsay, same within the homonym Elsay Lake, situated just upward from the mountain's spike, where a massive bath of spiritual resurrection was administered honoring her baptism.

The two diverse religions mingled, creating later the holy guardians of the sacred mountains, transformed in time in Templar lineage. (Originally named Mystery Lake, Elsay Lake became a mystery in the mystery; shrouding in legend its real ancestral origin.) March 16th was at hand, and the crew had only one week left before executing Elysa. A deceitful plan was concocted by Ravello to mislead the tribe and isolate the shaman's league.

"Captain, our only chance to fulfill this expedition is to eliminate those who oppose us in the name of Lucifer. We must act sharply and cleverly, before the witch's curse strikes. Inform your most reliable man as soon as possible about our plan, and do not tell anybody else. Ears are all over us. God will protect us from darkness," exclaimed Pietro, while donning his long tunic.

"As you wish, your eminence, whatever you command!" answered Alonso, snatching a little purse refilled with coins from the cardinal's dirty hands. "That will do it, your grace!"

They organized an expedition up the mountains, bringing their priests and the shaman's group. They desired to thank the spirits of the natives for being generous to them all.

March 20th at dawn they began the spiritual walking prayers toward the forest, while a reddish bloody sky created a horrific universal premonition.

CHAPTER LI

Forensic Challenges

September brought the DNA results of the first blood sample. Police could begin collecting the community's DNA from men and women, undertaking a huge effort in organizing sites for singling out DNA samples. Thousands of people showed up day after day sorted by age and gender, forcing forensic analysts to increase the pace of testing. Scientists used an electronic chip that could copy and analyze the models taken from a cotton swab.

Technicians collected DNA by swabbing the mouth, mixing the sample with a few chemicals, and warming it up. The final test was performed on a chip in the laboratory, a four-hour process for each person. Examiners used all the labs available in the city of Vancouver.

Jim Carter interpreted: "DNA of the pieces found on the floor was compared with the blood, matching perfectly. One of the killers was injured when struggling with the victim." Jim put great pressure on those more potentially suspected, making sure nobody could elude the test. Moreover, all the criminals recently convicted in that area were minutely assessed.

Although citizens were bothered by this unusual process, they felt safe and protected at the same time, because the law was getting closer to the unknown culprits; perhaps they were hiding among the population. Claudio and his friends underwent all the tests, as did their parents and relatives.

Time was rushing by and police enforcement was working day and night. September was almost settling the murderers for their six-month lethargy. Everything was falling again in an enchanted, dark lost dream.

"This is one of the most astonishing triangles we extrapolated up those hills: Elsay-Bishop-Cathedral peaks—that after the latest discovery in Rome we can think as the witch trial and its religious meaning," said Claudio to Isabel (The Spanish Inquisition accused more than 150,000 people, executing around 5,000. The majority were innocent people).

Maurice had opened their minds and hearts. Not everything was intelligible by the knowledge of books or paper if not completed with the spiritual meaning of our universe. Maurice revealed to them how all aspects of life had to be joined, before obtaining the true reality; the one he found with Armando in the history of time. In their travels back in history, guided by documents of people's past lives, the prophecies of the saints, and the stars' alignment, they found the universal alignment of the triangles of life, there on the map.

Isabel pointed out the latest research from Maurice: "Clairvaux Abbey is northeast (Malachy-Elysa Second Seal, 1609), Fontainebleau is northwest near Paris (*Pope Pius VII deposed by Napoleon 1812),* Avignon is southwest (the historical antipopes of the Western Schism) where the triangle is pointing down west, the sunset of the antipopes. Maurice even mentioned the city of Savona (Italy), southeast (where Pope Pius was deposed by Napoleon the first time in 1809), forming an opposite triangle pointing up toward Elysa, the Second Seal. Two opposite triangles like those painted on Andrew's home."

The mystical supernatural, the secret of occult prophecies, the powers of God and Evil and the material living world, were the keystone to opening this mysterious treasure of our poor existence.

A brush of truth, hidden in the dark time, was stroking the obscure canvas, uncovering forever the true meaning of life.

Tanis's portrait in Port Hurdy was irrevocably concluded, without the clear awareness of her last achievement. The eye of the universe was watching one of the most spectacular events in the world, never seen before in the history of mankind. There in a little black dot, deep like our macrocosm, the eye of eternal life. Tanis dropped the brush and fell into a state of unconsciousness that saved her life (she was spared for not watching the eyes of the universe); her body slowly touched the floor, while the brush was splashing the residual paints on the walls. A face of the past was turning around, looking for familiar faces, delicate on her velvety hands, moving in a leisurely, regal sloshing walking.

Two eyes scanning the depiction of modern life merged in the essence of the eternal past, sentencing the unrestrainable sound of time; a door of colorful delusional freedom, rejected and repudiated by the human art...a silenced masterpiece of genesis's creator undisputed of itself, a main cornerstone of the life.

CHAPTER LII

Prophets of Fear

Tanis Devine was the real descendant of the secret Templar tribe, a small group of people dating back centuries, which for some unknown reasons began to venerate the historical Templar cross. Four hundred years of honorable bloodline, passed to her by her father. She was indeed the last of the guardian shamans, oblivious protectors of the prophecy, after her sister vanished. They used to worship a mysterious lake enclosed in a map, from 6 in the morning until 6 in the evening, defending the land from an old, bestial curse legend.

Chan was reading a line to Meredith, working at her office: "Antichrist is a word combined within two roots, anti and Khristos. Anti means against or opposite of (in place of), while Khristos means Christ the Son of God, the Messiah (anointed one). The terminology originated by the Apostle John within the Book of Revelation, calculating Lucifer's coded number in six hundred and sixty-six: 666. John extrapolated the cursed number from the beastly name of the Roman Emperor Nero, the 6 as opposition to the 7 God number and its wholeness."

Music of a lost daze, dreams of Dante's *Inferno*—Claudio found himself in a dark wood. He was walking with his beloved doggie Leon on a narrow trail, going up the mountain at twilight. It was a steep, convoluted, obscure route, resembling everybody's life struggle. You cannot turn back. You must perceive its message of truth.

He was walking in a strange ghastly spell, while the eerie silence of after-life was heard all around. Time was whispering in the wind of the parallel universal existence. Claudio appeared in a clandestine covered area up the mountain, which all of a sudden opened, arraying a little flat clean water mirror. Leon disappeared between the dense bushes, and Claudio could not see him anymore. He perceived…barking loudly from a distance, as a human yelping voice of warning.

He eyed the reddish sunset light disappearing, and the yellow luminescence of moonrise ascending. An old man dressed in a long gray robe was slowly rowing an antiquated wooden raft, showing his shoulders to a little six-year-old girl gazing downward.

The barge docked on the opposite shore of the tiny lake, where the girl approached the land and walked on the water, reaching a small gravestone positioned beneath a tall double-branched tree. The youth could distinguish two dates and a name on it. It was engraved "Lysae" *1610-161…* Claudio could not read the missing number, continuing his perusal on the writings.

He was straining his view, trying to materialize the last digit when he became saddened! A noise of rising water washed away the memory of a dream within the dream, a vision he could now recall. Rome's Saint Peter's Square was flooding, and overwhelmed by the noise of the water, Claudio heard those old Latin words: "*Lacus, illa Lacus*" (the lake, she is in the lake), "*adiuvo, me amore*" (help me my love!)

Claudio widened his irises and saw the beautiful girl reflected upon the lagoon, he revolved suddenly away from the water mirror, but no one was behind him. After turning again his worried vision on the lake, a hideous, natural fiendish shape screamed inside his soul. He saw darkness blinding his mind, running hysterically away from that madness. He was aiming toward Leon's woofing, who suddenly appeared racing before him, in a leafy bedded trail. His steps were crashing numerous dry leaves, echoing within a deafening noise, while an obscure opaque figure was sensed behind the two, advancing in silence without touching the ground.

It was an encompassing oblivious antimatter, absorbing all the energy surrounding the forest. Claudio was outstretched by the sinister shadow, yelling in desperation. He twisted his head backward, realizing that nobody was chasing them anymore, returning thereafter his look to the leafed path! The ambiguous entity dispirited Claudio on the spot. He plunged deep into a lake of foliage, as if quicksand was swallowing his soul, evoking and awakening his dream.

The boy woke up not knowing if he was still dreaming, in a nightmare. In a hurry he washed his face with cold water, looking at the mirror! A water shape figure was framed in his eyes; he ran out of the room and went outside the street. He knew! He had to find that place up the mountain, and above all a lake.

Suarez exited from an old pastry shop near the Tiber River, carrying a well-packed box of desserts ready to be tested at Laura's. A nice bottle of wine had instead been purchased by Maurice, who assisted Laura in settling the table for lunch. It was still a warm September, with a cloudy sky veiled by a low atmospheric pressure. Maurice, watching from the window, said, "I can see the river level growing faster, a water bomb is exploding upon Rome, look at the thunder and lightning coming closer—they are playing a sinister doomed noise."

Maurice brought his hands folded together on his back, as the power went off in a long city blackout. He assumed, "I hope Armando can make it today, it seems outside we have pandemonium."

Suarez reached Laura's apartment all drenched, and luncheon was consumed indulging in the sweets and the wine.

A steaming coffee was served in prestigious china cups, releasing a strong, incensed aroma. Laura was observing her face reflected from the window, bragging a natural sincere beauty.

She was single and devoted to her career, skinny despite her brother. Her short black hair revealed a normal-sized head, adorned by two dark-brown eyes inherited from her father. Armando drew out from his carrying case a bound book related to the most important prophet's biography. He opened Malachy's chapter, pointing his finger upon it.

Maurice watched him and said, "What's happening, Armando! Do you want to read to us about the prophet!" He stared at them and read in a loud voice the entire original name of the saint. "Middle-Irish Mael Maedoc Ua Morgair, Modern Irish Maelmhaedhoc O Morgair. He was baptized Morgair and changed it to the Latin Malachus. Subsequently in English it became Malachy, Malachy Morgair. As you can see now, Elysa and the saint were both baptized with the same surname."

Laura and Maurice were startled—this was another important piece of evidence enforcing the real figure of Elysa.

The cleric added, "I am quite convinced that the Catholic Inquisition saw this as a further sign of doom in the coming of the antichrist—she was born predestined to be the rebirth of Evil, the temptress beauty of lustful darkness. Sealing her forever with the two saints-prophets was at that time the holy solution to expel Azazel (Lucifer) from the world. Only Saint Malachy could have sent back to hell. His malignant foreordained compatriot escaped from the Catholic Ireland (suffering the heretic Protestant curse), and concealed in Catholic Spain to spread the blasphemy of evil."

Armando stood up and went close to the window. The streets were flooded, and a few accidents occurred on the road's junction, while chaos and panic were displayed in front of his eyes.

CHAPTER LIII

The Arrests

In Rome water was threateningly seeping into every corner of the eternal city (the city of seven hills, the Babylon of perdition, according to the Book of Revelations). Water of life and death, water of resurrection and doomed destruction, rain pouring in the mountains feeding lakes and creeks, rivers and seas, oceans and clouds united from sky to ground.

Earth surrounded by infinite lines of streaming water that like slithering poisonous snakes infiltrated the living mortal life.

Laura turned to Father Armando close to the window, questioning, "Why did the church use the two saints' sigils, and not just the second seal—why a saint so far back in time like Malachy the Hebrew?"

Armando mumbled, "They had to unite the Old Testament (Deuteronomy) before the coming of salvation (Christ), with the New Testament and the coming of the final Judgment. They completed the Holy scriptures, unmasking the Evil one forever and sealing the beast in eternal damnation, far away in the water of the universe."

Laura added, "Rome and Vancouver were far away from each other, both in the terrestrial distance, in history and in the past events; but united by a unique vital natural factor of life, the water!"

Maurice intervened: "Rome in the Bible was called the Babylon on the seven hills, Babylon the Great, symbolizing a tantalizing evil female figure devouring the city in sins, the opposite of the Holy Mary, the mother of the Savior. The Evil has always been deceiving God to counter him and win the final battle of existence. It wants to survive forever, the fallen angel, the opposite side of the same coin."

Armando was aware that the truth had to be in opposition to what they always believed. It was not ancient Rome that was chosen to unleash the power of evil, but the youngest and faraway Vancouver, chosen by destiny of time, a long leisurely four-hundred year journey.

While in Rome the discussion was keeping our friends busy, in Vancouver a new alert spread around the city. A body was found in the forest, a female victim.

Jim Carter, the chief homicide detective, held an urgent press conference at the main office. It was a pivotal moment for the whole investigation and he spoke into the microphones, displaying an assuring face: "The body was found by a hiker in a remote place outside the North Shore area, past the Burnaby area. We are cooperating with the Burnaby police at the moment."

A reporter questioned him: "So the killers eluded the justice once again! What can we do to stop their escape—three homicides in a week…inadmissible," Carter replied rapidly, "We have one of the killers in custody! He has confessed already!" Microphones came closer to his mouth…the answer was unexpected.

"What! When did he confess? Why did the police not release such information to the media? Who is he then," the reporters demanded.

The chief said, "We could not release the news because we were looking for the murderer's accomplices, every dog has his day. They are trapped. We were waiting for his confession." Reporters were talking over each other: "how did you find the killer? What analysis did forensics do on the remains? Was she killed in a ritual?" Jim promptly read the forensic doctors' report:

"We were contacted by a phone call, a man friend of the victim informed us about her disappearance. He saw her last at a party with a man. We examined the remains of the burned body, it was consumed with a fire, and the woods used were not of that area."

A question surfaced: "What do you mean, not of that area?' Was she tortured and killed viciously like the others?"

Jim responded, "The wood was brought there by one of the participants; they were having a barbecue. Forensics examined the biological component of the lumber, it matched! That man used the material to burn the corpse after attempting an assault. After catching him, we could compare his DNA on a piece of plastic glove lost at the crime scene and a footprint—it was him 100 percent."

One correspondent asked, "Who is the killer then, do we know his identity?"

The detective said, "We told you everything, we are waiting for his confession about the rest of the guild, we've got them by the balls!"

It was a great moment for the community, and time was running faster. Jim Carter did not tell the press that the killer was an ex-boyfriend of the victim, who was previously sentenced for molesting and assaulting young women. This was the first victim sexually assaulted, different from the others in the North Shore hills. A feeble connection was guiding the investigators astray.

After Carter's conference, Dr. Lewis met secretly with Kevin Mesotti, revealing a disturbing truth: "My friend, what I am going to say to you is a secret to be concealed. You can use it when the time is ready, anonymously." "What is it about?"Lewis showed him a variant in the report: "The victim Darleen Satin, according to the forensic analyst, died choking herself before the fire completely blasted into the house—she was dead already!"

Kevin said, "What the hell! Did she commit suicide?"

Lewis glanced at him, saying, "I personally examined her, and found strong marks in her esophagus, as if somebody strongly pushed something until she suffocated. Smoke just helped. She was killed, my friend!"

Mesotti turned his face and stared at the doctor. "Why was it hidden? Who did that?" Lewis answered, "Jim Carter took care of it…difficult at first to establish the real cause of death."

Kevin said, "This is dynamite, evidence of a cover-up!"

Time, it was all about time. DNA results were released at last, displaying an unexpected verdict. Police enforcement and pool investigator vehicles were ready to roll, rushing with their blaring sirens to Claudio Verallo's house. The braking of wheels, followed by the squealing of tires resounded around the block, attracting the curiosity of the awakened neighborhood. Car doors were quickly and seriously slammed, while brisk steps were striding up the main stairwell. Armed police encircled the back alley, as others surrounded the entire building. Beacons of assorted colors were reflecting in the windows' glasses, creating a kaleidoscopic effect.

Carter was radioing his man, coordinating a possible SWAT intervention if necessary—everything was set up!

The detective's arm slid along his coat, reaching his gun sheath on the left side. His long, slim figure eyed the curtain of Giacomo's bedroom, enlightened by a feeble blue luminescence.

The assistant pounded the gate of the Verallos' principal entrance, neglecting the doorbell, as well as alerting the owner about a critical situation

"Mr. Verallo, your house is surrounded...you and your son are under arrest!" Jim Carter yelled loudly into the speaker. "We ask you to surrender and come forward with your arms raised!"

Giacomo dressed quickly, donning his tracksuit, approaching the porch to open the gate. He thought about some clamorous news discovered by police, when an agent suddenly handcuffed him, asking, "Where is your son?"

The door was ajar, and Claudio, who had just awakened, could not resist peeping in, remaining thunderstruck by his father's incomprehensible arrest.

Carter ordered the cops to restrain the young boy, while his father was loudly pretending a plausible explanation: "What's happening? Why are you arresting us? I don't understand what's wrong"

He replied, "It is routine—do not worry, we have to compare some DNA results with yours." Claudio countered, "What! DNA—you already got our family's genetic samples, I do not get it!"

The officer seemed different this time in his behavior, appearing less friendly and more professional, performing his job. Claudio insisted, as a hand was lowering his head, placing the youth inside the car's backseat, "Please—could you give us an explanation for this absurdity, you are our friend! Are you not?"

Giacomo was accommodated in a second car, divided from his son, talking to him from a distance.

CHAPTER LIV

The Saint

DNA showed on its composition the presence of some parts of Claudio's genes. Not completely present on the samples, but compatible with part of his chromosomal heredity. It was the same for Giacomo, as if the whole family was involved in Andrew and Duncan's cruel homicides. Tony and Michael went to see their family's lawyer, trying to give immediate assistance to Claudio.

The following day after the vehement arrest, Kevin agreed to receive Tony, backed by his lawyer who proposed the officer to submit his clients to DNA testing. The lawyer spoke: "In fact, during the previous blood collection, Tony was with his family in Los Angeles, California, missing the exam." Kevin replied, "Only the homicide detectives can authorize Tony and his family to be submitted to the police's forensic DNA laboratory—our hands here are tied up. This situation is going to be stopped! I can assure you of that. Your brother's arrest is the last mistake of Jim Carter. He is looking for scapegoats."

Tony said, "Carter said they have caught one of the killers, and now he has arrested my family. This man must be stopped, he cannot be trusted!"

Phones and GPS of the arrested were checked carefully, as were those of the witnesses and their cameras. Kevin and Ron contacted the press and photographers, asking them to hold their horses before releasing any hasty or wrong information. In the end, it was not possible for the suspects to have killed! Carter was confused and commented, "Why then was the DNA test positive? Who put it there? Who mixed the blood?"

Tony's and Michael's results revealed a similar situation! All the Italian-Canadian family had part of the DNA involved in that murder. No possible explanations were given; they were proved one hundred percent innocent, and unconnected with the facts—unexplainable to the scientists and the investigators. The only possible scientific answer was that some descendant of their family was one of the killers!

Carter: "The second DNA could be the one of the antecedent killer, murdered thereafter by the new slayer. They could have argued and moved to the city in disagreement, capitulating after. I have no choice now but to release the arrested!" yelled the officer closed in his office. Newspapers did not emphasize the matter, leaving the family out of the spotlight. Too much false evidences had already led them astray.

Isabel was brushing her long, reddish hair, framing her thin face embellished with a contour of tiny freckles, contrasted by dark-brown eyes placed on a small athletic body. She was preparing to finally shake and kiss her released love, going out for dinner and enjoying the tranquility of the beach restaurant on Marine Drive. It was September, and a full moon was reflecting a shining path along the ocean bed, a trail of endless light lost in the enchanted beauty of the dark ocean's horizon.

Claudio was mesmerized by the moon's line, a trail of revelation and love, mystery and hate. The clock of time was calling his soul, playing its ticking, historical forgotten bloodline; the call of the wild spiritual forest was echoing.

His mind was entranced in that vision, while Isabel was conversing with a hushed voice, absorbed by the magical evening. The night was over and Claudio could finally recede in his safe refuge, imposing on his troubled soul to rest in a long, muffled sleep. He motioned, touching some books from his desk that tumbled heavily onto the laminated floor. Some previous drawings of past dreams fell at hand, while he suddenly remembered observing them closer. He saw a smeared, mixed circle of colors, created from nowhere, as if self-made.

He got frightened and frustrated, deciding to doze on the large living room divan, sick and tired of everything, throwing the paper in the trash bin.

The boy had a sleepless, thoughtful night thinking of the only image he could see clearly on the portraits, that of Saint Kateri Tekakwitha. The Saint had a necklace with a cross, holding flowers on her hand close to her abdomen.

He commented the depiction in his mind: "The cross is the sign of God, but also the sign of the mortal life…a meaning of direction and guidance. The cross is aiming north (the North Star), where the light of sunset and the beams of moonrise donated the true light of revelation." Claudio remembered Armando mentioning the cross inside a circle, as an astrological symbol of the earth.

He continued, twisting his hair: "She had colored flowers around her (lilium, fritillaria, and others), two in particular were in her hand—*Lewisia Rediviva… Re diviva* (Revived) and the red rose. It is a warning given by the first saint of the New World, dead on April the 17th Easter time!"

TV News…

"The criminal released a second complete confession last night, claiming he was the only perpetrator of the gruesome homicide. He disposed of the body in that way to confuse the police. He clearly tried to conceal the body as the Spring Mountain Butchers did," the reporter informed. "He could not bring the body close to the North Shore because it was too risky, deciding instead to conceal it in the Burnaby area, in the forest. He was not able to replicate the serial killer's *modus operandi*, improvising a ritual fire…badly staged."

CHAPTER LV PART ONE

Sisters

Laura was chatting with her father after he was released. She longed to hear from Claudio. "Your brother left!" said an unnerved Giacomo.

His flabbergasted daughter replied, "He—what? Left where? Why?"

Her father said, "Don't worry, he is sharing Isabel's place as a student—he is paying with his part-time job at the restaurant. I think your brother wants to quit the university and follow his friend Ryan, a want-to-be detective." Laura puffed profoundly and comforted her father: "Relax, now, you need to calm down. I will talk to him after I finish with you, OK? How did you find out?" After a moment, Giacomo said, "When I was released, I went home and found his empty room. Leon is with him, too."

Laura reached her brother minutes later, pretending nothing happened. She disclosed to Claudio some pictures Armando Suarez found in the secret archive, regarding the Inquisition trial records. She exposed the cleric's plight: "He acquired them when he had permission to consult all the trial's files (in 1998 the Archive was opened). There were some old drawings displaying the tribunal jury and the inquisitors, performed by the historical novelists at that time. Three of them, even if in bad condition, showed some prisoners during the judgment. A date was noted (September the 17th was the only date disclosed, and was a birth-date of the prisoner). It is interesting to see how they were treated and how many witnesses were participating that day."

Claudio in excitement, "Could you send me those pictures with the scanner, please, I am very curious,"

Laura asserted, "Yes, sure! I was going to send you those images right away, altar boy!"

Claudio sneered when understanding what she was talking about. He then answered, "I'll be back home, give me some time to fix things up, OK?"

Minutes later Claudio was downloading the pictures on the computer screen. It was a slow process that saw Claudio's face turning pale: "Oh my God!" Two pictures unveiled a young girl with long hair standing up in chains, she was painted chin-up. The girl had a proud and strong pose, as if she was defying the jury.

The other image left Claudio's heart in pain. The lassie was in front of the jury and her beautiful face was full of bruises and tears, while a little girl was embracing her legs strongly in despair…laying on the ground with a rose left aside. The last image exhibited the women nudged by the guards, as the tiny girl was held by a cardinal, who kept pointing his finger on the condemned. The cleric's mouth was open as if he was screaming, warning the numerous people presiding the stormed chamber.

Claudio's pupils were overwhelmed in melancholic tears, as if he had entered the chamber's tribunal, feeling her love and desperation. Elysa was finally recognized by Claudio: "It is her, the beautiful girl of all my dreams and nightmares. I can finally remember her look in all my visions now." Claudio kept reading the notes on the computer: "Elysa's father was not part of the process, because he was already dead, and a name is mentioned (Elena, her 12-year-old sister), accusing under torture Elysa, depicting her as the only and real witch daughter of Lucifer."

The last paper at the end paraded again two names of the charged heretics (Elysa and Lysae Morgair), while the pictures always exhibited one girl, except for the little lassie upon Elysa's legs. "Who is Lysae, then?" thought Claudio, "if Elysa's mother had died previously?" Claudio's heart was broken because she seemed like a good girl and was convicted as innocent. The accusations were faked and created under tormented torture. His eyes were fixed on the images, noticing the sculptures of two lions beside the court and in front of Elysa. Claudio marveled, "The two lions—my God! The Lions of Vancouver Bridge, the Lions on the mountains range! I cannot believe this," concluded Claudio, presenting the wide pupils of a fascinated dazzled black cat.

The lions were a symbol of justice and holy power to the Catholics, which used to place the statues ahead of the accuser. They were the guardian angels of God's divine justice, with their eyes constantly opened and vigilant. "*Inter leones et coram populo*" (between the lions in front of people) was written inside the judges' court, a sign of church fortification.

In the eyes of Claudio the two Mount Lions peaks of Vancouver became the guardians of the city, facing from the north the accused. Later, after 400 years, the lions came back, roaring from the past in the wilderness of the New World. Claudio was almost ready to sleep when Isabel came back. "How are you!" she asked. Claudio was quiet and silent at the beginning, and only after a few minutes he began informing Isabel about Elysa's identity.

Isabel questioned Claudio: "Do you know about the origin and meaning of the name Elysa?" Claudio responded, yawning, "Not really, honey! But I feel you are going to tell me."

Isabel smirked, "It is a Spanish name, meaning 'consecrated to God! Elysa or Elisa has variants such as Eliza, Elsa, Elizabeta and others. By the way I found another variant, Lysae or Lisa!"

Claudio exclaimed, "Lysae? So it is the same name?"

"No!" said Isabel, "it is a variant. The name has always been used in Italy, Spain, France and England, our omnipresent countries in this story." Elysa, continued Isabel, "has an even older origin, and it is a variant of the Biblical name Elizabeth. It is of Phoenician origin, so that we have the Biblical and spiritual meaning joined."

Claudio countered, "How do you know that?"

Isabel said, "I have been doing some research about your secret mistress!" She laughed, while Claudio was not really happy about the joke; he seemed distraught.

PART TWO

An anonymous document arrived at the provincial homicide headquarters, a concealed report of a possible misjudged homicide. Jim Carter scowled at Roger, furiously brushing the whole desk of the numerous documents standing on it. Carter was now regarded as a bit of an oddity; he had finally burned his career in Vancouver.

Roger said to his boss, "If we leave now there is a chance this document will remain in our custody, but if we stay—"

Carter interrupted, "We cannot stay! A mole is working here, this is a warning! We must leave now and save us a bigger scandal. I screwed up. I trusted Dr. Lewis and the others."

The secretary said, "Those vultures—they are lost without your support, boss, your expertise is necessary to them. They are already in a blind corner." Carter was distraught and planned his dismissal, burning Darleen Satin's document right away. Carter said to Roger, "Listen to me carefully now, you will receive an urgent fax from my family doctor back home, it will say that my mother is sick and needs assistance. She has been ill for years and we can prove it. You will let everybody know, rushing to my office soon after."

While the homicide detective was silently leaving Vancouver, Morris the verger deposed the mysterious image within teak, covering it with a canvas…not to be seen. It was like a curse after all those people were brutally killed, and all his dearest friends died because of it.

Isabel and Michael arrived in the morning, requesting the church officer to scrutinize the image one more time. He agreed, although refused to come inside the room, entrusting them with the key to the teak while waiting outside the vestry.

The boys contrived therefore for a long time, appraising the icon and searching for answers. Isabel began focusing no longer on the image of the girl, but on all that was around her. She ascertained to analyze the front canvas details and the reflected facets in the water, within its angular shades and tridimensional aspects.

The "scotoma-impaired vision" had to be seriously considered on that occasion. Isabel said, "It was spring! It was March! The image is clear."

Isabel showed Michael the brightness of the miscellaneous, assorted colors, commenting, "You can see the position of the sunlight and the height of the luminous moon, trees and flowers around the fragile shape show an unmistakable springtime, as does the delicate light cloth she is wearing. According to the parchments, the two Malachys left Spain at the end of December (unusual for shipping, given the extreme weather conditions), navigating for at least two months before reaching the West Coast. It means that at the end of February they were here in Vancouver." Michael moved his head in a state of appeasement; he was seeing Isabel in a different way, and she realized that.

The female continued, "I feel both Elysa and the shaman's image were here at the same time, sharing the same destiny and mystery, a fused curse of the past."

Michael smiled. "I got a grip now, Isabel. After all, Meredith already mentioned the meaning of spring and Easter…the latter can change every year, it can be in March or April, so why March?"

Isabel smiled even more, as a hint of wisdom enlightened her hearted mind, proclaiming, "In March we always have the Equinox, the same day and the same month always."

Michael kissed Isabel! She replied in astonishment, "What are you doing? Are you out of your mind?" He replied, "Sorry—I am very sorry! I was overwhelmed by your hint and… you are gorgeous!"

CHAPTER LVI PART ONE

The Equinoxes

The spring equinox, the Easter equinox, the pair positioned everything back, closing the room and thanking the sacristan. They needed a break and a good coffee. Minds and hearts were beating and running, like time chasing its own destiny. Michael asked Isabel, "Are you living with Claudio now? Do you love him?" She was flattered, but said, "This is not your business, Michael. It is not relevant to our presence here! Are you jealous of your cousin's private life?"

Michael answered, "No! I am happy for him, but I never understood your relation with Claudio. You two do not look like lovers!" Isabel stopped, turning her face and displaying her long, beautiful hair, while Michael realized with more belief that he was indeed attracted to the girl and ready to challenge his cousin. "You are really weird, Michael! I thought you were in love with your computer—this conversation dies here!" The youth nervously wrung his hands and drove away with Isabel.

Jack and Luca showed up at Meredith's office, waiting for Michael and Isabel to come. Jack was complaining to his friend: "You are always late and careless, if you don't want to be part of this group anymore, so be it! I am tired of pushing and motivating you over this matter." Luca gave a cursory glance at him and replied, "You are pathetic! Remember that we are realtors and not detectives, we are losing too much time with this case, and no results yet!" Jack countered, "You are the laziest person I have ever known! You cannot finish a task, can you? We lost Darleen for this—it was an accident but she died anyway. I wonder how you can be so selfish." Luca defended himself: "I am just tired of this, no one seems to understand that—" Jack interrupted, "There they are—Isabel and Michael, I do not see Claudio!" Luca switched the subject: "Perhaps Isabel got tired of the dude and chose a real brain."

Minutes later they were sitting with Meredith and Chan, she took over: "March is for sure the strongest month in religious and spiritual meaning. It opens the equinox while September closes the equinox, six months. That is why the assassins choose this period—if we think they are real assassins!" "What do you mean by that?" exclaimed Michael. Meredith explained, "We all know that police never got real tangible proof of those hypothetical human beings, and they seem to all of us like ghosts. I want you to believe in facts and feelings you can see and perceive. The DNA is an example of unbelievable coincidence, because our friend Claudio and his family were arrested. Someone mysteriously inserted part of their DNA at the crime scene, yet they said it was of a bloodline relative. I think something above us is working here, something out of our scope, a strong source of historical spiritual energy never seen before."

Friends were fearfully observing each other as the medium was talking: "It happened to our dear friend Andrew Devine and I am sure Darleen's death has something to do with that." Meredith was exhaustive and concrete and all she said was true, as for the evidence and research they found so far. Police were focused on the DNA results, and the special laboratory was completing the elaborate exams on the dead blood they found in the last slaughter. Jack asked, "Do you really think Darleen's death is a mystery? They said it was a tragic accident." Meredith answered, "Kevin told me something classified! It seems Jim Carter is resigning and leaving Vancouver, they found out something about Darleen's real cause of death!" Isabel exclaimed, "Unbelievable! I hope Mesotti will let us know."

The police conference about the DNA was held at the City Central Department, explaining the 100 percent scientific reliability of the test. Dr. Lewis and his team were reading the forensic scientific report drafted by doctors and specialists of the laboratory. Lewis said: "The blood was examined completely, obtaining the mitochondrial DNA (chromosomes usually have close circular structures) which is haploid because only the mother's DNA is inherited. Subsequently the nuclear DNA or diploid was examined (linear and open structure, including forty six chromosomes) because it is inherited from both the mother's and father's DNA." The doctor was describing on the big screen the two double helixes of the nuclear DNA that remained the more complete and reliable. He continued, "The Verallo family is showing without any reasonable doubt that part of the cells, genomes, chromosomes and molecules are genetically part of the found DNA. The Bureau of Criminal Apprehension (BCA) and the Federal Bureau of Investigation (FBI) supported the police investigation, using techniques involving the nuclear DNA, and confirming the results. They even performed the DNA replication or duplication from the original one, which is only possible with live blood. DNA is unique, twins have two distinct DNA." A reporter asked, "What is your final conclusion, doctor, about the Italian family! Are they innocent or guilty?"

Lewis concluded, saying, "Detectives will evaluate this matter again. From my scientific point of view I can affirm that one of the killers is without any doubt a distant relative of the family, who probably moved to North America or South America a long time ago. I was informed that Italian police have already combed through their genealogic bloodline, and nobody was found living outside the country or in Europe.

A TV correspondent asked, "What can we deduce from that?" Lewis responded, "The only likely explanation is the existence of an illegitimate member of the family, due to an extramarital affair or a family secret. A valid hypothesis corroborated by the DNA, a strong one."

PART TWO

In Rome news traveled fast and Italian police partnered with their Canadian counterparts in tracing the DNA of the fugitives. They were genetically testing all the Verallos' distant relatives, commencing from the oldest-dated Vancouver homicide. Italian investigators encountered a brusque, similar case a few years earlier, when to capture the assassin of a teenager they tested the DNA of more than 18,000 residents of a small village. Armando and Maurice encouraged Laura in this particular moment of her life. She looked like a wizened, beaten soul, afraid for her distant kin. Claudio, surprised once again by the news…set the TV on a local channel. A native reconciliation event was organized at the southwest Marine Drive Musqueam Reserve (by the Fraser River and the Golf Club).

Indigenous artists of different first nations exhibited embellished artworks, representing peace and spirituality. One in particular was named, the depictions of Saint Kateri Tekakwitha. The saint was painted many times by different artists, and the portrait Claudio saw the first time was there, carried back from Vancouver Island. The program talked about the saint's beatification in 1980, followed by the saint's canonization in 2012. "We must pay a visit…" said Claudio…

CHAPTER LVII

Oak Street's Nightmare

Jim Carter finally resigned, silently leaving the investigation and bringing with him a small number of collaborators. He was temporarily substituted by one of the detectives from the homicide squad. Nothing surfaced about Darleen Satin's real cause of death. Happy to hear the news, Claudio decided to go running in downtown Vancouver along Oak Tree Avenue, turning left at 66th Street, where he terminated his training. He relented, walking slowly on muffled footfalls, when he noticed a clean, well-maintained building. It was a family respite center for elderly people.

An old man in a wheelchair was staring outside a wide, encompassing glass, decoyed by the youth's unexpected presence. He seemed allured from the view, looking for help. Claudio felt empathy and compassion for the shriveled senior while a big airplane was reflected in the glass in a landing position (the runway was visible from that place).

The youth was approaching the big window while waving his arm, as sunlight was shining upon the glass, shrouding the image with its strong reflection. Claudio saddened when for a moment saw his dead grandpa resembling the senior, it was just an illusion as a distant recall. The elder waved back, showing a sign of positive reaction and communication. He was a very old man, wearing a reverend's garments. For Claudio it was a sign of respect and understanding to a life lived already. He revolved and reached his car, turning on the engine before fastening the seat belt. He slipped his right hand along the belt, inserting it with a clicking noise. He unblocked the handbrake, thrusting the first gear in his manual system. The vehicle moved gradually, parading along the building's window, where the revered was frantically gesturing, as if querying the youth.

Verallo observed a figure approaching the grandpa from behind, choking him soon after with two atrocious burled hands. He was struggling helplessly while blood spurted from his mumbling mouth.

Claudio stopped his car immediately, rushing toward the ransacked living room. The sunlight obscured his view, while Claudio began pounding the glass and screaming for help. Clouds veiled the sun and the mirror showed again the old man smiling with a smirk—he was OK!

"What happened?" exclaimed a nurse outside the building's entrance, "Do you want to see Reverend Oliviero Sosa?" Claudio jumped back in the car in a curious, furtive manner, quickly leaving the place. "What the hell happened there? What is wrong with me?" he yelled to himself inside the automobile, disinclined to admit his precariously unstable state of mind, his sanity. He had relapsed in his miscellaneous allusions, reminders of female sinister hands wrapping around others' necks.

It was the second week of September, and the fellowship went to the outskirts of the golf club at the Musqueam First Nations reserve, for the art show. Jack and Luca drove with Michael and Meredith, while Isabel accompanied Claudio. Meredith told the bunch, "I received a call from Kevin—the boys are back in town! We are officially back in the game,"

Isabel said, gladly, "That is great news. Finally Mesotti recognized our effort in helping the community!" Meredith said, "We were lucky that Jim Carter screwed up so many times, and now the North Shore is fully supported by the Provincial Homicide Squad. The high echelons need collaboration and not attrition." Lunch was consumed at the banquet reserve, so that money could be collected to assist the talented artists; a small additional fee was requested to enter the display, while the group spread around looking for their line of portraits. Isabel found Saint Kateri representation.

Claudio confirmed that was the one he spotted before…scrupulously examining the image. All the details evinced the excitement of springtime, exactly the season when Saint Kateri had died. Some other images of the saint were a copy of the previous icon, although there was one more. A bewildering impression, Saint Kateri had someone eyeing her from behind, as if a simulacrum was added later to the canvas.

Claudio said to Isabel, "On the back—do you see it? Like a little abstract distant shape, there is a girl front-face with a white cloak. She is scanning Kateri from beyond, merged within her feet in a puddle of dark black water. Her resemblance is blurred and tridimensional as if she is coming from another dimension." Claudio turned his face to Isabel and said, "It is her! It is Elysa!" Meredith noticed, saying, "There is a name on the bottom! The artist who made it! Tanis Devine, she was the artist."

Claudio went looking around to find Tanis, asking for the Port Hurdy first nations. One of the leaders confirmed, "She was here this morning, placing the artifacts in order, and probably left the showroom without any notification. Over there she placed another of her portraits—take a look, perhaps Tanis moved to that side." Claudio and Meredith, followed by Isabel, came across the secret drawing Tanis completed, after her stepbrother Andrew was killed.

Claudio's blank stare froze like eternity, isolating from the material encircling world. He was a prisoner of the enigmatic riddles of the past, his mind was lost in love and his heart was dying in wisdom; in the last moment of mystery the eyes of truth were revolving once for all. Meredith grabbed Claudio by his jacket, while he was in dismay, like some loud Gregorian angelical music was playing in his ears. He came back from a parallel dimension and winced. Meredith ascertained, "Reconciliation! We were meant to be here today, guys! A superior power is leading us toward the truth; she wants to be discovered and helped!" "What are you talking about?" replied Luca. "I can feel now more than ever a spiritual intangible essence. I am an insightful medium, I know! Reconciliation is the name of this special event, and we have here today, for the first time, all three images simultaneously!"

A local guide was describing to visitors: "Both men and women could have been shamans (most often men). That big totem shows a shaman raising his hands, while a young girl is lying at his feet. The shaman is communicating with the spirits to heal and save a sick, dying girl. Performance masks and transformation masks were used for their sacred rituals (creation myths, institutional myths and ritual myths). Some of them are scary and threatening, half-human and half-animal," trailing some artifacts. "Transformers appeared as human beings with supernatural powers (great spirits), intertwined with water, fire, earth, and air. Stars, sun, moon and cosmos were always considered heavenly powers above us. The aboriginals had great respect for all the creatures of creation, prone to preserving the natural environment around them. Transformers were like incarnation of the Gods into animals," concluding.

The sun was behind the horizon, when Isabel said something that sparked Meredith's sleeping mind: "It is becoming dark sooner...in ten days the length of light and night will be perfectly the same!" Meredith's eyes opened widely, meeting those of Isabel. "Meredith what is on your mind?" asked Isabel "We got the seal at this very moment! Guys, we got it!" replied the medium. "*Ae Quinoctium*—same night," she added...euphoric. Meredith fetched a well-shaped apple from her bag, incising it in two perfect pieces, and then said, "United and apart forever, day and night."

CHAPTER LVIII

Unsealed spring

The Seal was about the equinox of eternity.

To Meredith, the Holy Inquisition wanted to settle a perpetual seal on the evil heretic witches. It was a Holy Eternal Spell seized forever in the Holy Easter, with the most important spiritual, astronomical and material event (Easter Equinox). The iniquitous Lucifer slammed between night and day forever, without a moment to get free.

It was the perfect seal for the Catholics.

"We know that it is between March 20th and 21st when everything has a specific meaning," concluded the medium.

Michael answered his phone. It was his father: "When are you coming back, Michael? Your uncle is here." Michael replied, "Giacomo is there! I didn't know, I am here with Claudio and we are having supper." Claudio eyed his cousin, careless about the conversation, as Michael continued, "If he can wait I will be there in thirty minutes."

Tony said, "He is not alone, he is accompanied with a lady, his new partner. Be discreet please! Do not let Claudio understand that. OK?"

Claudio distinguished Michael embarrassed expression, "What's up, Michael? My father is at your place?" Michael stared at Isabel and answered, "I was not supposed to tell you, but you will find out anyway—your father has a new girlfriend! She is living at your house since you left!" Claudio's orbs burst out, as if madness exploded from his brain. His mind collapsed on Lidia's final day, producing an unmanageable fury. In a hiatus of desperation he fetched a fork, eyeing deeply his cousin's face, tucking it in his hand. Isabel screamed as soon as blood spurted on the table, attracting the attention of customers, while Claudio was rescued, refusing any help.

"What did you do to your hand? Why—I do not understand that, you must be crazy!" exclaimed Isabel in panic, while Claudio took away the fork from his munched left hand, leaving the restaurant and pulling the tablecloth with him. A noise of broken glass resounded, while Jack apologized to the owner.

Meredith said, in disbelief, "I have never seen anything like that before, how could one inflict so much pain on his own body for no reason?" Michael was sorry. "I did not know what to do… after all he left his father's house for good. The man began a new life. My uncle is a young, good-looking man, a hard worker and a widow."

Isabel said, in disappointment, "There are no excuses for Claudio this time, he went too far; he should be on his own."

Meantime Meredith was reflecting about the spring and autumn equinoxes, and how they marked the midpoints in the sun's movement between the two solstices; it indicated the change between the four seasons, and the four equidistant points in the cycle of the sun through the year (four elements: water, fire, earth and air, seen on the cross). She read, "The sun has a spiritual meaning as we all know, the cycle of life and death. The spring equinox is a time of great confrontation between the forces of darkness and light, creating the opposition needed to attain immortality. The Church could have not chosen a better astronomical event (Christ was announced by a star's comet) to seal Satan forever, where the mysterious presence of the enchanted forest was not lulled to repose yet." Meredith's hands were calmly clasped over her chest, after bursting out her theories. She needed to be able to work under pressure and not get flustered.

Michael arrived outside Isabel's apartment, noticing that Claudio was not there. "Do you want me to come upstairs and check if psycho is there?" he asked her. She didn't appreciate the joke and replied, "It is not funny,

Michael! It is not easy to accept that your father has a new potential wife. We will leave Claudio in peace for a while. I am concerned about his hand!"

Michael, in disapproval, said, "He went to get first aid for sure, what a fool!" when up, Michael asked Isabel permission to stay for the night. She commented, "I don't think it is a good idea, your father will be worried!" He told her, "I am not a boy anymore. I could sleep on the divan if you don't mind, and wait for Claudio return. Come on, don't you trust me?" The girl said, "OK, I will give you a blanket for the night, but make sure to let your family know; they will panic if they do not see you." While the youths settled for the night, Claudio reached his friend Ryan at home. "What happened to your hand? Did a dog bite you? Let me disinfect it and put a decent bandage there, I have an occupational first aid level two," said Ryan. "I thought you were living with Isabel!"

Claudio said, "Yes sure, but I need to change again. Could I stay here and share the rent with you?" Ryan said, "OK for me, it helps both of us, and I don't mind the dog. Sleep here. I can give you a lift in the morning to pick up your stuff, ok?"

Kevin's face was rinsed with fresh water, while police had concluded all the possible DNA tests. They examined both women's and men's samples, even if the blood values found belonged to women (the killer could have changed gender in time or identity, yet blood cells would have remained the same). Ryan left Claudio outside Isabel's, ready to leave the apartment. He opened the door and was overwhelmed by Leon: "My dog, you waited for me all night. Who is sleeping on the divan?" Claudio poked him, "Michael? What the hell are you doing here? Why are you here?"

Michael was speechless, waiting for Isabel's intervention. She said, "I told him to stay! I was alone and afraid for what happened to you last night, that is why he is here."

Claudio glanced and said, "I see! You two didn't lose any time! My compliments indeed—what kind of friends do I have here! I am disgusted."

Michael, playing the part he liked, said, "It is not what you think, cousin! We are just friends—I mean, we like each other but..."

Isabel shouted, "Shut up, Michael! You are making things worse here! Where did you sleep, Claudio?" He turned his look to the window, while Isabel glanced outside the balcony, moving the curtains and saying, "You didn't lose any time, did you? You are leaving me alone, as you did with your father! You are the best at using people when you need something."

Michael found himself in the middle of a storm, gazing at the two angry lovers fighting to the teeth. Claudio replied angrily, "You are the one who replaced me in one night! I better leave this place now. I'll grab my stuff and disappear. That's your rent."

He launched dollar bills all over the place, dumbstruck, packing in a violent manner his stuff. Isabel slammed the bedroom door abruptly, exploding in a desperate cry. She loved Claudio very much.

CHAPTER LIX

Blood Lines

The last trace of a Ravello descendant was seen in the 1795 expedition, and after that a missing link...emptiness. Armando did not want to relinquish in his work, deciding to execute some further researches.

Armando observed, "Napoleon was called the antichrist by the Roman Catholics, when in 1804 crowned himself emperor of France and the Holy Roman Empire. In 1808 he invaded the Catholic Spain, declaring the kingdom of Spain a client state of the French Empire." Armando observed Maurice, and removing his reading glasses said, laughing, "Your Napoleon my dear... was a real troublemaker!"

Maurice replied with a clever smirk, "Who, that little armless man?" Suarez returned to his readings, "Napoleon then set out to dismantle Christianity and create what he called a new docile religion. He abolished both the murderous Holy Inquisition and the index of prohibited books, establishing a new Catholic creed, a new messiah and a new Christian calendar. It was a disaster for the Catholics, which got worse when Napoleon identified Year One starting from 1792, declaring Paris the real holy city, with Rome its subsidiary."

Maurice theorized, "the Roman church tried by all means to hide the most important secret documents from the greedy French emperor—that would explain why the expedition of 1795 showed the Protestant joining the Catholics (Britain and Portugal were supporting that part of Catholic Spain, which continued to resist the French). I suspect that perhaps the last cardinal inquisitor's identity on the West Coast expedition in 1795 was indeed kept secret and hidden from Bonaparte. After his defeat, the holy inquisition was reestablished, but its time was over and the cardinal ended their line of duty, bringing with them the conundrum of the past."

Armando surmised, when Laura joined them: "In translating the biography of the last Ravello, we observed that before being nominated cardinal, he was the bishop of the Holy Mary Church in Gravina, Puglia region (Italy). It was an old church of the eleventh century destroyed and rebuilt in the 1456, after an earthquake. The cardinal's relics and remains could have been brought there later by his family." Laura eyed Maurice approvingly, while Armando pronounced, "I have decided it is time to pay a visit to that church, I feel it is the last chance we have to find some lost evidence. Four hours' driving is not so bad." Armando contacted the main rector in charge of the church, which was collaborative and ready to help in any way.

September the 10th saw Rome under one of the greatest rainfalls of the last century (more than a hundred millimeters of rain in a few hours). Laura had to wear boots outside Saint Peter's, while subways, streets and garages were flooded. TV showed dangerous lightning, strong winds and fallen trees. More than ten people died that day in Italy because of the storm. Claudio was bewildered by Italy's rough weather, while Laura recalled to him, "In Rome floods were simply a part of life in the ancient times, where proximity to the Tiber left a substantial part of the city vulnerable to the river's occasional transgressions. I think water is the conjunction ring between Rome and Vancouver, and your vision was a perfectly prophetic sign."

Claudio asked, "Are you saying I am a prophet?"

Laura said, "Stop acting like a silly boy! How are you now? I am so sorry for your situation. I still cannot believe that Isabel and Michael turned on you, not understanding how difficult it is to accept a father with a new… they lacked sensitivity."

Dawn introduced Armando's vehicle driving rapidly to Puglia, passing over Mount Cassino Monastery and the city of Benevento, a trip to the past inside the mystic National Park of Murgia. Around 10 a.m. the clerics arrived at the church, while old ladies with veils on their heads were reciting with anguish and agony a guttural rumbling Holy Rosary. They entered… hidden framed eyes were scanning their furtive presence. The interior of the monastery had three naves divided by columns with burial capitals, each one with different names. The sacristy held a wooden-inlayed counter, where the sacristan was cleaning inside.

The verger in charge introduced himself, showing them by surprise another little chapel with three naves dedicated to the holy cross, just below the cathedral. "This hidden crypt is now called cathedral's relief. In it there are remains of frescoes of the sixteenth century, and a stone altar of the seventeenth century. It was originally an ossuary liberated in 1633 by Bishop Ricci and transformed into a church. Later, because of conflicts and wars, it became a secret shelter. Some relics over time remained inside the crypt, and under the old altar there was an aged name slightly erased with a date on it," explained the verger in his dialect. All of a sudden the chaplain showed up in a worried rush, exclaiming, "What are you doing, Mariano? You are not supposed to bring visitors here, it is a hazardous area, please leave now!" The verger, taken by surprise, retrieved, displaying a disgraceful look toward the priest: "Sorry for the inconvenience, but no one is allowed to enter down here! And…" Armando reacted, "Yesterday you told me that was possible to visit every corner of the abbey, how come now it is dangerous? Did an earthquake occur last night I haven't heard of."

The clerics directed down, while the priest positioned between them and the stairs: "I cannot let you in—please, it is an order!"

Maurice was fed up: "An order, our Lord Jesus Christ? Who called you from Rome?"

Armando said, furiously, "We have the authority to report you…know that! We can enter every place. Do you know who I am? Armando Suarez is my name!" The strong robust cleric pushed the priest over and advanced, followed by Maurice; they were closely glancing at him while giving him their backs. Armando bent to read, feeling a startled emotion. It was written in Latin: *"hic iacet ultimus Cardinalis Inquisitor de Familia Ravello"* (here is buried the last Cardinal Inquisitor of the Ravello Family), and under it again, Familia Verallo!!! Armando saddened in disbelief, frowning, when noticing an uncanny Templar cross sculpted beside the grave. He drew his hands to his head and said, "Claudio Ravello!" Maurice replied, "Ravello! Verallo! Who are they?"

Armando finally obtained his response.

Cardinal Ravello was Cardinal Verallo, ancestor of Claudio's unaware family from Rome. The bewildered cleric questioned the verger when outside the abbey, "Who called last night? We know someone called after we spoke with him. We can give you a reward for helping us; this is an important matter, my friend."

The man replied, hiding in the corner and glancing around him, "A phone call from Rome late night… I was in the sacristy cleaning, and I heard him talking. Whoever called must be a very important person of the vicariate." Maurice said, "We know that. Who was it?" Armando put 300 euro in the man's hand and said, "There is much more for you—God needs your help, son."

He concealed the bills and whispered, "From the Vatican—they called from there, the priest was talking to a cardinal! The only name he mentioned when saluting was 'Verallo!'"

The priest came back and enquired, "What is going on in the crypt? All that fuss for nothing."

Armando instead asked for the access to their church's archive; they were allowed and went looking for the cardinal's documents. "A parcel of the year 1795 specified that he was killed during his holy mission, and failed to achieve God's will." The papyrus exposed the accounts of local people who were killed, while some survivors were questioned by Captain George Vancouver, who never forgot the memory of that last expedition.

Ravello's name was later banned from the Church, disappearing in the Verallo.

When Napoleon ended the Holy Inquisition, the church took the opportunity to end its unwanted servers, and after the French defeat it was easy to hide the past's crusty secret, closing forever the Inquisition. Armando to Maurice…flabbergasted: "The oldest parchment we found in the parcel is a bizarre papal seal, unclear and different from those issued by the Roman and the Spanish devout. On the back we have a date, March the 20th, 1610, *In aequinotium sigillum aeternum*, the everlasting seal of the equinox."

CHAPTER LX PART ONE

Ghost Descendants

Armando neared Laura, looking in her eyes with his own reflection, "Only those who never die can remember where their eternal spirit once belonged." Maurice lingered in his thoughts, staring at Laura. Armando: "Warn your family and relatives in Vancouver…they are all in great danger." He was engulfed in his concern, adding, "We have to gather all our papers in a unique bundle, before we start losing tracks of our findings. We have not much time left, I fear! This unexpected twist in our investigation is a presage that things could still change and surprise us." Armando, in a talented active temperament, spurred Laura to action; while she informed Claudio about the incredible family descent, recoiling in the church close to her apartment… praying to God to protect her sibling.

Claudio swiftly reported to Kevin. The last expressed: "I didn't expect that—unbelievable! I, too, have something astounding to tell you. Keep it to yourself, we need that secrecy!" He stood up, moving his chair, revealing, "Our dear friend and paranormal expert Darleen Satin was killed. The fire was arson. That is the main reason why Jim Carter resigned."

Claudio dumbstruck, said, "That is a cover-up of evidence—he should be persecuted! The killer got lucky again, I cannot think of that." The officer exhaled, "It's too late to speculate, nobody knows except us." Claudio looked unnerved, while Meredith commented: "Too many surprises—as for our modern concealed schism in Rome, Claudio! It is creating a sort of silenced mystery, the fact that two popes are still alive at the same time."

Evening paused the frantic day, accompanied by a sweet tender music. Isabel was playing the stereo, while Michael was trying to dance with her. She looked sad while embracing her new friend. Her mind was flying on Claudio's dream, as a draft of forgotten love.

Reflecting from his window, Claudio was enjoying a beautiful view, pumped by a melancholic song. Ryan, with a tremulous voice, expressed, "You look lost, my man! You are thinking of her, aren't you? We should get out soon!" A different window displayed a pair working late. It was Meredith, mired in confusion and fear, working overtime in her office, while her assistant Chan was on the computer. Twilight showed on the horizon, while Chan was speaking from another room: "I read an article the other day, it gave me the creeps! It is about a paranormal expert living in the States. You should listen, my dear!"

The medium replied, "Spit it out, I can hear you, so what!"

Chan's expression was grave: "I warned you! It is scary, really scary. This medium named Anna was contacted by a family living in a so-called haunted house. She drove all the way down and spent a whole week in the house, using all the tools to investigate. After a week she left, discovering the real presence of a ghost. The house was freed at first but afterward it came back cursed." Meredith seemed quite annoyed: "Usually they have to return to those houses many times before the spirits are freed. It is not easy." He let out a long, slow puff, continuing: "That is what she did, but nothing changed until the truth came out. A horrible truth! The ghost was that of a girl, but a diverse girl with the body of an old woman!"

Meredith said, disgusted, "My God, what a monstrosity."

Chan, wearing a satisfactory smirk, said, "Yes, especially when the medium saw her! She left the house and followed Anna back home." Meredith's curiosity revived: "Finish it, please!"

He concluded, "She was obsessed and frightened by the ghost, undergoing mental therapy, until one day someone sent her an article from a corrective institute; it was about that haunted house." Meredith noticed twilight falling inexorably. He kept telling, with suspense, "The old article dated back around 1938, when a woman was raped in the house and her baby killed after. That girl was that little baby grown up as a ghost in the parallel dimension. She wanted to be remembered and loved."

Meredith was tense, "Why did she have the body of an old woman?"

He said, "Because her mother killed her for the shame, and died old with no remorse! Anna was found dead last week in Colorado…her head was severed and put on a doll, a baby doll!" The medium felt a cold shudder when noticing the keyboard's button moving on its own, a line of writing appeared in her pupils: "Darleen is with us down here, walking on the black flames of water!" She screamed, falling down.

Chan said, "Hey what is going on? You scared me like hell! I'm Sorry for the story!" She screamed again: "The ghost is here, the one who killed Darleen!"

Chan darted to the other room and helped Meredith, who said, "Look at my computer, there is a writing." "It seems real. Good try. I am impressed but not scared enough!" replied him

She pursued her lips disgustedly, "Do you think it's a prank? Listen… the airshaft!" A mix of unclear voices was surfacing from the channel, as if a crowd was having a nervous conversation. The studio was a sole, little building with no one around or near it. Chan checked the radio, putting his ears on the speakers. The voices were confusedly merging from the air channel. "I do not understand really! I will take my microphone and record it," he said. Meredith noticed the writing erasing. In a moment the noise dissolved, blowing a cold wind around the room. The pair stared at each other, as a supernatural entity exited the building.

PART TWO

Andrew Devine's and Duncan Wilson's funerals were held at their parish in the Squamish Nation Reserve. Friends of the tribes and community members participated at the religious services. A priest from Vancouver's archdiocese gave the last rites to the poor victims. Kevin convinced Claudio and his cousin not to participate at the memorial services, as they were indirectly engaged in the crimes. The boys wanted to honor their friend Andrew, and see if Tanis Devine and her father were there. Meredith, Jack and Isabel instead went to assist the ceremony, supervised by Mesotti.

Meantime, Chan noticed that something on the shaman's artwork was not quite right. According to the documents, Elysa was executed in the spring equinox of 1610 (March the 20th), when the calendar displayed a falling new moon; how was it possible then, to have a rising half-moon, perhaps a full moon, in the portrait? Chan pointed out, "When we have the last-quarter moon phase, moonrise after midnight, only the sunset light can be seen, instead of when it is in the first quarter with the moonrise at midday and the moonset at midnight. The full-moon phase (moonrise in the evening and moonset in the morning) is the best option for the portrait's star positions."

He paused, exhaling, "even if not completely clear, the moon on the portrait is a twice lie." Chan realized, the moon painted on the water was reflected on the opposite side from the one not painted in the frame, like an image reflected on a mirror. The moon was not descending (C) but crescent (D), going day by day in a full moon; a double moon trick well thought by the artist. Chan said in a modest tone, "The moon on the painting… around March 7th 1610, and not two weeks later, when it was almost new moon. Whoever the shaman…was still alive!"

CHAPTER LXI PART ONE

The Head of the Snake

The hand that draw the image based his work on the chronological revelation passed down in time by the natives, 400 years of legendary eyes of tales that witnessed the cruel event, surviving somehow.

Perhaps he or she made the opera after the execution, referring to a previous time. It was impossible to fully understand a portrait made 400 years ago by an unknown figure. It was a complex and tortuous decryption, similar to the one Armando and Maurice were going to perform.

In Rome, the trio was trying to verify all the weather conditions and astronomical positions during all the subsequent trips after 1610.

They were looking for further evidence regarding mistakes made on the first expedition. Father Larry appointed some notes about those trips; although he could not cease his research in Rome, his friends could conclude what he commenced.

Armando explained, relying on his intellect, "The trip has the number '40' sequences as we know, but they differentiate for days and moon phases. It seems as if they were trying to complete something unfinished…sick advised actions we could assume. March 20th -21st 1650 was a decreasing full moon, March 20th—21st 1690 an increasing full moon, March 20st-21st 1730, a last quarter decreasing moon, and March 20st- 21st 1795 a new moon crescent; all different in moon phases and Easter celebrations." Everyone was muffled with dubiety.

Suarez continued, displaying a seared personality: "The March 20st-21st 1770 expedition is missing (last quarter waning to a crescent new moon) because the Protestant English Empire took over the Catholic Spain, and only after the appearance of Napoleon, had England gotten closer to Rome again, making possible the last expedition of 1795."

A comment followed: "at least historical facts are supporting us!" Armando said, "After Cardinal Verallo's tragic death and the crowning of Napoleon as emperor, the church quit its mission and hid everything forever, until Larry the Irishman showed up in Rome."

Laura observed the differences between the first and the last trips, the Sunday equinox and the Saturday Equinox in order. It was nothing strange if Armando had not noticed a prophecy in between, regarding the Old Testament's Saturday, the day of the Lord…and the New Testament's Sunday as the day of the Lord. "It is not an incongruous coincidence, commencing with the 1610 day of the New Testament—Malachy the second, and ending with the 1795 day of the Old Testament—*Malachy the first*. It is a backward historical and Biblical voyage, prepared in a time of prophecy."

Armando stared at Laura, wearing a visceral look because her brother was the new present witness of the past.

"Claudio, witness of what," asked Laura, darning and mending her consumed shrouded lineage garment, thinking of her dear brother embedded in a daring, perilous situation.

Claudio was falling asleep in the dark night of Vancouver. Dreams visited the youth rather late as usual, plunging in an intense sleep of the past, an old remembrance of childhood: the Holy Mary of the Angels Church in Rome (Republic Place, in front of National Street), crowded with children on their First Holy Communion. Claudio was guided inside the cathedral by his loving mother, joining the youngsters divided in two long lines. Grandiose candles and incense created an esoteric atmosphere, while in the center a holy parade was held, displaying a holy sedan for the Virgin Mary. The holy chair was carried by numerous cardinals dressed in red, orange and black colors.

Claudio's mother vanished, while an eerie sinister music was played by a chorus of nuns on a mezzanine. A hooded monk dressed in dark brown was playing an old hydraulic organ; they were shoulder positioned. Claudio tried to peek at the chorus, noticing the nuns endowed with animal feet, while from the monk's robe a wicked tail was moving. The kid got scared and began looking for his Lidia.

The parade was coming closer, and the cardinals were approaching the two lines of children. Hundreds of sacerdotal and boys were parallel to each other, and could discern the lad moving faster, bellowing for his lost mother. The Holy Mary statue transfigured, appearing alive, turning her crowned head toward the child. Her face transmuted, and he distinguished a young girl with long, dark-blond hair!

All of a sudden, a big head of a treacherous snake revised her face. Two profound evil eyes stared in front of the crying kids. One of them was bitten by the snake, which held half of his body out of his mouth, while he was kicking and flipping his legs. The screams were echoing all over the church, while the chorus was playing and the cardinals were walking the monster. One of the clerics was eyeing Claudio, whispering something to him, while the snake swallowed the kid. His voice echoed as if it was burning in hell.

The obscure lips of the Cardinal whispered, "The seal, the seal—close the seal, my son!" The snake moved toward Claudio, losing the holy crown and trying to eat him alive, while everybody stared at him. In the depths of darkness and desperation a hand grabbed Claudio's shoulder, pulling him out of the parade, and running in a bright light of live water. He was thrown with a strong love outside the church, inside the fountain of the Naiads in Piazza della Repubblica, drowning deep down, while his mother's face was watching him going deeper and deeper in the origin of creation. His eyes could see Lidia from under the water for the last time. She was going away, above the fluid, while the head of the snake caged her like a malignant cancer, forever!

Claudio screamed, awakening from that horrible water tunnel of macabre life.

PART TWO

The night concluded, bringing the last week before the autumn equinox. Kevin received a phone call, and quickly directed to the laboratory. The second blood sample's astonishing result was ready. The forensic analysts were staggered by the outcomes, describing, "The blood is 400 years old. We used advanced, state-of-the-art technology (the same used on the relic of the Holy Shroud of Christ), obtaining a similar DNA with some discrepancies. In other words, inspector, the blood is in line with the previous one, a descendant of 400 years ago!"

Kevin was in total dismay, staring at Robert. "How it is possible that somebody preserved 400-year-old blood, and used it after slaughtering those people; what kind of insane professional slayers are those?" Kevin paused, walking tensely around the lab, continuing: "We could assume that someone kept the relic of the cardinal with him, and passed it down over time, until a madman decided to revive his ancestor's memory here in Vancouver."

The analyst winced, surveying, "After all, the Holy Shroud was kept safe for more than 2,000 years, and tested many times; creating an endless debate, and dividing people of faith."

Robert flinched nervously. He said, "This is too much to believe, I think we are going once again off track. We should focus on today's event, perhaps it is a coincidence."

The examiner expressed with a ragged voice, "My friends, DNA testing is the most reliable tool we have today… it is based on modern technology and scientific experiments—no mistake! We have tangible proof!" Mesotti viscerally complied, commenting, "I have to talk to Ron Taylor, see what he thinks. We are pretty loose now to investigate; in a couple weeks a new chief of the provincial homicide will permanently replace Jim Carter, leading the case."

Robert frowned, mulling over the various options, while Mesotti shook the forensics analyst hands thankfully, leaving the building in a rush.

Maurice Fredel donned his dress, while expounding his notion to Laura: "The church, relinquished after 200 years, when Napoleon declared Paris the new holy city of Catholicism. Rome considered at that point passing the blame to the new French emperor and his nation, which soon after was defeated, bringing back the Restoration and the lost memory of the 1610 expedition."

Laura, wearing her form-fitting trousers, winced, "How can we take that for granted? Can we really believe one hundred percent that those historical facts are intertwined with our killings in Vancouver?!" Maurice felt misled by Laura's doubts, and replied audibly, "Larry tried to darn the church's errors on his own, coming through a matter bigger than he thought. He forgot, however, that only a descendant of the bloodline could close the same parentage lineage."

Laura patiently listened, yawning audibly at Maurice's disquisition. She insisted, with a debatable discourse, "OK—I got it, but what do we have to heal or mend? What?"

Maurice was striving with his eidetic memory, saying, "Water!"

Like a slow current of air and fluids, water was drifting the fellowship downstream, in the abyss of damnation.

CHAPTER LXII

Possessions

Loris rapidly contacted his nephew in Vancouver: "Now you know, Claudio! You are the heir of an important ancient Roman family, fallen in disgrace for serving the Catholic Church!" An incongruous hiatus forsook the dialogue. Claudio spoke: "You knew uncle, you always knew?" "Yes, Claudio, your mother was the only one who discovered the truth three years before dying, by means of a cleric inside the Vatican State, whom I never met. Your mother acquired lots of information and important acquaintances there. For being a devoted and pious woman, she gained trust and respect from the new clergy. However, she was still afraid of the old mistrustful religious hierarchy, mindful and guardians of past history," explained Loris, in an epic, fervent voice.

"Who are they? Why after 400 years do people still care? I don't get it," outlined Claudio. His uncle, more than 9,000 kilometers away, tried to sober his vivid, naïve, rebel temperament.

"Time and space have no number to the spiritual world—past is like future and present seems not existing anymore. We are living in the future of the past, as it is right now for us, speaking on the phone." Loris continued: "Lidia uncovered…guidance in regard of your father's ancestors… never revealed to anybody; regrettably, all vanished with her in the secret silence of the church." Claudio apprised his uncle about the unreality of the conundrum, out of time and place. Loris nodded, "Do not forget your dreams, my dear, I am sure that your mom is trying to warn you and protect you; follow her line, a mother's line is always true. How could we possibly live in this displayed material world, without taking into consideration the spiritual unseen dimension of it, something different or even better?"

Claudio was still doubtful despite the numerous evidence he had. Lidia's death almost shattered his faith completely, enveloping the youngster in an insidious sigil of limbo. He attempted numerous times to establish a sort of supernatural contact with his mother, abusing of the intangible realm of plausible chances, without any response or proof from the so-called afterlife. He remained a prisoner of the domain of the possible. Claudio credited his uncle, replacing the receiver slowly and slamming his eyes remembering Lidia.

It was a raining day, March 9th, Claudio was nine years old and Lidia was rushing to the Bethlehem Church in Rome for a special Easter benediction. The little boy was sick with a fever, grumbling and whining. They entered the cathedral, while the din of heavy rain was subduing the squeals and howls of a woman, a possessed girl. The priest was a well-known exorcist who delivered free indulgences and blessings, and when he blessed the young lady, she collapsed into oblivion of obscurity. Claudio was framed with a horrifying sensation, running away toward the altar's cross, as the faithful were trying to restrain the possessed beast. The boy leaped onto the altar and touched the cross… the girl fainted and regained consciousness. She came after close to the little boy, caressing him and kissing him, while people were praising God for such miraculous grace.

Claudio remembered the girl's name after all those years: It was Elisa and she was visiting from Spain. Lidia took Claudio near a little, old black iron cross, said to be a powerful spiritual evil-expeller; The iron four-pointed cross was kissed by Claudio, as he did every Easter time (as an old Roman tradition).

He leaned, and while kissing the cross, pushed with his head the down side of the symbol of affliction. The cross detached from the wall and snatched Claudio's right cheek, spraying vivid red blood all over the dark black cross. The screams reverted inside the house of God! Claudio's remembrance of the past ended with his finger sensing the little scar on his delicate face, and those coincidental names (Elisa and Bethlehem).

"I think it is time for me to visit Vancouver, your family is in serious danger," said Armando, under a numinous red light. Maurice lingered, as if daydreaming, "I do not think it is a good idea! There is nothing we can do down there—it is a waste of time! Think of Larry and his replacement, they are both dead. No way, you should not go there!" expressed the priest in disagreement. Laura countered, "I agree with Father Suarez, he is the only one who really knows what to do! After all, thanks to him we uncovered documents and papers very important to the investigation. Claudio told me that police are using some of our information."

Kevin paid a visit to Giacomo's, forgetting about the arrest of his family. The inspector was welcomed, and was offered drinks accompanied by some snacks, after which they discussed the latest unexpected blood results. Mesotti had never seen anything like it before, not even when working as an investigator in the States.

He confessed, "Part of the blood samples were sent to the States, where I have some old scientist friends capable of deepening the research on that blood, as they lately did for the blood type found on the Holy Shroud of Turin in Italy. Secured in a vault in the Cathedral of St. John the Baptist. The scientists, after years of testing and studying the controversial Christ's artifact, discovered that the blood on the shroud contained male blood type AB, which matched the blood type found on another old relic known as the Sudarium of Oviedo (kept in the Cathedral of San Salvador, in Oviedo, Spain)."

Giacomo marveled, "I see you are well-informed about our holy relics, detective!"

Kevin was flattered, continuing, "the sudarium is a little piece of line cloth, thought to have been used to cover the head of Jesus Christ immediately after the crucifixion; unlike the Shroud of Turin, the sudarium does not display an image, however, it has bloodstains that later revealed the same type of cells found on the shroud. The blood found on the shroud could be 2,000 years old, while the blood type found in Vancouver's last crime scene were confirmed to be one of a living woman, and the other of the same type to be 400 years older. In the end, comparing all the results, they found some strange anomalies between those two samples sent by VPD."

Kevin stared at Giacomo and said, "They found that both the blood types, even if 400 years apart, are so close and similar in the DNA content that could belong *to the same female person-only one person!"*

"How is this possible, for God sake?!" Giacomo seemed muddled, pleasing Kevin to be more specific. The inspector was a practical man, and could not really explain to him all the spiritual meanings bound inside the vital fluid-type. He just said that this 400-year-old blood, according to the lab tests, never died, replicating itself! "What?" replied him, unsettled, "Do we have vampire ancestors?"

It was very difficult for Kevin to fully understand what the experts deducted from their complex research. A human body that was able to replicate its own blood cells and never die, a Nosferatu (unclean spirit). Giacomo was sure there was a mistake, as many times before he had seen on the news. "The man wrapped in the Holy Turin canvas suffered atrocious torture—we know this is true because of the creatinine and iron hydroxide particles found on the artifact, thanks to the latest technologies used by those laboratories. These particles are not found in a healthy organism," elucidated Mesotti. "Blood of any type tends to lose its antibodies over time. While some of them were found on the shroud, even if its DNA was old…badly fragmented; the same aspect was established on the 400-year-old blood type. That person in 1610 suffered a vicious torture, as for the particles found on the shroud's blood, reappearing later with a restored replicated sanguine fluid type. No dead blood can be replicated in the lab, only DNA of a living organism can be reproduced" extensively clarifying.

Giacomo glared at Kevin and said, "I am a Roman Catholic, and even if I do not attend every Sunday's service, I am in search of the truth every day, praying in remembrance of my lost loving wife. I am not familiar with resurrection, but I know that my wife didn't come back, and Claudio died within," in a tremulous voice, bursting in tears.

Kevin apologized, embracing him, while eyeing Lidia's pictures on the walls. He clasped Giacomo tight against his chest, while the vibration of their beating hearts reverberated within their rib cages. The thumping muscular pumps were alternatively intertwined by their human sound of cultural diversity, and past history, united in a unique feeling of reciprocal respect. Kevin saw a photo of Lidia standing hand-in-hand with her little son, on the day of his Holy Communion. Hundreds of children were all ordered in line, while a cardinal's parade was held. It was a wide ceremony that usually was offered by the Vatican, when the consecration had numerous participants.

Kevin read the name of Saint Mary of the Angels Church. He noticed by a coincidental circumstance, a sort of simulacrum impression on a depiction within the cathedral. The aged photo revealed a confusing image, situated above the little staircase, on the left side of the chantry, close to several cloudy hazed icons. Kevin separated from him, shaking his hand and patting his shoulder, drifting himself from the meandered heartbeat of the man.

Afterwards, the officer's pupils redirected on the image, driven by an unseen alluring essence; a dubious simulacrum disguised between the icons, resulting on Kevin's eyes a strenuous exchange of focusing and blurring. Giacomo asked, "Are you ok, did something enter in your eyes?"

"No, just tired, I presume. I need to rest. This case is killing me," replied him, thwarting his nervous actions.

PART FIVE

CHAPTER LXIII

Family vengeance

Tony was a mushroom seeker, and every year used to go along the North Shore trails looking for the good ones. He left after lunch for a couple of hours, parking his car away from the checkpoints. Although warning signs were distributed and allocated throughout the forest, he entered, walking on a path close to the Grouse Grind Trail. He headed northeast, while hikers were walking southwest.

Tony was in a zone between the Grouse Grind and Baden Powell Trails, walking gradually in silence. It was around 5:30 p.m. when he came back southeast, close to the military control point, deciding to linger in the woods. The sun was setting earlier that last week of summer, before the approaching Autumn Equinox. He sounded vaguely annoyed, while the clock displayed 6:30 p.m. It was time to go before twilight. His first steps were hampered, and he could not progress, as if he was bound fearfully to the ground. Tony could not discern clearly, shrouded in the dark, trying violently to heave his legs from the ground. The more he tried to haul, the more his feet and legs huddled like a vise. He began feeling an excruciating pain, while the bones were slowly cracking in a painful serious sound, shattering entirely.

Screams of rending cries were suddenly muffled by a piercing, sharpened-rock nails, penetrating and vibrating his voice, as dirty cold water was poured within. His arms tried desperately to move, when the blades severed his hands. While choking in the water, his lower throat was vertically slashed, allowing the liquid to overflow. His eyes plunged in the marauder's look, emblazoned with spraying ancestral hate…fading, a grotesque voice sighed… Ravello!

Night descended and Lyan was looking for her husband when Michael came back home from Isabel's. She said, "Michael! I thought you were with your father, where is he? Look, dinner is still on the table!" Michael's body tensed, "I have no idea, I was with Isabel. I thought you two were having dinner!" Lyan closed the kitchen cabinet, and moved to the sink, drinking a cold glass of water. She said, "I fear something has happened to him! We should call the police!" Michael knitting his brow, answered, "Calm down mom, do not panic! I know where he is!"

She nervously pursed her lips. "Please call your uncle right now!"

After realizing that Tony was not around, Michael immediately phoned Detective Kevin, querying desperately for help. His father was missing, while a gloomy obscure presence was upon them, watching the universe of windows.

Claudio was peering outside the skylights, reciting his favorite poem, "In the middle of the walk of our life, I found myself in a dark forest, that the straightway was lost." Ryan questioned, "You do really like Dante Alighieri! What can you tell me about his mysterious life?" The youth replied, wearing a taut smile: "This is the first verse of the *Inferno*. I began to follow the poet after my mother died. I was mesmerized by the character of Dante Alighieri of the Republic of Florence and his troubled life in the late middle Ages. He was a Guelph (favorable to the pope) and fought against the Ghibellines who approving the emperor." Ryan commented, "At that time everything was frightening."

Claudio believed within his heart and soul that the intricate and absurd chronicle was not at all a sheer coincidence. He sensed the need to accomplish more, exposing himself on the line of duty, as if Lidia was soliciting for it. In finding the truth about this account, perhaps he could have uncovered the true passageway leading to his mother's afterlife dwelling. He felt naïve and a dreamer, but he had nothing to lose. "Let us do it once for all," said Claudio to himself, looking his image reflected on the skylight's glass.

CHAPTER LXIV

Final Execution

March 20th 1610.

Cardinal Ravello secretly orchestrated the vicious assassination of the shamans' band, and that of Elysa! He assumed a plausible excuse to lure all the prisoners up the mountain, close to the lake. They decided to bless the expedition's return, honoring the spirits of the natives' land. All the elements of the shamans' sect were escorted by Cardinal' soldiers, and a small group of aboriginal warriors began their trip early that morning (the shaman's older son was part of the warriors). They wished to come back before the wraiths of darkness plunged upon them.

The cleric's purpose was to slay all of them upon the so-called Black Mountain, searching for his cursed lake.

"I will let you know when it is time, captain! Be ready to act swiftly before the warriors' reaction. Once they are defeated, we will take care of our business," whispered to Alonso's ears.

As soon as they climbed over the hills, the colonists forced the aboriginal guides to escort them close to Black Mountain, instead of going east of Cypress. The inhabitants considered that fraction of the mountain a place in which dwelled the evil spirits of the elements, and no one dared to adventure the territory before consulting the shamans and obtaining their permission.

The healer ceased the march immediately, ordering the crew to modify their direction. "We cannot keep going this way, it is forbidden! We have to go back to our regular trail, my people's journey ends here," declared the healer, as Pietro advanced between the tendrils of his obscure visions. "Your people have nothing to fear, you are protected by the holy sword of God! Obey the Lord's will and lead us to the lake of discord, I will free your land once for all," presuming.

"You said it, Ravello! Your God it is not ours, and here other entities are working. The spirits of our ancestors are..."

The cardinal yelled, disrespecting the chief, "There is only one God, the only truth possible. Your words are a blasphemy! You all obey now, otherwise..."

Pietro's eyes were filled with hatred, manipulating the situation with his tendrils of deceit. With a blink of an eye he gave Alonso the order to unleash the pandemonium. A fierce brawl started between the armed sentinels and the aboriginal warriors, capitulating with a terrible massacre. "In the name of the Lord!" screamed Alonso.

Time was needed to find the haunted lake (positioned between Cypress mountain and Cabin lake), called by the natives "Black Lake" (under Black Mountain...very dark in his color). Black Lake was chosen for its oval shape, the shape of a seal!

Elysa had to be executed and put in the middle of the lake, to create the first circle of Malachy the First's prophecy, while the lake itself created the second circle of Malachy's the Second's prophecy; forming a perfect oval seal of eternal damnation, where the antichrist could no longer escape. They reached the lake in the afternoon and prepared quickly for the execution. A wooden raft was created by the crew, while two crosses were assembled for the shaman chief and the black witch Elysa. The others were burned at the stakes placed around the lagoon.

"Your will be done," said Ravello, as the chief was crucified outside the lake and set on fire.

His screams echoed among the spirits of the evil past.

Elysa, in tears, put her hands on her abdomen, waiting the martyrdom. She was stripped of her original clothes and dressed in a brown native vest, while showing her hair braids going down.

"There is the woman" said Pietro, while observing the naked sensual body of her. The cleric always relied on his astute intellect, although a diverse feeling was flooding in his mind: "What's happening to my soul—why have you forsaken me, Lord?" The cleric murmured in his tempted mind, lured unexpectedly by the witch. He was attracted by her mesmerizing beauty.

Alonso was shrewd enough to perceive with admonition the pious man's perverse desire. He pretended not to see it, ordering instead his soldiers to build a Templar cross. (The Knights Templar appeared after the first crusade in 1119 and were persecuted and killed by the church after 1318. Templar was unjustly executed for blasphemy, heresy, sodomy and evil rites.) Ravello, distracted by the screams, ordered, "We don't want her to die like our Lord Jesus Christ, or upside down like Saint Peter, she has to be murdered as the antichrist."

Elysa's head was placed at the end of the north side of the cross, while her abdomen was at the center of the cross. Hands were nailed laterally coming down from the shoulders, while the crossed legs were nailed perfectly at the end of the south side of the cross.

"That is your fate, daughter of Azazel! You'll be sealed forever and ever," gazing at her sortilege.

Elysa and a second girl were carried and crucified on the raft, while Cardinal Ravello was reading in Latin the seal's exorcism on the spellbound Black Lake (two little eyes were hiding in the bushes). When at the center of the oval lagoon, the cross was put straight, and all of a sudden a guard disemboweled Elysa (she was praying in pain, her eyes closed), cutting her from the top down and tossing the cross in the water.

A double scream was heard between the air and the water's film, a squeal of malediction and obscenity. A bellow that those concealed eyes would never forget.

He had obtained what the Roman Church desired, and Elysa's blood did not curse the earth, instead dissolving and purifying itself in the water of eternal life. Blood mixed with water reflected the last red light of sunset, while the weight of the wood was slowly drowning down the abyss of life... seen from the sky of our human eyes.

Visions of creation widened from above the open sealed reservoir, as if it were a reel of sin and blood, a sigil of death and salvation. The twilight was descending at last, and the first stars were reflecting on the mirroring pond, creating an elliptical solar system in the water. Elysa's drowning corpse was red like the sun, and the reel of bloody water was spinning around like orbiting planets. "What's happening? What's wrong now? I can see the light of obfuscation!" Ravello interrupted the exorcism and approached the lagoon, discerning a captivating manifestation inside the lake. The Templar cross was resurfacing, speeding outside the exterior, bursting out as a created earthquake of waves of terror. "Where are the girls? Where are they?"

Three circles formed in the water, while the cross was spinning red in blood. Elysa's body was missing and the soldiers started running away from the perimeter; it was past six o'clock, late afternoon, the day of the last equinox of the world, the day of the second and last resurrection ever seen in the universe…a date that changed the world forever.

"Run and save yourself from the fires of hell and damnation!" screamed the guards.

Pietro dropped his book in the water, while the three circles became a seal of life, a solar system of creation and a womb of life and resurrection. The seal, like a human eye, closed its eyelid on the earth, reopening it forever in the universe.

Ravello was reasoning in his mind (the equinox has same night and same day today, March 20th) of a mistake or a conspiracy concocted by his enemies. Silence and obscurity tumbled on the black lake while his blood froze.

Elysa at that moment became unique, binding with the natural spiritual essences, joining the new and old worlds, good and evil, life and death.

The little boy's eyes behind the woods saw the truth, and ran away, far away, while screams of terror resounded all over the valley; a night of terror and darkness created by the unjust cruelty of mankind.

CHAPTER LXV PART ONE

Morgairs

The calliope hummingbird is Canada's smallest bird and symbolizes the spiritual enjoyment of life in its most profound sense of love, and although it has a miniature size, it can travel long distances.

Claudio was admiring one of the colorful birds outside the porch, feeding on the flowers' nectar of his hanging vase. The hummingbird was flying backward and upward, peeking up inside the flowers with its elongated beak. Sunset's rays filtered between the spaces of the fence, enlightening the transparent, miscellaneous colors of the pigmented petals…that like an x-ray revealed its inner reality.

The beak was grazing in a maternal womb, concealing however, the innermost precious nucleus.

For a moment Claudio with his seared personality, relapsed in his thoughts, reflecting upon Saint Kateri's depiction and the flowers held in her hand—close to her abdomen.

All those shards of hints and episodes were creating a predestined jigsaw puzzle of unexpected revelations.

Armando's flight took off from Rome, headed to Vancouver, while Laura and Maurice came back home revising their documents. She was really concerned about Tony. Maurice gazed in her eyes with the reflection in the mirror, saying,

"We have to find out the secret of this historical seal, before is too late." Laura had to restrain herself from contacting the family in Vancouver—it was too early there. Instead she went with Maurice, speculating about the coming of this predicted eschaton. The cleric had his own theories, and the one he liked lately was mentioned by both Testaments: "weather conditions!" he explained, tethered on his escritoire, "Those are signs of the times, as for the disasters of the last decades. Your brother's dream about Rome flooding is proof! Think about north Italy's hard rainstorm (many people died), or the most recent earthquakes in the center of Italy; what about the wildfires in Canada, bringing smoke and destruction? Cold and snow hit Europe and North America, Vancouver's winter 2016 was very hard." Added an unsettled Maurice, "Last week we had Hurricane Mary in the Caribbean and Florida, followed by three strong earthquakes in Mexico with more than 300 casualties," he commented with his passionate knowledge.

In Vancouver, Chan had filtered the weird shaft recordings, as if panning for gold. His device cleansed the noise, isolating the voices. A distant soft lapping of liquids was heard, while Meredith felt a frightening sensation from deep within her heart. Kevin was attentively listening, as if throngs of damned souls were screaming from a close cavern, echoing on a floor dressed with wet silt. Chan elucidated, as if bequeathing, "I don't know where those voices came from, but I invite you to listen and hold your emotions. This is a trip to the past! I am bewildered."

The computer kept playing, while their faces paled in fear. A sound was dooming their destiny. "Hear this, it's Latin. They are in a trial! I heard the words of a powerful man accusing a woman. Hear his voice now and listen to that name!" A suffuse mumbling crowd was despising… Meredith trembled in panic, while Mesotti balanced her perilous staggering.

"Are you all right?" asked the officer. "I feel sick, I am cold! It is cold in here," replied a clammy medium. Chan paused the recording, and grabbed a cover for her. It was warm in the room. Kevin said, "I think you got a virus! You look pale and tired." Meredith said, "Play that recording, please, I want to know!"

Chan continued. Chains sounded tremendously, while the girl was walking. She pronounced, as her feeble delicate voice silenced the chamber.

A tense, young, innocent vibration emanated from an archangel, distorted all of a sudden by the speaker. The power went off and a frightening feeling surrounded the building.

Mesotti, acting professionally, said, "Keep calm, I have my gun ready here if someone wants to play tricks. Activate the lights of your phones, I can barely see!"

Chan, reacting with fear, "Ok—here I am! What is that—my God! I saw a shadow moving back, close to Meredith. Move now!"

She screamed, "It is hovering over my head, I can feel a presence."

The officer loaded his gun and approached Meredith, while the electric power revived. None was there with them.

"I was going to shoot for God's sake, you got impressed by those recordings, how do you know It's not a prank?" said Kevin leaving in a hurry, while the recording vanished.

Meredith sighing, "Chan!" There was a brief silence. She said, "Take a look at my arm! Look at it!" He came closer, raising her shirtsleeve. "Who did that to you? You have a big bruise here, it is a hand."

An invisible, energized entity drained subsequently into the ground, as if the witnesses suffered visual and cognitive impairment. A mark of death was left behind, a plague of the past.

PART TWO

Claudio and Michael were finally reunited, craving to rescue Tony. The duo was contriving an immediate plan, proceeding up the trail.

Claudio said, forgiving, "Let's forget about the past, cousin, we have to rescue Tony before it is too late." Michael replied, "My mother is desperate, I feel frustrated Claudio. What if those criminals..." Claudio mired with optimism: "No, he got lost! The killers are hiding in the city now, not anymore up the hills." He noticed Isabel exiting a car, feeling a sentimental shiver of love, then said, "I leave now, too much fuss here, I will phone you later, ok? Don't panic...do not tell anyone our plan."

Claudio left briskly, while Isabel felt empty and delusional. "Did

Claudio mention me? I saw him running away. Did he say something about—" she asked. Michael, bothered, yelled, "No! He does not care anymore about us, he is just worried…" Isabel winced, "Calm down, Michael, police will find your father." Michael said, reluctantly, "Yes, sure, dead perhaps!" He cried, pushing Isabel away.

After a while Claudio drove to Meredith's, the last was using a satellite programs and 3-D maps. She located three lakes in perfect triangular alignment with the line traced from the Lions Gate Bridge. Meredith surveying: "The sunset's rays and the moonrise's beams point toward Eagle Lake, forming a triangle with Whyte Lake, and a northern lake. Take a look, Claudio!"

He neared, and exclaimed, "Wow! This tiny lake has a seal shape!"

No trails were detected on the satellites, and from above—slightly visible, albeit tall alpine trees were situated around the lake's perimeter…dense vegetation seemed to protect the lagoon from human eyes. Claudio switched his stare between the screen and Meredith's eyes, murmuring, "This could be the one!" while his words slid away from his conscience…

Armando Suarez, comfortably seated while flying, ventured in deducing the unusual third seal. The last was dissimilar despite the others, emblazoned with a Templar cross.

Laura hung up the phone, retaining a distraught and perturbed expression. She was terrorized for her family, whilst Maurice came through with something unexpected. He found on the document of the Pamplona trial a name related to one of the many charges: Elysa was accused. Maurice was reading: "A young novice was seduced by the witch in the house of God, trying to taint in shame the Ravellos' sacred name. The young man was the nephew of the Cardinal… Claudio!" Maurice paused: "Claudio born in Rome March 20th 1590.

Laura's pupils were blinking: "A cardinal and his nephew in 1610 condemned and executed an innocent girl, while a father and a son in 2017 were cursed by an evil prophesied witch. This is not a mere coincidence other than a real event."

Laura speculated, "I suspect the killer for some reason made a mistake, confusing Giacomo with Tony." She then lingered, "Claudio's life is in danger."

CHAPTER LXVI PART ONE

The Gap

Claudio was striving, evaluating his own answers, when finally the research showed some unpredicted natural evidence. Although the spring and fall equinoxes are considered to be on the 20th-21st, the real date when day and night are perfectly equal is on the seventeenth.

Isabel and Jack fathomed that sunrise on March 20th is at 6:30 a.m., while sunset is at 6:40 p.m., making the day longer than the night (12 hours and 10 minutes daylight, 11 hours and 50 minutes nightlight), creating a 20-minute void. Isabel explained, "Tha's because the time it takes for the sun to fully rise and set, which is in minutes, is added to the day and subtracted from the night, and therefore the equinox on March 20th lasts a little longer than 12 hours."

Jack continued, reading, "The earth's atmosphere refracts sunlight within refraction of the sun, and its bending of the light causes the sun's upper edge to be visible from earth several minutes before the edge actually reaches the horizon. The same thing happens at sunset, when you can see the sun for minutes after it has actually dipped under the horizon."

Isabel suggested, "We should inform Meredith about it, this is very important for the investigation. The killers are using those dates for their obscure rituals." Jack said, corroborating, "Yes, we should reunite the group." Isabel wondered, "By the way, where is Luca?" Jack replied, "Too busy with sales, he stepped back."

Hours later, Meredith dashed into Mesotti's office. She mentored, "The church was against any kind of scientific discoveries or astronomical speculation, Galileo Galilei's affair with the Roman Catholic Inquisition is an example. His tremendous ordeal stretched from 1610 to 1633, ending with his trial and condemnation."

"The inquisitors had condemned themselves, letting evil prosper on their ignorance and cruelty. The curse was spreading in the world and no one could seal it, as it was for the long-beaked mask of the Black Death. That is why the church tried so many times with its bigotry to close the curse, without relying on the knowledge of the heretic scientists. They failed, endeavoring to hide an abominable mischief," concluded Meredith, looking unnerved.

She was mired in her extravagant ideas, formulating her own version of facts, discussing within: "Claudio was born on the inaccurate day of the equinox, March 20th, as for his homonym. According to that, they cannot close the curse, the seal. Only a bloodline descendant born on March 17th could do it." It was a fantastic horror tale, narrated in a limbo of uncertainty.

Armando concurrently landed in Vancouver, bringing back the third seal after 222 years. He was a wise man, knower of ancient religious secrets and historical facts. His black hair and brown eyes showed a robust and confident framed face, placed on a vigorous sturdy and well-balanced body, a fifty-six-year-old man in perfect shape and with a good appetite. Armando came to Vancouver for the sake of his friend Larry, distinguishing a clear evil presence in that natural pure place of British Columbia. His eyes caged seriously, foreseeing the tragic events at hand; an instant of battling genesis between the sons of God, eternal conflict of creation.

PART TWO

Kevin, with his professional cadence, "Your father is willing to pay your tuition for the police academy! Are you ready to walk the walk, young man?" said Kevin to Claudio. Robert smiled while flipping his right leg, seated on a desk. Claudio's heart was hammering emotionally. "Is it true, dad? Do you really agree?" Giacomo replied, displaying urgency in his voice, "Yes my son, if that is what you want. I am waiting for you to come back home, your room is still there."

The youth frowned, "What about your new partner, does she live with you?" Giacomo in a swell of embarrassment replied, "She is just a friend, and spent a couple of night at the house. She does not live with me." He glanced over at his son, telling him, "We must go to the airport… Armando's flight is landing in one hour."

Claudio bolted upright, "I cannot come with you right now," he said. "I will see you back home with Reverend Suarez."

Hours later in the car, Armando had his eyes riveted on Giacomo… mentoring. He was sharply observing Armando's full lips waving in wisdom as he spoke, "The equinox diagram is forming a seal of rings: sun, earth and moon going around, and now that you told me about Isabel's intuition, it is clearer. Nevertheless, we cannot yet decipher this outlandish, unusual seal of the year 1610. It is very different from the two Saint Malachy's," asserted Armando. Giacomo's adrenaline rushed his system. He was frustrated about Tony, following Armando long dissertation. "Perhaps it is just an unfinished papal bull, even if to me in confidence it looks like a child's sketch," concluded Suarez, dabbing his lips.

Armando needed to refresh and have a bite before meeting Inspector Kevin, without falling asleep from the jet lag normal disruption.

CHAPTER LXVII

Witches

The officer preferred receive Armando in his office, letting the cleric reveal all his knowledge and deductions about this mystical case. It was not a coincidence perhaps that Armando felt the need to come to Vancouver just a few days before the autumnal equinox (Friday, September 22, 2017). The mystery deepened when Armando spoke about the shrouded figure of Elysa, and the strong supernatural belief that she was indeed the hills murderer.

The officers glanced at each other, choking back their emotions, skeptical about this grotesque figure. On the other hand, Meredith and Chan looked very concerned; convinced of Armando's story. Suarez gave a further disclosure in regard of the meaning of triangles, uncovering the female geometric aspect of the shape. "The pointing-down triangle is not only a female expression, but a more profound internal element of herself, woman womb and female pubes. She is warning us of her rebirth, like Christ in the spring of resurrection!" externalized Suarez, accompanied by his train of thoughts.

He gave some examples from mysterious unsolved cases around the world, such as killings or disappearances without logical explanations, possessions, haunted places or supernatural events. He mentioned the States, Mexico, Europe and even Canada, just to open Kevin's mind, preparing him for the afterlife's trip. The officer was dubious at the beginning… however he admitted the extravagances of this case. Ron Taylor and Robert Jones clenched their fists, bothered by the inexhaustible cleric's speech. After all, who was this guy coming from the Vatican, and giving direction?

After breaking the ice, Armando fired his preponderant theory, a crazy one: "Elysa is still alive, although she was sentenced by the Holy Inquisition in 1610 here in Vancouver! They chose the Spring Easter Equinox (the Vernal Equinox) like the symbol of Christ's resurrection and evil damnation, Day and night forever on the same length, but on the wrong day, the 20th instead of the 17th. Elysa cursed them, and unfortunately the seal did not close. She was bound here in eternity, and now she will be free forever in the spirit of darkness."

Ron puffed loudly, eyeing the ceiling, while Armando let out a soft gasp of surprise, continuing, "Think of the bodies' remains found in spring, think of the hour of death or the way they were killed…she is coming closer and closer, she is becoming stronger and stronger." Armando's voice thundered in a state of exaltation, as if the spirit of revelation was dialoguing within his soul, as a part of the spectators were enthralled by his strong perception and honesty of speech.

Mesotti stared over the officers, surprisingly corroborating Armando at last, "We have to remember the witnesses' confessions, the strength to drag the bodies so far away, the ability to survive without any trace, the sidestep of police and professional soldiers." The cleric fetched the ball, adding, "That girl Claudio mentioned, Tanis Devine—where is she? She knows something or she is something. That painting is important, very important. Whoever inherited and passed the old tale was present in the 1610 event, perhaps a bloodline descendant."

Kevin's mind was awakening, rethinking all the episodes. Armando was right, even if it was difficult to understand completely. He confessed that in the past he was an exorcist in the Vatican, and witnessed more than once supernatural evil possession. The Protestants, too, had their exorcists with their different rites. The priest said that 400 years had passed, and the seal opened completely in 2000, according to the prophecy. Kevin, moving his hand in midair, questioned, "How come people were killed even before 2000?"

Armando inhaled deeply, replying, "Before 2000 the sigil was not closed, but partially open for the fulfillment of the prophecy. Since March 20th 1610 it remained unclosed, waiting for the end of the second millennium. The prophet always talked about millennium (as for the year 1000). Elysa could kill only in a restricted period of time, the same time Jesus Christ waited for the Resurrection, three days from Friday to Sunday (down to Hell), while the witch had three days of life from March 17th to March 20th, bringing Hell on earth. Christ's Resurrection is the only one in history, followed by the rebirth of Evil. Doomsday is coming."

Armando steeple his hands, persisting, "Commencing from March 20th 2000, Elysa was revived by the evil spirit, having more freedom and power to kill from March to September, as Jesus was given power after his Resurrection. Elysa died when she was seventeen."

Wholly unexpected, Ron Taylor lost his patience: "I am sorry guys, but I think you are all having hallucinations here, what's wrong with you? What are we doing here, an exorcism!? This is it!? Do you think the homicide bureau will follow this nonsense? No disrespect for you, Father Armando, who came all this way down here, but I think this is a horror fairy tale, nothing more." Robert placed his arm on Taylor's shoulder, trying to sober the officer, who in a state of frustration abruptly left the office. He slammed the entry door, leaving quickly in a state of delirium. He could not stand Mesotti believing in those fantasies…he was dumbstruck.

Robert said, apologetically, "I think Taylor is tired and nervous! You know, the new homicide chief was assigned a few days ago, and a storm is coming!" Mesotti flabbergasted, "I was not informed! I did not expect a replacement so soon—anyway, I have something to include in our line here." Everybody was seated while a friend brought some coffee from the coffee shop. Kevin speculated, introducing some technical aspects, easing down a bit on the supernatural elements. He spoke about the two different methods of executing, and how they switched after 2000.

Armando, overlapping again the inspector, affirmed that Elysa before 2000 was murdering in memory of her painful past. "She memorized in time the painful tortures and assassinations, using by natural instinct her reborn ruthless revenge, until the completed resurrection of the new timeless Elysa. After that, in 2000, she received the perpetual evil spirit of hate, beginning a new visceral hunt on humankind. The only feature I cannot fully understand, from my humble spiritual and theological knowledge, is how Satan could resurrect a dead body, if only God is the creator of the universe," affirmed Armando. "There must be another truth that we cannot comprehend, the final revelation of the eschaton."

Kevin countered, "Does the Bible not affirm that Lucifer was once an Angel of God… made by the same essence and cast into hell after its rebellion?"

"Yes!" answered Armando. "But only God gave life with the holy spirit (without sin), and afterward resurrected himself with the same spirit of eternal life. Lucifer could only create a sinful reverse resurrection in eternal damnation—a reanimation of a living dying body, perhaps?"

Kevin was perplexed and lost, while Armando was indoctrinating him, revealing that the world had never seen such a thing. It was just a theoretical disquisition.

CHAPTER LXVIII

Letters of Fate

The long day was over, and before falling asleep Armando reflected on Maurice's theory in regard to the split personality of Elysa and Lysae…the last was seen as a stork image, black and white.

Only on some documents did this second mysterious name appear, with no date of birth. Suarez was focusing on Lysa, while the minutes ticked. "Who is she? Elysa's mother died, while her little sister Elena disappeared after the process. No documents mentioned Elysa's aunt or other relatives. Why had the 1610 exiled document contained either of those names?" Armando trailed off, a load of torment. Lysae was like a ghost, hiding somewhere.

A glorious knight was riding his horse, wielding a mighty, long shining sword, while protecting his body with a triangular white shield adorned with a red equal cross. The shield was turned from one side to the other, unchanging the cross in the alternating triangles. A Y letter in the middle of the shield divided the protection in three trilateral formations, each with a letter within. When the metal triangular screen was pointing downward, the two Y letters were positioned in the lower part, and a third W on top. But when reversed, the W shifted into an M. The warrior was approaching, displaying a frightening crash helmet, followed by a glorious, framed fighting armor.

An epic music was bursting within the woods, overwhelming the New World. The paladin was galloping to attack, defending two strong female arms wrapped around his abdomen, seated behind the soldier. Dust and dirt were kicked, scattered in the air by the horse's hoofing, striding on the glorious north mountain trail. The sharpened blade slipped high in the thin air, cutting a dense wall of mist, after plunging thereafter transversally with momentum upon Kevin's neck. His head was completely chopped at once!

A slow and deep violent sound reverberated in his auricles, as a succession of splitting nerves, muscle fibers, tendons and blood vessels; the noise of ropes diverged under a nervous tension. The blade spattered a cloud of reddish blood pouring on the green leaves, as a raining horror, as the broadsword's trajectory formed an ascending hyperbola, accompanying the hurling and rolling severed cranium in the sky. The dissected headless corpse was standing immobilized, blinded by the vision of life-and-death transition.

A fountain of blood was gushing from his neck, nurturing the eager terrain within his consumed life. His dying eyes were rotating from above, seeing the chevalier running away from the back, and a young lassie with long, dark-blond hair grasping him. For a moment the girl revolved her face, eyeing with a feral look the pupils of the flying skull. She was dressed in a white smeared robe with a look of sensual ambiguous charm, a whisper of love and hate blown by the wind of despair. The buoyant head fell heavily on the neck, banging with a contorted splash against the broken side, performing the last beat of the eyelids.

The iris's blurred vision discerned the horseman entering a church shrouded in flames, as outside the pillared temple two lions on guard were roaring furiously. The two burst in the fire of hell, followed by a chorus of innumerable agonizing screams of afterlife damnation. The cranium was balancing on the body, plunging soon after onto the ground with a closing thud... darkness at last.

Kevin awakened from his unexpected nightmare, meeting at the end his Knights Templar warning. "Holy Jesus, I thought I was going to die! Too much of this affair, I need to take a break. Dreams are like snores and farts, they remain in bed," the cop pointed out ironically, showing a less sarcastic glance after all.

⁂

The letter Y, caged and protected within Elysa's and Lysae's names, had a recondite and earnest meaning; it was a predestined symbol of inner resolution and profound wisdom. In mathematics is an incognita (mystery) associated with the number 12 (6-6) and placed in the 24th (6-6-6-6) position of the Italian Roman alphabet. Y has a spiritual connection with the tree, given its shape. Moreover it resembles a cross that unites the male and female, opposing. The three extremities equalize the number 3.

Kevin recollected his dreadful dream, and in particular the letter impressed on the Templar shield. He was muttering in his reattached head, as if heaving a massive load up. "We have to focus on the female being, and the shield to consider, is the one pointing downward. We have two Y as two girls, and the W could signify the females united! Yes, sure! But why when reversed is it so unclear and ambiguous?" The officer hauled his hair around his fingertips, feeling a sense of uncertainty.

Why had he experienced that haunted nightmare upon the North Shore hills? A warning or a message perhaps…He continued, perturbed, looking like a disheveled man: "The upward triangle has two reversed Y resembling inverted tree crosses, and the W is an M! Mother…inverted Mother?"

Appearing like a lanky figure on his shoulder, Mesotti lifted his eyes to the ceiling. "After all, Larry wrote about the possible existence of the Trinity antagonist!" Larry impressed in his writings the following quote: As the Holy Trinity is united forever, his adversary is divided perpetually. Kevin was puffing, closing his eyes like a scavenger collecting his discarded items. He was divided between the practical logical investigation, and the supernatural mysterious research. He left his place, and crouching on his haunches, went to the police station. He was ready to try his new service vehicle.

It was raining, and the streets were streaming with cars, while his windscreen was blinded by the pouring water. The officer squinted, activating the windshield wipers…noticing the formation of rivulets of rain every time the brushes lowered. Liquid rills were creating letters, erased soon after by the wipers. He was clearly reading the alternated letters Y and M.

"I am losing my mind! I am seeing things, I am imagining them. That nightmare was a symptom, a sign of stress. Taylor in a certain way was right!" his car drove away, while the plate number reflected on the avenue water's mirror... Beautiful British Columbia "2Y1-3M6."

Tanis Devine was the last in line, the ultimate blood descendant (born September 22th). She placed with a fishtailing movement, the two portraits side by side for a specific reason: the sacred and the profane. The last seal found by Armando, was instead like a childish drawing. At the center of it there was a cross, a Templar cross. At the base of the cross a line was going down, joining with a number zero...with a little tree inside. Above the cross on the left side there was a letter V, which had the left side thicker than the right. On the upper right zone of the cross were placed the letters *Alpha and Omega...*attached. The only Latin scripture was the word *Sigillum*—"Seal"—on the top.

Launching a fleeting glimpse, our eyes were trying to find out exactly what transpired from the old parchment shrouded in a mystery.

CHAPTER LXIX

Heirloom of Centuries

Michael and Claudio were connected to the Ravello's bloodline with a strangely different destiny. Claudio was born in Rome on March 20th 1999, and Michael in Vancouver on March 17th.

Elysa came to light September 17th, dying on March 20th, disclosing to Maurice the secret of the unsealed prophecy, and the only possible resolution. It was September 17th 2017, the only vatic day for closing the seal in eternity, and the evil created in it. Maurice draped his light jacket, convincing Laura, "Your brother Claudio is the bloodline's chosen one, because he was born when the inquisitors mistook the equinox, and therefore he could..."

Laura perched on the side of the armchair, staring at him. "My God, Laura," sounded a robust voice. She replied, startled, "What is wrong, Maurice!" observing the anguished framed face of the cleric. "I will tell you now about this kind of purification to be performed, I am not sure of the effectiveness of it. According to the Catholic liturgy... wait a moment, 6 is the hour we are looking for." Laura wrapped a shawl on her shoulders, as if protecting her daunted figure.

"You are scaring!" mumbled the girl. "How can we resolve this matter?" The priest silenced, while Laura reacted with fear, as if someone had yanked her hair, when she saw a few numbers on Maurice's table. Claudio 1999 at

6 p.m., was a reverse one like a reversed cross with 666**.** The union of dates, 20th and 17th, was a pivotal fact, creating the year 2017.

West Vancouver police task force received an emergency call from an alarm system detected (6:36 p.m.) near Whyte Lake Trail. The chlorine gas station was smashed from the outside, and the camera was completely off. A patrol rushed immediately to the place where the accident had occurred. The station, close to the Gleneagles community center, had the door shuttered, presenting the camera as broken. The recording of the accident was still intact. What the images showed later was just behind belief!

The few seconds' frame lasted an eternity. A dense-shaped mass of dark water stormed out of the woods, parading in front of the camera…displaying a monstrous creature inside the fluids. Two ebony yellow eyes thundered through the camera, while an open mouth showed sharp, rocked teeth, smashing it. Kevin's eyes sagged, observing the frame. Armando inspected that bobbing horrible savage demon. He was a priest and a man of God; he knew how to recognize those things. It was not a prank, and water was all over the place. Suarez's mind was prepared to glimpse the few seconds' abominable frame.

He hurdled from terror, moving briskly away from the screen, while darting along the outskirts of the building. He was repeatedly crossing his chest in a specific spiritual epic sign, screaming, "*Vade retro Satana*" (go away, Satan) writhing in spasms, as his words ricocheted. Police stormed outside the office, trying to calm the fugitive priest and restore order; he was out of his mind, in the uppermost level of apprehension. He was accommodated and kept safe in the police's first aid nursing station. Mesotti noticed the priest squeezing his holy rosary necklace, clutching it, and reciting Latin prayers of bewitching.

Only later he regained lucidity, displaying his recovered poise. Police believed he was in a state of trance, caused by the scary image on the video. Even if a mysterious phenomenon was recorded, they had to evaluate its real content with accuracy. Kevin regained a kind of calm demeanor, speaking to his men: "We better send the film to the TV lab…they will filter and extract every single bit of camera footage, creating various portraits of the film. I will take care of Father Armando. He is in distress because of the long trip and a sleepless night!"

Claudio was lying on the couch while caressing Leon, trying to gather his dispersed thoughts. He was studying a copy of the third seal, and his hands were slipping on Leon's coat, as his mind was walking on a lake mirror. The youth was reading a note written by Armando Suarez: "The Alfa and omega letters are the first and last letters of the Greek alphabet, and a title of Christ and God in the Book of Revelation. They are used as Christian symbols, often combined with the cross. The appellation of Jesus in the Book of Revelation says: I am the Alfa and omega, the beginning and the end; as for the opening and closing of the seal. The V letter is the symbol of victory used with the palm branch, as Christ's triumph over death. Behold, I make all things new! From the Book of Revelation as well…"

Claudio focused on the prophecies, remembering the spiritual meaning of trees and roots on the seal, ending with letter O. The last was a symbol of grief and tribulations of the crown of thorns that Jesus wore as he died on the cross. Claudio mumbled silently, "It is all clear now in my mind… we have a different seal that seems to glorify Elysa. Whoever mastered this sigil, it is not the same person."

Leon was snoring profoundly, making noises and twitching muscles, distracting for a moment the lad from his work. When his view motioned like a revving engine, crossing the seal again…he saw with naïve simplicity a map seal. It was a cartogram created upon an unfinished bloody sigil, by the hand of a surviving tiny sacred soul, bearer of an eternal united lineage.

CHAPTER LXX

The Unseen

Claudio babbled, when discerning a clear map and not a seal anymore. A triangle was obtained joining the three symbols on the map, like the one spotted from the satellites. The three points (three lakes) were…an arrow (Eagle Lake) a Templar cross (Black Lake) and a circle attached to the omega letter (Whyte Lake). The last was not a letter but a horseshoe—it was Horseshoe Bay. "Yes," exclaimed Claudio, using his versatile brain.

He glided on his computer, and from the satellites he could see how accurate and simple the chart was. The lake he was searching for was close to Black Mountain and Cypress Peak, it was the unnamed Black Lake. Claudio conjectured, glimpsing at Leon, while the blond carpet rolled his eyeballs toward the ceiling, "I finally understood the double meaning of the portrait, the one on the frame with no moon presence, and the other reflected in the water. "Yes!" he exclaimed. "They are completely different with their own disclosed truth."

The portrait immortalized the girl's execution, March the 20th, while the image in the water was a reflection of the girl's mind, of March 7th, a possible day to be remembered in her life.

Black Lake was named by the aboriginal inhabitants after the 1610 historical occurrence, when as reported by the local legends, every year in March the sea eagles were continuously flying on top of the mountain, circulating around the lake, never crossing in the middle. Animals were avoiding the lagoon, neglecting its water supplies… although carcasses were found on its perimeter.

Later in time, natives started dying in the springtime, suspecting a curse by the evil spirits of transformers. From that day on, the myth was passed from generation to generation.

Moments later, a phone call distracted Claudio from his intricate hard work in unrolling the depiction's wire coil. His sister was speaking on the receiver: "Our family has a strong connection with this seal and the cardinal's bloodline. You could cease the malediction with the support of Armando, do you know that?!"

Claudio replied, acquiescing, "The sigil is a map! I think I am right; it tells you where to go perhaps! Whatever is up there, me and Michael…" Laura, taken aback, interrupted abruptly: "You need Armando Suarez, by all means! Do not forget that! Michael? Why?"

It was September 15th, and in two days, according to the prophecy, Elysa would have been revived completely by the evil curse. Claudio had only 48 hours left before the lagoon unleashed its dreadful revenge. After Laura's phone call, Claudio felt alienated from the outside world, blurring his real vision. He was convinced he had to solve the conundrum.

Next morning, September 16th, Armando and Kevin caught the ferry at Horseshoe Bay, ready to reach Port Hurdy. Armando's phone buzzed. "I got an email from Maurice. He says time is closing… September the 17th" Kevin distracted: "How do you figure it out…tomorrow?" "Let me finish, the message is not completely opened!" nervously picking on his phone, followed by an invisible shadow…

Claudio drove his car to Michael's home. His cousin looked sad and hopeless about his father disappearance, a calamitous event.

Claudio told his cousin they had to scout Black Mountain and save

Tony. "Up there we go!" said Claudio with brazen assurance, appearing unhinged, "don't tell anyone. Nobody can help us!"

The boys prepared for the journey of their lives, without listening to Laura's directions. The crisis was climaxing with their intention to approach the forest.

Claudio then ordered, "We'll take a nap now! We need to sleep and rest before going up."

Not far away, at the North Vancouver Squamish Reserve, Morris Harrison was kneeling on the church's bench. He was praying intensely surrounded by a misty solitude. Dante's *Inferno* was finally at hand; ready to strike with wrath and rage, denying the true light of life, as only obscurity veiled the reverse sky of damnation.

Caronte (the ferryman of the dead souls in Dante's *Inferno*) left Dante Alighieri on the shore of the Acheronte River, and took Claudio's mother to the Roman Tiber River. The boy was now in Saint Peter's Square, in opposition to his previous Roman dream.

A legend would come true when the bronze statue of Saint Michael the Archangel at last came to life.

Two wide-open, thumping wings flew upon Rome, snowing feathers of clashing presage, while his majestic holy sword was wielded and brandished, reflecting the sun rays on the Tiber. Claudio distinguished his mother followed by a cleric (Father Larry) and devout people, marching in front of the castle, and aiming for the Vatican. For a moment Lidia revolved her view to Claudio, whispering mute words miraculously transported, and heard by the wind of love: "*Amore mio*" (my love). In a split second, the barrier between the material world and the spiritual universe crossed each other, Claudio wondered, "How come I cannot decide to run and touch my mother, who is restraining me!" Claudio could not decide because he was still alive and not free to experience the real life. He called his mother again and again! He saw Lidia's face turning pale and worried.

People saw Claudio standing there as if for a moment his love had breached the boundary of the afterlife... Love, love of wishing death, of being reunited with his mother once for all within the womb of eternity.

An eerie sensation of free will appeared in the form of obscure watered clouds, framed as dragons flying upon the sky. A slithering rumbled noise was heard inside the river, no more water was flowing in the eternal city: only the long serpent of perdition and temptation, ready to collect his revenge. The horrible snake wisely came out of the river's bed, showing its ruthlessness in swallowing those who were standing on the bridge. A shadow started running toward the snake… dressed like an aboriginal of the West Coast… It was Andrew, reborn in his original soul.

Lidia, from a distance, showed Claudio his uncle Tony, as Andrew with a proud jump tried to pierce the snake, which bit him instead. Lidia was holding a paper seal and was bringing her hand to her womb, mumbling a word: "the baby, the baby," while the snake was beheaded by the magnificent shining sword of the Angel.

Claudio felt free to run and went toward his mother like a thunder, while blood and water were flooding Rome. The battle of the creation was ending in the afterlife, ready to plunge to earth.

The youth almost reached his mother, when he realized that the serpent was still alive because it had three heads (Dante's image of the Devil was a monster with three heads: Judas, Brutus and Cassius, merged in a frozen black lake). He panicked, and in all that confusion could see only the fight overwhelming his dream. He came back to life in a state of bewilderment, with bloody eyes, not perceiving the sensation of reality yet; after all, what was tangible anymore in his mind? What was real was unreal and vice-versa. He had to prepare and go looking for the lost lagoon, comforted and encouraged by Lidia's message, and the encounter with Tony (Claudio realized his uncle's death) and Andrew.

For a moment he thought, "Father Larry! Was he there, too? I never saw him."

CHAPTER LXXI

Dante's Inferno

In Horseshoe Bay, the cousins were driving on the highway's upper level, targeting a possible path they could stealthily infiltrate. They had to reach Eagle Lake directly, continuing on to the unknown Black Lake, where no trail existed anymore.

Michael was reciting a verse of Dante's *Inferno*, assuming a taunting voice, "Abandon all hope, you who enter here," revolving his view on the upper hills…deriding Claudio. "You are not funny Michael!" replied a ridiculed Claudio. That saying was a bad omen…they were just at the beginning of an infernal journey, begun 400 years ago.

Claudio prepared his backpack, bringing with him all the religious objects of his dear mother, averting a trivial Michael: "Not all religions or movements firmly believe in the existence of the Devil, even the church is divided by those who believe it, and those who do not believe it. The only voice we should listen to is the one of the only truth. Christ spoke clearly about the eternal damnation, as the spirit of immortal sinner." Michael spoke with his overestimated loudspeaker voice, "So! What the hell are we going to do up there?! I am only worried about my father, all the rest are legends."

Claudio insisted, as if they were rehearsing on a back stage, "The seal! Even if what you said is true, the seal can be closed forever. The six months must be completed to fulfill the prophecy, and tonight is the 17th, the end of the second equinox, the autumn equinox; the six months embracing the two equinoxes." Michael dubiously persisted, "I am not impressed with your lavish, talkative brushstrokes, Claudio! I am confused about the reason, I cannot see…" Claudio interrupted, "I don t need to impress you! Day and night—same duration, remember… tomorrow is the day!" Michael felt a sudden knot in his gut, a true sensation of fear.

They were silent, commencing to ascend into the unknown, ushered by an inside courage. Michael swigged a glass of water in a single gulp, exhaling: "Up we go Dante!"

Two weeks before the execution, Elysa revealed an important secret to the newly acquired little brother, a secret to be revealed only in July. They went up to the forbidden area of Black Mountain, where they merged in the lake…water of joy and desperation…

Claudio and Michael were ready to meet their fate. It was 6 o'clock in the morning of Saturday, September the 16th. Claudio's eyes closed for a moment, remembering the last day of Lidia's life. He was a kid, and was running on the first floor at his uncle's. His mother was originally from Tivoli, and decided to spend her last days there, between the olive trees and the hills above Rome.

It was September the 22nd, 3 p.m., and Laura was looking for her brother, busy playing soccer with his friends. Lidia asked to see her little boy for the last time…the pancreatic cancer had extremely consumed her.

A warm wind was blowing between the curtains, swaying like sails in the sea, the last trip of a life. The kid kept running in tears, when saw his uncle Loris crying, telling him to rush: "*Corri, corri, mamma ti aspetta!*" (Run, run, your mother is waiting for you!) Lidia could see her son running from the window of the past. It was just a moment, a whisper of life. She was dying of a respiratory failure, and when her son entered the room, people were grabbing her in despair. She had the strength to bend her body, whispering the last word while staring Claudio's eyes… "*Amore* "

He screamed, embracing her. Claudio's eyes opened when Michael put his hand on his shoulder, it was time to go, time to see what life was about.

CHAPTER LXXII

The Challenge

Mesotti caught Tanis by surprise, while she was watering the garden. She seemed uncharacteristically alarmed. "Do you really want to see her?!"

Armando replied, baffled, "Yes by all means, it is a matter of life and death!"

Tanis raised her hands upward and said, "Bless be…the eternal rebirth of Elysa!" Kevin took her from behind, forcing the woman to confess: "Tell us once for all what you really know about the murders! Who is killing up there?" Armando tried to calm down Kevin, who handcuffed Tanis and brought her inside the house, looking for the portraits and her father. The priest complained, "This was not our intention, inspector. She is just a possible suspect, not a criminal! Let her speak and confess what she knows." Inside, a disgusting smell of death and decay made the two men almost puke. It was horrific! In the kitchen they found the dead body of Tanis's father, nailed feet and hands on the chair with rock spikes. His eyes were missing, while he was staring at the portrait standing upward in the room.

Kevin proclaimed, bustling, "Just a suspect? Look here at this monstrosity. You are under arrest now!"

Port Hurdy police intervened, arresting Tanis and seizing her property for investigation.

Armando's heart was pounding words of reflection, "We live in a material world, surrounded by the hiding parallel spiritual dimension. Today this concept has changed, because the supernatural dimension is chasing us, while we hide in our earthly weakness in disbelief!"

At the same time, the cousins were able to elude the soldiers, passing inside a narrow dry creek parallel to the Trail View Point, maintaining the approximate northwest angle direction on their compass.

It was a strenuous, unmarked slope trail, with rocks, pines and blind direction. Leon was their only defense and protector.

Navigating in North Vancouver's wild mountains was a grueling task even for expert hikers, and the lake they were looking for was high and impervious. It was a warm sunny day with a few clouds painted in the sky. Before lunch, with a big effort, they positioned up north, between Whyte Lake and Eagle Lake. A Y-shaped tree, replete with black crows, appeared in their view as an explicit sign of warning.

A majestic ebony raven stood on the uppermost edge of the tree, playing with its hoarse cawing voice. The dark black bird flew…followed by the raucous croaky crows, circling upon their heads in a circumference of creepiness and anxiety.

Michael could not take his eyes away from the birds, remarking, "They are so creepy! I feel we should come back cousin, I want to go home!"

Claudio asserted, "Are you afraid? Do you not care about your father? You never change, you are a kid."

He opposed, slating Claudio's reproaches, "I don't want to be part of this matter anymore. I was so stupid in listening to you."

Claudio realized his hard work was slated by Michael criticism, reacting, "You are a coward, my dear. I think Isabel would be disappointed by your behavior, a man is a man! If you want to leave, you can retreat right now. Good riddance!"

Michael succinctly covered his salient mortification. He responded, "Alone? I don't know where to go now, you are the navigator here! You bring me back."

Claudio did not bother at all, fleeting across the Baden Powell Trail, deciding to continue on the path. They rested for a moment, eating chocolate bars and drinking water, while Leon indulged in its cookies.

Numerous little lakes were around the area, all with different shapes and dimensions; they knew from the maps that keeping on the trail, Cabin Lake was on the west side, close to the track.

Subsequently from there, the only way to find Black Lake was to walk inside the Disbrow Creek, generated at Cabin Lake. Following a southwest direction, the creek merged inside the Seal Lake. It was 2 p.m. when the lads realized it was already late, and 6 p.m. was a dreadful number not to get across.

Michael was in distress, terrorized by twilight's obscurity, while Claudio was not afraid to die, thinking of his mother's death, and the fragility of life. They were there for a reason.

Before Cabin Lake they had a magnificent encounter with a little wild fawn, which Claudio approached. It was searching for food, and ended feeding from Claudio's hands. "What a wonderful creature!" exclaimed Claudio, "So angelic and peaceful—how could it be here with the evil spirits?!" It was one of the best experiences he ever had. Afternoon was slowly emerging, while they were approaching Cabin Lake, detecting the formation of the creek, steep and bursting with rocks. Water was cold and abundant at the beginning.

Michael slipped, falling ruinously upon the rocks, badly twisting his ankle; an unexpected sprain cursed their voyage. "Help me, please! My foot, I broke my foot I am going to die here," Michael cried.

Claudio could not relinquish now, he knew that only by uncovering the Evil one could he discover and believe in God.

Father Larry wrote in one of his documents found in Vancouver that the Devil has been hiding since he was cast out from heaven. His mission before doomsday was not to be uncovered!

Human beings in truth have fear of God and not fear of Evil, as weird as it can appear. For those who do not believe in God, Evil hides with his despicable cleverness, waiting to strike at the right moment.

For those who believe in the spiritual afterlife, Lucifer misbehaves differently, showing them the cruelty of material life, without encouraging God's intervention.

Larry said, "The angel of darkness will reveal himself only in the second coming of Christ, when everyone will follow Jesus. Before that, he will be shrouded in fire."

Every one of us one day...will be in the dark path of his existence, for whatever reason.

Laura personally endured her path when informed about Claudio's reckless, unhinged behavior. Maurice, striving to appease Laura's anxiety, at the climax of her calamitous situation, outlined a few aspects. "The day his nephew died in 1610, Cardinal Ravello was leaving with the expedition," pausing.

"What really moved me—was the fact that Claudio died at Santander, the harbor where the two Malachy sailed. Why was he there? And what kind of accident occurred?"

Maurice had noticed a new detail. Santander had a Horseshoe Bay like the one in West Vancouver, same shape (Santander's was bigger in dimension despite the little Horseshoe Bay in Vancouver).

Fredel was longing soulfully, framed behind his escritoire, glancing now and then at the clock. He continued, "His nephew darted there for a reason, and I suspect that he committed suicide perhaps after begging his uncle to spare Elysa's life. The cleric was described to be a merciless character, convinced of his celestial mission. Not even his nephew could change his mind, capitulating in taking his own life. He challenged his uncle's arrogance."

Maurice's suppositions could not purloin much longer Laura's tremendous inner concerns...she was surrounded by a sparse concentration.

The breeze of the past was surfacing from the water.

CHAPTER LXXIII

Forgotten Symbols

Two opposite bays apart, forming two omega letters, one conflicting with the other. Two ends without beginning, like the unfathomable way of killing of the monster…to be understood in all its aspects and shades.

Many features and clues were given by the slayers, bequeathed on the crime scenes and on the bodies of the victims. Maurice, from his spiritual and religious point of view, acknowledged: "Whoever the executioner… its performing an ancestral revenge on the meaning of life. The victims are tortured and slowly martyred, as if they are dying while being reborn at the same time. Smoke, fire, fog, water, trees and ground are part of the crime scenes where the victims are somehow connected or attached. They all died living, and lived dying."

Laura perceived that sensation in her soul, while Maurice added, "We know God acts on hearts, whilst evil on minds; God is the resurrection and the life, Evil is the damnation and death." Maurice suspected that Elysa's destiny was coming back home from west to east, as if she was thrusting the curse upon the origin of it, speaking to the spirits of the past. Two opposite forces facing each other, and creating a universal balance. Two reversed triangles pointing one on the other, filling the voids of creation.

The end and beginning was finally acquired in the States, at the national scientific laboratories, where the Alfa and Omega showed once for all, startling the scientists in their minds and beliefs. The same occurred for a picture obtained at the film laboratory in Vancouver: a frame of revelation and truth, closing the historical triangle formed between Europe, America and Canada.

Kevin's phone rang! Giacomo was desperate, supplicating for the officer's intervention: "The boys went looking for Tony, adventuring in those dire woods. I am begging you to alert Officer Robert Jones. We need to rescue Claudio and Michael before it is too late!"

Armando muffled his hands on his head, praying to the sky, "Protect them from their fatal destiny—God!" Kevin was tormented, "Why had Claudio not waited for us? What a fool! Initiative is a quality I personally admire in a youth, but when it changes into a reckless, hasty deed…"

Armando redirected inside the building to possess the portrait. It was past five in the afternoon and the sun was setting. He turned all the lights on to scrutinize better the colors and shadows of the artifact. It was his first and last chance to observe the eye of universal… The sunlight created a luminous film on the water, mirroring a blind reflection on Suarez's face. Blood was mixed with rose petals and sunrays, while the pale reflection of the moonbeams divulged a clear vision on what was under water.

Armando could not discern what she was admiring with her eyes, especially with her left eye, until… within the pupils?!

He was having tarnished sight, forcing his iris to go deep inside the black painted dot. The right eye showed the priest overlooking the girl, as if she was painting the future, while a dark sinister figure was approaching from behind. Armando could not turn; it was as if he was embalmed in a spider web.

The eyes were turning to transport him in hell, whereas feeling lost and abandoned, he watched inside the left eye before it was too late; there was hidden the truth, the only truth of the Alfa and Omega, his omega (his death).

Sunset tumbled as Kevin credited the local police, motioning in the house looking for Father Armando, and feeling once again the vibration of his phone, he answered, "Hello Taylor! I tried to contact you a moment ago, I need a favor. Giacomo called me! His son went up the trails with his cousin. I think they are looking for Tony, check and see if you can find them before the homicide squad steps in."

Claudio and his limping cousin gazed upward at Black Mountain's peak. Claudio was prone in relieving Michael's agony, tormented by a swollen foot with a black bruise. He was recalling in his innermost senses, his first unforgettable love. It was when Claudio was twelve years old and his mother became sick during the summer holidays. He was in the beautiful layout of the Puglia coastal shoreline, where the sea is as blue as the sky. Giacomo, given that his wife was seriously sick— decided to spend the last summer of their existence by the everlasting sea. Claudio was still unaware of Lidia's sickness, enjoying beach life and new friendships

The last week of his holidays, he went with his mother to attend a local traditional procession, performed in an church of the eleventh century (the last Cardinal Ravello's burial site). Orthodox costumes and popular historical music created a revival of ancient Christendom. Lidia whispered beside Claudio's ears "One day my love, you will come back to this sacred place, where your blood is embedded in the spirit of redemption. You will be looking for me and I won't relinquish you."

The child could not absorb entirely what Lidia was saying, distracted by the pompous scenography before his eyes. The statue of the Virgin Mary was parading, slowly moving in front of Claudio's gaze, when all of a sudden, like a majestic galleon unfolding before him, he saw a little figure staring at his face.

A sweet little girl, dressed in local costume appeared in the eyes of his heart, a platonic vision of pure innocent love. Claudio erased that episode from his inner mind, recalling it only now in the wilderness, within his free unchained heart. People were enthusiastic in seeing such an innocent, dreamlike love story, ending with the very last summertime of the purity… of blessed children.

Like a sound descending along the blurred stairwell of destiny…her name was Elisa! He was bewildered and caged in his pain—"Why did I forget those memories of my childhood?"

Michael was crying in despair because of his injury, fearing the treacherous night shrouding them in darkness. A thick mist was darkly encircling the area. He grabbed his cousin and stared at his tearful pupils,

Claudio was unhinged, out of his mind, confusing fiction with reality, fear with courage and uncertainty with self-confidence.

CHAPTER LXXIV

Down to Darkness

A dark forest descending through the stairwell of the haunted woodland, as a long winding mysterious path with no answers; a succession of shapes and shadows were running, chased by the sunset's rays, confusing their sanity and beliefs, knowing in their mind that something had been waiting for them.

When they arrived at the westernmost side of the creek, they noticed the formation of reversed trickles of water—as if an opposite pressure force was pushing backward. "The lake!" yelled Michael.

Leon scrambled among the bushes, disappearing from their mystified irises, while cold water was soaking their boots. It was the water lake. Vegetation was soupy and impenetrable at a point that obliged the fellows to pull back, away from the stream. Turning on the left side of the forest layout, they encountered an artifact in the middle of the blurred pine trees. It was an old totem carved and realized in a living tree, just at the bottom of it. No one could have noticed it, if they had not come deep down there, losing their orientation and sense of direction; it was a rough, curved work performed in details.

What they saw was frightening and compelling at the same time, even if a dim light was shimmering on the verge of the branches: a woman with long, loose hair framing her face, well-carved and distinguished. She was resting her shaggy, hairy, rutted hands on the belly of a little girl, facing them with two profoundly sculptured eyes.

She was engraved in a strange position, with her head staring at the ground, as if she was asleep or in a state of oblivion. On the far bottom, a little cross was sculpted (a Templar cross). Leaving the tree from their side, was the key to unfold the little hidden lake, were Leon was abundantly refreshing. They arrived finally around the tortuous lagoon. It was a struggle emerging from the dense glade, while Leon got bushes and branches in his face.

The oval lake appeared in front of their faces. Michael's arm was on his cousin's shoulder…Leon exhausted, was drinking water. Silence reigned all around the little obscure reservoir.

Its color was a sinister black, as if the lake was deep down the center of hell. A weird atmosphere of the hidden past was sinking on the place. Even if the sky was visible upon the lagoon, it was like the trees were closing on them, hiding the last light of sunset.

It was almost 6 p.m. when their watches and phones were drained from their energy, absorbed by an unknown source of spiritual exuberance. They were lost there, knowing that there was not a chance to go back home. Michael could not walk anymore, while Leon was in a state of agitation, releasing strange sounds of wailing toward the water. "I cannot continue, Claudio, I am wasted. You were right—I am useless here, I wish to go back home." Claudio said, "You are just tired—do not worry, I will not leave you alone, we will be back soon!"

Six p.m. on September 16th in Vancouver was 3 a.m. on the 17th of September in Rome.

Maurice and Laura were occupied conversing with Giacomo, eager to hear news about the boys lost up in the hills. Patrols and rescuers were conveyed near the sites, even if after 5 p.m. they were forced to retreat because of the bylaw restriction.

Laura had already indulged in three coffees, staying busy reading the files again and again. Giacomo, on the receiver, said, "Mesotti alerted the police, they are searching the area." Laura replied, "I am very upset with Claudio, I told him to wait for Armando and the others—what a stubborn guy he is!"

The night was closing upon the young fellows, ensnared in the deep dark of the forest. Laura, searching through the DNA results of her family, captured a discrepancy between Claudio's and Michael's values that awakened her bushed—slumbered mind.

She apprised Maurice and said, "According to the DNA results, Michael is endowed with a minor quantity of the Ravello's DNA values, while Claudio possesses more. Our family branches were different in time, and perhaps my cousin has sundry distant relatives."

Laura was obviously on Claudio's branch because of her father, and the fact that Tony was taken by the killer was no longer a coincidence for her. Michael, not Claudio, could have been the only one capable of closing the cursed seal. She was dying for Maurice's opinion, but he was busy reading all the trial documents, and the strange deed about Verallo's nephew.

Laura noticed the flashy tawdry clock pointing out September the 17th! She yelled, in an obliterating, scary manner. "Today is the day! Elysa is connected to the holy seal, sentenced in Europe!"

In Vancouver, Meredith was desperately trying to reach Kevin, while the inspector realized that his cell phone was dead. He then approached the living room, to talk to Armando. Six-thirty p.m. tolled in silence, as an obscure dusk was falling upon Vancouver…a spiritual cloak of darkness. It was almost new moon.

Time had passed since the officer reviewed Father Larry's map of triangles, flaunting the two opposite trilateral with a circle within and the number one inside it. A number two was outside the circle and caged in the triangle, followed by number threes on the angles of the pointing-up figure and number sixes on the pointing-down figure angles.

Larry could not finish his perceived hint on concluding the sealed cartogram, which changed as the time of destiny did.

The figures modified in a discrete secrecy as a more diverse complexity; the triangles shifted inside the circles within the number one inside and the number two in the circles as did the rest of the numbers…

CHAPTER LXXV

Revelations

Claudio and Leon approached the outskirts of the pool, while Michael, cold and in anguish seated on a shaped rock, trying to ease the pain. A masterpiece of life appeared in the easternmost shore of the lake, a mesmerizing wonder of nature…a unique sensational spellbound wood. Two similar trees were facing each other, slightly pulling back as if ready for a battle of love, while the body and the branches faintly bent backward, creating two opposite hyperbolas.

Boughs and leaves on top were coming back, closing in, assembling an awkward dome; a heart-shaped frame opened in the middle.

The bottom trunk of the trees was merged in the water, while the roots were joined in a tremendous crossing… overlapping of grumpy tubers, all trying to feed on the facing trees.

Claudio remembered instantly that the only place where he saw something similar was in his mother's birthplace in Tivoli, inside the famous Hadrian's villa, in an historical olive tree park.

It was called by the locals "the enchanted mystery of life," because at sunset the sun was positioned perfectly between the abdomens of the trees, creating a sphere of fire fusing the trees together. No one knew if it was formed by nature or by the gods.

Claudio could see the gloom posing on the sinuous peak of Black

Mountain, where the reddish color of the solar star mirrored the twin trees on the reservoir. He could corroborate with astonishment his belief that an ambiguous, double-malignant presence was acting within the glen. Claudio distinguished an antithetical divergent exposure of the plant, and began talking to his dog: "Look in front of you, the branches, boughs, limbs and twigs are turning toward the sky, beseeching for the sake of God, while the stand and roots are hauling the tree in the deep water. When seen on the poolside, the branches are imploring the obscurity and pulling the foundation of the plant away from the sky."

Sunset tolled its pendulum in an eerie hush, while the last star rays set upon Horseshoe Bay, filtering between the west angles and shooting perfectly in the middle of three. It was overwhelming and mystifying, seeing those shaky, dark-red sun rays coming from nowhere in the wood.

It was just a few minutes of oblivion and unconsciousness, enchanting animals and human beings alike. The beams began to wobble and disappeared one after the other, climbing in the following encoded sequence: 20-17-7-6-4-3-2-1.

It was a rotation cycle, unique in its formation, revealed by the unknown mystery of the mathematical domain: myriads of more than 400 years of combinations fulfilled by the last one.

Clamor was coming from inside the lake, a distant devilish sound deep in the roots of the earth.

Michael said, terrified, "What is going on, Claudio? Where are you? I cannot see you anymore, please!" He replied, "I am here. Hear that noise? We better..."

Water moved with wobbling vibrations, as if a cold, cynical wind was blowing upon the silenced surface. A sign took shape in the middle of the lagoon. It was a cross, a Templar cross, spinning and creating two circles around. One was a sphere while the other was oval-shaped.

Leon was barking loudly, pushing Claudio back with his head...the dog was protecting his master.

Claudio's eyes could see a silhouette forming on the cross, it was a subhuman shape made of slime and liquids, bringing its hands toward the sky. Fluids became clear and a feeble light was sparkling inside it. Claudio said, "My goodness, what is happening here tonight is just beyond belief. Am I having a new dream?" The fountain collapsed like a waterfall, revealing a girl attached with her feet in the stream. She was slowly walking, sliding in the water, dressed in an aboriginal garment and hair braids.

Moving in a contorted, sinister manner, her hands undid her hair, falling down her shoulders like two sailing, shrouded galleons.

She was enchanting, the girl in Claudio's dreams.

Elysa was coming back to him after all this time.

The youth, dragged by an insatiable unquenchable power, entered the cold lake, while Leon was holding his pants with the bite of its mouth. Elysa spoke without moving her lips, "Claudio, *amor meus*, my love!" (She was reviving in her drowned memory the lost love of her denied life). Claudio, as if captured by the embedded afterlife dimension, merged in the icy ebony water, heading toward her; the water level reached his thighs, diving Verallo's blue hands. Elysa was advancing with protracted arms, releasing a gelid, frigid wind of isolation.

The two were almost converging in an emotional reunion.

She lowered under the lagoon to equalize Claudio's height, when the youth, instantly guided by his innermost instinct, glanced over the liquid mirror of hell. She mumbled a mix of Spanish and Latin words, while trees' rooted legs were walking underneath the lake, connected to the deepest meander of unreality. He felt a shiver inside his soul, wakening from that mesmerizing spell, because his mother used to speak to her son like that. He suddenly put his hand in his pocket, clutching Lidia's holy rosary, and heaving it above his cranium. A scream echoed in the embedded reservoir, reverberating in the lost greenwood . Elysa's eyes transfigured in black water, she opened her mouth full of blood and hate, melting soon after.

Creeping roots from the earth were eradicated from the soil and the trees, converging at the center of the pond. A cross of lumber appeared outside the liquid film, joined by tubers and rocks, intertwining all together. Leaves were falling, while the wind was thrusting all into the circle. Claudio was pushed back by Leon, while Michael was screaming in fear, "Claudio! Get away from that thing, let us escape this nightmare, please, I cannot believe it is true, please!"

The creature was standing on the lake, advancing again with her abominable, unpronounceable entity. Claudio's blood was pumping frantically, as a fearful sensation was gripping his soured throat. A reddish haze was falling on the scene.

An abominable fiend beast was advancing, closing in on them, her legs were made of twisted, slimy roots, intertwined with bloody guts, thumping and pounding in respiration. The upper part was a breathing blend of rhizome, bark and sanguinary innards. The head was a horrific human mask, made of burned smoky wood and wrinkled pieces of flesh, eyes of dark black macabre reality, watching everything everywhere. Foot-nails, hand spikes and teeth were made of long, sharp rocks, screeching in an ominous sound of death.

A hand scratched on her belly, vomiting blood and mud.

Claudio jumped out of the water, running toward Michael, he tried to grab his cousin, hitched by slithering roots around his body; in a moment the beast yanked Michael inside the pond.

Screams of terror were smothered by frozen dark water. His cousin was drowning. There was nothing they could do, framed in the dark dense woods.

Claudio thought, "This is a nightmare, cannot be true. Wake up, Claudio, wake up now!" Michael bellowed afresh when brought to the middle of the circle, elevated after by the fiendish demon. One hand ripped his chest, extracting his beating heart and folding it back. Michael's corpse fell in the pool, disappearing. His cousin felt hopeless in despair, the bulging enchantress was deforming his body, emanating disquieting distortion.

Claudio screamed "it cannot be true! It cannot be real!"

Distant screams were lost in the meander of the dark woods.

Simultaneously at Port Hurdy, Kevin was proceeding in the room, whereas Armando's eyes saw the pupil's sigil reflected in the lagoon. He saw a womb hanging on an umbilical cord, hidden from the front part of the body!

CHAPTER LXXVI

Grotesque Genesis

In the States, the DNA labs had the blood results, bestowing a cell of the same cell. The only possible answer was a fetus. She was pregnant!

In Vancouver, the photogram was extracted from the last picture, granting clearly two little eyes inside the body mass of water and roots, it was a child closed in a sealed womb.

In Rome, Maurice turned to Laura and said, "I know now who Lysae is...and why two people looked like one. Elysa was pregnant because of Claudio Ravello—they were lovers, and that is the only reason why he committed suicide there. She was going to die with his son and bloodline! She had a baby that was killed with her, the seal was the womb!" The seal was a womb.

CHAPTER LXXVII

Ravello

1610, Cardinal Ravello was told by his illegitimate son Claudio (introduced as his nephew, because at that time many sex scandals were secretly hidden) about his intention to relinquish the religious novitiate life and opt for marriage.

His father was furious and afraid to be discovered, shrouding the whole family bloodline with scandals and dishonor. He decided then to use all his power and influence, exploiting his highly important rank in the Roman curia.

Elysa was accused of sorcery and witchcraft, while Ravello put all her closest friend and relatives to the gallows. No one had to know or suspect of the blasphemous affair of his secret son. Peter sent his felonious son away from that discreditable situation, relying more on his illicit second son living in Rome. He was a merciless and treacherous man, a false conservative clergyman who took advantage of the undergoing cleansing accomplished by the Spanish Inquisition. The more extensive trial of all time: The Basque Witch Trials.

Elysa miraculously survived starvation, and was found merged in a pond of purplish blood. Doctors discovered her unexplainable monstrous pregnancy, believing it to be the macabre and sinful work of the Evil one. The cleric thought as for the other that was the malignant spirit to have caused such a sacrilege, and not his son indeed. It was the first time in the history of church to assist in such spiritually evil adultery.

Elysa wanted to survive only to save and give birth to her daughter, striving and undergoing a struggle for life. She did what any good mother could do, protect and nourish her beloved womb. She would never again place her trust in humanity, defending and conserving her loving daughter until death.

Tanis's father paid with his own life the price of defiance, knowing the old haunted legend: "From those protectors of the cross, who dared to glance at the unwatchable (womb), death will rise from the abyss of hell." The old man was deliberately dying, anticipating the revelation of his warrior's soul reborn. Elysa had a troubled childbirth, transferring all the suffering and tragic effort to Lysae, via umbilical cord. Mind and soul were hardly put to the test, reacting and surviving with love and hatred at the same time. Lysae was six months old when her mother died in March, regressing of six months after her prophetic rebirth...that was why September was the last call for Claudio and his friends. The moon phase of March the 20th (1610) and September the 17th (2017) were showing an equal segment, a last-quarter moon cycle closing the prophecy in a dark coincidence, finalized by the encrypted numbers transmitted by the solar system.

Vancouver Black Lake

The beast swiveled, enshrouding the umbilical cord hanging from her abdomen. She was bearing beneath the filmy surface a sealed body, clutching the bloody pulsing cord with her curled, clawed fingers. It was conserved and protected inside the placental seal, moving and breathing with a beating heart. Claudio understood that at the end, the seal was a womb, a mysterious and unforeseen womb. The demon was caressing and kissing an innocent fragile creature, wrapped in love...her placenta. She was dripping blood and tears everywhere, and in all that mystic dark horror, he felt for an instant compassion and mercifulness, as if he was admiring an angel, an angel fallen from heaven. At that explicit moment Claudio remembered the tombstone date engraved in his lagoon's nightmare, a missing number, a zero. Lysae 1610-1610 never born, never died! The Alfa of the east sunrise, the omega of the west sunset…

She was born within her mother's venter world, but dead for the outside material life, reversing after in dying inside the mother's womb and living outside the universe…when Elysa was disemboweled.

Kevin could not locate Armando within the room, noticing for a moment the image on the painting repositioned. It was an optic effect perhaps, and the inspector kept looking for the clergyman.

The lab image in Vancouver disappeared from the screen, while the expert vanished with it.

The blood samples in the States were erased, obliterating the researcher personnel.

CHAPTER LXXVIII

Reborn

The truth was just within their minds, blurred by the confusion of the events, and it was not a fortuitous coincidence. Laura, sensing an essential sound of fear circling the air, was listening to Maurice. "The resurrection of a non-born creature in a dying living mother is the anti-resurrection of life, the antichrist. A seal created by himself and not by the will of the church. The cruelty of man in the name of God defied the Almighty, allowing the Devil, in a tiny fraction of time, to open the seal forever." When dying in despair, Elysa was praying to God to save her innocent daughter, feeling abandoned like Christ on the cross. She lost her faith, and God could not intervene, while the black angel came from the foundation of the earth, saving in damnation the womb.

The profound material and spiritual substances of Mother earth, were joined by the evil spirits of the sacred mountains, giving life from the bowels of the globe. Lysae, beginning in 2000, was reborn completely at her mother's age (seventeen) at the time of death. Elysa, thanks to her daughter's resurgence, never died completely, remaining in the unique limbo status of existent prenatal condition; they were two existences in one, never dying and never living, apart and joined forever.

Claudio could not discern anymore the creatures on the lake, paralyzed in a state of preservation. Everything froze, as if the clock of the universe was for the first time ceased by the sealed enchanted spell of eternal creation. Material time could no longer handle the sound of spiritual eternity. Good and Evil were part of the same everlasting creation, in their opposite meaning, and Claudio was in the focal point of it, in the lagoon of transitional motion.

CHAPTER LXXIX

Martyrs

Midnight plunged on the lake, reawakened from the spell, while in the sleeping Vancouver, September 17TH revealed Sunday of revival.

Elysa was slowly absorbed by the umbilical cord, generating an inverted-genesis process, feeding again for the last time the loving bag of placenta. A big oval sphere was now standing in the middle of the lake, freed forever from earthly bondage. The Zenith Sigil lifted, stirring close to the water's surface, surrounded by a halo of universal energy, whereas inside the transparency of its magnificence—a unique grown body—was sealed in a fetal position.

Claudio was freezing in hypothermia, surviving clutching Leon to his chest. He was in a state of unconsciousness, swallowing his warm saliva and no longer able to speak. He was exhausted.

The entity moved, and two dark-yellow eyes opened suddenly, gazing in wonder. The sealed sphere dove violently in the water like a falling meteorite, vanishing into the deepest mystery of unreality.

A squealing shiver of muffled crying was heard, it was a baby crying.

Whimpers reverberated in the deepest lagoon, increasing and multiplying in a deafening, infantile chorus, enfolded by the density of the fluids;

Claudio could sense the guttural rumble of vengeance, turning his body muscles in a rigid, cold emotion.

Cramps framed his legs, while his tired face became pale and lush with tears. Those children's yelps were piteous cries, seeking a denied justice, neglected by the human badness through the millenniums.

All was swallowed up in the funnel of darkness, disappearing in the blink of an eye, followed by a second explosion underwater, spreading a dim light of the cosmos, dissolving into obscurity.

The Zenith Seal was broken, unsealing all its appalling secrets, divided at last from his original 400-year source of energy.

"Father, all is accomplished!" A voice awakened the numb, torpid consciousness of Claudio, benumbed by the cold woods.

He reacted, trying to reach the backpacks, crouching and snatching his cousin's clothes and jackets, while with his frozen hands, he dressed himself in an onion military-style, adding more socks on his gelid feet. Chills and quivers accompanied the youth in an endless horrifying night, suspended in the limbo of the coming death.

Leon towered over his friend, debilitated by the wilderness of pure nature, while dawn was finally showing at the east, giving them the option to escape from that unreal place.

Their only option was to advance northeast, trying to find the trail and subsequently Cypress Bowl Road. Step by step Claudio was gaining confidence, guided by Leon through the dark woods.

Light was shining from the east as a blissful path of salvation.

He did not hesitate anymore, walking briskly toward the incongruous glint of the sunrise.

Claudio was stripping off his pants, turning nervously back, fearing an unknown backlash. The two clambered upon the cliff-side, overlapping the pass in a staggering rate, arriving at the end on the road! He had outlasted the spawned legend of the shaman's curse.

A military pickup spotted Claudio and his beloved dog on the road, rushing them to the closest emergency outpost on Cypress Bowl Road, at the Cypress viewpoint.

Giacomo and his friends, alerted by Kevin, stormed to the place, where police cars and ambulances were assisting the bushed friends. Sunrise was luminously shimmering upon the blue sky, while Claudio was surrounded and kissed by his family and friends.

Giacomo's eyes riveted on him, asking for Michael: "Thank God you are alive, my son! Where is your cousin?" Claudio said, remorsefully, "I endangered him. We were nestled in the woods and could not retreat. Michael got injured and could not walk anymore," sobbing in despair… trembling.

"We were deceived by the emblazoned seal on the zenith, we mistook everything!"

Giacomo yelled, letting out all his desperation, "Where the hell is he! For God's sake, no! No!" He cried in desperation because he understood by the distressed look of his son that Michael had died! Kevin intervened in a conservative, polite manner, consoling Giacomo and sending Claudio immediately to the North Vancouver Lions' Gate Hospital, "Poor Lyan—who is going to tell her now?!"

Isabel made her way through the crowd, embracing Claudio in tears. "I love you. I have always loved you Claudio!" vented Isabel, whispering in tears.

Claudio's eyes had seen something unthinkable to explain or understand. It was a nightmare, a loving nightmare, like those he used to have as a child after his mother's death.

Elysa died like a martyred saint. When she realized the evil spirit was coming to possess her soul, she refused to let it in, and tried to die, but because Lysae had to live by her love, she could not end her own life, allowing the evil to enter and transform the little innocent creature.

In time Lysae possessed her mother's dead body, using the power of everlasting hell; abandoned and rejected from the same men of faith she used to trust and believe.

Jesus Christ said, "For many will come in my name, claiming, 'I am the Christ,' and will deceive many."

The Zenith Seal, as for the twin trees in the lagoon, had an ambiguous double meaning, fused in one truth. The left symbol (the arrow of Eagle Lake), were also two triangles penetrating each other, united in one. The right symbol (Alfa and omega of Whyte Lake and Horseshoe Bay) were two letters combined in one, as was the Templar cross in the middle. The crucifix was created crossing two distinct pieces of wood, in one. At the bottom of the cross, two roots joined together the center of an oval shape… a womb, with a tree inside; the tree of life (the one Claudio saw in Black Lake) where the witch remained well-hidden for all those years.

CHAPTER LXXXI

Fulfillment

The ambulance was converging on the highway, as the boy was lying on the stretcher closing his eyes to rest. He stayed enveloped in the warmth of the tender blanket. The vehicle's undulation cradled him to sleep, when warm hands gently stroked his soul.

He opened his eyes on the Peak of Black Mountain, admiring Vancouver and the Pacific Ocean from above. It was sunrise, and all of a sudden the sun's rays fired in to the sky, colliding with the zenith of the equator, closing the last equinox of 2017 and opening forever the Zenith Seal—Vancouver, September 17.

The zenith was considered the highest point on the imaginary celestial sphere, in the vertical direction opposite to the gravitational terrestrial force of the nadir, the opposite force balancing the world.

On March 20th, 1610, Elysa died as a victim at the eyes of the Lord, never knowing her child. Day and night were apart forever, as triangles pointing in opposite directions. Life and death chased one another in the "circle" of life, facing love and hate in the middle.

Elysa was six months pregnant when executed, transmuting the remaining three months of earthly expectancy in 400 years of spiritual, apocalyptic sustenance.

By the Inquisition's will, she was taken to Black Mountain to be sealed forever in damnation, without touching the sacred earth. She plunged into the entrance of the gaping hellfire of perdition.

The cleansing water of Black Lake was the only plausible passage from the living world of God to the deathly self-creation of Lucifer; her blood, guts and body were purified forever in water, without infecting the ground. The lagoon was believed by the natives, and later by the Catholics, one of the gates of hell, deep until… *Inferno.*

Cold dark water at the beginning and red vicious fire at the end, which one day would have boiled for the coming of the apostate…

Lysae was still an innocent creature, living in the intangible seal of the universal cosmic water, not able to oppose her pure love to anybody. It was a *final reversed gestation, an inverted resurrection in defiance of God.*

Jesus Christ came into the womb of a hearted Virgin, resurrecting after death as only the Everlasting Spirit could perform. The Fallen Angel finally accomplished what he ever yearned for…in heaven, before being cast out into the earth: "Eternal Resurrection." His evil spirit entered a "living, minded, dying body, giving life to an unborn fetus," generating an antithetical resurrection.

Jesus died and was resurrected. Lysae never died or lived. She was feeding her mother forever to survive. She was in her mother to meet her one day, but met herself when reborn. Lysae was the evil one for the sake of mankind. After 2000, Malachy's last prophecy was fulfilled and she reached her mother's age of seventeen on September 17th 2017; the two bodies united, and Elysa was reborn again in Lysae, always apart.

CHAPTER LXXXII

Family

1609 Navarre, Spain

Elysa was conversing with Claudio two weeks prior the persecution of her family. The young couple desired to contract marriage shortly, choosing to live forever, joined by their coming baby.

She was pregnant, and no one knew about their secret, it would have been an appalling dishonor, a disgrace for the Roman cardinal.

They had to marry before revealing the truth. It was December, and the couple decided to name the newborn.

Claudio placed his hand on Elysa's abdomen and said, "If it is a boy he will be called Michele (Michael, meaning who is like God), if it is a girl she will have your mother's name (Lysae, meaning God is my oath)."

Michael was chosen because in the New Testament, the archangel led God's armies against Satan's forces as reported in the Book of Revelation, becoming "Michael the Archangel." He was the healer and protector of the army of the Almighty against the forces of Evil. Michael is mentioned three times in the Old Testament by Daniel, the prophet.

They stood up from the bench, walking away on the road of creaking leaves, while the last autumn wind was sweeping their destiny forever. A feather was cradling, pampered by a flying cold wind, a dark one.

And I, who collected the black plume of destiny, followed the lovers from far behind, closing my consumed book, and plunging after in a day-mare of never-awakening.

EPILOGUE

The Beginning of the End

Claudio recovered as Leon, leaving the hospital three weeks later. Police searched the area without solid evidences or facts, despite Claudio's feedback and narration of the weird circumstances.

Kevin grinned when listening to Claudio's contorted visions, because he was not confident, even if the lad never hesitated in his version.

Investigators did not find any carved totem, or twin trees inside the impervious, recondite lagoon, it was a very deep little lake, but no more than that. Research into Michael's disappearance was in full-throttle, and police thought Claudio had a nightmare from being worn out and dehydrated.

No trace of blood was found around the area, it was a place very difficult to reach…unknown to hikers or hunters; military officers were somber and humorless despite Kevin's sense of hilarity, they thought Claudio was hiding something in regard of Tony and Michael disappearance. He was once more under investigation after this last incident, for being the only witness to his cousin's uncertain murder.

Kevin took the boy aside and asked him confidentially, "Claudio! We are friends and have been helping each other for long time on this case—if you know something or are afraid to reveal it, please! Let me know. How many people still have to die before we uncover the truth? So far we have discovered scrolls, documents and papal seals. Do you know about Father Armando?"

Claudio replied, "No! I thought he was back in Rome after I left the hospital. I was expecting him to visit me. My father did not say anything about him. Where is he now?"

Kevin's facial muscles turned rigid, while swallowing in distress. "He vanished from Tanis's as soon as I went looking for him. He was seated in front of that goddamned portrait and evaporated from nowhere."

Claudio stared at Kevin with a sense of foreboding, and his apprehension for Armando was evident. The inspector knew that, even as he studied Claudio's reactions to his tortuous questions—after all, he was a cop.

"I told the truth, I swear to God! All I said is real, with my eyes. The horrible creature was inside her."

Too much to accept as true…not conducive at all…!

Kevin eclipsed the whole truth from Claudio, omitting the bewildering, unexplainable disappearing of the scientists in Vancouver and in the States, all gone the same day at the same hour—hard to believe. For this reason he decided to release Claudio for the moment, keeping him under surveillance, as ordered by his superior.

The new chief in charge of the Provincial Homicide Investigation, Danny Carson, convened with Inspector Kevin about Claudio situation. The commissioner was doubtful about the youth's version.

"I think Mr. Verallo is acting brilliantly! I want to be more specific, inspector. This month we reviewed all the files concerning the case, and found some interesting neglected patterns."

Mesotti said, participating, "We checked all the possible connections and hypotheses regarding the enquiries, all of it!"

Carson continued, "Yes I appreciated the work of the entire police department, but as we all know, mistakes were made from both sides! Darleen Satin's death evaluation was one of them."

Kevin agreed, telling him, "Unfortunately we all make mistakes, sir!"

Carson elucidated, "As I was telling you, we think that Claudio is seriously involved in this mystery; he was the last one to have seen his uncle Tony, and his cousin. They both disappeared up the hills, and Claudio was there by coincidence!"

Carson reinforced his version, "Of course! We are still investigating, but we need to watch the boy closely. He is under surveillance—keep that in mind!"

Was Claudio a con actor and a clever deceiver, hiding a contorted, surprisingly evil mind? Who was Claudio, indeed?

PROLOGUE

The End of the Beginning

Women were regarded for centuries by the church as the eternal source of sin and perdition, the cause of the original and primordial sin—and as for "Eve," they were punished and doomed forever.

Elysa was seen as the new Eve, and her womb, when discovered, was a treacherous symbol of female perdition.

Thursday, October 26th, forty days (Jesus walked on the earth for forty days after his resurrection, before ascending into heaven) after the abominable events, Claudio was strolling on the boardwalk of the West Vancouver seaside, an extension of the Ambleside Seashore Marina. It was a warm, cloudy autumn afternoon, with no rain coming from the sinuous, curling mountain range. Claudio's favorite day time was in the fall season, when the slumbering, invisible spiritual masses of condensed fluids vaporized, floating in the atmosphere above the material ground; shrouding our minds and imaginations in a magic spell.

The lost, immense truth of the cosmos up in the sky was hidden, as well as its mysterious creation, which confused our fragile feeble existence. Faith and hope were weakened by the emptiness of the universe.

Claudio felt more confident, embedded in the sky's blanket of fantastic, daydreaming imagination, and all was kept safe and pampered from the menacing swinging pendulum of time-lapse.

Astounding art rocks—pyramids were performed along the sea cliff on the beaches, dazzling people with their perfectly-built balances, geometrical shapes of numerous differentiated forms.

Claudio's mood was burlesque and sarcastic, commenting a few awkward configurations, sprinkled by the foam of the ocean's resounding, rumbling waves. He was captured by that magical, authentic atmosphere.

A couple of art rocks resembled geometrical, astronomical shrines, exposing at the top ends pointed-up triangles.

Claudio bewildered halted in front of them, mumbling: "Why all the pivotal triangles we took into consideration had a pointing-up position… at the end this arcane phenomenon was based on the female essence!"

He turned north, considering the last tiny triangle of all, the one on the Zenith Seal.

Claudio shrugged off those strange, freakish introspections from his shoulders, continuing along the shore until the end of the sea walk, where Dundarave Park begins.

The sun was setting, reflecting a purplish, shimmering star-way from west to east. The solar sphere burst into the waving water, while the crashing fluids of creation were emanating a bombastic, rocked sound from a distance.

The star rays enlightened the way. Claudio was captivated by this privileged scenery of nature, noticing the circles of luminescence blended in the blushing crimson of colors.

An oval seal form emerged from the bay, revealing itself inside the astonished iris of Claudio—it was her!

He ran and got closer to the shores, while people were assisting at his foolish, weird behavior. Children were enjoying the park's playground, and customers were indulging in their orders on the restaurant porch; a few elderly people observed the youth muttering and yelling on the rocks.

A mother was trying to sober her little kid, wanting to climb an oak tree. The boy was lively and stubborn, distracting Claudio for a moment.

He remembered Lidia when they were back in Rome. She used to take her son to the *Castle Saint Angelo* front park.

For a moment he lost the living sphere floating in the water, retracing it beneath his eyes. He became agitated, trying to attract the attention of all. Someone pointed fingers toward the water, calling for a sea lion or a killer whale, while Claudio, out of his mind was screaming the words, "The witch, the witch, Elysa! She is free! Help me!" People moved away from the shore, calling the emergency number for a mentally sick guy having a panic attack, or worse.

Claudio completely lost his marbles, merging in the cold water to scan the creatures, while the little boy could not climb the tree, commencing pulling his mother's leg and lamenting insistently.

An old lady bent toward the child to distract him, asking for his name. Claudio saw the entity exiting the placental seal, unattached to Elysa's vanished corpse, plunging into the freedom of the ocean's sigil.

Claudio discerned the body at the very end, before the monster disappeared deep underwater in the Pacific Ocean, proceeding east.

He watched clearly a male creature abandoning his unsealed womb.

A male seen only now in his real features…the real and only true son of Elysa.

Claudio whispered, "All this time looking for the truth, and when finally we thought to have discovered it, our own eyes deceived us at last!"

With the voice of innocence, the child answered the old lady: "My name is Michael, Michael!"

Michael, the nonaligned Archangel of Hell! Deceiving once for all the Holy See…ready to unleash the power of the Inferno!

A white feather candidly fell from the sky into the ocean, touching the everlasting eye of the twilight of deception.

To my Mother, the light of my darkness

God is an opening light, immersed in his freedom of infinity, always widening the existing brilliance of love. We close our eyes, walking in trust toward the death of our not-conceived life. Our materiality is ensnared into the dwelling of Evil, deep down inside the earth, sealed in a claustrophobic fear of terrestrial existence. Obscurity, darkness and narrow-mindedness, which imprison us in the profound mouth of the iniquitous malign. We cannot see it, as we can never trust in our heart, the deceiver of all masters, afraid to live and die, in the entrance of uncertainty.

All the vicious foes of the world will be floating forever in the spiritual love of the universal immensity.

Al Crown

ABOUT THE AUTHOR

Al Crown is a poet, writer and author of the new Novel *The Archangel of a Black Feather* which is the first book of the series *Grotesque Wings*. He lives and work in Vancouver, British Columbia. Driven by a deep passion for history, different cultures and nature, Al has travelled extensively in Europe and North America finding the inspiration that gave life to his characters and make his stories intriguing and unique.

Lightning Source UK Ltd.
Milton Keynes UK
UKHW040941260919
350504UK00003B/214/P